A View To The North

Also By Robert Rea

SunDreams

A View To The North

A NOVEL BY

Robert Rea

MapleLand Press
Bracebridge, Ontario, Canada

 For information contact MapleLand Press, P.O. Box 1285, Bracebridge, Ontario, Canada P1L 1V4 E-mail: maplelnd@muskoka.com

Cover Paintings: Richard Robinson
1030 Dickie Lake Road, R.R. #1
Baysville, Ontario
Canada
P0B 1A0

* For more information please see 'About the Cover Artist'

Canadian Cataloguing in Publication Data

Rea, Robert, 1964-
A view to the north

ISBN 0-9686997-2-3

I.Title.

PS8585.E3218V53 2002 C813'.6 C2002-900345-8
PR9199.4.R43V53 2002

Published by MapleLand Press
Printed in Canada
First Edition: First Trade Paper Printing: June 2000
First Edition: Second Trade Paper Printing: October 2001
Second Edition: First Trade Paper Printing: April 2002

NOTICE

This is a work of fiction. Names, characters, places, and events either derive from the author's imagination or are used fictitiously. Any similarities to actual places, events, or persons — alive or deceased — is purely coincidental.

FIRST EDITION ACKNOWLEDGMENTS

The author gratefully acknowledges the following for their help in developing this novel:

Wendy Hosick, Susan Simmons, Ted Currie, Terri Buwalda, Shirley Berch, and especially, Louise MacLeod.

SECOND EDITION ACKNOWLEDGMENTS

The author wishes to thank Marilyn Smart of Orillia for her tremendous support and encouragement, and the many readers worldwide who, through conversation and letters, offered both praise and suggestions for how this novel might be improved.

AUTHOR'S FOREWORD TO SECOND EDITION

In the nearly two years since its release I have learned much from publishing *A View To The North*, this period abundant in lessons, insights, and, most notably, surprises. In this brief note I wish to share a few such experiences.

To begin, I was initially much puzzled at seemingly the vast majority of readers interpreting the novel quite differently than I intended. From the outset in developing *A View To The North* I wanted to create a mainstream novel that explored the complexities of our emotional relationship with wild, non-human nature. I had spent years studying this subject matter and felt it could provide the foundation for both an interesting and important novel. Especially so considering the gravity presently bestowed upon environmental issues. "It's very much a 'woodsy' novel," I would typically proclaim at signings when introducing the book to potential readers.

But, soon after publishing, I discovered something peculiar: 'woodsy' was almost the last word used in reader responses! Most were enjoying the novel far more for its social aspects — the circumstance of a family coping with tragedy, the politics of a tiny lake community, and, particularly, the challenges of an urban-to-rural lifestyle change. "It's all about the grandmother adjusting to country life — isn't that obvious?" claimed one Canadian reader in person, dumbfounded at my naiveté.

Other authors may sigh at the above account and proclaim such an experience is normal and to be expected. And I would agree; all readers bring a perspective uniquely theirs to any book, and therefore take something uniquely theirs away from it. Nonetheless I was not quite prepared for just how different readers' reactions to the novel would be from my expectations. I was also not prepared for something else: that in time I would see those alternative interpretations as equally valid. I would come, that is, to recognize new facets of my own novel.

The result has been a greater understanding of the nature of fictional composition and the creative process. Specifically, I've come to believe authors, like perhaps all artists, inject as much into their works unconsciously as they do consciously. I've also come to feel published writing travels a two-way street; that you not only send your works into the world but the world, in response, often sends its own versions back. Artistic expression, in other words, is an act of both giving and receiving.

The above naturally leads to a second insight I would like to share, one concerning the act of publishing itself. I hope the following will be of particular value to others aspiring to see their own literary work in print.

A common refrain in the publishing industry is "write your first novel, publish your second." Although I might have once professed the same, I could no longer. Since releasing *A View To The North* I have received countless appraisals of my strengths and weaknesses as a writer, and these I would clearly not have received with an unpublished manuscript stashed in a drawer. Granted I would still have benefited from professional evaluations, but with all respect I don't believe these equal in value the myriad offerings of normal, everyday readers. In light of such diverse feedback gained through publishing I've come to believe an author's second work is perhaps only better *because* he or she published a first. Put another way — I once saw publishing as the end result of an author's writing tools; I now see it as a writing tool in itself.

In closing, I wish to thank all past readers for sharing their comments concerning the first edition of *A View To The North*, and I do hope readers of this enhanced second edition will follow in their footsteps. For me, writing entails never-ending learning, and study now very much includes that curious role played by readers. With such in mind, and borrowing the words of a certain young friend, I continue to investigate the matter.

Robert Rea
April, 2002

For those who wander the woods,
but equally for those
who haven't even considered doing so,
and never will.

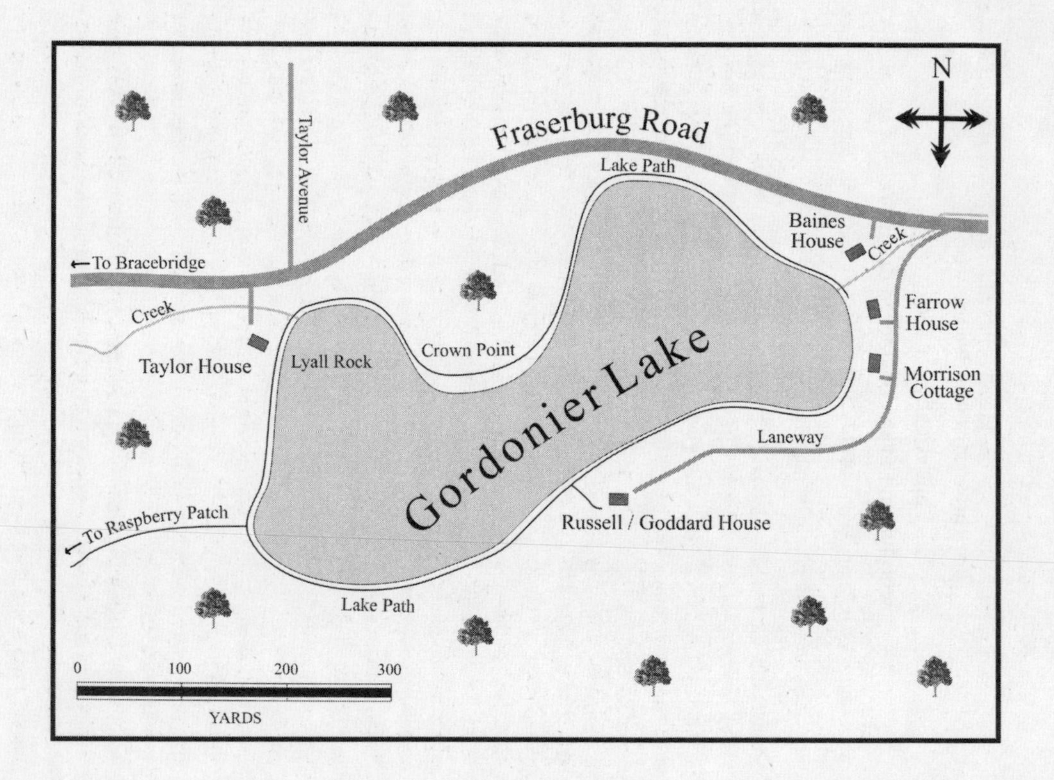
N
Fraserburg Road
Taylor Avenue
Lake Path
← To Bracebridge
Baines
House
Creek
Farrow
House
Morrison
Cottage
Creek
Taylor House
Lyall Rock
Crown Point
Gordonier Lake
Laneway
Russell / Goddard House
← To Raspberry Patch
Lake Path
0
100
200
300
YARDS

PROLOGUE

It was on a sunny August afternoon several summers ago that I took the plunge. Ironically, I intended the weekend visit I made with my wife Carrie to Gordonier Lake to serve as a break from building a house. What actually occurred, however, was the birth of my most ambitious construction project yet.

Gordonier Lake, a mere raindrop nestled amid a vast expanse of thick Muskoka woods, was the setting for much of my childhood. My parents and aged grandmother still live there, in fact, and the weekend visit Carrie and I made was by no means our first. It was also not the first I shared with my wife some of my childhood experiences. While driving to the lake, and while later hiking around it, I again strived to have her understand what happened to me at this place, and why I felt those happenings important. As usual, though, I wound up frustrated; there was simply too much to say and my talk degenerated into, as my fellow hiker so tenderly put it, "woodsy ramblings." But then came the event making this particular visit exceptional. Moments after I resigned on this afternoon and began my usual mope, Carrie uttered a challenge: "So why don't you try telling the *whole* story in writing, Lewis?"

Now I normally enjoy challenges, but I must admit this one threw me for a loop. I was, after all, a bloomin' house contractor, not a writer. Wanting to write my story and being able to were, I knew, two very different things. When I presented this argument to Carrie, however, she soon pointed to the real problem. After politely hearing me out my dear wife proceeded to voice her best imitation of our neighbour's chicken coop. Cruel, perhaps, but effective.

That August afternoon, then, marked the beginning of two years of reminiscing and writing, two years of pulling together the key episodes I believe formed the most important span of my childhood. The resulting story shares learnings associated with growing up, with meeting new people, and unfortunately, with devastating family tragedy. Most significantly, however, this story is about learning how we as individuals feel, both consciously and unconsciously, toward wild 'Mother Nature', that realm of forest, water, and sky largely uncontrolled, as yet, by humanity. It is what I learned in this respect that unquestionably produced the deepest impact on my adult life. It is also concerning this particular area of learning, and its everyday effects on me now, that I most desire to be understood — not only by Carrie but by others as well. "Why do you always study the way woodsy places affect people, Lewis?" is a frequently heard question I hope to now answer.

In many ways writing this story proved a learning experience in itself; the sheer vividness of my memories alone reinforced my awareness of just how influential the years at Gordonier Lake were. At times, though, this task was painful. Relating one's past in depth requires essentially reliving it, and so through my writing I experienced once again the great highs, great lows, and consequently, profound confusion permeating my childhood in Muskoka. At her wedding my younger sister Judy described our early time at the lake as "the years when heaven and hell shacked up together." And although I know she referred simply to her own childhood experiences, her words were nonetheless also applicable to mine.

Despite relived pains, I feel quite rewarded having made this effort, and feel very grateful toward my wife for pushing me to it. In my heart I also allow, if I may, that an old Gordonier Lake friend is pleased with me. It is therefore in a decidedly positive light I now present to Carrie, and to you, a somewhat more organized and complete account of my "woodsy ramblings."

Part One

1

My tiny brother Sean delivered the final news. He was waiting for me under our designated maple when school let out, and his squirming stance told me something was up. Just as he had some four years earlier when announcing the arrival into the world of our sister Judy, he seemed about to pee himself.

"The offer's been 'cepted, Lewis!" he blurted out when Joey Farnsted and I were still thirty feet away.

Instantly I stopped and glanced right. My wide-eyed friend was studying me in return.

Knowing my brother sometimes confused his facts, I said, sternly, "You're sure, Sean? You're *absolutely* sure?"

He nodded. "Some people phoned at lunch! You missed everything by going to Joey's!"

Seeing his unwavering gaze I collapsed to my knees and merely stared at the grass. And as though he stood fifty yards away I heard Joey, mocking my grandmother, say, "Jesus, Lewis! You guys really *are* moving off to the sticks!"

This afternoon was in mid-June of 1975, the year Sean turned seven and I turned ten. The offer my brother referred to was one my parents made on a house in Muskoka, a district about a hundred miles north of our current home in Scarborough. My shock over his message was my grandmother's work, but I'll get to that later. For now I'll tell you the very idea of our family moving to Muskoka came as no surprise whatsoever. I had three good reasons for feeling this way, and each concerned my father.

The first was that Dad grew up in Muskoka, spoke fondly of his childhood years, and led me to believe he wanted his kids to do likewise. A second reason, supplied by my maternal grandmother, was my father only left Muskoka for lack of year-round accounting work. Given the chance, Grandma Layton contended, he wouldn't hesitate to return. The final reason concerned the argument that would arise when my father inevitably received his job opportunity. Although my mother and grandmother were city-bred and never showed the slightest desire to move, Dad would win any dispute with Mother, Grandma Layton insisted, by simply yelling louder.

I received my first hint we might actually move to Muskoka in late fall of 1974. As I often did as a boy I struggled getting to sleep one evening. My clock showed almost eleven when I quietly climbed down from my bunk atop Sean's and crept to the bathroom. While drinking some water I heard my parents talking in the basement TV room below me. By the tone of their voices and the way they overlapped I knew they were arguing. This was rare and something they did only when Grandma Layton was away. Although I sensed they wanted to keep quiet, sound carried well in our small house and a nosy oldest child had no problem overhearing the occasional word. One of these words was "Muskoka."

After that night I never again heard my parents argue, but during the following winter months I did sense a definite tension between them. At supper they rarely talked, and on weekends seldom did much together. All this convinced me they were having the very dispute my grandmother predicted. My nagging question was: would my father win?

The answer came, finally, in mid-May. I arrived home from softball practice one Wednesday afternoon to discover the rest of the family sitting at the kitchen table. This was early for my father to be home, and spread out in front of him was one of his office files.

"We have an announcement," he said quietly. "One we hope you'll like."

Mother, with Judy in her arms, offered a pained smile. "How do you feel about moving to Muskoka, Mr. Farrow?"

I can't recall my exact reply — something politely favourable is all I remember. Fortunately it didn't matter because my parents were apparently not expecting much of a response. To them, after all, their news came to me as a complete surprise.

Dad soon confirmed my suspicion: that someone in Muskoka offered him a job. Ironically, it proved with the same accounting business for which he'd worked before moving to the city. A once-fellow employee of my father now owned the business, and could offer steady work.

"And really — it *is* a good job," Mother added brightly when my father finished explaining. This she said for her mother's benefit, of course, but to no avail. Grandma Layton merely rose from the table, vented a lengthy sigh, then grumbled to herself the rest of the evening. It was a sour mood we'd have to get used to.

With this big decision behind them my parents turned to finding a house in Muskoka. Selling in Scarborough was not a problem; the son of the Walshes, our immediate neighbours to the left, had a long-standing offer to buy our place. Buying a house up north was another matter. My father's job was to begin in mid-July and this gave my parents only two months to find something.

Not until their third house-hunting trip, in early June, did they find a place to their liking. They arrived back in the afternoon on that Saturday with news they'd placed an offer on a house at a lake some five miles outside Bracebridge. A tiny black-and-white real estate photo my mother produced showed a compact house on a fairly wooded lot with, as she put it, "woods and more woods" surrounding the lake.

Hearing about a house on a small lake was shocking. I'd always assumed living in a Muskoka town was a compromise my father would have to make before getting my mother's consent for the move. I judged he'd argued a great deal more, and a great deal louder, than what I heard the previous fall.

With a house chosen the only remaining issue was whether the owners would accept my parents' offer. My grandmother did everything she could to convince me moving north was still very much in question. While my parents looked at houses Grandma Layton repeatedly declared, "They probably won't find anything." When they did she said, "They probably won't get it." Therefore not until that Friday afternoon in mid-June did the reality of our moving to Muskoka completely register with me, and with Joey Farnsted.

"This means you're gonna get to do everything up there, Lewis!" my friend said as he lay on a bed of old leaves. "And not only for some measly afternoon, either, but all the time!"

"Yeah, might be good," I muttered, downplaying as best I could. Then, as I'd been doing too often in recent months, I began fidgeting, picking up a maple leaf from the previous fall and spinning the stem between my fingers.

Joey and I were now nestled in the Lord Roberts Woods, a small patch of maple-dominated forest between the open grounds of Lord Roberts Public School and the railway corridor. It was a place we invariably wound up after school each day — even rainy days.

"Think you'll get to go way back in the bush, Lewis?!" Joey said.

"Don't know what I'll get to do," I replied quietly, and dishonestly. My parents had already briefed me on a full range of activities — from swimming to forest hikes.

"You know, there might even be spots nobody's ever been to — like in the Yukon and stuff!" Joey's eyes now began glazing over, like my father insisted mine did when talking about exploring.

"The lake isn't far from a town, so I doubt it," I said, lying again. I felt certain there'd be no end to unexplored spots.

Joey, apparently sensing this fib, turned and focussed two sharp brown eyes. "But I'm sure you'll discover *something*, Farrow."

Joey Farnsted was both classmate and close neighbour. Despite differences at times we shared an unquenchable thirst for exploring. Together we'd concocted and executed countless exploring missions within and beyond our neighbourhood. Our yearning to 'investigate the matter', as I was fond of saying, occasionally led us into trouble. After hopping several fences too many one fine August morning, for example, the police duly escorted us home, and over the next week Joey and I explored our respective bedrooms.

My shared interest with Joey put me in a predicament when the issue arose of our family moving to Muskoka. Here I was, on the verge of my greatest exploring mission yet, and Joey couldn't join me. He would never, I knew, so much as get to visit; his parents were even more anti-rural than my grandmother. I also knew, however, his curiosity about country life equalled mine. Over the previous several months he'd enthusiastically helped me speculate on what I might encounter up north. Indeed, most of the bears, moose, giant trees, and wild Indians were his contributions. He was green with envy over my opportunity and when with him I couldn't help feeling guilty. But his envy, ironically, made it impossible to share with him another problem, for fear I'd look unappreciative of my 'good fortune'.

The truth was, as the months passed since receiving that first hint of our moving north, I'd become increasingly apprehensive. For all my curiosity, I also worried what life would be like outside the city. Thus my giving only a half-hearted reply when first asked by my parents about moving. My concerns naturally included my mother and grandmother, but that issue aside for now, I feared for myself.

In the great expanse of my ten years I had not, even once, been truly outside Metropolitan Toronto. That I was a rural greenhorn is an understatement. True, I'd spent considerable time in the Lord Roberts Woods, but I was already wise enough to realize a small city woodlot was no substitute for the 'real woods' I was headed for.

Now you might suppose journeying to a land of unknowns is precisely what a young boy much into exploring would dream about, and to some extent concerning Muskoka, I did. My problem was the issue of escape: what if I hated the woods? While exploring my city neighbourhood, if I discovered something I didn't care for I went home. But in Muskoka, my caring for home itself was questionable, and part of an exploration lasting indefinitely. Therefore, along with Joey Farnsted and guilt pangs over how lucky I was to be moving to the country, I was plagued with worry. "How can you be so bloody ungrateful, Farrow?" I'm sure Joey would have hollered. It was enough to drive a person to fidgeting.

So, when Sean delivered the news you can understand how desperate I was to change the topic. Luckily, a light went on inside my head. Without a penny in my pocket I said, "Feel like going to Howard's for an ice-cream, Joey? I'll spring!"

"No, Lewis!" Sean broke in, as I knew he would. "You promised we'd stay for a bit!"

"Why don't you just live up there?" Joey barked at him. "Then you wouldn't be bugging Lewis and me all the time."

Sean, his twig-like arms tensing up, glared down and snapped, "The only one bugging Lewis is you, dummy!" He then promptly returned to peering through his binoculars.

My little brush cut brother sat perched well above Joey and me in a beech tree, monitoring a robin's nest in a maple some fifty feet away. The nest sat on a well-sheltered branch about twenty feet off the ground, and every year a pair of robins used this choice spot. By climbing slightly higher in his lookout tree my brother could watch the birds through a pair of binoculars he'd received for his fifth birthday.

Sean, quite simply, was a bird fanatic. His preoccupation began at age four when he saw some older boys use stones to knock a nest out of the choice maple. He tried rescuing the two nestlings surviving the fall, putting them in a shoebox filled with grass, but the birds soon died. Ever since, he diligently watched all the new nests.

Now although I sympathized with Joey on this afternoon, my brother definitely did not. He believed Joey helped knock down the robin's nest, even after hearing Brenda Farnsted insist her son was home at the time.

"So...how's the nest, Sean?" I said, trying to maintain this new focus.

"There's only two babies left now!" he answered, again glaring down at the bird-killer, who was obviously responsible.

Joey's eyebrows rose. "I didn't touch any birds! Why would I?"

"When we get to Muskoka there'll be all kinds of birds!" Sean added, as though my friend wouldn't stand a chance of killing them all.

"How would you know? You and Lewis have never been out of the city even once!"

Sean swivelled his tiny feet on his branch, dangerously I thought, and gave Joey a hard stare. "I know stuff!"

My friend returned this stare, then looked toward the school. "You don't know the first bloody thing. You don't know —"

"I know there's *birds*!" Sean broke in. "So you shove it, Joey Farthead!"

"Old lady bird-watcher!"

A pause from my brother, then the expected, "You're just mad because Lewis is stronger'n you." This was the little bugger's standard response when running out of things to say in any argument.

Joey, who'd heard this line many times before, croaked, "*What the heck does that have to do —?*"

"He's stronger!" Sean quickly repeated, and with that returned to his birds and ignored us.

Thankfully we spent the remainder of that afternoon in relative peace, Joey seemingly content daydreaming about Muskoka and Sean seemingly content in his lookout tree. For me, however, this peace was only outward; although I'd finally succeeded in distracting Joey, doing so didn't rescue me from my worries, or my fidgeting. Indeed, listening to my co-explorer only increased my awareness of my anxiety. I believed what he'd said to my brother he could as easily have said to me: that I didn't, and couldn't possibly have had, a clue what I was headed for. And, looking back after all these years, I know just how true that was.

2

Ann Bernice Layton, my dear, one and only grandparent, had lived with us since I was two. My mother urged her to move in soon after my grandfather, a gentlemanly lawyer, passed away following a long and miserable bout with cancer. This move was only the second in my grandmother's life; her one other experience was as a newlywed, when she moved out of her parents' pristine, elegant townhouse and into a nearby pristine, elegant townhouse with her husband. From what I experienced living with her, and from what I knew of her past through stories and photographs, she led as proper, cultured, and urbanized a life as I supposed a person could. My father put it best, perhaps, when he once quipped, "That lady be through and through city folk, Lewis."

For the most part I believe Grandma Layton enjoyed living with us, and this had been mutual, also for the most part. She did maintain some stringent rules for her grandchildren. Woe to that child, for instance, who left the bathroom less than immaculate, and "improper vocabulary" invariably earned one the chance to tidy one's bedroom. Ironically, her exacting ways could also be pleasing at times. She had, for example, a very refined and stylish way of making beds. I don't know how she managed it, but after five minutes of precise folding, tucking, and fluffing her masterpiece would be complete and you'd be spoiled beyond recovery. She also was a mouth-watering cook, evidenced best by my father's ample belly.

Quite predictably, my grandmother's urban refinement

brought her tremendous grief when it came to the issue of leaving Scarborough. The belief my father would someday push our family to Muskoka was a major thorn in her side, and simple mention of the matter made her blood boil. On many occasions I'd witnessed her having tea with our retired and similarly prudish neighbour Rita Walsh, expounding on the shortcomings of rural life. She'd sooner be relieved of her precious china collection, it seemed, than suffer "living in the Godforsaken sticks."

Although not as blatant as my grandmother's, I also found my mother's dislike for rural life obvious during our family's urban years. She was much simpler in her tastes than Grandma Layton and far more open-minded, but I believed she was ultimately no more inclined than her mother to move. I partly based this belief on her never having expressed any interest in leaving the city, either permanently or even as an excursion. Mostly, however, I based such a belief on a habit my mother had when outdoors.

On some afternoons after school Mother paid a surprise visit to Sean, Joey, and me in the Lord Roberts Woods to check for, as she put it, "cigarettes, jackknives, and other contraband." During these shakedowns there invariably came a time when she spent a full, silent minute staring at something nearby — a tree, leaf, or insect, for example. She kept her head absolutely still, with her long, shiny brown hair hanging lifeless, her youthful, pretty face completely expressionless, and her small green eyes mysteriously vacant. She seemed, in short, utterly out of place in this setting.

I believed strongly my mother only finally consented to moving to Muskoka because she simply ran out of steam battling my father. I didn't feel even for the sake of us kids, as I understood my father's motive for the move to be, my mother would pleasantly accept this lifestyle change. The possible future consequences of her having consented purely out of fatigue were also not lost on me. By age ten I'd already observed twice in our neighbourhood what could happen when husband and wife vehemently disagreed over a period of years. In the same light, I could obviously see a family disaster brewing with my grandmother as well.

One evening about four days before hearing the final

announcement I decided to confront my mother about the move. I did so shortly after Sean and I went to bed and she, as always, came in to check on us. My brother had fallen asleep quickly so I felt the moment was right.

"Mom, think ... Grandma's thought of not moving with us? Or thought of moving back to the city eventually?" I blurted this out only several seconds after my mother arrived at my bunk railing.

Enough light came from the hall for me to see a quizzical look form on her face. "Don't be goofy, Lewis," she whispered. "Of course your grandmother is coming with us, and staying."

"But ... she could get her own place, or maybe move in with the Walshes. They'd take her in." I hesitated, then let out nervously, "They'd take *you* in too."

Mother leaned closer to the bed. "Now you're being completely silly, mister. Of course she and I are moving with the rest of the family. Your grandmother especially; she'd face anything to live with her grandchildren — you know that." After studying me a moment she added, "You're worried she and I will be miserable — aren't you?"

I turned away and stared at the ceiling. "Maybe."

At this my mother sighed, and out of the corner of my eye I caught her glancing toward the hall. She whispered, "I want you to stop worrying. Start thinking about all the things you'll be doing in Muskoka. I know darn well you're curious about what it'll be like up there."

"Maybe," I said once again, in as reserved a tone as I could manage.

"*Maybe*, Mr. Explorer?"

I faced my mother. "But ... even if I do like it, that doesn't mean you and Grandma will. You might get sick of living up there, and then ..."

I heard a deeper sigh now; my mother fiddled with her long hair while apparently mulling over something. Finally she said, wearily, "There's more to this moving situation than you know about, Lewis, and I'd like you to simply accept that for the time being. This is one occasion when I'm asking you not to *investigate the matter* — okay? Just let things be."

"There's more to —?"

"No questions!"

As my mother uttered these words I noticed a definite mischievous sparkle form in her eyes, the hall providing just enough light. It was like she'd concocted some evil plan of revenge against my father and would get the last laugh. As quickly as this mischievous sparkle formed it disappeared, however, and I was relieved.

I said, "Can I at least ask about Grandma?"

"What about her?"

"Think she'll be okay?"

Mother paused, once again seemingly collecting her thoughts. "My mother ... is more adaptable than you realize, more adaptable than she herself perhaps realizes. She accepted a major change in her life after your grandfather died, for one thing. You simply haven't been around long enough, Lewis, to see how your grandmother can always find something to her liking in virtually anything. She may never admit it, but I'm confident she'll eventually enjoy more up north than simply her grandchildren. You just wait and see."

To this I only nodded, and after receiving a standard peck on the cheek, Mother said, "You get to sleep now, Lewis Farrow — no one wants you being a grump in the morning," then slipped out of the room.

If my mother was right, and my grandmother would eventually adjust to life in Muskoka, you'd never have bet on it seeing her at supper the following Friday, on the evening of the big news. Any and all optimistic doubts she'd maintained about our moving had clearly disintegrated, and she was now in deep and obvious pain. She hardly touched her food, and in the first ten minutes alone my father received enough dirty looks to tarnish him forever. Since we'd invited our neighbours the Walshes over on this evening, we ate on our more spacious back patio, and my grandmother soon began escaping to the kitchen for lengthy stretches. Mother, in turn, took to sending me in to help her. 'Helping her' on this evening meant simply listening, and she was only too glad to give me an earful. Her most common line, uttered at least five times, was, "We're headed right down the pipe, Lewis — mark my word!"

When dessert time thankfully arrived, my father, using dieting and a "TV problem" as excuses, made his own escape with Jack Walsh. And they had no sooner disappeared into our basement than Grandma Layton reappeared from the kitchen, of course. With a mighty "harumph" she motioned toward the house with her sharp chin and said, "Can you believe all this supper malarky, Rita? He seems to think there's call for a celebration! I'm amazed he hasn't got this Donald Nelson character joining us tonight."

She was referring to my father's new boss, who Dad had told us about since his Muskoka job became public knowledge, and a person she naturally already hated.

"Now, now, Annie," an equally urbanized Rita Walsh replied half-heartedly. "Surely this can't be all *that* bad, can it?"

"Yes it can," Grandma Layton grumbled as she plunked herself in a patio chair. "It can be and it will be." After a long groan and pulling at her precisely-curled silver hair, she added, "Oh, Rita ... I told you this was coming — I told you! Bruce was bent on moving back from the day he moved away, and now he's taking the rest of us *right down the pipe with him — mark my word!* Moving to this Godforsaken Muskoka is simply ... *ridiculous!* Who the heck wants to live in the sticks? It's like regressing a hundred years! If I didn't need my grand—"

She broke off, glancing lovingly at my sister, and Judy, seemingly oblivious to what our grandmother was about to admit, soothingly offered, "But you can take all your cooking stuff, Grandma!" She was referring to our household's forty-seven kitchen gadgets.

"Might not be any point, dear." Grandma Layton stared skyward with her world-is-ending frown. "The water and electricity probably cut out every hour on the hour, and the bugs will soon have the run of the kitchen. We'll all likely be filthy bush animals inside a year." With that, and another long groan, our dear, one and only grandmother began jabbing viciously at a piece of homemade blueberry pie with her fork.

Her rant could easily have continued the rest of the evening had it not been for what my mother did next. Before my grandmother mustered the energy for another round, Mother turned and whispered in Judy's ear, who then quickly slipped from her chair and went inside. A moment later the living room record player came on. Playing was one of my sister's dance tunes — I don't recall which.

Some explaining is required here.

In her youth my grandmother was quite committed to ballet. Her background in dancing was actually still very much apparent; despite now being in her late sixties there remained a definite grace to how she walked, even to how she ate. I was therefore not shocked when learning her childhood beginnings in dance led to her becoming a ballet instructor, nor that she retired merely a year after I was born. I also was not shocked when, seconds after Judy took her first unaided step, my grandmother came out of retirement and started teaching her how to dance.

Now as wonderful as this may have been, when it came to dancing my grandmother had a habit I found odd and often embarrassing. Whenever Judy performed the instructor would raise her arm and trace the dancer's movements with her perfectly-manicured right index finger. It was a strange thing to see even after countless occasions, and apparently involuntary on my grandmother's part. When my sister danced Grandma Layton drifted off to another and more refined world, becoming seemingly oblivious to all else around her.

So with my kitchen sessions not succeeding in calming my grandmother, I was embarrassed but not overly surprised my mother tried the dance approach. What did surprise me was this tactic worked even on this evening; Judy had been dancing on the lawn barely three minutes when the great dance finger rose.

"Keep her goin', Jude," cheered a tongue-in-cheek Jack Walsh, who had returned with my father by this time. "More of those twirly things, I think."

From behind Mother's chair I overheard Dad whisper to her, "Aren't we the clever one."

Even with the Walshes present I honestly feared a snide reply to this comment, considering my father was responsible for Grandma Layton's pain. Instead my mother's eyes assumed a familiar mischievous sparkle, and after licking her finger — her right index finger, I might note — she simply added to an imaginary score above her.

3

During all the years we lived in Scarborough, there hung in a corner of our basement a large black-and-white framed photograph of my father at the age of perhaps nine or ten. Wearing only shorts, he is hanging by his hands from the branch of a large birch, his feet dangling some ten feet off the ground. Besides a devilish grin you can see a dazed excitement in his eyes, the look, as my mother once told me, "of a child on Christmas morning." I don't know whether anyone besides the two of us paid much attention to this photograph; Grandma Layton, I'm sure, would only reluctantly acknowledge its existence. For me, however, it came to epitomize a particular side to my father, and not merely one he had as a boy but one he still very much had on the brink of forty. Also, I could see in this picture a physical resemblance to someone else — the same tangled brown hair, the same smoky blue eyes, the same stocky build, even the same darkly-freckled forearms. I could see myself in this picture, that is, and so, I came to suppose, could my father.

Ever since I was old enough to understand him Dad had shared with me stories of growing up in Muskoka. The particulars of these stories are now lost on me, but what is not is the manner in which he told them. His voice, even his entire overweight body, became energized. He spoke louder and faster, he sat rigidly upright and was extremely expressive with his hands, and he sometimes talked for hours. What made his story-telling manner remarkable was, first, how it compared with his normal manner:

lethargic in body and reserved and business-like in disposition. Second, he showed this great enthusiasm toward growing up in Muskoka despite this period of his life being marked by tragedy. When he was eleven, both his parents died in a horrific car accident and he was thereafter raised by a not-too-pleasant aunt and uncle. In light of this history my father was not one from whom you'd expect to hear lively, happy tales of childhood.

Now in relating what I've just told you to our move, it is not relevant merely in showing how my father desired a return to Muskoka for his own sake. He wanted the move first and foremost, I believed, for the sake of his kids. He wanted Sean, Judy, and me to experience the same joys he'd experienced, for us to one day be able to tell our own kids lively, happy tales. And it was because of this unselfish motive that I didn't resent my father pushing my mother to move. It is also why I sympathized with his suffering.

During the several months leading to the final news of the move, I noticed Dad was often quiet and downcast. Reserved may have been normal, but not quiet and downcast, and I sensed the Muskoka issue was wearing on him. His glum mood didn't surprise me, mind you, because as mentioned earlier, serious disagreements between my parents were rare. My grandmother aside, my father had never liked doing things my mother didn't enjoy. Other than the dispute over Muskoka their twelve year marriage had been a good one, and I knew it hurt my father deeply to disturb this fortunate situation.

So it was in a strange atmosphere — half of me drawn into his excitement, the other half drawn into his depression — that I made my first trip to Muskoka. This occurred on the first Saturday of July. We were moving the following weekend and Dad wanted to do a few things inside the house while it was still empty. Sean and I quickly reserved seats in our family's green Buick, but we proved the only ones to do so. My mother and grandmother decided to stay behind to continue boxing up household belongings, and Judy had a precious swimming class to attend. So it was only the three of us who headed north on this sunny Saturday afternoon, leaving right after Dad finished a morning at the office.

Of all impressions of this day the strongest was how quickly we left the city behind. Despite my enthusiasm toward my father's stories I always had difficulty fathoming how the rugged, woodsy setting of these tales could lie a mere hundred miles north of our home in Scarborough. Toronto seemed to me as a child almost a universe unto itself. That this urban giant could give way to immense tracts of woods in a mere few hours I found difficult to believe. More than once I'd pondered whether my father's stories were somewhat tall in stature. But, in seemingly no time on this afternoon the universe of Toronto gave way to farmland, which in turn soon gave way to the rock-riddled forests of Muskoka, and the view left me gazing in stunned silence. "Quite the change, isn't it, Lewis?" my father commented while eyeing me. Apparently someone else also realized an element of vindication to this trip.

About fifteen minutes after reaching our new home district we left the highway to enter Bracebridge. From my father I already heard it was a small, approximately 100-year-old community of eight thousand, and was packed with cottagers and tourists in the summer. I also knew that a popular attraction for the town was a small amusement park called Santa's Village. Located exactly halfway to the north pole, this, I learned, was where the big guy spent his summers.

The town was jammed, and we made our way up the store-packed main street at a crawl. Finally Dad hung a left onto Kimberley Avenue. This street met the main one at a shallow angle, and wedged between the two was a small, richly-grassed park. Its dominant features were a war memorial and an ornate bandstand. On Kimberley, facing the park, was a long line of old brick townhouses, and we soon pulled into the driveway of one such house.

After backing the car in close, saving dreaded "extra work," Dad opened the Buick's trunk and we each grabbed whatever box of files or books we could manage. My father then slowly led the way into the house through a side door. A stylish sign on it read, "Nelson Accounting & Bookkeeping Services."

Nelson Accounting proved tidy but small — half the first floor of the townhouse. Leading off a tiny waiting area were a washroom, storage room, and two private offices facing the park. In the larger office, one sporting pots of Marigolds, we found my father's new boss, a pale, slender man with silver-rimmed glasses and thinning, slightly graying black hair. Sitting at his desk, he was smartly dressed in a navy blue suit, studying some papers while talking on the phone. As we approached the other office he looked up and waved, and a minute later joined us.

"What's this? Working Saturdays, Donny?" my father said as he took my box and placed it on a filing cabinet. "A real company man."

"Won't be working them much longer," he answered with a sly grin, and he kept grinning as Dad feigned a short cry.

When my father finished introductions his new boss said to me, wearily, "No offence, but seeing you makes me feel ill. Last time your Dad and I worked together we were just kids ourselves."

Dad said, "It feels that way now, at least."

Don Nelson poked at my father's ample belly. "Somebody had a lot less of this back then, I know that."

When his boss stepped out to answer the phone, Dad took a seat in his desk chair and swivelled to face the park, where several kids my age were tossing a football. I could see that despite joking a few minutes, he again looked glum. He sat silently for several minutes.

"Nothing much has changed from this vantage point, I see," he said when the boss returned.

Don went to the window. "Oh, the town's grown since you left, Bruce. It's not exactly Toronto, I grant you, but ... there're things going on."

"Grandma should like it here in Bracebridge, at least," I offered. "So should Mom."

"Grandma will like that bandstand, Dad," Sean quickly chipped in. "It looks ... fancy."

At this Dad slowly swivelled around in his chair. "What do you say, Donny? Do these two have potential in sales?"

His boss smirked. "Show some faith in Val, Bruce. Things will work out."

"God I hope so," Dad replied with a pained smile. "Because the move's a done deal, isn't it?"

Don said, "It's a done deal, and it's for the best," and my father merely nodded before swivelling back again to study the park.

We stayed at the office about another hour that afternoon. Dad began organizing the books and files we'd brought from the city, and gabbed with Don on numerous topics, most concerning business. I noticed during this hour that whenever the conversation returned to the issue of our moving, Don glanced at me, almost nervously at times. I sensed he wasn't sure what he should — and shouldn't — say in front of my brother and me. This reminded me of my mother saying I didn't know everything concerning the move, and the office visit provided me with a touch more insight into this mystery. Whatever knowledge I didn't have, Don Nelson apparently did, and his involvement, and nervousness, suggested the importance of this knowledge went beyond my parents.

When we were back on the road we slowly retraced our way through town until reaching the highway. But instead of turning back onto it, Dad crossed and started up a roughly-paved hill. "This is the Fraserburg Road," he announced. "The lake is about five miles."

For the first mile of this road the land was mostly cleared and was divided into a handful of old-looking farms, a few with cattle grazing near the road. Soon the pavement ended, however, and we entered thick woods. Bits of gravel sprayed against the underside of the car, and occasionally we rumbled over a washboard section of road. None of this distracted my brother and me, though; we all but had our faces pressed against the car windows. Unlike on the highway, where we merely looked *at* the woods, we were now most definitely *in* the woods. What Sean thought of all this I didn't know, but for me this forest, just begging to be explored, was enough to briefly erase any worries I had regarding the move.

My father, in contrast, looked more downcast than ever. I

supposed the woods reminded him just what sort of place we were moving to, and how against my mother's grain that place was. Revisiting his childhood home also likely made him reflect on his past, and in turn made him consider how much he owed my mother. She, after all, had been his saviour, the one rescuing him from a life filled with misfortune. I heard, directly and indirectly, about all such hardships. As mentioned, sound carried well in our small Scarborough house and often I'd overheard my parents speaking of my father's past. At times I'd gone out of my way to overhear.

When Dad was eleven his parents attended an evening school concert, one in which he proudly played the trumpet. In a cheerful mood the family took a different and longer route home than usual. The road they chose had only a gravel surface and was very winding. Dad's father wasn't concerned; he'd driven it many times. But, halfway home, he failed to negotiate a turn.

Drifting sideways on a long gravel curve, the big blue Chrysler smashed through a wooden fence at the road's edge and entered dense bush. Frantically pumping the brake Dad's father missed the first trees, but after glancing off several small maples the car struck a large one directly.

Joseph Farrow's head went straight through the windshield; he was killed instantly. Dad's mother, in the front passenger seat, survived the initial crash but was severely injured. In the back seat my father miraculously suffered only a broken right arm and cuts to his arms and face. He was trapped in the car, however; badly dented, the doors wouldn't open. He couldn't smash any of the rear windows, and his mother screamed in agony when he tried climbing out the front.

Few people lived on that road so there was little traffic. Worse, the Chrysler was well into the bush. Over an hour passed before someone saw them; a man stopped to check his truck's engine, and waving his flashlight about caught sight of the Farrows' car.

It was too late for Judith Farrow. She had serious head and internal injuries, and on that cool November evening my father could only helplessly watch her die. What it was like trapped in that dark car — seeing his dead father, and listening to his mother's cries of agony — I can not imagine. I do know that to this day my father never speaks to me of the experience. Although bearing scars on his face and arms, and paying tributes to his parents through his kids' names (Judy, of course, was named after his mother, and my middle name is Joseph) he has never once directly mentioned to me his family's horrific accident.

My father's aunt and uncle, the infamous Uncle Doug and Aunt Paula, fought to become his guardians. Why, no one knew; they proved terrible parents. I overheard few details, but of all those lively, happy tales of Muskoka my father told none included mention of his aunt and uncle.

At eighteen, and fresh out of high-school, he moved into a Bracebridge apartment. Taking accounting courses by mail while working at a restaurant, he landed a job with Harris Business Services. Grandma Layton, years later demanding an explanation from my mother about why Dad left Muskoka, told me that after four years with Harris' he was laid-off. Unable to find other accounting work, he decided to move to Toronto.

City life was almost entirely new to my father; he'd visited Toronto only a handful of times with his parents, and never with his aunt and uncle. Job hunting was quite different than in a small community. In Bracebridge a prospective employer already often knew my father's background when he walked in the door. Such was obviously not true in the city, and my recently-moved, Muskoka-bred father had a difficult time convincing anyone he had much to offer, or intended to stay long. What jobs he did land proved duds, and he had half a dozen in his first three years. Understandably, his confidence dwindled to nothing and he became extremely depressed; he had no real family and seemingly no real future ahead of him.

But at a small staff party thrown by one city employer, he met an attractive young woman, three years his junior, named Valerie Layton. She'd come to the party with a friend who was the company's secretary. As the story goes, when she met my father the two hit it off immediately and began dating. Friends believed they had nothing in common other than both being only children, and a framed photograph of the couple during this early dating period had 'Lonely Onlys' hand-written across the bottom. Yet they got along extremely well, announcing their engagement less than a year after meeting.

It was not, however, smooth sailing from here on for my father: his fiancée's mother didn't have a problem with his personality, but she definitely did with his background. She felt certain from the day she met him he would eventually lead her daughter back to Muskoka — it was simply a matter of time. Her suspicions were only strengthened when my father took my mother to politely visit his aunt and uncle several times before they retired to Vancouver. My mother, though, was not moved by any of Grandma Layton's pleas for "basic sense," and proceeded to marry Bruce Farrow the autumn following their engagement. Soon after this she also helped Dad land a decent accounting job through an old friend of her lawyer father. And when a few years later yours truly along with several other accomplishments arrived, my now securely-employed, newly confident and wisecracking father was again living a life with joy in it. Without question, Valerie Layton was the best thing that ever happened to him.

So, here we were on this Saturday afternoon in 1975, heading for a new house my mother obviously didn't want, and basically forcing her own beloved mother to do likewise. I could only conclude the bond my father had with Muskoka, and his desire to see his kids raised there, was extraordinarily strong.

Successfully rounding a long curve in the road, Dad poked my arm with his finger, then pointed to our right. There, behind perhaps fifty yards of bush, was a small patch of dark blue water. "That's the lake," he said casually. "The far bay — you'll soon see the rest."

Gordonier Lake was tiny; later I learned it was only a third of a mile long. Despite its small size, it did have an interesting hourglass shape, and the shore was mostly lined with solid woods. I could see only four houses. One of these sat well back from the lake, built atop a hill on the southern shore, directly across from where we were driving.

Soon after passing the house closest to the road, a tiny bungalow with 'Baines' hand-written in yellow on an eye-catching purple mailbox, Dad slowed the car and turned right onto a narrow gravel road. This led us back toward the lake, and between us and the main road a tiny creek flowed. When we soon turned away from the creek and main road, I looked to the side of the laneway opposite the lake and saw the rocky land rose sharply and was thickly wooded.

We'd driven maybe a hundred yards when a small gray house with blue trim came into view, and Dad pulled into a slightly overgrown gravel driveway. "This is it," he said quietly. "Like it or not, it's our new home sweet home."

Jumping out of the car, Sean and I raced out to the front lawn, with our father following at his usual lethargic pace. Our lot proved to offer a nice view down the lake, with a house on either side of us barely visible through a buffer of trees. "Private, at least" is how I hoped my grandmother would respond. Such optimism didn't last long. As Sean and I approached the water the grass became spongy and several frogs hopped out of our way. Also, the shore was jagged from erosion and lined with patches of pickerelweed. So much for pleasing Grandma Layton.

Following this quick look at the lake Dad steered us back toward the house. During this return trip I discovered something I hadn't noticed from the tiny real estate photo: two small dormer windows jutting from the roof.

Coming to an abrupt halt, I said to my father, "It's two storeys?"

He nodded. "We have two bedrooms upstairs, and that's where we're putting you kids. You'll be spoiled rotten."

We went in through a small porch on the driveway side. Leading off this porch was the kitchen, then a main room with a woodstove and large picture window facing the lake. At the back of the house I discovered a bathroom and two bedrooms, along with a screened room at the corner farthest from the driveway, one Dad referred to as a "Muskoka room." He explained it was a room designed primarily with spring in mind; a place where you felt out-of-doors but didn't get eaten alive by mosquitoes and blackflies. This led to a small deck, and a wooded back lot. The most striking feature was a huge white pine some fifty feet behind the house, a towering monster dwarfing the surrounding maples.

Back inside, Sean led the way upstairs, which were U-shaped and adjacent the kitchen. We found the two bedrooms large — enormous, actually — compared to those in the city. The dormer windows not only provided much light, but offered excellent views of the lake and surrounding woods. At this time, at least, I felt "spoiled rotten" was correct.

After exploring inside another half-hour we went out onto the front deck, which sat low to the ground and spanned the full width of the house. Here my father decided we should have our first Gordonier Lake supper. Sean retrieved a small cooler from the car and we sat at the edge of the deck, beginning with salads Dad made for us.

By this time evening approached and the lake had become glassy smooth. From everywhere came the sound of croaking frogs, and the cool, pine-scented air was refreshing after the hot, stuffy car ride. None of this seemed to phase my father, mind you. His expression remained glum, and he ate slowly and mechanically with his plate resting against his pot belly. As always, an old scar high on his left cheek, one from his family's car accident, stretched slightly while he chewed.

Wanting to raise his spirits, I said, "Mom and Grandma might come to like it in Muskoka, Dad. They really might."

He turned to me suddenly, as though I'd interrupted him deep in thought. "Thanks, but enough is enough, Lewis. We'll see."

"Grandma will like the house — it's ... big!" said Sean, our father's request obviously not registering.

"Yes, your grandmother will like the house," Dad echoed cheerlessly. Quickly turning, he fired something at me taking me completely by surprise. "Don't ask about anything Donny did or said today either, okay?"

"Don't —?"

"You heard me."

I dared to meet his stare but soon looked away, pretending the matter was closed. This was impossible, of course; for the rest of the evening the mystery of 'what I didn't know about the move' would consume me. I would not get to the bottom of it until years later, but I will share with you what I knew at this early stage, including what my father said to cap our conversation on this evening. In words I felt had an almost eerie relevance to my worries concerning Muskoka, he whispered, "As I said, boys — like it or not, this is our new home sweet home."

4

My father's mood was better on the Sunday of our first Muskoka visit. Indeed, so 'cheery' was he that shortly after breakfast he announced no further need for Sean's and my 'help' painting trim, and suggested we enjoy the great outdoors. Any hurt I felt over this dismissal, however, was quickly overwhelmed by interest in our shoreline. Here my brother and I spent several busy hours catching frogs and water spiders, luring sunfish to the surface with bits of bread, poking about in the pickerelweed patches, and generally getting filthy dirty. If we missed anything it was not for lack of enthusiasm on my part, since I endeavoured to thoroughly 'investigate the matter'.

I'd first heard this favourite phrase of mine, I should explain, at the age of six during an after-school TV show. After repeating it several times it also stuck with my parents, and henceforth they often teased me. 'Investigate the matter', in short, became my signature phrase, that perhaps best expressing my passion for exploring in all senses, from "missions" around our city neighbourhood to peppering chosen victims with questions. "The devil's private journalist," my father once tiredly quipped.

During the latter part of this first Muskoka morning my thirst for exploring quite typically degenerated into snooping. When my interest in our front shoreline waned, I lured my brother into a thirty-foot ribbon of bush along our property's right edge, between the lawn and creek. Once through and standing creekside we could, as I expected, scrutinize our neighbour's small bungalow.

This was the place I earlier noticed 'Baines' written on its purple roadside mailbox. Studying this residence, Nosy Parker that I was, I immediately sensed the Baines family was not exactly rolling in money. Faded yellow paint peeled from the siding, the tiny front porch appeared ready to collapse, and the overgrown 'lawn' was almost equally as wild as the surrounding woods. Parked in the driveway, too, was a rusty brown pickup filled with old, water-stained lumber. Curiously, in spite of this rundown look there were signs the owners were not particularly low in spirits. Besides the flashy mailbox, a tidy line of plastic cartoon characters lined the porch windowsill, and above the porch door an orange sign read 'Cathy's Castle'. For all its obvious wants the place unquestionably exuded a certain cheerfulness.

This overall positive impression, however, did not last long. Catching me completely by surprise, a tan-haired, heavy-hipped young woman wearing torn jeans and a wacky, green and yellow batik shirt suddenly emerged from the porch and strode quickly to the truck. She didn't notice the creekside spies, and before she did I yanked Sean behind a bush with me. I did this just in time; prior to reaching the truck the woman suddenly came back toward the house, facing us. Her appearance made me particularly glad my brother and I hid: her face was red and her cheeks noticeably wet. Returning to the truck she viciously fired a hammer into the back, then spun her tires on the gravel driveway when pulling out. Startled by this, I kept Sean hidden with me until she turned onto the Fraserburg road, heading away from town.

Fearing trouble, I never mentioned this incident to my father at lunch when he inquired into what precisely Sean and I had seen and done that morning. Sadly, my brother was pathetic at keeping secrets, and I think Dad soon suspected his sons were withholding information. Before getting a chance to interrogate, however, he was distracted by an old silver Buick clunking past on the laneway. It pulled into the place left of ours, opposite 'Cathy's Castle'. Further putting Sean and me in the clear, this time three snoops peered through the trees, catching a glimpse of a fifty-something couple exiting the car — a tall, blonde-haired lady and a short, wiry man. We didn't need to strain our necks long, mind you, because within a minute of this lady yelling "Heidi Ho!" she and her cigarette-smoking husband were standing in our kitchen. "New neighbours — I'll be goddamned!" the man blurted out before receiving a nearby elbow. And so it was we met Reggie and Carla Morrison.

Carla, to begin, struck me immediately as very ladylike. She wore a flower-print dress, kept her short blonde hair neatly curled, and her fingernails looked professionally manicured. She was the sort of person, in other words, I sensed my grandmother would like. One aspect of her appearance not seeming particularly ladylike, however, was her footwear: beneath her dress were tall green rubber boots. I'd noticed them as she approached the house and it was all I could do not to snicker. This reaction wouldn't have raised offence anyway, I soon realized, because as she walked her eyes never once left the ground. Midway through visiting her husband quietly offered an explanation, and warning: "Carla's real, *real* squeamish about frogs, snakes, bugs, and any other bloody thing that crawls or slithers. You'd be wise to always keep that in mind."

Reggie Morrison seemed an odd match for his wife — a small, quick, excitable man reminding me of boxing referees I'd seen on TV. Unlike Carla's quality dress he wore bargain-basement green pants and a plain white shirt, both mended at that. Also unlike his wife, and despite his modest appearance, he had about him a distinctly proud and even boastful air. He kept his slightly-graying black hair neatly slicked back, and he boldly scented our kitchen with the sort of cheap after-shave my father loved but my grandmother didn't tolerate. "Blue-collar Willie duding his way to the races on pay-day," that same grandmother would later scoff.

For the most part Reggie was jovial and mischievous on this afternoon. He managed, for instance, to make the eldest Farrow child briefly believe school started two weeks earlier in Muskoka. But there were also moments when I saw another side. Sometimes behind a perpetual veil of cigarette smoke you would see a face strikingly dark and grave. One such instance was when my father inquired about the couple from whom we'd bought the house — the Elliotts.

"But you'll miss the old ones, of course?" He said this to Carla as she and Reggie had a look at our back deck, and immediately after she expressed pleasure over having new neighbours.

She first glanced at her husband, then said with a touch of red, "We hardly knew them, I'm embarrassed to say."

My father's eyes lit up. "Hardly knew them! They had this place fifteen years, did they not?"

Carla frowned. "I maybe talked to them four times in those fifteen years, though, and you don't miss people you don't know. Reggie knew them a little better, but not much."

It was then, when Carla turned to her husband for comment, I noticed the change in him to which I've referred. After a long puff on his cigarette and exhaling through his nose, he cast a dark, grave face on my father and said, quietly, "The Elliotts pretty much kept to themselves, Bruce."

Carla, apparently finding nothing unusual in his severe look, quickly added, "We've long looked forward to having sociable people next door. That's why Reggie and I were so eager to meet you this afternoon. It may sound terrible, but we're glad the Elliotts left. Good riddance to them."

Sounding slightly concerned my father asked her, "Any idea *why* they left?"

She shrugged. "One of the few times I talked to Linda Elliott was just before she and Greg moved, and she hinted the reason was money problems. I can't claim that was the case for sure, though. Did they mention anything to you, dear?"

Her husband only slowly shook his head, grave face remaining. Even more puzzling, shortly before the Morrisons returned home and he and I were alone a moment on the back deck, I noticed him casting this same expression on the woods behind our place. And I considered being mistaken, but it seemed he paid particular attention to the huge pine.

That evening the Morrisons insisted on having us to their place for supper. We cleaned up before heading over, and were glad we did because the interior of their tiny red cottage proved immaculate. "A strictly no-slime zone," Carla announced. The layout of the cottage was similar to the first floor of our house, with several bedrooms and a bathroom in back, and a kitchen and main room out front. They explained they'd built the cottage themselves and that it had been a kit, delivered complete on one truck. "A regular do-it-yourself special," Reggie declared. With a proud smile, and as though they now had wheelbarrows full of cash, he added, "We hardly had a bloody dime back then."

We ate at the kitchen table, adjacent to a large window, and my father chatted with the Morrisons on numerous fronts. All was pleasant until he asked Reggie about his job. His wife quickly interjected and explained he worked as a shipper-receiver at an automotive parts plant in Toronto, then just as quickly changed the subject, launching into how the weather had been lately. But my father soon innocently returned to the issue of jobs, and the more questions he asked the more somber and agitated I noticed Reggie became. When he excused himself to "look after something outside," Carla whispered, "Sorry, Bruce. You couldn't have known, but work's a touchy matter with Reggie these days. We're into union problems at the plant again." Dad never mentioned work after Reggie returned, but the damage had been done: he hardly spoke the rest of supper.

In light of his somber mood I was surprised when after supper Carla pushed him to take everyone out in his boat for a lake tour. She emphasized it being *his* boat, and until he badgered her she showed no intentions of joining us. Finally, however, on went the green boots and out we all ventured.

Reggie's boat proved an old wooden rowboat, and one definitely hurting. The seats and gunnels were cracked and splintering, the oarlocks barely remained attached, and as we soon found out, it leaked. About the only thing this craft had going for it, seemingly, was size — it was large enough that even clad in the life-jackets Carla insisted everyone wear, we had no trouble finding room to sit. Dad and I occupied the wide stern seat while Sean sat with Carla up in the bow. Reggie took a well-worn middle seat and looked after the oars, and in no time had us well out into the lake.

The surface was very calm, and despite a sour rower being somewhat jerky with the oars the boat sliced through the water smoothly. The air had become cooler and fresher, and everyone took deep breaths. Other than faint squeaks from the oar locks we were completely silent the first several minutes, all of us merely soaking up the lake and woods. Indeed, we were so quiet that a large bird, one my father later told me was a great blue heron, flew past us surprisingly close, its huge bluish-gray wings slowly wafting the evening air.

For the next half-hour Carla gave us a nonstop commentary on the lake and its residents. We learned, for instance, the Morrisons were the only cottagers, everyone else remaining year-round. Two such full-time residents were Ed and Laura Russell, the couple who owned the house up on the hill. Another was Marie Taylor, the owner of a green two-storey house nestled among trees at the far end of the lake, a place not visible from ours. Marie and her late husband were the original owners of all the lakefront property, but after building the laneway at the opposite end they gradually sold lots. The Morrisons were the first buyers, building their place in the late forties, followed soon by the Russells, then the Elliotts, and most recently Cathy Baines, the single young woman living across the creek from us.

It was right after mentioning Cathy that Carla inquired into whether our family had yet seen or met her, and I desperately tried to appear innocent. Luckily my brother was absorbed in studying the darkening shoreline woods and didn't hear this question; I imagined him suddenly blurting out, "Yeah, we saw her, Mrs. Morrison — from behind a bush!" Anyway, when my father answered that we hadn't yet seen or met Cathy, Carla explained why she was curious to know.

"I don't want to appear nosy," she began hesitantly. "I only tell you this so you'll be sensitive to her situation. Her aunt has become quite ill with cancer, and the two are very close. As kids Cathy and her sister spent summer weekends in Muskoka at their aunt and uncle's river cottage, farther down the Fraserburg road from this lake. The uncle passed away years back, and her aunt is about all Cathy has in the way of family other than her sister."

"Her parents are both gone, are they?" my father asked.

"Not really, but they might as well be. Cathy doesn't get along with them, I'm afraid. They're rather strict with her."

"Or they try to be, at least — she's a lamb who's jumped the fence," Reggie piped in, his first time speaking since we left the dock. "Turned her nose up at a top-notch career job with her father's law firm to live at this lake and just work at a bakery in town. Probably gave up a spot in a hefty will, too, for all you know."

Carla glared at him. "Perhaps, but I believe we're now getting a touch gossipy, aren't we, dear?"

"Just telling Bruce so he'll be sensitive to her situation," Reggie answered with a mischievous grin.

His mood had lightened decidedly since we'd begun this lake tour. Slowly but steadily he'd recovered from the supper conversation, evidenced not only by his teasings about Cathy but also by how smoothly he presently rowed.

My father asked, "So how old a boat is this, Reg?" He did so, I should add, while using a small plastic ice-cream pail to bail out some of the inch and a half of water soaking his and my shoes.

"Had her almost thirty years," Reggie boasted, his cigarette dangling from his bottom lip. "How old she is I don't know. Picked her up at an auction the summer we built our place. I can tell you this — she's still just as good as the day I bought her."

Carla added smartly, "What he's saying is that this tub leaks as bad now as the day he lugged it home. I've been trying for years to get him to buy something new, but he's too stup—" Breaking off, she shouted, "Don't be doing that, you dirty bugger!"

Through his usual veil of cigarette smoke Reggie smirked devilishly, and without turning, said, "Somethin' wrong up there, Carla?" He then eased the bow away from a large patch of pickerelweeds.

The sun neared the trees at the lake's west end, and after Carla informed us she was an "early to bed, early to rise" person, she asked Reggie to turn the boat homeward. On the way, though, we passed the rocky point of land half responsible for the lake's hourglass shape, and here the captain suddenly brought his precious craft to a full stop. He proceeded to provide me with a quick lake commentary of his own. "We call this spot Crown Point," he announced, then explained, impressively and at length, how her majesty occasionally made a visit. "Plants herself in a lawn chair down by the water, she does, with a big white hat on and a big jug of iced tea between her knees." Gazing across the lake and smiling tenderly, he closed with, "The silly girl really loves the birds here."

I must sadly admit I didn't see through this story quite as quickly as the one he told about school starting early in Muskoka. In fact, such was the quality of this second performance, I beg you to believe, that fifteen minutes passed after this lake cruise ended before my father managed to set me straight. And so it was an evil pastime was born for Reggie, and one he would nurture my entire time at Gordonier Lake.

Before sending us to bed that night Dad took my brother and me up to the Russells' place on the hill. Insisting the absent owners wouldn't mind, this was a walk the Morrisons recommended, and it didn't take us long to discover why. Although the Russells' house was not particularly striking — a small, slightly rundown brown bungalow — the view from their front deck certainly was. For one, you could see most of the lake from here, allowing you to better appreciate its small size and hourglass shape. More significant, however, was the view their deck offered of the woods surrounding the lake; even from this much higher vantage point you could still see nothing but solid bush in all directions. I don't believe I was alone in being mesmerized by this sight. My brother, holding Dad's hand, stood several minutes just as silently as I stood, staring in utter awe.

Once nestled into our sleeping bags on our new bedroom floor, he and I also talked briefly that night. One issue was the future of our bunk beds. When I proposed separating them, considering our much larger room, Sean immediately raised argument. "Brothers are s'posed to have bunks!" was one offered excuse. I finally gave in, but not before demanding one condition: that we trade places. I was sick of climbing in and out of bed.

Silly as this discussion might seem, it exemplifies well how things were between us. I didn't feel myself worthy, but without question Sean looked up to his big brother. His both promoting and defending me could be amusing at times, but mostly it was embarrassing. His rebuttal to Joey Farnsted about my being "stronger'n you," for instance, always left me red-faced, and it was because of such remarks I sometimes referred to him as "the little bugger."

And little he certainly was. Although at seven he was slightly taller than four-year-old Judy, he was no heavier, and this became evident when he and my sister had a 'disagreement'. His skin-and-bones frame also made him a favourite victim of school bullies, and of teasing, kids often referring to him as the "brush cut runt of the Farrow litter." Somehow I had escaped such a predicament; although cursed with darkly-freckled forearms, I was blessed with a stocky build for a ten-year-old, and of this my brother was keenly aware. At supper he often mimicked me bite for bite, claiming food must surely be my "secret."

With the bunk bed issue settled Sean raised another issue on this evening I found rather more surprising, and rather more unsettling.

"Lewis? Think ... we'll live at this lake forever, or just a little while?"

Turning in my sleeping bag to face him, I answered, "We're probably here forever, and at least for a long time. Mom and Dad can't go buyin' and sellin' houses every two seconds, you know."

"Yeah, I know."

"Then how come you're asking? Didn't you like those people we met today?"

"I liked them."

"Then why?"

Sean didn't answer, and was silent a moment. The light in the hall was still on, however, and so I was able to watch him during this time. His eyes darted about but he kept his head completely still, a standard reaction when he was very nervous. The reality of our moving, I supposed, had now sunk in with him too.

A slight quiver in his voice, he said, "Think ... there'll be lots of stuff for us to do around here, Lewis?"

"Should be, but I guess I don't know yet," I softly answered, albeit reluctantly. Really I wanted to shake him silly and shout, "With a lake and ten trillion acres of woods around here you're wondering whether there'll be stuff to do?" But instead, deciding he needed comforting more than big-brother lecturing at this time, I tried to think of something about our new home he would find especially appealing. Luckily, I remembered why, in the months leading to the move, I'd never worried much about him not enjoying Muskoka. Doing my best to imitate his tone I quickly said, "I know there's *birds!* So you shove it, Joey Farthead!"

Thankfully this brought a chuckle from the other sleeping bag. Sadly, though, Sean was soon quiet again, and I was at a loss how to help. Too, for perhaps the first time ever, on this final night of our first trip to Muskoka I believe he was just as long getting to sleep as his older brother.

5

The following weekend proved incredibly hectic. The trouble began early Saturday afternoon when the movers, after driving no more than fifty feet along the laneway, slipped into the ditch. By the time a tow truck pulled the van out and the movers unloaded, it was nearing dark. Grandma Layton was sour enough already, but this accident drove her sourness to a level we'd previously not witnessed. On Sunday she whipped the whole family into a frenzy cleaning, unpacking boxes, and arranging and rearranging furniture. "I will *not* be living in a bush-hut!" was her most frequent line, voiced with added volume anytime my father was nearby.

On Monday afternoon, after considerable pleading, my grandmother at last granted me a reprieve and I resumed exploring the exterior of our new home. Along with Sean, though, I now had to contend with my little sister. My mother decreed I keep an eye on these two, and Judy, in her usual bold, determined way, wound up pretty much dictating where the three of us went. She also was bent on "finding more stuff" than her two brothers — typical as well — and rubbing in any successes.

My dear, four-year-old sister had an exceptionally competitive nature, one both heralded and despised by the rest of the family. On the positive side her competitiveness was undoubtedly responsible for her excelling in swimming. By age four, with the help of our Scarborough neighbour Jack Walsh, a swimming instructor, she could already swim as well as many kids twice her age. The problem was she clearly recognized such skills and was prone to showing off. Since poor winners tend to be poor losers, she could at times be the witch of the century. Fortunately for Judy, winning was the norm, especially when competing at virtually anything with her oldest brother. Through sheer determination or sometimes uncanny luck, she always got the better of me. Being six years her senior I found that hard to take, you understand, and became prone to seeking revenge by toying with her vulnerable side, and this she certainly had.

My sister, to put it mildly, had quite an imagination. For the most part our grandmother kept it in check; no "silliness" allowed in Judy's ballet, for instance, and her appearance was kept equally conservative — plain clothes and a simple ponytail for a hairstyle. In two main ways, however, her imagination still shone through.

First, it was our family's belief her imagination was responsible for her being a frequent sleepwalker. "Wayward wanderings of a wayward mind," was my grandmother's diagnosis. I only heard secondhand about most of my sister's wanderings, but those few I did witness I devilishly lodged in my memory for future reference. Most notably, one Saturday night in Scarborough I returned upstairs to find Judy in our dimly-lit kitchen, apparently in the midst of baking muffins. I won't claim she was making much progress, but she did have a muffin mix down from the kitchen counter, had it open, and had poured some onto the kitchen table. Sufficient evidence for me, and she paid dearly the next morning at breakfast.

My sister's imagination also manifested itself through art. Since about two she'd produced a steady stream of pencil crayon pictures on Bristol board, her medium of choice. To this day I've never encountered anyone, young or old, who drew odder pictures. Gravity, perspective, realistic colour, and basic common sense had no bearing in Judy's artistic world. When she was three, for example, she presented my mother — her official appraiser — with a picture of a purple dog riding a flying, six-legged giraffe through a green sky filled with staplers and teapots. Not, I believed, the workings of a normal mind.

Such held true on the Monday evening following our move, when Judy revealed her first Muskoka work. Mother visited her room to deliver laundered clothes, and Judy saw her opportunity. Pushing the appraiser down on the bed she presented her with a large yellow sheet of Bristol board. I witnessed this from my own open-doored room, and treasuring opportunities for revenge over lost competitions, decided to offer an appraisal of my own.

Judy's drawing was a classic. The basic scene was normal and predictable — our new house and the surrounding lake setting — but that was where any normality or predictability ended. It displayed: a levitated red house with triangular windows and a bus parked on the roof; Z-shaped black grass with giant chickens running around everywhere; an orange lake with candy canes floating in it; and lastly, an assortment of what I'm sure were upside-down trees with blue leaves.

Judy, standing on the bed with her arms draped over the shoulders of our seated mother, who was holding the picture, said, "Think it's a good one, Mom? Think maybe it's the ... *best* you've ever seen? Eh, Mom?"

Mother studied the drawing and, as usual, the only wrinkles yet on her pretty face — those at the back of both cheeks, likely formed purely through these appraisals — deepened. "It's ... got some ... *snap*, sweetie," she declared.

The great artist beamed a confused smile. "Snap?"

"What I'm saying is ... you ... chose ... some nice colours! Very nice colours, for sure!" Mother was doing well so far, I thought, but then came the big slip. "And ... those flagpoles with bushes around them look dandy."

As I let out a loud, malicious laugh my sister growled, "Those are *trees*, Mom!"

"They're dumb trees, though!" I couldn't resist adding, still laughing as I watched a puzzled-looking mother turn the picture upside down. "Since when the heck are the leaves blue and at the bottom like that?!"

"Since I decided!" Judy snarled. "I can make my picture any way I want. What's it to *you*?"

Sarcastically I answered, "Embarrassing!"

"Yeah, well go pick your nose, Mr. Freckly Arms!"

"Midnight Muffin-Maker!"

"Enough!" our mother ordered, but Judy was not about to be bested by a mere stupid brother, and we continued trading several more nasty remarks. All might have blown over had I not made the fateful mistake of giving her long brown ponytail a slight tug. I didn't pull hard, but by the way she howled you'd think I'd ripped half her scalp off. No doubt she was faking, I assure you, because the instant Mother began scolding me out snuck a tongue. Nonetheless, only I was found guilty.

Off to my room my mother sent me, Judy victorious once again.

It was on the sunny Wednesday of that week — my father's first day on his new job — that I met the Russells. On Grandma Layton's direct orders my mother and I were raking "every last Godforsaken leaf and twig" off the lawn when these hilltop neighbours suddenly appeared and introduced themselves. Surprising me even more was when Cathy Baines showed up several minutes later. "Security in numbers," this group declared.

Cathy, to begin, I found hard to believe was the same person I'd seen on our first trip to the lake. In complete contrast to the angry, tearful face I'd witnessed that morning was now one boasting the widest, most joyous smile you could imagine. Her smile was powerful enough to be contagious — one making you simply unable not to smile back. I also now saw more of her wacky side, that prompting the purple mailbox, orange 'Cathy's Castle' sign, porch window cartoon characters, and loud batik shirt. On this fine morning she wore huge, untied work books; two different coloured socks — blue and green; yellow shorts speckled with tiny silk-screened pineapples; and a blatantly ill-tucked Army surplus shirt. She wore, in short, the sort of clothes Judy would dream up. "I'm afraid she simply drums for a different marcher," Laura Russell later quipped when catching my mother and me staring.

Now for all her wacky, childish appearance and demeanour, I

sensed quite soon Cathy was not lacking in the intelligence department. She had piercing blue eyes, and nothing seemed to escape her attention. She also was not lacking in toughness. There were lingering clues to the first mood I'd seen her in; a hint of pain in her eyes and dark spots under them. But besides maintaining her incredible smile, never during this morning did she even allude to her aunt's illness, and through the Morrisons' account I knew she was suffering badly.

As for her companions, they struck me immediately as a couple fitting right in with the lake setting. Unlike Carla and Reggie Morrison, who seemed rather cityish, the Russells — both wearing hiking boots, jeans, and heavy sweatshirts — seemed very rugged and rural-minded. Ed Russell especially struck me as woodsy, his black beard and weathered skin giving him a classic 'woodsman' look, but despite thick glasses his tomboyish wife seemed equally comfortable in wild surroundings. And this initial impression proved accurate; even though they appeared only in their early fifties, they'd lived at the lake close to twenty-five years. "We were just kids when we built here," Laura Russell informed us. I soon realized that in those approximately twenty-five years they had acquired quite a knowledge of Gordonier Lake and the surrounding area. Both could, when coaxed, expound at length on virtually anything my mother or I asked. "That particular blue jay has been around here six years," was one comment. They also gave us a detailed introduction to the lake's great blue heron, which my mother and I had seen while raking.

For the next half-hour our visitors continued gabbing with my mother. Fascinating topics ranged from the quality of bread at Cathy's workplace to the price of new truck tires for the Russells' "Midnight Blue" half-ton, apparently the envy-of-the-lake vehicle. I was just getting ready to sneak away, in fact, when conversation turned to something I found almost unbelievable considering the Russells' great knowledge of their home: they planned to retire to British Columbia in several years. The couple owned a photography studio in Bracebridge and had already agreed to sell it to a long-time employee. Evidently Cathy Baines found this move unbelievable too, because it was while the Russells explained their intentions that I saw the first hostility between these lake residents.

"We're simply due for a change," said Ed. "We set a course for early retirement and once we do in a few years we're on our way. Some friends out in B.C. are taking us in until we find our own place."

"This, at least, is the plan," Cathy said with a smirk.

At this Ed's unbearded upper cheeks almost instantly reddened. Slowly, with his eyes closed, he said, "No, it's not the *plan*, dear, it's the *fact*. Embed it in your frigging brain, and —"

"I'm afraid Cathy, and Carla Morrison next door to you here, don't think it'll happen," Laura broke in, using only a slightly calmer voice. Sarcastically she added, "And of course, they're major authorities on what goes on in our heads."

"Yes we are!" Cathy defended, beaming a smile at my mother and me. "Even if Eddie and Laura do leave — which they won't — they'll be back before they even need to do laundry."

Steam seemed ready to come out Ed's ears, and Mother quickly said, "Sounds very nice. Bruce's aunt and uncle retired out west and they ... sure like it."

This was a complete lie: my mother hadn't spoken to my father's infamous aunt and uncle for five years. But her comment calmed the Russells, and conversation turned to something else catching my attention.

Ed had politely promised an elderly lady living farther down the Fraserburg road he would pick some wild raspberries for her. Not seeming thrilled about this chore, I promptly offered my services. I'd never picked a berry in my life, of course, but I let on I was an old pro. My mother — kind enough not to reveal this fib — sadly declined Ed's offer to come along, insisting her mother would not appreciate her absence. But Ed's next innocent comment left her doubled over in laughter.

"Hell — bring your mother along then, Valerie. Has she hiking boots of any sort?"

My mother laughed so hard I feared she'd hurt herself. Wiping tears and regaining her voice, she said, "Sorry, sorry! It's just that, Mother's not particularly ... *woodsy*, and we had a crazy weekend. I'm not sure she's even been to bed yet. Mind you, she'll wear out eventually and be much better after a sleep."

Both the Russells and Cathy looked puzzled.

"She's not too happy, you see," Mother continued, awkwardly. "She ... she's scrubbing the bathroom caulking with my husband's toothbrush right now, for one thing."

More puzzled looks.

"Tell you what — I'll ask!" my mother said in desperation. Turning toward the house she yelled, "Mother!"

A moment later Grandma Layton, my father's toothbrush in hand and perspiration dripping from her chin, appeared at the porch screen.

After a deep breath my mother delivered, "One of our wonderful new neighbours is taking the kids into the woods berry-picking tomorrow, Mother, and he'd be delighted if you went along."

"*When hell freezes over*!" came the curt reply, and the source stomped back into the house.

My red-faced mother turned to Ed. Waving both hands to emphasize he disregard what he'd just heard, she said, "Don't worry — like I said, she'll conk out eventually."

6

Flanked by my brother and sister, and raring to go, I banged on the Russells' side door immediately after breakfast the following morning. "*Holy Christ*!" we first heard quietly grumbled, this through a small nearby window. Then a softer voice. "It's seven-thirty, Ed — what the hell did you expect?"

Moments later a bearded neighbour opened the door, groggy-eyed and wearing only pyjama bottoms. Sarcastically we now heard, "Hey guys! Is the sun up yet?"

"The sun's right over there, Mr. Russell!" Judy innocently answered, pointing through the trees behind the house.

A night-gowned Laura Russell, nudging herself a place in the doorway, smiled sympathetically. "I'm afraid you kids will have to come in and wait a few minutes. We're not the earliest risers in the world anymore."

To this Sean offered the last thing I would have. "We can go home if you want, Mrs. Russell?"

"Don't be silly. Ed's about to rush off and get dressed — aren't you, dear?"

"Of course ... sure," he muttered, plodding away. When he was out of earshot Laura gave me an embarrassed, apologetic look and whispered, "Fifteen, twenty years ago he would have been getting you out of bed to go on this hike. I'm afraid times have changed, Lewis."

A long half-hour later we headed out. The trail to the raspberries began behind the Russells' house, and being quite impatient by this time I forged ahead of the others. I hadn't hiked twenty feet, however, when my brother and sister came to a sudden halt.

"What's that thing, Mr. Russell?" Judy pointed to what I already guessed was an outhouse.

Ed's eyes widened. "Never seen an outhouse before?"

My sister shook her head, and Sean embarrassed me further by asking, "What's it for?"

Ed smiled at me, then turned again to my brother and sister. "That was the bathroom back in the days before we had plumbing."

While Sean and Judy held a private conference over this revelation, I distracted Ed by saying, "Why, though, is it painted light blue?"

"Laura did that for a laugh one year to dress it up. But there's not much point now in trying to save it — it's had the biscuit. I'm planning to pull it down soon."

Judy, evidently gaining little insight from my brother, broke off talks and asked with a disbelieving tone, "If that was the *bathroom*, Mr. Russell, how come there's no curtains on the window?" She was referring to a small one on the back wall, visible through the open door.

"That's so you can see when you're in there," he answered.

A crease formed in Sean's forehead. "But ... somebody could peek!"

As Ed enjoyed a hearty laugh, and I considered crawling under the house in embarrassment, Laura poked her head out a back window. "What's the problem?"

"Outhouse peekers!" her husband announced, and she looked at us strangely.

The thrill of the outhouse soon wore off, I'm happy to report, and we began hiking the trail. The first segment proved to lead down the hill to the shore of the lake. Here our trail met another Ed explained simply circled Gordonier Lake. We followed this lake path until reaching the end of the far bay, then resumed walking the trail leading to the raspberries, heading straight into the western woods.

It was about eight-thirty now and the day had become bright. As we progressed along the trail, however, the bush gradually grew thicker and dimmer, and soon the forest floor was only speckled with what sunlight poked through the canopy. The air changed too; away from the breezy lake it now carried a blended scent of pine and damp earth. As for wildlife, all we saw was the occasional bird, roused from its tree, ironically, by the sounds of my bird-loving brother stumbling on rocks and tree roots. Seeing nothing but birds was both surprising and disappointing. Between wildlife shows on TV and Joey Farnsted's speculations about the Muskoka woods, I honestly expected to see deer, moose, bears, and wolves all within the first hundred yards. "So where the heck were they?" I kept asking myself. A city boy with much to learn, I was.

Reminded of Joey, I began wondering how my old exploring buddy would react if with me on this hike. I even pondered the things he'd likely say, such as grumbling, after not seeing any large animals, "Let's just keep going and going until we get to the good stuff, Lewis." Or how, as always during our city adventures, he'd have to stop and lift something heavy every ten minutes simply to prove I wasn't really "stronger'n you," as my brother claimed. Thinking like this made him feel almost with me on this day, and that in turn made me feel better. His long face the day our family moved, and I'd raced to his place to say goodbye, had stayed with me. So too our chat the previous day when, in final desperation, my friend dreamed up a wide assortment of crazy ideas about how he could visit me. He could, for instance, jump a northbound freight train passing the Lord Roberts Woods. But I knew it was hopeless; he wasn't going to jump a train, and his thoroughly city-minded parents would as soon have allowed him an excursion to the moon. All I could do to share with Joey this particular exploring mission was try writing him a letter sometime, and on this first Muskoka hike I resolved to do just that.

Now not only did I learn things about the woods on this morning, but also about our lake's rugged photographer. The first was that he was difficult to keep up with in the woods. He never stopped, or even slowed, to look at anything. I also learned he wasn't particularly talkative; many times I asked him questions but always received very short and unenthusiastic answers. For all the wonder his three young companions felt on this trip, and for all the hiking experience he obviously had, he seemingly couldn't have cared less about anything around us. This was particularly evident when we reached the end of the trail, and in a large clearing across from a shallow creek, the promised patch of wild raspberries.

"So," Ed announced sarcastically, "this is the pot of gold at the end of the rainbow."

Not exactly knocked over by this introduction, my brother, sister, and I quietly followed him across the creek, stepping on a series of smooth stones obviously placed there for this purpose. When across I handed Ed one of two plastic bowls I'd been carrying and we began picking, Sean and Ed filling one bowl, Judy and me the other. My first few berries I popped into my mouth, and found them somewhat more tart than the store-bought ones I was used to, but nonetheless tasty.

I was not tall enough to see the entire patch, but assuming it stretched across the whole clearing, it was large. Only Ed dared to venture inside the patch, coaxing Sean with him; Judy and I stuck to picking from the perimeter bushes.

We had picked and sampled the berries diligently about fifteen minutes when Ed, drawing close, surprised me. "So have you met Kevin Taylor yet?"

I shrugged. "Kevin Taylor?"

"Marie Taylor's grandson, a boy your age. Reggie and Carla didn't mention him?"

I stopped picking. "No."

"Kevin's spending the summer at the lake with his grandmother. He was here last summer as well."

"He's here for the whole summer?"

Ed nodded. "But don't expect to see him too often. He keeps to himself, and you need to remember that when you meet him. Don't be offended if he isn't too sociable."

"So why's he like that?" I asked, already somewhat put off.

Apparently sensing some hostility in my voice, Ed answered, "Easy, Lewis — easy. Kevin has his reasons. His parents went through an ugly divorce, and now he's having, well ... problems living with his mother. His father lives way out on the east coast — in Nova Scotia." Before I could inquire further, Ed added, "It's not my business to say anything more, though. You'll meet Kevin eventually, and I'll leave it to him to decide what he wants to share."

"You can't tell —?"

"No, I can't help you investigate the matter, Lewis Farrow," came a firm reply.

Ed had obviously been briefed the previous afternoon.

Upon filling the bowls we crossed back over the creek. Here I took a seat with Ed on a large nearby boulder. Several birches shaded this spot, convenient because the day had grown quite warm. Nothing slowed Judy, though; removing her shoes and socks, she waded into the creek. She then tried catching some minnows she'd discovered. My brother merely knelt beside the creek and watched.

Soon after sitting, and out of exploring habit, I flipped over a small rock with my feet. It sat about six feet from the creek, and nestled in a moist cavity of soil were two small, lizard-like creatures — both black with tiny reddish-orange spots. "What are those things?" I asked Ed, pointing at my find.

"Salamanders. Haven't you kids ever seen those before either?"

I shook my head, and Judy, who'd approached us with Sean, said, "Is it okay to touch them, Mr. Russell, or are they ... poisniss?"

With a chuckle he answered, "You can touch, but be careful not to hurt. You should also put them back soon or their skin will dry out. They need moist skin to even breathe — they don't have lungs."

When this comment produced three surprised looks, Ed

reluctantly treated us to several minutes worth of explanation about salamanders. His talk was similar to that the previous day when he and Laura told us about the lake in general. There seemed no end to the Russells' knowledge of their wild surroundings. I also noticed this knowledge was very particular and obviously gained from experience, not merely from books. For example, Ed didn't just know about salamanders, he knew about *these* salamanders. "Those little guys have lived under that rock for years," he informed us, and to this I could only shake my head in amazement.

After Sean, Judy, and I each had a turn holding them, Judy put them back in the soil cavity and I gently replaced the rock. My sister then returned to the creek and resumed trying to catch minnows, with Sean once again silently looking on.

After watching Judy a moment, who came about as close to catching a minnow as catching a crocodile, Ed said to me, "I'm gathering from all this that before moving you kids hadn't spent much time outside the city. Is that right?"

Seeing no point in trying to maintain yesterday's declared reputation as a seasoned wild berry-picker, I quietly admitted, "Hadn't spent *any* time outside it."

"Never?" Ed asked, and when I looked up and nodded I saw his surprise. He may have deduced by now we were green to the woods, but evidently didn't suspect we were quite this green. Stroking his bearded chin, he said, "Then I'm curious to know — what do you think?"

"I'm liking it so far. I used to go exploring a lot in the city, and I've always wondered about Muskoka. My father used to tell stories about living up north." Already believing I knew the answer, considering Ed's lack of enthusiasm on this day and his desire to move, I nonetheless asked, "What about you? Do you like living at the lake?"

Ed frowned, staring down at his worn hiking boots. "Once upon a time, Lewis — once upon a time I did. For instance, Laura and I, along with our son Jimmy, made this trail. We discovered the raspberries while I was taking pictures during our fifth summer here, and decided to cut a trail to them."

"How come you don't like it now, though? You seem to know pretty much everything. I think it's neat around the lake, too. Haven't seen what I thought I'd see, but —"

"I envy you, then. Laura and I were once the way you are now. But, let's simply say a lot of years have passed and we're really looking forward to going somewhere else. In fact, we can hardly wait."

"So you're sure about moving in a few years?"

Ed scowled. "Yes, *Cathy*, we're sure."

I should have seen this reaction coming, of course, and trying to make amends, I said, "She really teased you yesterday, didn't she?"

"Oh, she and Carla Morrison have been doing that since the day Laura and I made the mistake of suggesting we'd like to live elsewhere. I did my best to bite my lip with Cathy yesterday, considering the rough time she's having with her aunt being ill, but there's no question I'm sick of the teasing. She and Carla apparently think if they bug us enough they'll change our minds."

"And they won't?"

"They won't."

Turning to study my brother, who along with being quiet was still doing nothing but watching Judy, I said, "What about your son Jimmy. Has he already moved away?"

"Years ago, but not for the same reasons Laura and I want to move. He met and married a German girl on a little tour of Europe he did after high-school, and he spends most of his time now on the other side of the big pond. 'Jermany Jimmy' we call him."

"Did *he* like living at the lake?"

"I think so."

"So why don't you and Mrs. Russell?"

Ed glanced at me wearily. "I'm not prepared to spoil your outing today, Mr. Farrow. I want you to enjoy Muskoka, and I'm envious if you do. Just be satisfied with knowing we once, at least, liked living at good old Gordonier Lake."

"Yeah, but —"

Precisely as his wife said earlier, Ed solemnly added, "But I'm afraid times have changed, Lewis."

We headed home a short while later, the return trip quieter because I didn't even bother asking questions. And I believe keeping my attention strictly on experiencing everything around me was responsible for my noticing something peculiar. As Ed and my brother walked ahead of me I saw the older studying the younger closely. Sean continued walking clumsily on this day, and as he scanned the forest he seemed oblivious to these stares. But when I drew closer to Ed I saw a look on his face that puzzled me. He was not observing my brother with the sort of affectionate, amused gaze with which our father sometimes watched his kids when they were experiencing something new. I might have been mistaken — and I later mused over this possibility — but at this time I would have sworn Ed wore a pained expression as he watched my frail little brother. It was a look of concern, a look of worry.

7

On Friday evening of that week everyone on the lake threw a housewarming party for our family. The Morrisons were first to arrive, endearing themselves to my parents with a bottle of wine, and the rest of the lake crew soon followed. To my surprise, this crowd included Kevin Taylor and his grandmother.

Tiny, gray-haired Marie Taylor immediately struck me as exceptionally friendly and helpful. Before anyone even introduced her she'd given me a warm hug, and despite needing a cane she took part in all jobs concerning the party. During the evening she also chatted with my mother and grandmother like she'd known them thirty years. Grandma Layton especially enjoyed our elderly neighbour's company, and declared she'd take this "dear, frail woman, deprived of civilized life" under her wing.

Kevin, on the other hand, was virtually his grandmother's opposite in the social department. Within minutes of arriving he planted himself on the edge of our front deck and only rose again when Marie said they should head home. He spent almost all his time whittling small nearby twigs, blatantly showing off a camping knife I learned his father recently mailed from Nova Scotia for his eleventh birthday. Even with plenty of teasing by various lake residents he never showed the slightest hint of a smile, and all together said maybe three words.

So naturally I didn't expect to see much of Kevin Taylor that summer. But this proved true only for the next few days. On Monday afternoon, while Grandma Layton had Sean and me tidying our room, Mother yelled for us from downstairs. We found Kevin standing in the porch.

"So ... you guys wanna come over for a swim or what?" he muttered, studying the kitchen doormat.

Despite his obvious lack of enthusiasm, I wanted to forward his surprising initiative and so led my brother upstairs to change. Soon the three of us started along the Fraserburg road, heading toward the west end of the lake. This walk proved quiet, since Kevin had little to say when I asked him what he did around the lake for fun. "Nothin' much, really" was the longest reply I received. Most of his attention seemed focused on keeping his unbelted brown corduroy shorts from falling down. His poor, ill-fitting clothes were something I'd already noticed at the housewarming party. There he'd worn a tattered yellow shirt and baggy jeans with the leg bottoms folded up three inches. At that time, and during this swimming trip, I also noticed Kevin himself didn't appear in very good shape. He was about the same height as me but easily twenty pounds lighter, his face was thin and pallid, and his dandruffy black hair looked like it'd been trimmed with garden shears. "Kevin looks junky," my brother would later comment, and I had to agree.

When we arrived at his grandmother's place he led us past a pale green two-storey house to a large lakeside area of exposed bedrock. Here we found Cathy, Judy, and a sandy-haired girl about my sister's age. Katie Howard lived at a small lake half a mile farther down the Fraserburg road; earlier on this day Cathy introduced her to Judy.

"Welcome to the official swimming hole, boys — compliments of Kevin!" Cathy trumpeted while floating on her back about twenty feet from shore. In keeping with her other outlandish clothes, she wore a blue one-piece suit with several dozen orange and yellow fish embroidered into it.

Kevin only nodded in reply, then sat in the shade of a large pine growing in the grassy centre of the bedrock clearing. Here he took off his shoes, socks, and shirt — exposing a full set of ribs. While Sean and I sat and removed our clothes, our sister, wearing her expensive yellow "racing suit," stomped along the shore to where we were sitting. "We didn't need any dumb boys here!"

"We can come if we want!" I snapped at her. "Don't go thinking this is your own private spot, Miss Swimmer!"

Before she could argue back, Cathy said in a soothing voice, "But Kevin wanted them over, sweetie. This was his idea — *remember*?"

To this my sister grumbled something indiscernible and went back to playing with Katie. As for me, Cathy's rather forced comment revealed to whom I truly owed my invitation this afternoon. Kevin apparently realized I'd watched the cat leave the bag, too, because when I glanced at him he immediately turned away.

We were soon in the water, which proved cooler than I expected. It also had an earthy, rainwater scent surprising me, although it obviously shouldn't have. I needed to wake up and realize the lake was a far cry from the warm, chlorinated swimming pools in Scarborough.

Since my brother was not yet a strong swimmer (a fact Judy often reminded our family) I kept an eye on him, and so did Cathy. By her comfortable back-floating I'd already surmised she was a Muskoka swimming hole veteran. I supposed her experience came from those many summer weekends at her aunt's cottage.

Examining a small stick of driftwood, she said to Kevin, "Before I forget — your mother came out searching when you were getting the Farrows. I promised I'd tell you."

Kevin quickly turned. "What did she want?"

Cathy shrugged, but with a distinctly worried look answered, "Don't know, Kev."

He gazed at her a moment, then turned away and started swimming, rather aggressively, I thought, farther out into the lake. He only paused on occasion to yank up his shorts. Whatever his mother wanted, he apparently was not eager to learn.

Heading farther out from shore myself, I turned and floated on my back like Cathy and studied the Taylors' house. It was a green, dormered two-storey similar in size to ours, but with this house the gable wall faced the lake. The front wall boasted an elegantly-trimmed second floor balcony accessed through two clear-finished cedar French doors. Although the balcony and doors struck me as additions, since they were much fancier than the rest of the house, they did provide a touch of class to the place. At the housewarming party I learned Marie Taylor's late husband Lyall built this house himself several years before marrying, and had been quite proud of it. Although I felt this pride justified, one portion of the Taylors' yard detracted from the appeal of the whole residence. You could see remnants of Lyall Taylor's career as a building contractor. Beside a rundown workshop with a faded 'Taylor Contracting Ltd.' sign above the door was a variety of half-covered and sloppy piles of old, water-stained lumber. Evidently Marie also recognized this as an eyesore, because I learned it was here Cathy got the lumber I'd seen in her truck during my first visit to Muskoka.

Another thing I learned about Marie at the party was that she'd been extremely close to her husband, now deceased eight years. Laura Russell told my grandmother and me that a large silver locket Marie wore — and allegedly this tiny, elderly lady always wore — held a picture of her and Lyall. Also as a memorial to her husband, she dubbed his favourite swimming spot, the one causing him to build where he did, 'Lyall Rock'. But perhaps most significantly, Laura claimed she didn't move only because she strongly associated the house with Lyall. I believe it was this final revelation that prompted my grandmother's remark about Marie being a "dear, frail woman, deprived of civilized life."

Having been so close to her late husband I worried Marie might not like our large, noisy group at Lyall Rock on this day. Suddenly I spotted her approaching from the driveway, with Carla Morrison following closely. Like at the housewarming she took short, cautious strides using a dark brown cane that contributed greatly to her aged, frail appearance. Hanging in front of her blue dress was the heavy silver locket.

"How was town?" Cathy asked her when she reached shore.

"Busy, busy," Marie replied, adjusting her fancy flowered hat as she studied each of us in turn. She smiled and said, “I see you’ve got the whole gang using the pool. That’s nice,” and instantly I felt silly for thinking she’d be annoyed.

“Hey, like I’ve said, compliments of Kevin,” Cathy again trumpeted while glancing at Marie’s grandson, who was swimming back toward us.

Marie turned to Sean and me. “I came over to ask you boys if you’re for hire. I’m getting a big load of firewood in tomorrow and it’ll need stacking. It’s work too tough for me these days, and Kevin hates doing it on his own.”

Stopping his swimming, Kevin gasped, “I don’t mind, Grandma — really!” and when I glanced at him he again turned away.

Undeterred by this, Marie said, “So what do the Farrow boys say?”

Getting a nod from Sean, who perhaps out of empathy had already adopted our tiny neighbour as a second grandmother, I said, “We’ll help.” Later I would be glad; I learned she was quite a worrywart about winter and perpetually concerned about her firewood supply — even in midsummer.

“That’s much appreciated, thank you,” she said with obvious relief; she turned and started back toward the house. Halfway there she stopped and briefly faced us again. “Help yourselves to the fridge — I’m off to bed.”

Swimming close to shore near Carla Morrison at this time, I whispered to her, “Off to bed? Already?”

“She has a nap every afternoon,” she whispered back. “You’ll need to be a little quieter from this point on. Her room is the front one, the one with the fancy balcony.”

About five minutes after Marie went inside a younger woman suddenly appeared from the house, jet black hair and a narrow face identifying her as Kevin’s mother. She pushed open the screen door so hard it banged against the siding, and strode briskly out to Lyall Rock. I noticed she wore much nicer clothes than her son — white slacks and a fancy purple blouse — and her hair looked recently styled.

"Kevin!" she screamed. "You get inside right away! What the hell do you think this is? I gave you work to do while I was making those calls!"

Kevin peeped, "But I'm only —"

"You're only goofing the hell off is what you're doing!"

Marie, from her balcony, shouted, "Debbie! For God's sake leave him be! He has company over — the new boys on the lake."

"I don't give a goddamn who he has over!" Debbie snarled, spinning around to face her own mother. "He was told to pack my things up and the little bastard didn't. I have to meet some people in the city, and now I'll be late."

"Don't you talk in front of these children that way!" Marie shouted. "And these *people* you're meeting I don't care to hear about either."

"I'll talk however the hell I want, and these *people*, for your information, are way above you, dear." Nose high, Debbie turned back to her son. "You! Get in that house — right this second!"

Kevin slowly swam to shore and got out, and as he passed his mother she gave him a hard slap on the head. "Don't you *ever* pull bullshit like this on me again!" She then followed her son inside, grumbling other things I didn't make out.

As you might imagine, this incident left the rest of us rather quiet and uncomfortable on this afternoon. "Let's go home, Lewis," both my brother and sister whispered when we were back on shore, and I thought this a good idea. Cathy and Carla also talked, and I overheard one comment. With a sad and deeply frustrated tone to her voice, Cathy gazed toward the house and said, "I know, Carla — I know. *Christ* I feel sorry for that kid."

Despite that less than pleasant experience, from that day forward Sean and I chummed with Kevin almost every day. We learned his mother was only visiting for that one afternoon, and thereafter the mood at the Taylor house greatly improved. Our new friend still wasn't particularly chatty, but nonetheless, if Sean and I didn't call on him he'd invariably call on us. Besides delighting his grandmother by stacking her precious firewood, we swam regularly at Lyall Rock, and often played soccer or softball on our spacious front lawn. Our most memorable occasion, however, was the Thursday after our first swim. That evening Reggie Morrison let Kevin and me go out on our own in his boat, and while everyone on shore laughed and hollered, I put on a pathetic display of first-time rowing. "Let Huck have a try, Tom!" my smart aleck father bellowed from our front lawn. The good part was even Kevin started laughing, the first time I'd seen him do so.

Now during this span of time I developed a growing sense he was withholding information from me. His deep brown eyes occasionally looked secretive, as though he had something up his sleeve. Turned out, I was not mistaken.

The afternoon following the boat ride, right after watching Marie cane her way upstairs for her nap, Kevin led Sean and me across the main road and down a narrow, overgrown lane. He quickly explained his grandfather had made this little road for getting firewood and jokingly dubbed it 'Taylor Avenue'. That's all he explained, however; I asked him three times where we were going but he wouldn't answer.

Resigning, I decided to simply go along with this game and turned my attention to our surroundings. Taylor Avenue, to begin, was apparently lengthy because I couldn't see its end. I also couldn't see far through the woods since the land was hilly and rich with young trees. About the only specific thing I did notice was an assortment of rusty engine parts lying beside the road, along with yet more partly tarp-covered piles of old lumber.

The first surprise came when we reached the end of the firewood road. While I looked around for a reason for coming here, Kevin continued, venturing into the woods. I could see no trail, but he had seemingly no problem determining which way to head.

The thick forest was difficult to move through. Nonetheless Kevin hiked quickly and my brother struggled keeping up. Like on the raspberry-picking trip he kept stumbling over rocks and roots and getting whipped by branches. After he tripped over a fallen maple and did a complete face-plant, I had to ask Kevin to slow down. "I'm okay!" Sean clamoured as he wiped muck from his face and studied his scraped knee.

At last, reaching the peak of a ridge, I received my first hint to our destination. Climbing a large boulder to gain a better view, I shouted to Kevin, "There's another lake back here?"

"Shh!" he said with a hushed voice and stern look. "You don't have to go tellin' the whole stupid country!"

Leaping off my boulder and doing a wild, rolling landing, I jumped up and said, "So what's it called, Kev?"

"Don't know if it has a name," he answered, pawing the ground with his toeless running shoe. "Don't think anybody's given it one."

We soon reached the lake. It seemed about the same size as Gordonier but longer and narrower. Also, far more white birches grew here — solid stands in places. The biggest difference, however, was the number of houses and cottages: seemingly none.

Kevin led Sean and me along the shore. It proved rocky and steep and worrying about how clumsy my brother had been this afternoon, I ordered him ahead of me. I didn't worry long, though, because we soon came to a sandy flat stretch. We also soon reached something obliterating anything else on my mind: about thirty feet from shore, nestled amid a stand of young birches, was a tiny cabin.

"Holy cow!" I yelled, racing ahead.

The cabin looked very old. Alongside it thick bushes had grown up, and the siding was mossy and rotten. One end of the roof had collapsed under the weight of a large branch broken off a huge nearby oak. Inside, two legs of a rusty little woodstove had pierced the floor, a cot and table supported mounds of smelly animal droppings, and the one small window on the lake-side wall was broken. The place, in short, was a mess, but that in no way dampened my enthusiasm. A cabin deep in the woods, half-rotted and stinking or not, was the sort of thing I'd dreamed of finding in Muskoka.

"What's this place?!" I said to Kevin when he and my brother caught up.

"Just a place I found last summer. I think it's an old hunting cabin." Kevin said this as he pulled his prized camping knife from his pocket and began whittling a birch twig he'd picked up. Occasionally he glanced up, making sure his knifeless companions were watching.

"You mean some hunters might come here?" said Sean, his eyes lighting up.

Kevin paused with his knife. "No, no, *no*! Nobody's been here in a long time."

I said, "Sure?"

"I'm sure. Nobody comes to this lake besides me, and you're the first people I've invited."

"Doesn't your Grandma mind you coming here?" Sean asked.

"She doesn't know," came the predictable answer. Kevin then stared at us. "And she's not gonna know, either. Don't even go tellin' your parents my Grandma sleeps in the afternoon, 'cause that's the only way I get to come here."

Sean scowled. "We *won't* blab."

Despite this vow I decided, in light of his history of not keeping secrets well, to later reinforce the need to stay quiet. But for now I had another concern. Worried about not being granted future visits and thinking a little carpentry knowledge might be my ticket, I peered inside the cabin again and said, casually, "Those joists need replacing, for starters."

Luckily this remark did throw Kevin for a loop. After pocketing his camping knife he took a long swipe over his nose with the back of his already dirty hand, then said, "Joists?"

I pointed to the boards supporting the floor, and after studying them Kevin looked at me sternly. "How do you know stuff like that?"

"In the city my father and I helped a few families on our block make decks. Dad showed me all kinds of things."

"Lewis is the best carpenter in Toronto ... or anywhere!" Sean declared, chin high. No questioning, I reminded myself, the little bugger was handy at times.

I said, "Didn't you ever do any carpentry stuff with your Grandpa, Kev?"

"No," he answered softly, scratching his dandruffy black hair. "I was really little when he died."

"Maybe ... I could help you fix this place up, then! We could make it our own fort!"

Kevin scowled. "It's not ever gonna be some stupid fort, Lewis! Only little kids make stupid *forts*. This place is a cabin! It's *my* cabin, too, and I don't need your stupid help with it!"

Following this outburst I stayed quiet, but blatantly studied the half-rotted cabin door, which lay on the ground.

Finally, after also studying the door a moment, Kevin grumbled, "I don't know — *maybe* you can help fix it up. But it'll still be mine no matter what. It might not be the greatest place in the world, but it's mine, and *not yours*." Despite this emphasis concerning ownership, what came next registered even more. Stomping away he quietly said, seemingly as much to himself as to Sean and me, "And it sure as heck isn't my stupid mother's, either."

8

Over the next several weeks Sean, Kevin, and I visited the cabin almost every day, each time slipping away the moment Marie began her afternoon nap. As promised, with some old lumber, nails, and tools Kevin "borrowed" from his late grandfather, I began helping him make repairs. We started with the collapsed end of the roof, after removing, with difficulty, the heavy oak branch responsible for the damage. Work proceeded slowly because we only dared stay at the cabin about an hour and a half each visit. Another problem was Kevin proved very unskilled; he usually needed three tries at driving a nail, and was hopeless at sawing lumber. Even Sean faired better at these tasks — a fact not lost on Kevin. "Might as well forget this!" he muttered angrily one day as we were about to leave the cabin and he assessed our afternoon's work, which amounted to pathetically little. I began to wonder whether I'd promised more than I could deliver.

Slowing our progress with the cabin even further, I must confess, was my inability to resist occasionally exploring the new lake and surrounding woods. This I did with my brother only, since Kevin wanted no part in "stirring stuff up everywhere and getting dumb people's attention." At first I was puzzled what he meant, but after several lakeshore journeys I began to understand. I came to believe what he'd said about no one visiting this lake other than ourselves; at no time did I ever find any evidence of human presence. The cabin aside, the lake and surrounding woods had to them a wild purity even my ten-year-old mind appreciated, and I eventually vowed to myself to keep them that way. Never did I leave anything behind during my exploring trips, and even endeavoured to erase any footprints. I also never complained when Kevin insisted we take a different route to the cabin each day to avoid developing a path.

Now over the course of these several weeks my brother acted strangely. He continued stumbling often while hiking, a clumsiness he didn't exhibit in other activities. He also showed little enthusiasm toward exploring, and on several occasions even made silly excuses for returning to the cabin, such as "to check on Kevin." Lastly, he never commented on any birds we saw, and this was the main reason I felt he'd enjoy these little jaunts.

The root of his behaviour finally came to light the Friday of our second week visiting the cabin. On this overcast afternoon I managed to persuade Kevin to grant me a half-hour "off work" so I could explore the creek flowing into the lake, which entered at the east end. My brother and I had only hiked several hundred yards along shore, however, when he surprised me. Suddenly stopping behind me, he said in an angry voice, "I'm ... not going today, Lewis. I don't want to."

I spun around. "What's the heck's wrong?"

He stared at some nearby bushes. "Nothin's wrong. I just don't wanna go with you."

This wasn't the first time my brother backed away from one of my exploring ideas; out of boredom he'd done it in the city with Joey Farnsted and me. But studying him now, I noticed he kept his head perfectly still while his eyes restlessly darted about.

In disgust over this telltale sign, I said, "You're scared? You've gone chicken-shit on me?"

"I'm not chicken!" Sean fired back, his face turning red as he gave me a rare sour look. "And don't call me a chicken-shit ... Bonehead!"

The look may have been rare, but the remark represented an all-time first. "*Bonehead*!" I shouted, hardly able to believe my ears. "You're calling *me* a boneh—?"

"Leave me alone, Lewis! I'm going back! I'm going ... and you can't stop me!" With that Sean turned and stomped back along the shore, as usual stumbling at one point and almost winding up in the lake. As for me, after snapping several dead tree branches in half and heaving a large stone into the lake, I decided to heck with it and carried on toward the creek. No way a chicken-shit little brother was spoiling my fun.

And so ended Sean's participation in my exploring missions around the cabin. Not only did he refuse me that afternoon but consistently thereafter. As much as I was disgusted with him and determined not to let the matter bother me, it did; to put it mildly it left me confused. Having been such a fanatic about birds in the city I found it bizarre the woods scared Sean. But confused and in need of answers as I may have been, I never said anything to my parents or grandmother; I felt the issue of our moving to Muskoka was sensitive enough already. Out of desperation I did approach someone, however, and that was Ed Russell. I now had a hunch the worried look he'd worn while studying Sean during our raspberry-picking hike had to do with him seeing a problem I didn't.

This hunch proved a good one. On the Monday after my fight with Sean the Russells started their summer holidays, and that sunny morning I helped Ed do a two-year-in-advance-of-moving shed cleaning. Getting right to the point with my questions, I learned he was indeed aware of my brother being scared of the woods. Before I could inquire further, he stunned me with another admission.

"Your mother knows too, Lewis." He said this right after passing an old camp stove out the shed door, and I almost dropped it.

"My mother knows! How the heck would she know?"

Ed dragged a musty, sloppily-rolled tent out and heaved it into the 'Midnight Blue', the pickup already half full. "She became aware your brother was having problems shortly after your family moved to the lake. It seems he's woken up a few times after nightmares. She talked to me to see whether I'd noticed anything, and I had. I could see the fear in him the day I took you kids to the berry patch."

"He's woke up with nightmares! I haven't seen him getting up at night!"

Ed shrugged. "Then you must have slept through the times he did."

"My mother never said anything!"

"No, and she didn't tell your father or grandmother, either. She also insisted I not say anything to them, or anyone else. I didn't even tell Laura." Ed stared at me. "And you won't be telling anyone — *correct?*"

"I'm not the one who has problems keeping secrets!" I answered defensively. "Anyway, why would my mother not want my father knowing?"

"I have no idea, but she was adamant he, especially, not be told."

Hearing this surprised me, to say the least. I thought my mother would have loved to present my father with direct evidence the move had been a bad idea. In fact, having seen those mischievous, sparkling eyes the day the Elliotts accepted our house offer I'd have bet on her confronting Dad.

I said, "I promise I won't say anything, so could you tell me *why* Sean is scared of the woods? 'Cause I don't get it. He hasn't seen anything scary yet that I know of. He —" I broke off, almost mentioning things we'd done at the cabin.

Passing out a folding camp chair, Ed said, "I'll tell you what I told your mother, but it's ... tricky. I've experienced the same brand of fear myself, and I've seen it before in someone else. About five years after Laura and I built this place a nephew of mine spent the summer with us. He was nearly the same age as our son Jimmy — six or seven — and we thought the two would have a ball together. But it wasn't long before poor Gordie was having problems much like your brother's having — nightmares and becoming less and less keen on going into the woods. On two occasions I tried chatting with him about what was wrong but he never had much to say. He didn't hide he was scared — he admitted that — but he couldn't tell me what the problem was."

"So what do you think was wrong?"

Ed stopped working. "My feeling is he found the woods intimidating, Lewis. Do you know what that word means?"

"Sort of. But *why* would he find them that way?"

Ed left the shed and pointed with a long rugged arm to the woods surrounding the lake. "Take a look at all that, Lewis, and tell me it doesn't seem like the woods stretch damn near forever."

I didn't; I'd already developed this impression the final evening of our first trip to the lake.

"Try telling me," Ed continued, "those woods don't seem awfully big and powerful. If you do then I say you haven't been deep enough into them yet. Wait until you go tens of miles and see if you don't get a little nervous. I've been back that far, and I've felt intimidated — damn right I have. You feel so small and powerless against the woods; it gives you a taste, I'd say, of how life was for people thousands of years ago. You realize that without our inventions, like guns and bulldozers, we're pathetically weak and vulnerable."

I considered this, taking in the view of the distant woods, then said, "Maybe, but ... Sean sure hasn't been back that far."

"Ah, but in his mind he has. When you're as young and tiny as him even a half-mile into the woods would seem halfway to hell."

"He wasn't scared of the woods when we lived in the city, though. He loved the Lord Roberts Woods."

Ed shook his head. "You're not getting it. It's a matter of size, of magnitude. That tiny patch of woods at the end of your block was nothing compared to the woods here. Am I right?"

I nodded. "But like I said before, he hasn't seen anything scary yet. I don't see —"

Ed breathed deeply, pulling at his beard. "You're thinking there's something specific your brother's afraid of, and I'm claiming it's simply the sheer vastness, the sheer *strength* of the woods that's scaring him. They make him realize just how tiny and fragile he really is. Just like Gordie, though, I seriously doubt your brother could explain his problem. It's too abstract a fear for kids that age to understand. But not understanding their fear doesn't stop them from feeling it; they might not *think* it, but they can *feel* it. I could talk to your brother about his fear, but like I told your mother, I doubt it'd help." Ed paused, eyeing me. "And you, Mr. Farrow, also don't understand what the heck I'm talking about — do you?"

I shrugged and angrily said, "*I* think Sean's just being a stupid wimp. Maybe —"

Ed broke in with a harsh voice. "Then your brother is more experienced with the woods at this point than you are; he's discovered something in Muskoka you haven't yet. You could learn from him, you little bas—" He stopped himself, and after a deep breath, said in a softer voice, "How about showing him some sympathy. He's your younger brother, for Christ's sake."

"He's a stupid wimp is what he is," I grumbled, not loud enough for Ed to hear clearly, but he frowned nonetheless.

After this discussion I was lost what to think. I hadn't understood Ed's explanation about my brother, and not having understood it, had a hard time believing it. Any doubts I had about Sean having nightmares, though, dissolved on the Thursday following this talk. That night I woke suddenly to see my mother tiptoeing through my dark room toward the bunk beds. She had just passed a creaky floor board and I knew this was what woke me. Waiting a few seconds for the cobwebs to clear, I looked at the lighted clock on my night table. It was 1:25 a.m.

Knowing this was far too late for my mother to be making a routine check on my brother and me, I whispered, "What's going on?"

She inhaled sharply before whispering, "Oh! Sorry! I took the wrong route on that crummy floor toni—"

"What are you doing?"

"I'm ... getting your brother's pillow."

Not fully awake, I didn't connect. "Getting his pillow?"

Mother knelt beside my bed, Sean's pillow clutched under her arm. "He's sleeping with your father and me tonight — he's had a bad dream. Must have been that TV show you two watched."

She was referring to a program on ghosts we had watched after supper, so I knew she was making an excuse. My brother had seen plenty of shows like that in the past with no problems. I believe she knew I detected a fib, too, because after giving me a peck on the cheek she quietly but quickly left the room. Apparently she satisfied my father and grandmother with her reasoning, however; at breakfast the next morning no one spoke a word about the whole incident.

9

During the following days I never told Sean I knew, nor bothered him about what he did or didn't do at the cabin. I still thought his fear silly but after Ed Russell saying he didn't understand it, I didn't see any point confronting him. This decision proved insignificant anyway, because soon after his latest nightmare our cabin trip routine that summer suddenly came to an end.

The following mid-August Sunday morning Kevin's mother showed up unexpectedly and informed her son his summer at Gordonier Lake was over. She was hardly out of the car when she began yelling at him to "get his shit together." He didn't seem surprised by this sudden change of plan nor did he argue. "She's going on some stupid business trip and I don't fit in," he soon explained. "I have to stay with one of our cruddy neighbours because she won't have time later to come get me." When I asked what sort of business his mother was in, he wouldn't answer. He simply stared at his shabby suitcase and continued packing his equally shabby clothes.

With Kevin gone cabin trips naturally stopped. It being his place and most definitely not mine, after all, I didn't feel right going without him. This left my brother and me spending our remaining summer days playing sports or doing assorted activities with other lake residents. Marie Taylor made it clear we could swim at Lyall Rock anytime we desired, and during the following hot week we desired often. One notable occasion was a Friday afternoon when Judy coaxed our very white-skinned father to join us for a swim, his first since we'd moved. He'd been working long hours settling into his new job and was enjoying a rare afternoon off. Also with us was Reggie Morrison, joining us by boat shortly after arriving from the city. Despite our urgings, he didn't swim but merely chatted with my father.

The first hour was only a showoff session for my sister. Having basically lived in the water this summer her swimming skills had improved noticeably, and she was eager to reveal this to Dad. Her behaviour was predictable, of course, but what happened late this afternoon certainly was not.

On shore and just about to head home for supper, we suddenly heard several splashes behind us. I moved in time to see yet another one in a tiny pond behind Lyall Rock, some ten yards away. A narrow four-foot-long crevasse in the bedrock connected this pond to the lake.

Reaching the pond we instantly saw what made the splashes. A large bass had entered, apparently to feed, although on what we couldn't see with the bottom stirred up. When we drew close it must have detected us because it swam quickly toward the lake. My father's large white foot in the connecting crevasse stalled that plan, however, and the fish retreated.

"Whadya do that for, Dad?" Judy shrieked. "It wants out!"

"Settle down, sweetie. I'm only looking at it." To Reggie he said, "That's a decent-sized bass. I'm happy to see there're nice ones in this little lake."

After a silent minute watching the fish, which now stayed still, Judy said, "Think maybe it's looking for a new house or somethin', Dad?"

"Bass don't have houses, Judy," I said, all-knowingly. "It only went in there to eat stuff."

"Like what stuff?" Sean asked.

"Maybe it —" My father broke off because the bass now made a second and much more desperate attempt at escape; desperate enough that after weaving through numerous small pond boulders at lightning speed, it launched itself out of the water and managed to clear over four feet of bedrock next to my father's foot. All this with only perhaps six feet of shallow, obstacle-filled water to build up speed. We quickly turned to watch it, and I swear if I'd blinked I'd have missed it, so fast did the bass reach deep water and disappear.

"Can you *believe* that?" my father gasped before breaking into a crazy laugh.

"It ... jumped right out of the Godforsakin' pond!" Judy announced wide-eyed.

Studying the lake, searching in vain for any sign of the Olympic-medal bass, I said to my father, "Didn't exactly think it would do that, Dad."

"Me neither. Didn't think it would dare try, for one thing. How about you, Reg — ever see anything like that before?"

Our neighbour only shook his head, and this was a second surprise on this afternoon. Considering his penchant for telling tall tales I expected a doozy of a fishing story. But he said nothing. Too, he wore the same dark, grave face he'd worn the afternoon I met him, when he'd stared at the woods and huge pine behind our place.

I believe my brother and father were with me in considering the bass's escape an impressive feat, but we left it at that. My water-loving sister, however, proved a little more than impressed. The very next evening she announced at supper, in complete seriousness, that her newfound ambition was to become able to swim as well as a fish.

My brother's problem seemed silly enough, but this declaration pushed me over the top.

"Who cares what a stupid bloody *fish* can do?" I shouted across the table. "Chasin' minnows at the raspberry patch was dumb enough, but this is the stupidest thing you've ever —"

"They can jump and swim anywhere in the lake they want — right to the bottom, even — and as fast as they want!" my sister shouted back, green eyes flaring. "That's how I'll be able to swim soon too — so shut it, Lewis Penis-Brain!"

I had only once before seen my grandmother's rear dentures fall out, so this evening brought the count to two.

"Both of you get to your rooms this instant!" she screamed after recovering her teeth from her mashed potatoes, and continued to scold for the next fifteen minutes.

She sentenced us to two days in our rooms, without chance of parole, for our "dreadfully improper vocabulary." And two summer days of imprisonment were two very long days. Worse, when granted a release I shared with Cathy all that happened, and she tore a strip off me as well.

"Okay, wise-ass! Your sister's four! And by the drawings I've seen an extremely imaginative four at that!" I was helping load more of Marie Taylor's old lumber into her truck.

"But you don't think it's stupid, though? Wanting to be able to swim as well as a fish?"

After battling a heavy board, Cathy said, "Haven't you ever in your life wanted to be another animal, or at least wondered what it would be like, Lewis? Think of all the things some animals can do that you can't. Don't you envy them for those things?"

"Like what? I don't really care how well a fish can swim compared to me."

"Fine, but wouldn't you like to be able to climb a tree as well as a squirrel, or be able to jump twenty times your body length like a frog? Or how about carry fifty times your body weight like an ant? Think about that one — being able to carry that whole pile of lumber at once." She pointed to the five-foot-high stack we were drawing from.

Taking a page right out of my father's manual, I said, "That's what forklifts are for."

"That's so true, *Bruce*. Thanks so much for indulging me." As we lugged over another board Cathy added, "I, for one, remember a winter I saw a moose in front of my place early one morning. It stayed a good ten minutes before wandering off. I thought about how that moose spent the whole winter outside, and how tough it must have been to be able to do that. It made me wish I was that tough." She stared at me. "Am I getting anywhere?"

I smiled and shrugged, and Cathy said, "You're a waste of effort, Penis-Brain."

On the Thursday of that week I paid a visit to the Morrisons, who'd been up all week on summer holidays. Reggie was pondering new rowboats in a brochure Carla picked up and supposedly wanted my input. Clearly this was only to quiet his wife, because ten minutes after beginning our perusal, he dozed off. But thus I gained a chance to chat alone with his wife, something I'd looked forward to since Kevin went home.

About one nanosecond after she presented me with a glass of apple juice, I said, "So what exactly does Kevin's mother do for a living?"

I didn't expect this question to startle her, but it obviously did. Coughing through a mouthful of tea, she choked, "Why, may I first ask, are you concerned about that?"

I wanted to say, "I'm concerned for the same reason you are," but instead said, "Just wondering."

"Just wondering, huh?" Carla paused, staring in disgust either at her kitchen window view of the pickerelweeds, or perhaps over what was on her mind. Finally she said, carefully, "What ... *exactly* she does I'm not sure, but what I do know is she has a not-too-admirable occupation."

"Not-too-admirable?"

"That's all you're getting out of me, mister." The lake's early riser raised her hand for emphasis. "The last thing I need is Marie mad at me."

"She'd get mad at you for telling? It's that bad?"

"Probably all ninety pounds of her would clunk me over the head with a cane, and I thought I told you it was case closed."

More concerned than ever for Kevin, I pleaded, "At least a hint?"

Carla offered only a cold stare — one clearly indicating she was staying quiet concerning Debbie — then sent me to wake my boat-buddy. But I had no doubt she knew all. On the way to the living room I recalled Cathy's words at Lyall Rock: "I know, Carla — I know. *Christ* I feel sorry for that kid." Kevin, quite apparently, was in an even worse predicament with his mother than I first realized.

I left the Morrisons about seven-thirty. It was late August and already night was approaching. This evening was also chilly, and after shivering slightly I stopped to do up my jacket. Fighting a bad zipper, I heard the faint sound of honking geese. Sure enough, a moment later a flock of perhaps twenty appeared above the north woods, heading south. They were in V-formation but not flying very high, and as they passed overhead you could even hear their wings wafting the cool air. I watched these huge birds, transfixed, until they disappeared over the Russells' hilltop. And yes, no doubt whatsoever, I wished more than anything at that instant I could fly with them — along with a certain young friend — to virtually anywhere on the entire earth we decided to go.

10

On the final Friday of August our family attended its first Gordonier Lake corn roast. Tradition held that each lake household host this event in turn, and this year it was Cathy's. Not wanting to miss anything I went to her place, joined by Sean and Judy, about five o'clock to help with preparations. Being present early had both pleasant and unpleasant consequences. Indeed, along with making treasured acquaintances, I almost got myself into the worst trouble I'd ever been in.

To begin with the pleasant, soon after greeting the early Farrow clan Cathy received a major surprise: her sister and aunt arrived from Oakville. No one heard them pull in, and when Andrea, a taller version of her older sister, appeared on the lawn with sweet little Aunt Jenny, I swear Cathy jumped three feet in the air. Turned out this was a surprise her sister and aunt had long planned. "I don't believe you two!" she shrieked as the three hugged, kissed, and cried a solid five minutes.

Cathy's aunt was clearly ill. She had a drained, fragile look; her cheeks were pale and sunken, flesh sagged under her throat and tiny arms, and her short, thoroughly gray hair was sparse and straggly. She also was unsteady on her feet, Andrea having to hold her arm. Nonetheless, Cathy soon pulled my brother, sister, and me aside and quietly reminded us about her aunt's condition. "She's no wimp, though. So don't overdo it pampering her." I later found her remark odd because pampering their aunt was exactly what she and her sister did all night. Aunt Jenny, as Cathy instructed us kids to call her, received nothing less than royal treatment.

The unpleasant element to this evening arrived from Kingston about seven. Unlike her aunt and sister, Cathy already knew her parents were coming to her corn roast. At our place a week earlier she explained that since her very controlling parents always attended she loathed hosting the corn roast. On this evening I learned why. When a green Mercedes pulled into the driveway, she whispered, “The sergeants have arrived,” and sure enough, within minutes her life became utterly miserable. For his part a silver-haired and suit-wearing “Lorne M. Baines,” Aunt Jenny’s younger brother, began circling the house and lecturing Cathy’s boyfriend Rick on what a dump the place was. When meeting Rick he struck me as far from meek, but he merely followed his girlfriend’s father around the house, nodding politely at everything said. Meanwhile, an equally formally-dressed Patricia Baines went to work inside, loudly barking rapid-fire orders at Cathy regarding the corn roast, and occasionally offering snide remarks about her secondhand furniture.

This continued a full hour. Nothing Cathy did, past or present, escaped criticism from her parents. Some comments were only mild, but they accumulated. The result was tears from Cathy, which she tried concealing but I noticed, and me learning something: that in only our family’s short time at the lake, I’d bonded with her. I clearly displayed my feelings through what I did to Lorne M. after he delivered yet another nasty remark: I fired a cob of corn.

“What the hell?” he shouted, spinning quickly to face me, his hand on the side of his head that I’d pegged.

Standing next to a corn-covered picnic table, frozen in utter disbelief over what I’d very suddenly done, I could only stare back.

“Why the *hell* did you do that? What the —?”

At this instant Cathy came to her front screened window. “What’s going on?”

“This little bastard just whipped a cob of corn at me!” her father blared. “Not that I should be surprised — if you live in a dump you get dump neighbours!”

"Whipped corn at you? Don't be ridiculous — look behind you, Dad! He was only trying to toss it in that garbage can. Must be a bad cob."

Cathy's father turned and stared at the can, one I too only noticed at this time. After giving me an evil eye for several long seconds, he grumbled "Jesus H. Christ! Stupid bloody kids!" and stomped away without examining the perfectly good cob of corn.

And finally I could breathe again.

Incredibly, no one mentioned anything to my parents or grandmother when they arrived. Too, when the entire lake crew was present the event actually became enjoyable for a while. Aunt Jenny seemed to have a good time, and my brother, sister, and I found the tasks of tending the fire and cooking the corn rather fun.

It was about nine-thirty when — for me, at least — things again took a turn for the worse. Seeing Cathy up to her eyeballs in mother-ordered chores, I offered to take a pot of coffee out to a group seated mostly at the picnic table. This group consisted of Aunt Jenny, Andrea, my mother, and black poodle-haired Patricia Baines, who'd refused the picnic table and opted instead for a fancy padded lawn chair she'd brought.

When reaching the table I heard Patricia, sitting forward in her throne, say to my mother, "We're disappointed — there's no denying it. We tried to steer Cathy in the right direction, but apparently we've failed."

"There's nothing wrong with her, Mother," Andrea immediately argued back, and when she saw me she sent her eyes skyward.

Her mother countered in a hushed but stern voice. "Don't claim there's nothing wrong! She's completely out of control!"

Andrea scoffed. "That's exactly the point. She —"

"Haven't been to a lovely occasion like this in years," Aunt Jenny broke in, grinning slyly at my mother. "Neil and I went to the occasional corn roast on the river, but that's a while ago now."

"We held a couple of crazy bashes ourselves," Andrea added cheerfully, nodding politely when I motioned with the coffee pot. "Remember the time the cops showed up because of Uncle Neil and Tom Hutchings singing so loud? And the time your glasses fell into the corn pot, and we let you fish around half-blind with the tongs trying to get them out?"

"Lord yes!" said Aunt Jenny, chuckling while bringing a finger to her eye. Sighing, she said, "I sure hope we can make a trip out to that cottage tomorrow. I hope I'm up to it."

"You'll be up to it, Auntie," Andrea said tenderly, reaching out to hold one of her aunt's frail hands. "We'll go, and you'll be fine."

"We only wanted her to do something a little more substantial," Patricia continued with my mother, scowling at Aunt Jenny and Andrea. "She could be putting her education to better use. Lord knows we gave her enough. All this childishness — dressing the way she does, working at some silly bakery, and living ... *out here* — I'd say it's about time she grew up and got serious."

"Yes, I understand," my mother quietly replied, staring down at the picnic table.

Then came the tense moment.

When Mother passed on the coffee, I looked after good old Patricia. The second her cup was full she snapped at me, "You march inside and tell Cathy to quit slouching and get on with serving those pies I bought. This is ridiculous — having a lake boy serve coffee for her."

No, I won't tell you I considered dumping hot coffee on Cathy's mother, but I certainly was on the brink of a harsh remark. And this time I obviously wouldn't have escaped unscathed. Fortunately my mother, as always, sensed her son's disapproval, and motioned with her chin for me to move on to the rest of the crowd.

As I started away, and Bitchface carried on complaining about her oldest daughter, Andrea grabbed my arm and whispered in my ear, "Welcome to the club, Lewis. Cathy and I are lifetime members."

Much to my approval, Patricia and Lorne M. Baines left about eleven. By this time Aunt Jenny had retired to bed, and Grandma Layton, Sean, Judy, and Marie Taylor had also called it a night. Cathy and Andrea, however, were only getting warmed up. Both of them dove right into the sauce, and within an hour alternated between bouts of laughing and crying. The last time I saw them they were sprawled out side by side on the front lawn, gazing at the "gazillion billion stars," and I wouldn't doubt that's where they slept.

The following morning Aunt Jenny was fortunately feeling well, and we left for her cottage about ten. My brother and sister already had other plans, so it was only me joining Cathy, Andrea, and their aunt. We went in Andrea's car — a fancy BMW I was initially afraid to even get into so plush was the leather interior. Cathy, although seemingly even more out of place than me, took the wheel. True to form, though, she wore giant sunglasses with florescent pink rims, and every time I looked at her I snickered. I was the only one doing so, however; her wardrobe was obviously nothing new to Andrea and Aunt Jenny.

We drove along the Fraserburg road, heading away from town, until reaching what I learned was the south branch of the Muskoka River. Immediately after crossing the bridge we turned right onto a narrow gravel road cutting through the woods alongside the river — 'Cridiford Road', a sign read. We now travelled slowly, passing cottages on both sides of us, all of these tiny and modest. I found this surprising considering the money in the Baines family; apparently dear Aunt Jenny didn't share in this wealth. My impression was soon reinforced when Cathy slowed the car to a crawl and turned right into the overgrown driveway of a small brown cabin. Trees, bushes, and Lyall Taylor's old lumber crowded this driveway, and to avoid scratching her sister's definitely out-of-place BMW, Cathy eased in only far enough to get us off the road.

I found the cabin lot appealing. The entire front of the property was bare bedrock and sloped gently down to the river, which ran only about fifty feet from the cabin. Both the back section of the lot and the far side of the river were thickly wooded, and no other cottages were in sight. It was a spot striking me as very woodsy and peaceful.

The cabin itself looked quite rundown; the windows frames wore little paint, and in many places the siding was split and moss-covered. When we reached the tiny side deck Cathy warned us to avoid several broken planks, and after unlocking the side door she had to lift up on the handle to get the door open.

We entered a tiny kitchen. Indeed, the entire musty-smelling cabin was tiny. Furnishings were equally modest: chairs made from two-by-fours, a hole-ridden couch, and dusty paint-by-numbers. The wood floor was unfinished, including inside two closet-sized back bedrooms, and only a rough ladder served the attic bedroom, Cathy and Andrea's private domain as kids. Despite its shortcomings I felt the cottage would be fun; you wouldn't worry about wiping your shoes before entering, or worry about breaking anything. As Aunt Jenny commented later on this day, only slightly exaggerating, "If it's breakable, it's broken."

On a main room shelf I discovered pictures of Andrea and Cathy when close to my age. They were engaged in a wide array of outdoor activities, from swimming to mud fights to canoeing on the river. Spotting me Cathy came up and said dryly, "Those were times during my childhood I was actually alive, Lewis." Without elaborating she continued opening the cabin windows.

We soon had lunch, one we'd brought in a large cooler. We ate on a large, crude picnic table in front of the cabin, the legs cut to different lengths to level it on the sloping rock. Tragedy almost struck when the seat on one side suddenly gave way under Aunt Jenny. Luckily Cathy grabbed her in time, and we then opted for chairs, which proved only slightly better. Once settled I became simply an observer during this lunch; Aunt Jenny and her two nieces talked nonstop about old memories at the cabin. As on the previous evening the three laughed and cried a good hour. At one point Cathy croaked, "What the hell would we have done without this place, Andie?"

After lunch she and Aunt Jenny went for a riverside walk along Cridiford road. Andrea and I didn't join them; after Cathy's sister secretly whispered, I suddenly wanted her to take me canoeing. We didn't head to the river right away, though, but stood a moment in the driveway watching her ill aunt slowly amble down the road, with Cathy holding her arm. When they were out of hearing range I inquired about the canoeing idea. "Simply giving Cathy some time alone with her, Lewis. We're both close, but my sister especially." Continuing to watch her struggling aunt, Andrea said, softly, "Walking that road was always Aunt Jenny's favourite thing, and I'm sure she's thinking the same thing as Cathy and me — that maybe this is her last walk." Wiping her eyes while angrily scraping the driveway gravel, Andrea added, "Goddamn that hurts to say."

Like everything else at the cabin the canoe had seen better days. Regardless, we carried this craft, which I recognized from the living room pictures, down to the water and were soon afloat, miraculously suffering no leaks. Painted on both gunnels was 'Cathy and Andrea', the letters badly faded. Andrea explained her aunt and uncle had given their two nieces this canoe as a present one summer.

With me in the bow and her in the stern we began slowly paddling upriver, staying close to the thickly-wooded shore. The day was getting warm so we stayed within the shade offered by the shoreline trees, and the occasional drip of cool river water off my paddle also helped. This, of course, was my first time canoeing, and I didn't exactly master the art immediately. Andrea had to spend several minutes coaching me how to paddle, but I soon got the hang of it.

It was after travelling about a hundred yards upriver, and passing another tiny cottage, that Andrea suddenly stopped paddling and said, "So did you know you can get up to five years for corn cob assault, young man?"

I almost tipped the canoe.

"Corn cob assault?" I said, as innocently as I could.

Receiving no response I looked back at Andrea. While straightening her fancy-styled tan hair, she stared at me with a devilish grin. "I was right behind you, Lewis Farrow."

"But I —"

"Don't worry! Right behind you in more ways than one; Cathy too. She quickly figured out what happened, and told me later that in her head she jumped up and down and cheered like hell after you did that."

"She did?!"

Andrea nodded. "Pretty ticked off were we?"

"He was bossing Cathy around and saying rotten things about her! So I —"

"Oh, I know," Andrea broke in while resuming paddling. "I've been witness to that my whole life."

"How come they aren't that way with you?"

"They used to be. I've just fallen into line more than my sister. Compared to her, my parents see me as an obedient daughter. Plus, being the oldest, my parents have always put more pressure on Cathy. They never really allowed her a childhood to speak of — constantly pushing her into stricter private schools, never allowing her any real toys, and damn near having her bounce quarters off her bed every morning. That's why I think she's now childishly rebellious at times, such as the way she dresses; she's making up for something she was denied."

Watching several ducks swimming ahead, I said, "How come *she* didn't fall into line, though?"

I looked back at Andrea again and she answered with noticeable embarrassment. "Because she has about ten times as much backbone as I have. She was willing to do without having money, and that was something I have to admit I'd have a hard time doing. Basically put, I've lived in a wealthy family all my life, Lewis, and it's difficult to live not-so-wealthy after that. How Cathy can stand living the way she does I'll never know. You need to realize — she and I grew up in a massive house with maids, a chef, a swimming pool, and tennis courts. Think about that, and then about the way she lives now."

This stunned me; I hadn't realized Cathy's parents were *that* wealthy. I couldn't imagine her living such a ritzy lifestyle.

I said, "And Cathy gave all that up?!"

"She did."

"Her place at the lake, though, isn't ..."

" 'Cathy's Castle' isn't much of a castle?"

I turned and shyly nodded. "So *why* did she give all that wealth up?"

Steering us away from a long overhanging pine branch, Andrea motioned to the river and woods. "This place was the basic reason."

I stopped paddling and faced her. Apparently communicating my confusion with my expression, she said, "Cathy and I used to come to Muskoka all the time with my aunt and uncle, and things were ... well ... *different*, to say the least."

Already having guessed this but asking anyway, I said, "You mean your aunt and uncle weren't bossy like your parents?"

"God no!" Andrea laughed, dabbing playfully at the water with her paddle. "My parents gave them a long list of rules for my sister and me, of course, but my aunt and uncle ignored them. Regularly we stayed up late playing board games, and sometimes after Aunt Jenny and Uncle Neil went to bed, Cathy and I climbed down from our attic window and went skinny-dipping. We used to think our aunt and uncle didn't hear us, but I've come to believe they did. They simply didn't like spoiling our fun."

"Didn't your parents come to the cottage too, though?"

"Only once. Too busy getting richer. They saw this place as mere playground, and were far too serious-minded for anything like that."

"But if they thought that way ... why'd they let you and Cathy come?"

Andrea beamed. "That was Aunt Jenny's doing. Instead of suggesting to my parents Cathy and I needed a break from them, she suggested my parents needed a break from us. It worked, too; she wound up bringing us to Muskoka virtually every weekend, and for the whole of her and Uncle Neil's summer holidays. It was, without doubt, the greatest gift she could have ever given my sister and me — especially poor Cathy — and we've never forgotten what she did, or her cottage."

As Andrea wiped a tear from her cheek for seemingly the tenth time since I met her, I said, "So you and Cathy really loved this cottage?"

"We did, but not right away, mind you. Like I learned about you last night, we'd never before left the city in our lives, and when we first arrived at the cottage we thought we'd been sent to the end of the earth. We didn't realize how liberal our aunt and uncle would be with us. But having said that, it was Mr. Fox who really sold us on this place."

"Mr. Fox?"

Andrea grinned. "Early in the morning on our second day at the cabin Cathy looked out our little attic window and spotted a fox walking along the shore. After that we watched for him every morning we were here, and he never failed us. As soon as we woke we'd head straight for the window to watch Mr. Fox."

"And what did he do?"

"He trotted along the shore, sniffed at the ground here and there, backtracked once in a while, and sometimes just lay for a moment yawning."

"That's all?"

Andrea nodded, then gazed upriver, watching a loon. "Soon, that's all we noticed a lot of things doing around the cottage. But what we saw at the root of it is what caused Cathy and me to fall in love with this area. It's also what caused my sister to eventually forfeit the family fortune, and build that quaint castle at Gordonier Lake."

I stared at Andrea, who returned it and uttered something making me smile every bit as wide, I believe, as Cathy: "Freedom, Lewis — freedom."

11

Kneeling on the Morrisons' dock and whistling a tune unfamiliar to me, my father sank his accident-scarred right arm in the water to his shoulder and drew up a large bunch of pickerelweeds, roots and all. "Hooo!" he said, covering his nose with his left arm while plopping the weeds into our wheelbarrow. "*God* these things are smelly."

"How much are we gonna do, Dad?" said a rubber-booted Judy, worriedly studying our fish-habitat destruction.

"Just a little more, honey. We need to do enough so it shows from the Morrisons' kitchen window. That's the one Mrs. Morrison seems to look out the most."

"Think this will help much," I said, plunging my arm into the cool, murky water. The weeds were dying but still slimy with algae, and you had to grip tightly to uproot them.

My father shrugged. "Don't know what else we can do."

Reggie Morrison soon came across the lawn from our place. He wore the same sober expression he'd worn the last several long hours. When reaching us Dad said, "How's she doing?"

"Managed a cup of tea now, but Val damn near had to hold it for her. Little Sean is in there telling knock-knock jokes — that's helping." Squinting behind cigarette smoke Reggie studied our chosen pickerelweed patch, now significantly smaller. "Don't go straining yourselves."

"We'll finish this patch," Dad said firmly, peeling a brown fragment of dead weed off his bare chest.

"It needed a little cleaning out anyway, I guess; the boat was getting cramped. But it's a bloody shame you feel guilty about all this." With that Reggie strolled toward his cottage.

We'd been through a bad morning this cloudy Sunday, the day following the trip to Aunt Jenny's cabin. Not long after breakfast my mother sent me to keep an eye on Judy as she played along the shore of the lake. Knowing she could easily do this all day, I only let her go as far as the Russells' dock before demanding she turn back. While passing the Morrisons' on our return trip Carla, dressed in old, paint-smeared clothes, poked her head out her front door. "Could I borrow your muscles a minute, Lewis. I need help moving a table and it'd be a shame to call Reggie just for that." Her husband was currently cruising the far end of the lake.

Judy and I went inside and followed her to a heavy living room table, which was tucked against a corner. "I need it pulled back a few feet so I can get at the wall to paint," she said. Never one to be left out, my sister joined in, setting the shoebox she was carrying on the table.

We'd only pulled it back about a foot when a leg caught on the edge of a floor tile. This made Carla fall on her rear end, but with no apparent harm she merely gave us a jovial "Oops!"

The table leg getting caught, however, caused the shoebox to also fall.

Now I knew Judy had two frogs inside — I'd seen her put those in — but I didn't know that previous to her amphibian friends, she made captive a small garter snake. And apparently it loved being introduced to the frogs because it was in the middle of swallowing one when the shoebox spilled open on poor Carla's lap.

At parties for years after, my father claimed the scream arising from the Morrisons' place on this morning actually rattled our living room window.

"That should do it for this load," the same father declared, plopping another handful of conciliatory weeds into the wheelbarrow. Rising to his feet and stretching his back, he said to Judy, "So tell me — did you not think the snake would eat the frogs?"

"I thought he'd make friends!"

My father eyed me, grinning. "Oh, he was happy to make friends, all right."

"One frog got away, though. I put him back in the lake."

"That's nice, Jude." To me Dad said, "While I think of it — what'd you do with the dead snake? We don't want Carla stumbling over it on her way home."

"It's in there." I pointed to the ribbon of bush between our lot and the Morrisons'.

In the midst of screaming and scrambling Carla trampled the garter snake and half-swallowed frog with her feet — her bare feet, I might add.

Thinking back on the incident, I said to my father, "Why do snakes eat like that, anyway? I mean, swallow things whole?"

"Not having teeth to chew with might be one reason, but I really don't know. Why?"

"Just seems ... strange."

After I'd emptied the wheelbarrow behind our shed and returned to the dock, Dad knelt and resumed pulling. He whistled nervously, as he had the entire job.

"Why do you always whistle?" I asked him.

Continuing work, he said, "Picked that up off my father a few years before he died. Our lake was loaded with leeches, and Dad taught my buddies and me to whistle while we swam. He said it kept away the 'creepy-jeebies'. He might have only been playing with us — I'm sure we looked pretty silly, three or four young boys whistling as we swam — but it did seem to work. Having said that, I never got over the leeches entirely. I still cringe at them, so I still whistle."

I knelt on the dock again but hesitated before resuming work. Leech stories I didn't need; I'd already salted one off my freckly right forearm this day, and was becoming less keen by the minute about weed-pulling. The stench and slime also were not helping.

Finally, psyching myself up, I again plunged my arm into the cool, muck-scented water. I went as far down the slimy weed stems as I could to ensure getting the roots.

Just when I'd tugged a handful loose a small bullfrog jumped out from the shore underneath the dock. It bounced, wet and slippery, off my bare shoulder, then scooted down into the silty brown ooze of the lake bottom — to where, I couldn't help speculating, the water snakes were waiting.

"What?!" Dad said when I let go of the weeds and jerked my arm from the water.

"Nothing," I answered, and after several uncontrollable shudders, began shakily whistling the same tune as him.

12

September arrived on schedule and Sean and I now faced adjusting to a new school. Our first challenge was becoming used to riding a bus; it took over half an hour to get to Muskoka Falls Public School, a far cry from our two-minute city walk. Worse, my brother had problems with bus sickness, unloading on our seat several times, and our popularity suffered accordingly.

Although Judy was not yet five, my mother decided to enter my smart little sister into Kindergarten. She took the big bus in the morning and came home at lunch in a van, or "the limo," as Dad called it. Grandma Layton worried about this early start, but my sister easily broke into the school routine. On her first day she and her friend Katie Howard stepped off the bus and marched across the courtyard like they owned the place, and by morning recess seemed to have befriended half the school.

In contrast my brother and I were on our own the first few days, and during this time I especially missed Joey Farnsted. It wasn't until Wednesday we finally made some friends. Two were sandy-haired twins from my class: Lenny and Brian McKellar, the first identical twins we'd ever met. Soon after, Sean became friendly with several boys in his class, so by the end of that first week we'd settled in.

A snag, however, was an ungainly black-haired boy one year my senior — Scott Graham. For whatever reason, this kid immediately decided to hate me. He wasn't big for his age and could hardly have been deemed a school bully, but nonetheless did seem determined to get the better of me.

My first run-in with him came on the Monday of my second week. Lenny McKellar and I were beside our class portable when he approached me. "You can go right back to the city, Asswipe! We don't need you at our school!"

"We'll live wherever we want, and it's not your school, Dipshit!" I naturally fired back.

Scott stared fiercely and I countered, but before anything more could happen my teacher, Mr. Gerard, came out the portable door and broke us up.

For the next several weeks we continued trading harsh remarks, but it never went beyond that. On the Thursday of our third week, however, things erupted. During afternoon recess that day, Sean, the twins, and I were walking across the front courtyard when Scott came running past chasing a soccer ball, and my brother accidentally tripped him.

"What'd you do that for, Stupid?"

"Shut your face!" I said. "He didn't mean to."

Scott glared at me. "Shut *your* face, Asswipe! You're just as stupid as —"

He broke off, because at that instant my tiny brother took a flying leap at him.

Sean was half his size, but he still managed to knock him over. The only person more surprised than me at all this was Scott, who, with a stunned look, quickly shoved my little brother off. He then got up and took a wild swing. Jumping between them I took this in the chest, and after grabbing Scott he and I fell and started fighting on the ground. This battle was brief, however, because Mr. Gerard again arrived on the scene, pushed his way through a crowd that had formed, and broke us up. He sent Scott in one direction and my brother and me in the opposite, with both parties swearing at each other.

Amazingly, no one made a visit to the principal's office, but this incident was by no means over. By the time school let out my brother had developed a nasty lump on his head; it seems when he dove he hit his head on Scott's knee. Grandma Layton turned as red as a beet when her two grandsons arrived home. Even at supper, when the lump had all but disappeared, she was still fuming.

Trembling in anger, she snapped at my father, "Now are you going to call that boy's parents or am I? That was a heck of a lump dear Sean had!"

"He was the one who put the lump on his head!" Dad replied, waving his fork at my brother. "He was the instigator. Isn't that right, Champ?"

"He was only sticking up for Lewis!"

Dad scoffed. "Since when does big Lewis need Sean fighting his battles for him?"

"But you get mad when people bother him, don't you, sweetie?" my much calmer mother said soothingly to Sean.

Dad chuckled. "Sweetie? How cute — a champ who's a sweetie!"

"Leave him!" my grandmother said harshly.

Dad, with a devilish smirk, said in a resigned tone, "Yes, I suppose I should, Mother. When I think about all this, if Lewis wasn't so yellow he would have nailed this Graham kid in the first place."

Sean immediately looked up from his plate.

"Yup," Dad continued nonchalantly. "Must be rough having an older brother who's a complete wimp."

He stared straight-faced at Sean a few seconds, then stuck his bottom lip out and made a fist. Instantly my brother scooted over and punched him on the leg, and he wailed in fake pain.

"You're only encouraging it!" Grandma Layton blared, and in disgust stomped off to her room.

After frowning at Dad my mother capped this supper by saying something making this whole incident sting even more for me, albeit I'm sure unintentionally. Whispering in my ear, she said, "What's it like being ten feet tall, Lewis Farrow?"

My father may have joked at supper, but later that evening, right after having me go out to the shed with him to "move some boxes," he was far from jovial.

"You keep cool, Charley, and I'm dead serious now."

"Keep —?"

"Don't pretend! I've been watching you. There's all but steam coming from your ears. Don't go starting something tomorrow — you hear me?"

"He might —"

"Hey! Did you hear me?"

Quietly, but far from happily, I answered, "I heard you."

I tried, I honestly tried, but to no avail. The following Monday Scott and I got into it full force, and it was ugly. Dipshit went home with a scraped back and a black eye, while Asswipe suffered a cut on his forehead and a bruised leg. The net result was my parents confining me to my room after school the rest of the week. Confining me to stew and become even more uptight about Scott Graham, that is. I also wasn't thrilled with my brother at this time, even though one night during my prison term the little bugger whispered from his top bunk, "Sorry, Lewis." Indeed I was still miserable when, at the end of this week, I encountered an equally uptight neighbour.

When we didn't see the Morrisons for about a month after the garter snake incident, my mother started worrying Carla was seriously upset with us. She tried calling her in the city several times but never got an answer. At last she and Reggie showed up on the Saturday morning following my bad week, and to my mother's relief, shouted her standard "Heidi-ho!" from the car while passing on the laneway. Only several minutes later, too, she green-booted her way to our place and plunked herself down in a kitchen chair.

"I've come to hide, if you don't mind."

"Uh, oh!" said my mother, pouring her some coffee.

Carla sighed, glancing out the window toward her cottage. "He's been miserable for weeks."

"When we didn't see you we figured Reggie must be upset about something," Dad said, putting down his Toronto Star and winking at me. "What's up?"

Carla scratched her hair. "What's up is Reggie's union. The problems brewing in the summer when you met us have now reached a boil — the 'S' word is definitely in the air. We don't even answer the phone anymore there's been so many people from the plant calling to see whether Reggie has any inside knowledge. And if he didn't have enough to contend with, two fellows arguing about the union problem got into a fistfight a week ago in his shipping-receiving office and half wrecked the place. He's still sorting out files from an open cabinet they tipped over."

"A fistfight, huh? Seems there's a lot of that going on." Dad smirked at me while saying this and I countered with a scowl.

My mother asked, "Has Reggie ever considered going somewhere else?"

"Once upon a time. He worked so hard to get the job he's got, though, I don't think he could ever bring himself to leave. He's been at this plant twenty-three years and I don't know whether he could handle going somewhere new and basically starting over. His plant's car parts are all he knows."

"Tell him if they strike, Val could get him a moonlight job where she works," Dad quipped. "I hear they're looking for another bagger."

He was referring to a job as a grocery store cashier my mother landed in early September in Bracebridge. This was a type of work she'd done before yours truly entered the world, and although I believe she was a bit rusty at the till, she was doing well. She'd already got herself a bank loan and bought a used car — a red VW Beetle.

After Carla heard a quick boast about this job and car, she said, "I'll mention the bagging idea to him, Bruce, but I somehow doubt customers would enjoy his current mood. 'Golly, Mrs. Jones, I seemed to have squashed your bread. Maybe you'll just have to kiss my ass'."

Chuckling, my mother said, "Well, I'm sure getting away for the weekend will help. We should all get together tonight and play some cards — Reggie might enjoy that."

"That'd be nice, and sure, we'll do that," said Carla. "From experience, though, I can tell you these things tend to solve themselves. You'll see."

"Tell you what," said Dad, glancing at me. "Along with another guy who's been miserable lately, I'll go over and talk it out with him."

Carla looked puzzled, but simply said, "That's appreciated, Bruce, but you don't need to. Like I said — he'll be okay."

"You underestimate us. We'll have a man-to-man with him."

"Oh, please!" my mother scoffed.

Undaunted, my father rose from the table and headed for the porch door. "C'mon Lewis — we're going on a mission." Before stepping out he turned back to Carla. "Should we be taking weapons?"

"You'd be wise to give him a wide berth, in all seriousness. He's pretty wild right now."

We found Reggie attacking his shed door lock with a hammer.

"Stupid goddamn thing!" he roared, kicking the door so hard he fell down. He rose with a whimper, his normally slicked back hair sticking up in places, then again whacked the lock with the hammer.

"Um ... missing a key there, Reg?" said Dad.

"It broke off in the stupid goddamn lock!" he quickly answered before taking another vicious swing. This time the lock and hasp broke off and fell to the ground. Storming inside, Reggie yanked open a red tool-box my father and I knew held assorted plumbing gear.

"Closing up?" Dad asked.

"Might as bloody well. I seriously doubt we'll be up again."

"Something ... wrong at work, by chance?"

Reggie stopped rooting and squinted at my father. "The wife blabbed, did she?"

"Only concerned, I think."

Evidently not finding what he was looking for, Reggie dumped the tool-box on the shed floor. Dad silently watched a moment, then said, "Things are touchy at work, are they, Reg?"

"Touchy as hell," he snarled. Waving a screwdriver at us for emphasis, he added, "But I don't go dumping my friggin' problems on neighbours."

My father held up both hands. "No one's accusing you of that — we came to you."

Reggie paused from his search again and gazed into space. "*If* you're asking, though ... I just don't know about this plant anymore, Bruce."

"Hang in there — you're not far from retirement. Another ten years will pass before you know it, and then you can do anything you want."

"Only ten years, eh? I feel a heap better."

With a tiny wrench Reggie left the shed and headed toward the back of his cottage. My father took several steps in the same direction, apparently about to offer help, but stopped. "We need to head home now. You should come over and play some cards tonight."

"Sure ... cards," Reggie grumbled as he slipped under the cottage. And a moment later he was banging away at something else.

Following that failure, which I, a recently dubbed 'Smiley', did nothing to help avoid, Dad and I kept our distance. Reggie did come over that evening to play cards, but he was quiet and withdrawn and Carla soon took him home. On Sunday he did nothing but row around the lake. After supper that day my father decided to have another try at settling him down, and insisted Smiley come along. We reached him just as he returned to his boat.

"How many laps you plan on doin', Reg?" Dad said.

"Wasn't planning on doing any." He motioned with his thumb toward his cottage. "She won't let me do anything else — I thought for a while I might be having supper in the boat."

"Mind if we come along?"

"Not at all," came the surprising reply.

Dad and Reggie sat on the big stern seat while I sat in the middle. I was in no mood to row but my father insisted, saying the captain must be tired, and I needed the practice.

"We may need to get the whip out," he declared after I'd nicely embedded the boat in a thick patch of pickerelweeds near the Russells' dock. In frustration I started chopping at them with an oar.

"Easy!" Dad yelled.

"It's okay, Bruce," Reggie said while lighting a cigarette. He glanced at my still bandaged forehead. "I understand you've had some troubles yourself?"

I gave my father a hard look, and he said, "Not me! Your grandmother blabbed last night."

Reggie continued. "You're having problems with some kid at school, are you?"

I grumbled, "This one guy's being a dip— ... being an idiot."

"Two guys, as far as I'm concerned," my father added.

"Well, hang in there, Lewis," Reggie chortled as he got the boat unstuck for me. "Another ten years will pass before you know it, and then you can do whatever the hell you want. Just another ten years — right, Brucey?"

To this Dad only frowned.

For the next half-hour we slowly made our way around the lake. My father did almost all the talking, bringing up everything he could think of to raise Reggie's spirits. When he got down to commenting on the fine cover design for that year's phone book he seemed again destined for failure. Early in this cruise, however, I saw something my father evidently didn't: that Reggie's spirits had already risen. Gone was the strained face he'd worn earlier, and he struck me as quite comfortable simply watching the shoreline. It reminded me of our first lake cruise, when after being so uptight he'd gradually unwound and begun making jokes. I was perhaps particularly inclined on this evening to notice Reggie's change of mood, because although to a lesser degree, the same had happened to me.

Right after leaving the end bay and reaching her Majesty's bird-watching post, I paused for a rest. Unlike the end bay, which was well shaded and becoming dark, we were back in the late sun. It was then, basking in this soft light, that I realized just how quiet and calm the lake had become. The shiny surface was broken by the occasional fish rising to feed, but even these circles somehow added to the lake's peacefulness, so smoothly did they spread out. The autumn woods around us were almost silent, and their bright oranges, reds, and yellows made Smiley actually earn his name a moment. I even saw, like during that first lake cruise with Reggie, the lake's great blue heron pass, its huge wings once again wafting the evening air slowly and rhythmically, similar to how I'd been rowing lately. And although I won't claim I suddenly wasn't upset at Scott Graham or my brother anymore, I will claim I could see the makings of it.

Perhaps all I needed was a few more laps.

We arrived back at the dock again that evening to find Carla loading things into the Morrisons' old silver Buick. Without so much as a glance at us she casually continued this chore as we dragged the boat out of the water. While flipping it onto two wooden beams lying at the edge of the lawn, Dad whispered, "I have to confess something, Reg — when we didn't see you for a month Val and I worried Carla might be seriously ticked off about the garter snake thing. Did you have to push her to come to the lake?"

Reggie's bushy eyebrows rose. "Push her? Coming up was her idea — I was in no mood. She's been the boss the whole weekend."

"Really?!"

Shortly after this he bid us adieu and left to get ready to return home. Once inside his wife approached, as usual carefully inspecting the grass in front of her green boots as she walked. Sticking his chest out, Dad quietly said, "So? Mission accomplished. He's settled right down."

"Oh, I see," Carla whispered back, giving my father a superior smile before gazing out over a now brass-coloured Gordonier Lake. "You're taking the credit for that, are you?"

13

The first real snowfall that year came in late November. One Sunday morning I woke to see several inches of snow coating the pines near my side window. Dad soon entered sporting a mischievous grin, and before Sean or I became wise he'd jammed stinging handfuls of snow down our pyjamas. This was a declaration of war, of course, and we later countered his attack with snowballs.

That first snowfall proved to have friends, and by midweek my brother, sister, and I were doing what we'd long looked forward to: tobogganing on the laneway hill. Our favourite time was after supper, when we'd coax others to join us. Cathy was a regular, but we managed to lure everyone except Grandma Layton and Marie Taylor at least once.

My mother's first evening of tobogganing was one in early December. After supper Judy went right to work sweet-talking, and within twenty minutes had Mother flying down the laneway hill with her on a four-footer. She soon recognized a problem, however, and that was our mother quickly tiring from climbing the hill. Only six runs completed, and her enthusiasm obviously weakening, Judy had to officially declare a break, and ran home to Grandma Layton to get hot chocolates.

When she returned everyone flaked out on the snowbank at the bottom of the hill, a spot softly illuminated by the Russells' laneway lamppost. Everyone except Judy, that is. She quickly downed her hot chocolate and began making obligatory snow angels in the untouched snow behind us.

Cathy said to my mother, "You do realize these guys are only getting warmed up?"

"Yes, I'm aware," she answered wearily, rubbing her snow-panted legs. "I'm hoping bedtime will save me."

Judy quickly sat up. "But that's not for a while — right, Mom?"

"No, I suppose you're okay for a bit. Are you making one of those for me?"

"I'll make one for everybody." Out of amusement we all watched Judy a minute. She applied the same creativity to her snow angels as she did her drawings; in addition to wings she blessed her angels with rockets instead of ears.

Cathy said, "Considering how your mother is, I guess you didn't get to toboggan much as a kid, or make snow angels, did you, Val?"

Drawing my quiet brother into her arms, she said, "Actually, I did my fair share. My father had a lawyer friend in Haliburton, and whenever he visited he'd take me along. The lawyer's two daughters and I would toboggan on the hill behind their place. We had a great time."

It was my turn to suddenly sit up. "You went to Haliburton when you were little?"

"Probably a dozen times. I spent a week of summer there some years as well."

"Did Grandma go too?"

My mother grinned. "No, I assure you she didn't."

Haliburton County, I knew, was adjacent and similar to Muskoka, but I still had to ask, "And there were woods at this lawyer's place?"

"*Yes*, Lewis. Real live woods. Acres and acres." She stared at me. "I never told you I was *completely* new to the country. Is that what you thought?"

I shyly nodded, and Cathy said, "I think you've done a number on the boy, Val."

Sean, from the confines of my mother's arms, suddenly blurted out, "So Dad wasn't being mean getting you to move to

Muskoka, Mom?"

His question startled me even more than my mother's revelation; I had no idea he was aware of the conflict between our parents. He also hit directly on the nose, no less, the very question on my mind at this moment.

After musing, as seemed her habit regarding our move, my mother said, "Let's just say your father and I came to an agreement, Sean." Her eyes then assumed a familiar mischievous sparkle, one I hadn't seen since that evening I'd questioned her about the move. Glancing at me, and sensing as always I had further questions, she firmly added, "And that's all I'm prepared to say."

The following week the Christmas season went into full swing. One evening I helped my father string lights along the porch fascia while my mother helped Judy and Sean create a winter scene on the kitchen window with coloured paper. The big event, though, was getting a tree. The Russells had a patch of spruce behind their place and generously offered us one. They were quick choosing theirs, but the Farrows needed a good fifteen minutes. At last we agreed on a nice symmetrical seven-footer, and after I chopped it down everyone helped drag it home. "Just like in the storybooks," my father giddily declared. We set it up beside the living room window, and Grandma Layton, disgusted at having a real tree in the house, reluctantly helped decorate it.

Christmas rapidly approached. On the evening of the twenty-third I took Sean and Judy to Cathy's to deliver a card and a wrapped box of candies. She greeted us with her usual wide smile and warmly welcomed us in. In keeping with the season, she wore jeans with green and red tassels sewn into them, clothing that brought grins to her three young visitors.

"Why thank you very much!" she said, accepting the card from Judy and the present from Sean. "Can I open these right away?"

"No!" Judy all but screamed. "It's not Christmas yet!"

"You can't open them unless you get really hun—" Sean added, before an older brother clamped a glove over his mouth.

As we took off our coats and boots I said to Cathy, "When are you leaving for your parents place?"

"Tomorrow right after finishing at the bakery. Then the season's joy begins." She breathed deeply.

"Wanna stay with us?" my brother offered. "Santa's coming to our house!"

Cathy rubbed her chin. "Sure about that, mister? He might have a rough time."

Sean instantly scowled at her. "He'll make it!"

She must have already heard Santa Claus was a serious issue with my brother. His prime concern was where the big guy would land his sleigh and eight trusty reindeer. With such a steep roof on our house he ruled that out, and with so many trees on our lot he didn't feel it offered enough room; the driveway was too short, and you couldn't rightly expect Santa to carry many toys in from the laneway. It was something that started keeping him up at night. Finally, at supper one evening, standing so the family would recognize the gravity of his message, he announced a number of trees around the house would have to come down; that was all there was to it.

Upon removing his winter gear he gave our host a nasty parting look, then wandered off with Judy to look at a modest living room Christmas tree. I followed Cathy to her "yard sale gem" kitchen table, where a green, expensive-looking reading pillow lay on a sheet of pink wrapping paper.

"Is this for your Aunt Jenny?" I said, running my hand over the silky fabric.

Yanking my obviously dirty hand away, Cathy cheerfully announced, "Yuppers. I always get her something nice — she deserves it — and I thought a reading pillow would be the cat's meow this year." As she said this she struggled to maintain her smile, and her eyes fluttered.

Her aunt's health had recently worsened. The night we had my mother out tobogganing I'd overheard Cathy whisper to her she feared this Christmas would prove Aunt Jenny's last. Thus my mother sending her kids on a special visit this evening: we were to do what we could to spirit-raise. But she also warned against being unnaturally nice — sharp-as-a-tack Cathy, she insisted, would easily detect this.

With that in mind, looking out the kitchen window I casually said, "So where's Rick?"

"Went into town to get a few things," Cathy answered vacantly, back at work wrapping the pillow.

"Is he going to your parents' place with you?"

She smirked. "Of course. I don't get all the fun to myself."

Apparently noticing me studying a punch bowl on the kitchen counter, she said, "I'd offer you some of that, but ..."

"Dad let me try some wine once."

"Um ... Rick made that, Lewis. It's a little beyond wine. In a hardware store they'd sell it as paint stripper."

So much for that. Turning away from the punch bowl, I noticed a nearby cardboard box sitting on the floor. Inside was a two-foot circle of plywood, and glued to it was an assortment of small items from the woods, such as stones, chips of bark, a tiny piece of driftwood, acorns, and tree cones. There was even a crayfish shell.

"What's this?" I said.

Cathy glanced toward me. "That's a little collection my sister made at the cottage one summer when we were kids. Uncle Neil called it Andrea's 'Stones, Bones, and Cones' collection."

"Was it for a school project or something?"

"No, she simply liked collecting things. I brought that back from the cottage, and I'm going to wrap it and take it to the city. Andrea and Aunt Jenny will get a kick out of it."

I looked into the box again. "But it's only rocks and tree cones and stuff."

With a defensive tone, Cathy said, "I suppose. But Andrea was really fascinated by basic stuff like that. I'll tell you this — your mother was sure fascinated by that little collection when she was here yesterday. She stared at it forever. That's not the first time I've seen her do that, either."

I turned to Cathy. "Can't say I've ever seen anything like that. And I've kind of known her ... forever."

"Maybe you haven't paid enough attention. I didn't with Andrea until Aunt Jenny said something."

Still not a believer, after giving the collection a final look, I shrugged and said, "Sorry — can't see the big deal in it."

"Well, then I guess you're not the sort who sees a big deal in it, Lewis. But I'm telling you Andrea and your mother *are* the sort." Cathy tore off a long strip of tape and paused a second, smiling. "This might sound kind of goofy ... but have you ever wondered what it'd be like to describe everything on this planet to beings from another world?"

"But they wouldn't speak English. They'd speak ... Martian or something."

Cathy frowned. "Yes, I know that, *wise-ass*. I'm asking you, like that time I mentioned envying other animals, to use a little imagination. Just imagine you could visit another world and talk with beings who lived there, and they asked you to describe what your world looked like. They wouldn't know anything about it, so you'd have to start with very basic things."

I nodded, glancing again at the punch bowl.

"Take a tree for example," Cathy continued, waving her strip of tape toward the young maple outside her kitchen window. "You'd say something like, 'There are these things that ... stick out of the ground, branch out in every direction and sprout thin little things called leaves, get bigger over time', and so on."

I studied the maple. "That's makes a tree seem pretty weird."

"Yes, but they *are* weird! That's exactly what I'm saying. Most people see trees all the time, and they lose touch with their weirdness; they lose touch with how amazing even the basic idea of a tree is."

I faced Cathy again. "So what does this have to do with Andrea and my mother?"

"My sister, and it appears your mother, are the sort who *don't* lose touch with the basic wonder and strangeness of things. First I thought your mother was simply not used to the country. But when I made inquiries the evening we had her tobogganing and learned she'd often visited Haliburton, I threw that theory away. I've come to believe it's merely in some people's nature never to become numb to what's around them. And ... I admire and envy them for that." Cathy finished taping, then again looked at me. "Do you know what I'm saying, Lewis?"

"You're saying Rick's punch has made you want to talk to Martians about trees?"

A green bow bounced off my head, and Cathy moaned, "When will I ever learn?"

We left our apparently drunken neighbour's place a short time later. As we put on our coats and boots she came to the porch with a large shopping bag. Smiling, she silently handed it to Judy, and while she held it open the three of us peered into it. Inside were three brightly-wrapped presents.

"Are these for us?!" Judy asked.

Sean didn't need an answer; he was already hugging Cathy's leg.

Much to my brother's relief, Santa found the Farrow homestead and negotiated a runway just fine that Christmas. About 5:00 a.m. the little bugger shook me awake, then bolted out of the room and down the stairs. Seconds later he sounded the alarm, and within a minute had the entire family up.

So began what proved a fine Christmas Day. We spent most of it inside. Mother started reading a book on interior decorating my father gave her, Judy enjoyed a new crayon set Santa somehow knew she needed, and Dad helped Sean and me start building a nifty balsa-wood plane. As for Grandma Layton, she spent most of the day baking; the whole house smelled of fresh rolls. This was nice except she had a hang up about when they were to be devoured. Her story implied they were for supper. "She's torturing us, Lewis — plain and simple!" my father grumbled, returning to my room after a third failed attempt at swiping a few.

On New Year's Eve everyone on the lake gathered at the Morrisons' cottage. The union problems at Reggie's plant were recently resolved, putting the couple in quite a festive mood. The second our family arrived, in fact, Carla gave us brightly-coloured paper hats, and wouldn't leave us alone until we put them on.

That evening my mother let Sean stay up to midnight for the first time. Fearing a battle, she didn't tell him he could until after Grandma Layton took Judy home. He was glassy-eyed when we counted in the New year, but successfully impressed me by hanging in there. Shortly after the arrival of 1976, his new found freedom came to an end and Mother escorted us home. It was snowing by this time and even during the short walk from the Morrisons' the party hats received a good coating. When we arrived Sean and I were both sent directly upstairs, and predictably, about one minute after my brother's tiny head hit his pillow he was fast asleep. Before attempting the same, I slipped back downstairs, wearing pyjamas and slippers.

"What's up?" my mother whispered from the still unlit living room.

"Thirsty," I answered honestly, padding to the fridge.

"You wouldn't be stalling on me, would you?"

"I'm not."

I filled a glass with water, then returned the jug to the fridge. While drinking I turned toward my mother. She was kneeling in front of the living room window, looking rather lonely and downcast.

I went to her. "Is Dad coming home soon?"

Her eyes still on the window, she softly answered, "He won't be too long. But I'm not worried; he can have his fun. It's New Year's Eve."

"Want the Christmas tree lights on?" I headed for the plug.

"No, that's all right."

"How about ... playing a game? I'm not too tired."

Mother shook her head, then motioned with her arms for me to sit in front of her. When I did she wrapped her arms around me, warming me with her thick sweater.

"What's going on?" I said, scanning the snow-covered lawn and lake for something out of the ordinary.

"Shh," Mother whispered. "Just watch."

She'd turned the outside light on, and the bed of snow in front of the window was gleaming white. The light also brightened the falling snow, and I watched the flakes slowly descend and settle.

I soon looked up, expecting my mother to meet my glance, but she didn't. Her eyes remained fixed on the falling snow, and her unwavering stare made her seem virtually entranced. She was watching the snow, I realized through Cathy's remarks, in utter fascination.

Most surprising was not her expression in itself, but its familiarity: it was the same fixed, blank look I'd seen many times in the Lord Roberts Woods, and had, it seemed, many times misinterpreted.

And so my mother treated me, I thought at this time, to the best Christmas present of all, the final touch to what proved a thoroughly enjoyable season. For the first time I felt optimistic she'd enjoy Muskoka. Sadly, this gift would prove a mixed blessing: her expression on this evening was one I would greatly miss in the unfortunate years to come.

For now, however, we simply sat and watched the snow fall, my mother contemplating who knows what, and me contemplating how to describe it all to Martians.

14

When the holiday season was over we entered the heart of the winter. January and February brought periods of very cold weather, much colder than I ever experienced in Scarborough. Many nights the temperature dipped to -25°F, and occasionally reached -40°F. We also received much more snow. Although this year the mean level never exceeded three feet, I came to believe my father's childhood stories of years with five. Muskoka, in short, was an area of Ontario receiving more than its fair share of winter.

Since November I'd looked after Marie Taylor's driveway and firewood, visiting right after school or in the evening. When I finished work she'd always invite me in for a snack, even when I'd recently had supper. Sitting me down at the kitchen table she'd serve perhaps a slice of pie, then chat about things in the news, school, or whatever Kevin was up to lately. Although I did honestly enjoy these visits, talking with her was a habit Laura Russell encouraged from winter's outset. "The company does her good," she declared one afternoon in November, and I came to know well what she meant.

I was already aware Marie was a worrywart about winter, but not until these midwinter months did I learn just how uptight she actually became. Not a visit passed when she wouldn't check her woodstove at least twice, and similarly her outside thermometer. On especially cold days she tended to pace, slowing caning back and forth between her kitchen and front windows facing the lake. Lastly, she was very strict about my winter clothes; she might rewrap my scarf, for instance, exchange thick hand-knitted mitts she'd given me for Christmas with dry ones, or demand I don another pair of heavy socks. And so touchy was she in this final respect that in midwinter a serious rift developed between her and my grandmother.

The precipitating incident occurred in late January, on Judy's fifth birthday. My parents threw a tobogganing party for her, inviting fifteen of her friends from school. With so many five and six-year-olds to contend with, Cathy, Laura, and predictably, Marie, all offered their services. This trio conveniently arrived before the parents delivered their kids, and were thus present for the party's move to the laneway hill.

It was when about half the kids, my sister included, had slipped out the porch door that Marie, above the din of kindergarten voices, suddenly shrieked, "Hold the show!"

Equally as suddenly the kids still inside became dead silent, staring at this frail, elderly lady with obvious fear. You could have heard a pin drop.

"What's the matter, Marie?" my grandmother asked, pausing while helping one boy tie his boot laces.

"What's the matter?" she answered. "These kids are not dressed well enough to go tobogganing!"

Grandma Layton looked puzzled. "My grandchildren have been out many times dressed as they are, and all the parents knew it was a tobogganing party so they'd have dressed their kids properly."

"Well, they most certainly are not!" Marie said matter-of-factly, folding her tiny arms.

It was at this moment I saw the first signs of anger in my grandmother. Her eyes bulged a second and her upper lip trembled slightly. "Marie! What —?"

"I want all the children back in this kitchen this very instant!" she declared firmly. She then poked her head out the door to yell at everyone outside. Since all these kids were now on the laneway laughing and yelling, they didn't hear this call. So, Marie put on her coat and boots and went outside. Watching from the porch door, I saw her using her cane to point the kids back inside. She even went up the laneway fifty yards to herd in the last few, Sean one of these strays.

A rosy-cheeked birthday girl was among the first to return, and she immediately said, "Everybody's waitin', Mom! Aren't we going?"

Pulling her into the kitchen, Mother quietly said, "Just a minute — okay, sweetie? We'll go in a minute."

Now few issues were more sensitive with my grandmother than her ability to look after kids. She was perhaps especially sensitive at this time because she'd just nursed Sean through a week off school with chickenpox. Right after hearing her granddaughter's plea, and while Marie remained outside, her pot came to a boil. In only a slightly hushed voice, she said, "How ... *dare* she suggest I don't care for my grandchildren properly, or anyone else's children for that matter! *How dare she*!"

Getting me to coax her upstairs, where she wouldn't be so easily heard, Laura tried calming her. "Please don't take offence, Annie. Marie's completely and utterly paranoid about winter, and this is one way her paranoia reveals itself. I've seen this with her before — I assure you it's nothing personal."

Perhaps not listening, or deciding to ignore this plea, my grandmother continued with, "If she spoils this party for these dear children I will never, *never* forgive her! This is outrageous! All the children are fine to go out!"

"I agree!" Laura replied. "But Marie ... has a problem. I'm begging you to simply let her fuss over the kids a minute and then Val and I will take everyone to the hill. A few minutes, Annie — please!"

Thankfully my grandmother conceded, and as Laura promised the party went ahead as planned. What proved a fine day for Judy, however, did not for my grandmother and Marie; three weeks would pass before they spoke again.

In mid-February Marie's sister, Fledda Garrett, arrived from Barrie for a two-week visit. She drove up on a Friday evening, and to my surprise, had Kevin with her. "The poor kid needs a break from that mother of his," I heard her whisper to Marie. I would soon learn, however, giving Kevin a break was not the primary reason for her trip.

When Marie brought her to our place on Saturday afternoon to meet our family, I heard the two had gone clothes shopping that morning. Fledda — a loud, robust woman you would hardly have believed was frail Marie's older sister — had persuaded her younger sibling to buy herself a new dress, a purchase I knew she could scarcely afford. This she modelled in our living room during tea, her large silver locket looking especially impressive in front of a fancy green dress. "Looks like a million bucks, doesn't she, Annie?" Fledda trumpeted while her blushing sister twirled around in the living room. To this my grandmother brightly answered, "Simply *beautiful*, Marie!"

A touch too brightly, I felt.

Despite efforts made by both my grandmother and Marie to pretend all was well between them, all was obviously not. This afternoon social was their first since the birthday party incident, and had to it a definite artificial politeness; pleases and thank-yous were overstated, as were compliments. These were not normal relations between the two. From the evening of our house-warming, when Grandma Layton declared Marie a "dear, frail woman, deprived of civilized life," they'd developed a close friendship. They visited each other often and could chat nonstop for hours; they sometimes lent one another clothes, and were continually trading romance novels. I was glad for this friendship and it pained me to see it troubled. As I soon learned, it also pained Marie's sister.

On Sunday Kevin invited me to sleep over. Fledda was taking him home early the next morning to return to school, and as usual with limited time, he'd made the most of it. All day long we'd tobogganed, snowballed, and wrestled in the snow, and were both extremely tired. Tiredness had never guaranteed me getting to sleep easily, however, and that night, while Kevin slept like a log beside me, I lay awake.

Fledda also ordered Marie to bed early on this evening,

arguing correctly she looked worn out, but the elder sister had company; she invited over my grandmother. The two had tea at the kitchen table, seemingly innocent enough. But so it was my winter — and winters thereafter — would be forever changed.

That evening I heard a story about Marie. The spare bedroom Kevin and I shared was directly above the kitchen, and through the floor vent I overheard Fledda talking with my grandmother. For the first half-hour these two spoke of numerous grandmotherly topics ranging from cooking to dancing, and I paid little attention. But then the issue of Marie's winter anxiety arose, Fledda daring to raise this sensitive topic, and she proceeded to tell Grandma Layton a rather lengthy story. This tale I heard in broken sentences; the storyteller spoke softly, evidently not wanting her sister upstairs to hear. By slipping quietly out of his bed and lying with his head near a floor vent, however, a nosy young man could just manage to listen in.

To begin, I learned Marie and Fledda's maiden name was Bryant, and they'd grown up living on McKay Lake. This lake was about three miles farther down the Fraserburg road from Gordonier, and much larger. Large enough that even in the 1920's everyone on the lake didn't know everyone else — at least not well. One person the Bryants hardly knew was an elderly lady named Emily Kinsley.

One November afternoon when Fledda was visiting — at eighteen she was already married and living in Bracebridge — they happened to spot Emily outside. Although she lived on the far side of the lake they could still see clearly enough her struggling to carry a pail of water from shore back to her tiny house. They only knew several things about her: she was ten years widowed, something of a loner, and her health had recently declined. Loner or not, seeing Emily struggle on this autumn day, Rebecca Bryant decided she'd pay a visit, and took her two daughters along.

That visit went well. They found Emily pleasant and hospitable. Young, kindhearted Marie especially developed a fondness for this elderly lady, and before leaving offered her help.

Although grateful for the offer, Emily was reluctant to accept. This didn't surprise the Bryants: she was obviously ill, but her still thick calves and forearms suggested a person unaccustomed to needing help from anyone to do anything. They also found her strong-minded and unselfish — a combination making her hardheaded about not imposing on others. Nonetheless, after considerable pleading she did finally accept Marie's offer, but not before getting her to agree to something. "I'd like you to promise that if ever tiring of coming over, you'll tell me. I don't want you thinking that once started, you're committed forever." Marie made this promise, not even considering what Emily said a possibility.

She began visiting almost every day, walking over right after school. Besides cooking supper she washed dishes, did laundry, and cleaned the house. She also did Emily's grocery shopping, joining Rebecca once a week.

Now during her first visit she learned of another helper — a woman in her thirties named Trudy. Because of school Marie never did meet her; she apparently visited only during the morning. Not meeting her, however, did not prevent Marie from developing an opinion. From what little she saw accomplished she suspected this woman was more talker than helper. She often left dirty dishes in the sink, and seemingly did little else. The worst thorn, though, was a notebook.

During Marie's first visit, Emily explained Trudy kept track of her hours in a small notebook so she could eventually be paid. This annoyed the younger helper to no end; she never even considered accepting payment from her ill neighbour and was disgusted by the thought of Trudy doing so, especially considering her laziness. But, for Emily's sake Marie merely bit her lip and continued.

That winter proved particularly cold, and her walks to and from the Kinsley house were often painful. A harshly cold wind frequently blew off the lake. While visiting her family Fledda sometimes went with her sister to Emily's, and said they often had to walk backwards much of the way, the wind was so cold.

One such occasion when Fledda joined Marie was on a brutally cold day in early February. By late afternoon the temperature had already dropped very low, and when the two girls began their dark walk home from Emily's it was nightmarishly cold. The lake wind was so frigid they found talking difficult, and when it blew especially hard they had to stop and curl into balls at the side of the road. It was by far the coldest walk either had ever experienced.

By the time they reached home Marie, also quite thin in her youth, looked half-frozen. Her mother and much stronger sister helped remove her coat and then stood her near the woodstove. Soon after this, when removing her boots, they realized she was in trouble: she'd developed severe frostbite in both feet.

From all her walks to Emily's her boots were worn out, and since her family was far from well-off she hadn't complained. Her mother took her to a doctor the next day but there was little he could do. In time Marie developed gangrene in both feet, and needed half her toes amputated from each.

Her days of helping Emily Kinsley were over. Indeed, that windy winter night changed the rest of her life. Nonetheless, Emily's plight became Marie's main concern. Rebecca already worked long hours and arrived home each night completely exhausted, so she was unable to take over for her daughter. Her husband was working in Huntsville at this time, and living in Bracebridge made Fledda also unavailable. All she could do was inform Emily what happened, and this she did the evening following Marie's accident. Although returning with news that Emily insisted all would be okay, Marie was not convinced, and knowing well Trudy's laziness, began worrying night and day. Adding to her frustration was her inability to gain any news from the Bryant's lakeside window; Emily kept her drapes closed at night, and Marie couldn't tell whether her place was lighted.

When Fledda visited several weeks later, and said she'd check on Emily, there was no holding Marie back. Off the two sisters went on what was a casual walk for Fledda; she felt certain Emily was fine. When they arrived, however, they found Marie's worst fears realized: no tracks led to or from the house. Marie limped inside as fast as she could, Fledda holding her arm, and what the two girls found took their breath away.

Poor Emily Kinsley, curled up in a ball with merely a blanket around her, lay in front of the cold woodstove, frozen solid.

Marie gently put a corner of the blanket over the elderly woman's bluish, frost-covered face and open eyes, then collapsed onto the floor beside her, sobbing uncontrollably. Her deep sorrow, however, soon turned to deep anger. "Check Trudy's bloody time clock and see if there's an address!" she screamed to her sister. "The ignorant, shit-for-brains *bitch*!"

Fledda quickly fetched the notebook, in its usual place on the kitchen shelf. Flipping through it while returning to the living room, she said, "There's no address in here that I can see. In fact, there's —"

Marie ripped the book from Fledda's hands. Going through it, a look of shock formed on her face. "There's nothing —!"

The notebook pages were empty, and inside the back cover was handwritten, in faded ink: Emily Joanna Kinsley.

"There never was a Trudy," Fledda whispered to my grandmother. She had risen and was standing at the kitchen sink, and I now heard her better. "Thinking the whole thing through the following days, Marie and I sorted out what happened. Everything pointed to Emily's pride. Here she was, a person who'd been strong and capable all her adult life, suddenly becoming ill and needing help. Her pride made her reluctant enough to accept enthusiastic help, but the prospect of *un*enthusiastic help was evidently too much. 'Trudy', we came to believe, was an attempt at insurance against this.

"I don't think Emily trusted my sister's promise she would quit if no longer interested in helping. I believe she sensed Marie wouldn't stop helping her regardless of how she felt — she was too kindhearted. She wouldn't stop, that is, unless she was certain someone else was helping, and that's where Trudy came in. Emily invented this other helper to allow Marie to quit with a clear conscience. Every day she did what she could around the house to make my sister confident all would be okay if she wanted to quit.

She didn't succeed at this, of course; being ill she wasn't up to much, and so dear 'Trudy' wound up striking Marie as pathetically lazy.

"Now I believe Emily's claim that Trudy was accepting payment was simply an effort to persuade Marie to do likewise — once again, Emily's pride at work. I doubt this lady had gone a day of her adult life taking charitable help from anyone. And she could indeed pay: in her dresser we discovered an envelope of money with 'Marie' written on it.

"Finally, when my mother delivered the news that Marie could no longer help — nor anyone else in our family — I think Emily was simply too proud to make a plea for help elsewhere. Someone surely would have if she'd asked, or had my mother ask, but evidently she couldn't bring herself to do that. When my mother left after telling about Marie's accident I think she adopted the attitude she'd either manage on her own, or cease living altogether.

"Marie was messed up for ages, Annie. Blame was the central issue — I know because she often used me as a sounding board. For a while she considered Emily a victim of herself, someone who rode her pride to her grave. As time went on, though, she increasingly admired the resolve and unselfishness of the woman she helped; Emily may have been a victim of herself, but it was an honourable self. Marie rightly didn't turn the blame inward, either — what else could she have done? So more and more she blamed what happened on a third party: winter. It was the true culprit. Those harsh winter winds, by disabling her, surely brought about Emily's demise, and this dear lady freezing to death only added salt to the wound. I'm sure to this day Marie can still close her eyes and see that frozen blue face staring at her.

"So, she became bitter and paranoid during winters thereafter. You might think it odd she still has a problem after so many years, Annie, but she's plagued with a constant reminder of the incident with Emily — as soon as she wakes every morning, and her feet hit the floor ..."

Fledda brought a hand to her eyes; telling this story had taken a toll.

"My God — the poor thing!" Grandma Layton gasped. "Can you not get her to sell and move somewhere that doesn't get such rough winters?"

Fledda sighed. "I've been trying to do that since Lyall passed. But Marie strongly associates this house with him; he built it and treasured it. I'll never get over how she consented to living here in the first place — especially on a lake — but that's simply her love for Lyall at work, I think."

"How about you moving here?"

"I could — I'm widowed like Marie — but like you, Annie, I couldn't stand living away from my grandkids. No, the best I can do is visit a few weeks in the winter and try relaxing her; get her doing things she especially likes — baking, knitting, buying clothes, and so forth."

"Who all know about her accident?"

"Kevin, of course, and so does Laura Russell, but that's it for people on the lake. It's something Marie's pretty sensitive about, and something she's been sensitive about a long time. You must remember — this happened when she was sixteen."

Grandma Layton moaned. "I simply feel awful. The way I've ignored her the last few weeks, the things I've said about her ..."

"But you didn't know, and you couldn't have guessed. What happened to my sister isn't something everyone goes through, thank goodness."

"Yes," my grandmother quietly agreed. "Thank goodness is right."

After that evening winter was not quite the same for me — not this one nor any since. One way hearing about Marie's experience affected me was through winter dress. Consciously and unconsciously, I began bundling up better when going out. Marie continued her inspections, but adjustments became seldom. I could only shrug when she asked one afternoon, "What's come over you?" Mostly, however, hearing about her background made me much more conscious of the cold and its potential effects. Especially when working at her place; here I was, after all, doing essentially the same thing she'd done for Emily Kinsley.

A notable evening was one about a week and a half after hearing that late-night story, and one just before Fledda returned to Barrie. After supper that Friday I went to Marie's to shovel the driveway. In late afternoon we'd received about three inches of snow, and trying to impress upon Fledda that her sister would be well looked after, I decided to do the driveway right away.

Even after Fledda took me inside ten minutes to warm up when I'd finished, and despite being well dressed, I still shivered constantly as I walked home along the moonlit Fraserburg road. Several times I had to stop and adjust my jacket and hat. When reaching the middle of the lake swirling, face-stinging gusts of wind blasted me and I had to walk sideways. These gusts sent sprinkles of powdery snow down my jacket, making me shiver even more.

During this walk I found myself painfully considering the story Fledda told — of Emily Kinsley freezing to death, of Marie walking this same road, facing the same harsh lake winds. I began marking every step.

When at last I reached home I found only my mother's red VW Beetle in the driveway. All the lights were off inside except one in my grandmother's bedroom, and after removing my winter things I went to her room. Poking my head in, I found her sitting up in bed reading, her fancy pink quilt drawn up to her chin.

"Get Marie looked after?" she said, looking up from her book.

"The driveway's done, and her wood's stocked up. How come everybody isn't back yet?"

Grandma Layton shrugged. "It's Friday night — the stores are open late and they're still shopping. Your mother called not long ago, though, and said they'd be home soon. Why?"

"Just ... thought they should be back. Thought maybe they went into the ditch or something."

"Well, while you're incorrectly thoughting, could you stick another chunk of wood in that stove for me? It's cooling down in here. And could you close the living room drapes, too? That seems to help."

"I will."

"Oh, by the way, Lewis —" I poked my head back in my grandmother's doorway. "Did Marie happen to give you a novel to bring over? She mentioned wanting to lend me one."

"She was already in bed."

"Fledda?"

I nodded.

"I suppose that's best." After a deep breath, my grandmother turned to her book again and whispered, "The poor thing."

I stirred the coals in the woodstove with the poker before adding a large chunk of birch. Swinging the door shut again, I went to the living room window. I had the drapes half closed when a gust of wind blew in from the lake. It rattled the window and made powdery snow sprinkle down from the edge of the roof. Before pulling the drapes fully shut, I stared at this snow a moment, suddenly reminded of New Year's Eve and watching it snow with my mother. But on this evening, even amidst the warmth of our house, I couldn't help shivering as the tiny flakes settled in front of the window.

15

I believe I'm safe in declaring spring that year quite unlike any our family previously experienced. As the days grew warmer and the snow slowly disappeared, we responded far more intensely to this change of season than we ever had in Scarborough. My mother and grandmother, for example, went on several near-bankrupting shopping sprees, and I learned the Midnight Muffin-Maker made four late night appearances in April alone, twice wearing a new swimsuit. As for my brother and me, we took to sprinting wildly up and down the laneway, screaming our heads off. A normal spring for the Farrow family this was not.

I believed there were two reasons for our family developing such strong spring fever this year. One, quite probably, was sheer relief over the end of the previous season. With Scarborough winters comparatively mild our first in Muskoka was an abrupt change, and especially so for my grandmother and me since learning Marie Taylor's background. But another and I believe even stronger reason was our exposure to this contagious disease through what I thought the least likely of sources: Bruce Farrow.

Since we'd moved my father had unquestionably undergone a slow, steady metamorphosis. Indeed, so slow and steady that not until this spring did I, or apparently anyone else, notice his changes. First, he'd slimmed down considerably since we'd moved. Unlike the afternoon I'd met his boss, Don Nelson no longer took pokes at my father's stomach, and him being the "Ed Allen of Fraserburg" actually became a running joke. He now made even more wisecracks, a change you enjoyed only when not on the receiving end. Lastly, he had far more energy and ambition than I remembered him having in the city, or during our first summer at Gordonier Lake. He now began without hesitation projects around the house that previously he said he'd "start sometime." In early April, for example, he jumped headfirst into building a firewood shed, and later even spent a weekend lugging stones from the creek to surround a flower bed for my grandmother. "Wonders never cease!" an amazed Grandma Layton responded. The only times he'd ever been similar to the way he was this spring, it eventually occurred to me, were those in years past he'd told stories about Muskoka. That excited, energized story-telling manner had now become, in short, normal for Dad.

This miraculous change in my father was peculiar enough, but something else I found even more so: he almost completely denied having changed. His loss of weight he couldn't refute, of course — he'd bought many new clothes — but that he'd become more of a smart-ass, or especially, that his energy level had increased, he vehemently argued against.

"I fully, *fully* intended to do some jobs around this house!" he ranted red-faced at Reggie Morrison one day. "So don't feed me this bloody 'turned over a new leaf' crap. I've dropped a couple of pounds, I grant you, but I'm still ... *me*."

"Okay, okay — didn't mean to upset you," Reggie replied in a soothing tone. After stepping out our porch door, however, he added, "Actually, I only came over hoping to get your autograph, Mr. Allen." Luckily he ducked in time, and my father's polished office shoe sailed directly over his head.

A particularly memorable day with my 'new' father was one in early May. At his tenacious urging, he, Sean, Ed Russell, and I went out one afternoon to cut and haul some firewood using a reluctant neighbour's half-ton. With Sean and me riding in the back of the 'Midnight Blue', we journeyed about halfway down Taylor Avenue to an area with much standing deadwood. This we didn't do easily, mind you, and I came to understand Ed's lack of enthusiasm. The firewood lane proved very soft and several hundred yards in from the main road we became stuck. Fortunately, after rocking the truck back and forth a dozen times and swearing as often, he managed to work us free. "All part of the fun, Eddie my boy!" I heard my father brightly declare up in the cab. The response came in a decidedly less bubbly tone. "Yeah, yeah — whatever you say, Farrow. Let's just hope your goddamn elastic band finishes unwinding soon."

We worked diligently several hours, Dad running the chain-saw and the rest of us hauling. It was about three o'clock when Ed, after developing a sore back, pleaded for a break. This we took at a shady but dry patch of bedrock about twenty feet from the truck. When I say 'we' I don't include my father; he hadn't stayed still all day, and remained standing, gobbling several apples, as the rest of us sat.

Once settled with my back against a maple, I looked up to the top of this and other trees around me. They were now in leaf and provided some shade from the sun, which was summer hot on this day. The spring season was still evident, however; the ground mostly remained damp and spongy, and while working I'd discovered some ice lingering in a rock crevasse. There was still that musky thawing smell to the air, too — the fresh air of spring making it difficult to stay inside.

"We've done well," Dad declared, surveying our work, which amounted so far to about a truck-load and a half. "There's a bit of punky stuff but —"

"But it's all firewood, and that's why we're here." Ed mimicked a line my father had uttered twenty-seven times this afternoon.

Dad, at last taking a seat on the bedrock, gave him a stern glance. "Well hey! I've got a woodshed now — why not fill it?"

"This is true. And it's amazing how that woodshed appeared out of thin air. Last year you said you weren't going to bother. You said it'd be too much work."

"Damned if I recall saying that! I had a woodshed in the works from the get go after the move! Here we bloody well go —"

"All right, Bruce," Ed broke in with a defeated tone. "Only

trying to figure you the hell out — sorry I brought it up."

Soon after this, my brother, who like me had been sitting against a tree, moved and rested his tiny head on my father's knee. If this was indeed out of nervousness it represented about as serious a reaction to the woods as my brother was displaying these days. I was not aware of him experiencing any further nightmares during the winter, and he'd just as readily contracted my father's spring fever as anyone else in the family. Babyish as putting his head on my father's knee seemed, I felt it minor compared to nightmares, and I was optimistic this coming summer he'd be fine. For this I was glad; being down Taylor Avenue on this afternoon definitely wet my appetite for returning to the cabin.

I believe Ed also sensed a change in Sean because this spring he'd often encouraged my brother during his outdoor activities. Too, not long after my brother joined our father, he said, "I saw you running up and down the laneway this morning in the new shoes. You really like those babies, don't you?"

Sean grinned. "They're neat ones."

That morning my brother wore outside for the first time shoes he'd received a month earlier for his eighth birthday. My mother spotted him ogling them in a Bracebridge shoe store and decided to buy them. What caught his fancy were the soles: they boasted various-sized star patterns. Up until this day, though, Grandma Layton had only allowed him to wear the shoes in the school gym, so he hadn't been able to explore their full potential.

"Just be wise and don't get them mucked up, Starman," my father warned. "Your grandmother's testy enough as it is."

Ed said, "I think Valerie mentioned Annie's been on a major cleaning mission lately. Is that right?"

Dad moaned. "It's been awful. She wrote off all last weekend with a big spring cleaning — I wanted to start building some deck chairs. This party will be the death of us yet."

He was referring to Grandma Layton's 70th birthday party, which we were holding the following Sunday. Originally we'd intended to make it a surprise party, but my brother, as usual, was unable to keep a secret, slipping up one night at supper. From then on my grandmother hounded the rest of the family about "improving" the house and yard; she was worried sick what her friends might think. In late winter she joined a ladies' euchre club in town, and I emphasize 'ladies'.

"I hope you got her something nice, at least," Ed said. "For all the housework she does you owe her that, I'd say."

Apparently taking offence at this comment, Sean lifted his head from our father's knee and declared, "We got her nice stuff, Mr. Russell! A fancy new quilt and a wicker chair for her room!"

"A bloody expensive wicker chair, too," Dad calmly added, carefully scooping up some mud with a small piece of bark. "I had to hit about twelve stores in the city before I found a chair that met all Val's specifications."

"You went to the city for it?" said Ed. "I'm impressed."

My father stared at him in disgust. "*Pulease*!"

"You mean you were there on business again? You've been to the city a fair bit then — haven't you?"

"About six times since March." Dad carefully patted his mud down with his fingers. "No choice in the matter, though. This one guy we're looking after is only in Muskoka during the summer, and Donny doesn't like the idea of losing him."

"You can't simply call him?"

Dad shook his head. "Wouldn't be the same. And anyway, my old neighbour Jack Walsh likes getting together once in a while. He's always got something planned when I visit, so I don't go just for the sake of accounting work."

My father's frequent city trips this spring had been yet another recent change in him I'd found peculiar. This was because after both working with and watching Dad during early spring, I came to believe strongly it was not merely the change of season inducing his changes: it was the lake and woods themselves.

I noticed, for starters, after tiring from working outside he seemed only to need several deep breaths of pine-scented air to become reinvigorated. Never in the city had any amount of outside air affected him like this. I also noticed his rate of work coincided closely with any movements in the bush around us. If he caught sight of a chipmunk scampering across the forest floor, for example, or a duck taking off from the lake, his own movements seemed to keep pace. I felt he must have been affected this way since we'd moved, but only during this spring, when the lake and woods were especially vibrant, did I realize their effect on him. And yet he never complained to anyone when he had to make a trip to the city, leaving the place that he'd obviously benefited from so much. He seemed, in summing up, not only largely oblivious to his changes, but also oblivious to what brought about those changes.

I learned on this firewood job that the lake's hilltop resident shared my curiosity in this respect. After my father's last comment, Ed, uncharacteristically attentive to the woods, began studying some deer prints we'd discovered right after stopping for our break. These prints were one of perhaps a dozen things around us I'd earlier seen him observing — others included a pine sapling, a few early mosquitoes, and the forest canopy. Now gazing at the deer prints, he said quietly and seemingly as much to himself as to my father, "It's strange ... you don't even seem to recognize what's doing it to you. I've never encountered anyone so moved, and yet so unaware."

"What's that you're mumbling about, Eddie?" Dad had removed my brother's head from his knee and risen.

"Nothing, Bruce — nothing. Only mumbling."

Evidently not distracted by this comment, the moment of truth arrived and my father made his move. The saddest part for me was that even knowing it was coming, the bugger still hit me right in the chest. The mud, too, was wet enough to leave a big dark smear on my shirt. Not that I paid much attention to this smear, mind you, because less than a second after Dad pegged me I was on my feet and chasing him through the bush.

"Get'im, Lewis!" Ed roared from behind us. "Head'im off at the pass!"

I needed this cheering because I quickly discovered just how in shape my father had truly become; even with him laughing hard as he ran, for the life of me I couldn't catch him. I would, you might wager, equally as soon caught that spring buck.

16

Grandma Layton's 70th birthday party proved quite the occasion. In addition to everyone on the lake, all seven ladies from her Euchre Club attended. All these ladies, too, wore fancy dresses and jewelry, and all apparently had gotten their hair done. "They've made the rest of us look like complete slobs!" I heard Laura Russell whisper to my mother, who sighed and said, "You should tell Mother."

We had a rather big supper. My grandmother insisted we all eat at the same table, and the one my father and I concocted was close to twenty feet long. Her seventy-candle cake seemed almost that long too; it was all my brother, sister, and I could do to bring it over from the Morrisons' place without dropping it or getting burnt. Dad, apparently wanting to emphasize the number of candles involved, added to our problem by closely following us toting a fire extinguisher. And during all this, of course, we had to help sing "Happy Birthday."

After cake Grandma Layton, looking like royalty in a new red dress and gold earrings, sat on the living room couch to receive her presents. Besides the wicker chair and quilt, she received perfume from Cathy, a night gown from Marie, a small rug from the Russells, a bracelet from the Morrisons, and shoes from the Euchre Club ladies. All agreed, however, the best present was a Bristol board picture from Judy. It depicted a purple-haired Grandma Layton standing in front of a stately round townhouse, with perfectly-trimmed orange hedges and a tuxedoed butler (blue-haired) playing a giant harp. My grandmother said, "If this is what's ahead for me, sweetie, then by all means, bring it on," and this earned her a good laugh.

After she'd opened all her presents and we'd served coffee and tea, I hoped the evening's main events were over. But then, what I'd feared might happen, did happen: she had Judy do a few dance routines in the living room. And yes, the great dance finger made an appearance. It was embarrassing.

"Don't be snickering at your dear grandmother," Laura Russell said in a scolding tone as we watched from the back. I noticed, however, she held her hand in front of her mouth while speaking.

Shortly after this fiasco, when Grandma Layton and the 'girls' had started a major chat in the living room, a group of us escaped to the back deck for a breather. Along with me were Dad, Reggie Morrison, Ed Russell, Sean, and Cathy.

"This is quite the do — haven't seen this many fancy plates and cups and hairdos in ages." Reggie whispered this through a veil of cigarette smoke as he gazed through the Muskoka room screen at the party. It was the first time he'd spoken since moving to the deck. Up till now he'd stared at the huge pine in our back woodlot with the same grave face he'd shown the afternoon I met him, and after the jumping bass incident.

"Hey — we're amazed Mother didn't have us lay carpeting along the driveway," my father said. "That's about the only thing she didn't gloss over."

I said, "No, she had me rake it."

"She had you —?" Dad broke into a laugh.

"She's only trying not to look too ... backwoods," Cathy said defensively, waving her Fred Flintstone mug at our back lot. "I've seen some of the houses in town these ladies live in — they're about as fancy as houses get."

"Well ..." said Dad, "at this lake it's a rustic theme through and through, so why fight it?" Leaning forward in his chair, he held out a bottle of Scotch and said, "Care for another snort, Eddie?"

"Why not," he answered, holding out his glass. "Can't do me

any harm. I've been seeing *stars* lately anyhow."

Cathy pulled a smiling Sean into her arms. "Yes, I've been seeing a lot of them too, buster. I hope you don't intend on wearing those shoes to rob a bank."

"The boys are only getting warmed up for the summer," said Reggie, turning to me. "Not too far away, you know. Pretty soon you'll have your buddy back." With a devilish grin, he added, "If, mind you, he can make it out to the lake," and this remark brought a chorus of laughs from all present. All, that is, except me.

Reggie had done a classic number on me during a lake cruise earlier on this day. Soon after leaving the dock he reported, in deep distress, that he'd just learned a beaver dam had burst and the subsequent flashflood had washed away a section of the Fraserburg road between Gordonier Lake and Bracebridge. Weeks might pass before we'd "regain contact with the outside world." Sadly, I bought this tall tale and for a good hour after returning to shore stood at the end of the laneway, flagging down cars in an effort to gain news of the crisis.

But, out of apparent sympathy, Dad let the matter rest and said to me, "When's Kevin arriving, by the way?"

"Right after the end of school. He's coming up by bus."

Cathy said, "I told Marie I'd take her into town to meet him. Everything's planned, but she's still a little worried about him taking the bus on his own."

"He's getting big," said Dad. "He'll be all right."

"I suppose, but Kevin getting big might be exactly the problem; he's old enough to get ... ideas." In a whisper only I could hear, Cathy added, "I'd bloody well take off from that bitch of a mother too."

Downing the last of his beer, Reggie said to Ed, "Hey — before I forget — I've got a bone to pick with you, Mr. Russell."

Ed grinned at the rest of us. "Uh, oh. What'd I do now, Reg?"

"When the Great Investigator and I were out this morning on this year's maiden voyage, we stopped at your place because I needed to use a certain facility. All that was fine and dandy except the certain facility wasn't bloody well there anymore."

Ed chuckled. "You don't say, Reg!"

"What's this?" asked my father.

Ed turned to him. "I tore down our old outhouse a couple of days ago. Sean here helped me."

"A veritable landmark on the lake, and he goes yanking it down without an official lake meeting," said Reggie.

"That veritable landmark was falling down all on its own. If you'd used it you probably would have wound up down the hole."

"Yeah, yeah." Reggie flapped his hand at Ed. "Somebody here is itching to go. Are you marking the days off on a calendar?"

"No, I'm simply trying not to leave everything to the last minute."

Reggie snorted. "'Last minute' he says. A year still to go, and they're already cleaning up, and just had to start with the outhouse."

"Yeah, well that's tough, Reg."

Reggie smirked. "Tough for me? Wait till you cut your lawn, neighbour."

"I'm sure *Mother* will be the most disappointed of all," Dad said, raising his voice. "She always claimed that outhouse was one of the finest she'd ever used."

We all looked through the Muskoka room screen, but saw no reaction inside.

Cathy frowned at my father. "One of these days, Bruce Farrow, that dear lady will tar and feather you ..."

The party came to a fairly abrupt end shortly after eight that evening. The Euchre Club ladies all came in one big white Cadillac, and the lady who owned it — Nora Keaton — didn't like driving the Fraserburg road at night. So, with darkness setting in they all bid us farewell. The entire lake crew stood out in the driveway seeing them off, and the evening seemed to have come to a close.

About three minutes later, though, Nora Keaton was back.

"I'm afraid we've had a mishap," she said with a pained smile as she stepped into the kitchen.

My father rose from his chair. "A mishap?"

"I ... sort of went in the ditch," Nora continued, then put her hands on her freshly-styled hair.

Turned out, she'd gone in the ditch at the same spot our moving van had gone in — right where the laneway bent to follow alongside the creek. She'd done an equally superb job, with the Cadillac's inside tires buried in mud right up to the axles. But on top of this, one lady — Fran Hollings — had fallen while getting out of the car, and her fancy silver dress was caked in mud. When my parents and I reached her she was standing on the laneway with a stunned look on her face, scooping wet mud off her dress and pantyhose.

"Oh my God, Fran!" my mother said, grabbing her arm. "Are you okay?"

"May—be," she answered quietly, maintaining the same stunned look.

Seconds later Grandma Layton, still in high heels, arrived and proceeded to have a fit. "Come inside, come inside!" She put her arm around Fran and led her to the house, coaxing the other ladies to do likewise.

When they were all in the house, Dad stared at the laneway ditch. Unlike his good humour when we became stuck on Taylor Avenue, he now grumbled, "Stupid goddamn bush muck!"

"It'll be all right, Bruce — I'll get the truck," Ed Russell said, and with that started home.

Despite his good intentions we were over an hour getting Nora Keaton's car out of the ditch. The one rope he had kept breaking, and when it didn't the tires on the 'Midnight Blue' merely dug holes in the soft laneway. Not even several rounds of vicious swearing by my father seemed to help. Finally, after spending ages jacking up the ditched side of the car and putting more and more planks under the tires, we managed to pull a now very dirty white Cadillac back onto the laneway.

Back in our dining room, where Grandma Layton and her friends were having tea, Dad proclaimed, with a smear of mud still on his forehead, "The management humbly requests there be no more off-roading adventures this evening. We thank you in advance."

This remark brought a good laugh from everyone at the table. Even Fran Hollings, dressed in some clothes my grandmother had lent her, now chuckled over the whole incident. But as we saw this gang out the door again that evening, I heard Fran say to Nora Keaton, in what I thought only a half-joking tone, and in hearing range of Grandma Layton, "Get me the hell back to civilization."

Later that evening, after Sean and I finished a mandatory lengthy bath and put on pyjamas, our grandmother came into our room to change our beds. She no longer wore her royal attire, but even without jewelry and wearing one of her everyday dresses, she still looked elegant. We helped her pull the old sheets off but knew enough to leave the rest. She was the great master of bed-making, you may remember, and for several minutes my brother and I watched her practice her craft.

At last I said, "Dad says we're gonna fix up the laneway, Grandma. He says he'll order some gravel and we'll fill in that bad spot."

"Sure — that'll be nice," she answered quietly while neatly tucking a sheet under my mattress.

"And ... I'll clean my shoes," offered Sean. "I won't get them dirty again, either." He was referring to how he'd mucked them up while helping with the car — he insisted on being the official flashlight holder.

Continuing work, Grandma Layton said, quietly again, "No, that's okay, dear. You have your fun in them."

I offered, "Mom said she's gonna get Mrs. Hollings' dress cleaned, too."

"I'm sure everything will work out okay." Grandma Layton hesitated, then added with a faint grin, "She was showing it off, anyway. Maybe it serves her right."

It felt good to get a smile out of my grandmother on this evening, even if it only lasted several seconds. She'd been very downcast since her friends left and I felt more sorry for her on this evening than ever before. I knew how important she'd viewed the occasion, considering her extensive preparations, and obviously in her mind it had proved a complete disaster. I must admit that on this evening I came to understand just how against her grain our new home was. After we'd rescued Nora Keaton's car, I'd studied the moonlit muddy ditch, creek, and surrounding bush, and they impressed upon me how unrefined our Muskoka home was compared to the city. I tried to imagine someone getting stuck like that on our street in Scarborough and couldn't. The laneway, indeed the entire lake setting, seemed so primitive. I thus became glad for my grandmother getting her fancy birthday presents, for the Euchre Club ladies attending her party, and even for Judy's dance routines.

When Grandma Layton finished my bed I immediately lay down. As always on these occasions I pressed my face into the clean, lemon-scented sheets and breathed deeply. Turning onto my side and watching her do Sean's top bunk, I said, "Grandma?"

"Yes, dear?"

"This house'll end up okay ... eventually. It might even come to be like the one we had in the city."

I thought she might set me straight about this notion, and on this evening wanted her to let loose, but she surprised me by softly replying, "That would be very nice, dear. That's a very nice thing for you to say." And without another word, she picked up the old sheets and slipped quietly downstairs.

17

Despite his grandmother's worries about him running away, Kevin arrived at the lake for the summer via bus and Cathy's rusty truck on the Saturday after school ended. Right in keeping with Marie's worries, however, he came directly to my place, dressed in grubby jeans and a ripped blue T-shirt, and immediately said, "Been to the cabin yet?"

That set the tone for the summer. He and I, along with my brother, resumed visiting the cabin regularly, once again sneaking away the minute Marie went upstairs for her afternoon nap. Kevin had big plans: he wanted to completely repair the cabin — the roof, the floor, "the whole shebang." Each trip we hauled a few old boards from the jumbled piles lying along Taylor Avenue. My friend insisted the lumber would rot away anyway, so it didn't seem to me like stealing. Same for cans of rusty nails we took from his grandfather's workshop, and for some old door hinges we happened upon.

Unlike the previous summer we started making some real progress. Kevin became increasingly excited about the project, and began speculating on just how far we could go. At one point he proposed carpeting, which seemed a possibility, but whenever mentioning electrical and plumbing I always wandered away until he "got a grip."

On one such afternoon, midway through July, Sean started an argument with Kevin. He and I were talking about how we'd repair the cabin floor when my freshly brush cut brother suddenly appeared at the doorway.

"You don't be talking to Lewis like that!" he said, his twig-like arms tensed as he scowled at Kevin. It was a look he'd often presented to Joey Farnsted, the "bird-killer," in the Lord Roberts Woods.

Kevin looked wide-eyed at me, then at my frail brother. "Don't be talking like how?"

"Don't be telling Lewis what to do, *Mr. Boss.*"

"I was only talkin' to him! I wasn't tellin' him to do anything!"

"You just shove it, Mr. Boss!" Sean had turned away and was scraping the ground with his tiny shoe.

"Yeah? Well you can just shove it too!" Kevin looked at me again and shrugged.

"You think you're such a hotshot," my brother grumbled before stomping out to the shore of the lake. There he parked himself on a rock and wouldn't say a word the rest of the day.

From then on Sean stopped visiting the cabin with Kevin and me. He either stayed home or played with Judy and Katie Howard. Although he didn't seem mad at me he made it clear on several occasions he wanted nothing more to do with the cabin. At no time, however, did I bother challenging him. I'd already figured out he'd merely concocted the fight with Kevin because, being scared, he needed a way to get out of going to the cabin. I was also very disappointed, having thought he'd overcome his fear, and disgusted with him more than ever. My little brother had become downright pathetic.

Grandma Layton was quick to notice Sean's change of interests and soon notified my parents. Less than a week later my father raised the issue one evening following supper. Sean and Judy were outside playing, so it was only my grandmother, my parents, and me left in the kitchen. My father and I sat at the table, Grandma Layton did the dishes, and my mother wrapped up leftovers.

"Are you and Kevin not getting along with Sean these days?" Dad said, finishing a section of his city paper. "I hear he's been doing his own thing lately."

"He had a bit of an argument with Kevin, and after, he said he wouldn't do stuff with us anymore."

"What started that?"

"I don't know." In desperation I added, "Maybe it's because we're older or something."

"Maybe it's because he doesn't care for the things you're doing," Grandma Layton piped in. "Maybe he's a little more sophisticated than you two."

My father winked at me. "There's some wishful thinking if I ever heard it." He then picked up his paper again. That was a relief, because I feared he might follow my grandmother's lead and start probing into what exactly it *was* we were doing. But bothering me after this conversation was a worried look I'd seen on my mother's face, one reminding me she was well aware of Sean's problem. While I was sure she didn't know about the cabin, she nonetheless had made the connection between my brother's problem and his change of companions. It was her potential probings, therefore, that I left the kitchen table most fearing.

On the first Saturday of August, Kevin's mother showed up for a visit. Debbie arrived in late afternoon while I stacked firewood with Kevin, and the way his eyes lit up told me this visit was unexpected. Immediately I also received a hint about how bad relations really were between him and his mother. Not only did he not go to the driveway to greet her, his mother didn't offer any greeting herself. She merely stormed straight into the house, then seconds later stormed back out. As usual she wore clothes far superior to those she provided for her son — a fancy green blouse and gray slacks, and expensive-looking leather sandals. She'd also apparently had her short black hair recently styled.

"Where's Mother?" she snapped at Kevin.

"She has a nap after lunch every day," he answered quietly. "She'll be up soon, though."

"Oh, goddamn right she'll be up soon." Debbie glanced at our stacked wood. "What is this stupid malarkey?"

"Stacking Grandma's wood."

"And I bet she isn't paying you a bloody cent — is she?"

Kevin stared at the woodpile and scratched his dandruffy black hair. "No. I wouldn't take money from Grandma. Even if she had lots."

Debbie scowled, snorted something I didn't make out, then turned and stomped back in the house. When she was out of earshot I said to Kevin, "Is she mad about something?"

He slowly shrugged, staring at the woodpile. "Who knows."

Debbie was miserable the rest of that afternoon. We heard her arguing inside with Marie, and later she pounded out to her big silver Ford and roared away. Within half an hour she returned, however, and continued battling her mother.

Kevin had already invited me to stay for supper and sleep over. His mother being how she was, I assumed these plans cancelled. But, perhaps feeling company would help matters Marie insisted I stay, claiming her daughter was simply uptight about several things and would eventually calm down.

She didn't. At supper she hardly touched her plate, and abruptly left the table several times to make phone calls upstairs. This brought pain to Marie's thin face, and the third time Debbie rose I heard her mother say under her breath, "What the heck is she up to now?"

When she returned from this call she said in a very cocky tone, "You now have no choice but to lend me the money, Mother. I told Maurine it was a done deal."

Marie, staring down at her locket, answered, "If you think I'm a bank with bucketfuls of money to hand out, you're mistaken, missy." Glancing at me a second, she turned back to her daughter and added, "Regardless, I don't think this is really the time to talk about it."

"Oh, *please*!" Debbie scoffed, giving me a hard look. It was at this time I noticed redness around her eyes. I also noticed how fidgety she was — for about the fourth time she rearranged the ceramic dancers in a centre-piece Grandma Layton had given Marie. And believe me, I was old enough to know what state she was in: she was stoned out of her mind. Realizing this, I speculated on her "not-too-admirable occupation," and on what the money and phone calls were about. I will tell you in advance, too, that my speculation proved correct — Debbie, bless her heart, was a two-bit drug dealer.

After finishing her supper Marie said softly, "Have you looked at any new apartments, Debbie?"

"What the hell for?" was the curt reply.

"I thought by fall you intended to be out of the neighbourhood you're in?"

"Nothing's wrong where we are." With a smirk and her usual superior tone, Debbie added, "It's a fine, upstanding neighbourhood, Mother."

Marie pleaded, "But Kevin ... !"

Debbie merely shrugged, and when the phone rang yet again, she said, "That'll be for me."

Marie said, "Please, Debbie. Could you not —?"

The plea was to no avail; the daughter carried right on up the stairs, treating her mother to another nasty look.

When she was gone Kevin quietly took all our plates to the kitchen. Marie, leaning toward me, whispered in the saddest voice I'd ever heard from her. "I'm so sorry about all this, Lewis."

After supper Debbie's mood only worsened. She started drinking heavily and became increasingly irritable. At barely eight o'clock she ordered her son and me upstairs to bed and began arguing with Marie again. "Don't be telling me how to raise that little bastard!" she shouted several times, and about a dozen times screamed, "It's none of your goddamn business what I do for a living!" For Marie's part, one notable rebuttal was a harshly delivered, "If I had the money and steam to take him full-time, believe me I would!"

This went on a full hour. At one point we heard a big crash, then a thump, then Marie asking Debbie whether she was okay. Unfortunately this merely earned her another earful.

Only several minutes after that Debbie pounded her way upstairs and burst into our room.

"You!" she yelled at Kevin, slapping at the ceiling light switch. "What the hell bullshit have you've been pulling?"

"Leave him alone, Debbie — please!" Marie pleaded from the hallway.

Kevin sat up in bed, rubbing his eyes in the suddenly bright light. "What did I —?"

"You get out of that bed!" his mother screamed, "Right now, you little bastard!"

"For God's sake, don't get into this tonight!" said Marie, trying without success to draw Debbie back with the handle end of her cane.

"*Right now*!" Kevin's mother screamed again, this time at the top of her lungs.

He did as ordered, and for my friend's sake I won't tell you what I heard coming from downstairs that evening. I will tell you he was gone about ten minutes, and when he returned he merely lay on his bed again, trembling.

Nervously waiting a minute, and not hearing any indications of Debbie returning to our room, I dared to whisper, "You okay, Kev?"

He didn't answer a moment, but rubbed an arm that would be very bruised by morning. "I'm okay," he finally croaked. "But she's sure isn't."

The events of that incredibly fine Saturday left me in quite a predicament. Despite being disgusted with my brother, I'd begun feeling guilty about visiting the cabin without him and intended on telling Kevin this. Seeing just how bad things were for my friend, however, I found it impossible to disappoint him. Also, I felt Sean's feelings were silly, but certainly not Kevin's. He was perfectly sensible in wanting to run away to the cabin; I saw how it offered him a refuge from all the social evils in his life. Even at eleven I could see how the wild purity of the cabin setting translated into a wild innocence. No one beat you there, no one swore at you, and no one dealt drugs. I also knew if he was to live there, he needed my help; he was useless on his own.

So, I tried getting Sean to come back to the cabin. If he went regularly he just might, I optimistically thought, overcome his fear. I raised this issue in bed one night about a week following the incident at the Taylor house, and right after Mother was in to check us.

"Kevin's mother's a witch!" I quietly declared. "And since his grandma's too old and poor to keep him all the time, he's gonna move into the cabin one day." Hoping I'd fostered some sympathy, I added, "Maybe if Kevin let us, we could too. You've seen how he can't do much stuff on his own — he'd need our help."

Sean quickly moved to the edge of his bunk and looked down. "Live there! We couldn't live there, Lewis!"

"How come?"

"'Cause ... it'd be too cold in the winter."

"There's the woodstove, and we could cut lots of firewood."

"But ... but you guys haven't got the walls all fixed — right?"

"We're close. We still don't have a window, and we need more lumber for the floor and back wall, but that's about it."

Sean didn't respond, so I said, "You know, you can come back with us anytime. Kevin wouldn't mind — he's never said nothin' bad about you."

"Kevin can shove it. I'm not going again." My brother rolled onto his back and out of view. He was quiet several minutes, then whispered, "Lewis?"

"Yeah?"

"If only you lived with Kevin, think you'd come visit once in a while?"

"I don't know. If I came back, Mom and Dad would make me stay, and Kev'd have to live by himself."

"I guess," Sean said. He then became quiet again, and stayed that way.

As usual I lay awake quite a while. I assumed my brother long asleep, but a good half-hour after we finished talking, I heard a quiet cough above me.

18

"To twenty-five agoniz— ... oh so lovely years with Eddie and Laura," a slick-haired Reggie Morrison trumpeted, beer glass held high.

An elbow brought about his stutter, and raising her own glass his wife instead offered, "To twenty-five years of the Russells putting up with us." The sound of clinking glasses followed.

This toast set the tone for the summer's corn roast — at least, for how it began. Since this year was the Russells' twenty-fifth anniversary of living at the lake, we held the event at their place. Cathy and Carla, the ring leaders of the occasion, made it clear early on that the hilltop residents were to be treated as celebrities. One of the things they pushed for was old pictures, and the Russells had a mountain of them. About seven, when we had the fire going and corn ready for the pot, Cathy led me to Ed Russell's photography den. From there we carried eight of perhaps fifty large albums out to the picnic table. Here — some sitting, some standing — the entire group assembled to view them.

The vast majority of the pictures the Russells took while hiking and camping with their son Jimmy in the woods surrounding Gordonier Lake. Marie Taylor explained such was true for the remaining den albums. "Absolute fanatics, Lewis." This you could not doubt; besides the huge number of photos, the Russells displayed consistently pleasant expressions when a photo included either of them. Their former enthusiasm amazed me considering their disinterest at present. Most notably with Ed; if not for obvious similarities in his appearance you'd hardly have believed it was him in the pictures. But despite this great contrast in enthusiasm, Cathy and Carla seemed determined on this evening to pretend it didn't exist. "They live for romping in the woods around here!" the lake's earliest riser commented using typically present tense. It was as though the Russells hadn't changed one bit.

Now I noticed early during this photo album session that the celebrities of the evening were not particularly keen on taking part. Only when asked about a particular photo did they comment, and more than once I saw Laura give Cathy and Carla sour looks behind their backs. I didn't have to wait long to learn why. About an hour later, when it became too dark to look at them, my father had Kevin and me take the albums back inside. We entered through the side door, that nearest the den, and discovered my mother and Laura in the kitchen. They didn't notice us step in, however, and as we put the albums back on their shelf we overheard these two talking.

"I only wish to hell they'd leave the issue alone, Val," Laura said in a hushed voice. "We've decided to pull out of here and that's that."

My mother's softer voice. "Don't you think you're over-reacting somewhat? The way I interpreted it was that Carla and Cathy only want you two to stick around."

"Sure, and we're flattered! Absolutely! But there comes a time when you hope friends will simply accept you've made a decision to do something and not continue to question it. You haven't seen the history behind this — Carla and Cathy have been hounding us to stay since we first mentioned the idea of moving. What they did tonight was their favourite tactic, one they've used about six times: trying to get Ed and me caught up in our memories of this place to the point we change our minds."

"And that will never work?"

"Never work. Ed and I have had enough, and all this second-guessing business will do is make us sour toward long-time friends, and we've no desire to leave thinking like that. We care about them as much as they care about us, but both Ed and I feel they're showing us disrespect when they second-guess us like this. Enough is enough."

By eleven o'clock the crowd had thinned somewhat. Marie and Kevin had gone home, and so too had Grandma Layton with Judy. Sean also was no longer part of the festivities; he'd refused to go home without me and now lay sound asleep on the Russells' couch.

Most of those who stayed took part in a noisy card game in the kitchen. Laura initiated this event, and in light of what she said to my mother, I sensed her intent was to keep the mood pleasant and conversation off the topic of moving. Ed, on the other hand, made no such attempt to disguise he was uptight. He remained quiet, and rather than taking part in the card game he stayed with me at the fire, slowly pushing back beers.

It was while I added several more sticks to the fire that Cathy's boyfriend Rick suddenly appeared. Stopping beside Ed's lawn chair and staring at the crackling fire, he said, with apparently sincere concern, "Cathy ticking you off, Eddie?"

He didn't immediately answer, but eventually uttered a very reserved, "Perhaps." He then turned in his chair and gave Rick a suspicious look. "She didn't send you out here on a scouting mission, did she?"

"No, no — I'm not an accomplice. I'm only a curious person." Rick winked at me. "Only curious to know why you're so fed up with living at the lake. You're ... sure you're taking off?"

After choking through a swig from his beer stein, Ed wiped his bearded chin with his sleeve and answered, "Yes, for Christ's sake, *we're sure*!"

"Sorry! Don't rip *my* head off!" Rick pleaded while sneaking me a grin.

"You people need to understand, this isn't something we decided overnight, you kn—" Ed broke off and yelled to Reggie, who was currently heading away from us across the dark lawn. "Little Sean and I trashed it, Reg. Remember?"

"Oh Jesus!" he grumbled, then did an awkward turnaround,

spilling some of his drink, and slowly stumbled back inside again.

Rick said, "Golly, if you've torn down that lovely baby blue outhouse, I guess that confirms it."

Ed pointed a rugged finger at him. "Don't you get wise with me, mister."

I nervously jumped into the ring. "Don't you think you'll miss everyone on the lake, though, Mr. Russell? I mean, you haven't known our family very long, but what about Mrs. Taylor and the Morrisons, and Cathy?"

"Oh, we know we'll miss everybody, Lewis. That was the part about moving making it tough. Finally, though, we decided that, well ... changes have their costs."

"But Cathy and Mrs. Morrison sure seem to think they can get you to stay."

"Oh, those two are sure of themselves, all right. They argue we belong in Muskoka and simply don't realize it. It's the old 'you don't realize how much you need something until you lose it' bit."

Rick said, "And that's wrong?"

Ed exhaled loudly, then said in a tired voice, "Once upon a time Laura and I were exactly like Lewis here — we loved exploring the woods. You saw the truck-load of pictures we took. But, as the years passed we became less and less interested. Now it's reached the point where we're downright sick of it. It's the same old thing over and over again — nothing changes — and not even wanting to stay near close friends outweighs wanting to simply live somewhere *new*."

I countered with, "Sure doesn't seem boring to me, Mr. Russell."

"Yeah, well — give it time. This place is all great and wonderful to you at this early point, but a few years down the road ..."

This I couldn't fathom. "You really think I'll eventually get sick of this lake?"

After polishing off one too many beers, I thought, Ed looked at me sadly. "I really wish I could tell you that won't happen, Lewis."

With the corn roast behind us Kevin was on his last legs for the summer; the witch was picking him up the next Saturday. Wanting to savour his remaining time in Muskoka, every day of the week following the corn roast he insisted we go to the cabin. There'd be no silly exploring jaunts, either; he expected some work out of me. "Stuff has to get done!" he declared. On Thursday, however, he had no choice but to concede some lost time. It rained periodically that afternoon, and sometimes hard. This left us with nothing to do but work on the inside walls. Since we had little lumber remaining at the cabin, I spent most of this time listening to Kevin dream out loud about how great the place would be when completely finished. I was therefore glad when he at last conceded we should go home.

On this day we'd been blessed with extra cabin time. Earlier, Mother, Grandma Layton, and Sean had taken Marie Taylor into town and they weren't due back for several hours. That, at least, was the plan. When I arrived home I was shocked to see my mother's VW Beetle in the driveway. I soon discovered her alone in the Muskoka room, slowly flipping through a magazine.

"You're back already?" I said, allowing more alarm to my voice than I should have.

Mother, continuing to peruse the magazine, said, "Marie goofed on her doctor's appointment time, so we weren't in town long." She then added, with a penetrating green-eyed stare, "Why? Were we supposed to stay away?"

"No," I answered quietly, wondering whether Marie was interrogating Kevin at this moment about where we'd been.

After a final glance at me, my mother looked toward the living room. "Where's your brother? Out on the lawn?"

"Where's Sean? I haven't seen him."

"You haven't seen him?!" Mother put down the magazine and eyed me. "He said he was going to Kevin's to play with you two! That was over an hour ago!"

I shrugged. "We ... haven't seen him."

"He said he was sure you two were inside. He mentioned something about a board game."

I didn't know what to say this time, and merely shook my head and shrugged again.

My mother stared at me another moment, then shot up out of her chair. She yanked open the Muskoka room screened door and ordered me to follow her outside, where for five minutes we both yelled for Sean while circling the house. We had no luck, however, and I then followed Mother into the kitchen. Here she immediately picked up the phone.

"He might be at Cathy's, or the Russells'," I offered, watching her dial Marie's number.

"Can't be! I finished talking to Cathy on the phone only ten minutes ago — he wasn't with her — and I saw the Russells in town!"

Strangely, we received no answer at the Taylors'. After letting their phone ring what must have been at least a dozen times, Mother hung up and said, "You go over to Kevin's right away and see if he's there!"

As she began quickly dialling another number, one I didn't recognize, I said, "I'm sure he's *around*, Mom. Maybe —"

"You just get over there. This is more than an hour ago I'm saying he went to find you and Kevin, Lewis. More than an *hour*! And Sean would never play around the lake on his own — I know that for sure!"

"He might —"

"*Never*!"

My mother all but screeched this final word, and I saw panic in her eyes. I froze a moment, completely frightened by her look. It wasn't until she put her hand over the phone and shouted "*Get going*!" that I snapped out of my trance, and now without the slightest hesitation, turned and darted out the door.

I ran at full tilt to the Taylors'. There I found no sign of Sean, only Grandma Layton helping Marie put clothes on the line and Kevin stacking more firewood. They had a radio on, explaining why they hadn't heard the phone.

After quickly informing them of the problem, Kevin drew me aside and whispered, "Think he went to the cabin?"

It sounded possible, so we immediately ran down a rain-muddied Taylor Avenue. At the cabin we scouted around for tracks and called for Sean countless times, but saw no sign of him and heard no answer. Finally we headed back, running all the way again and stopping only when we reached the main road. At this point I didn't know where we should try next.

In the midst of catching his breath, Kevin said, "How about with Judy at Katie Howard's place? Think he might have gone there?"

I didn't answer, however, because at that instant I noticed something in the mud near our feet: star patterns. They led down Taylor Avenue, toward the cabin, and I quickly realized we were in big trouble.

19

"How many times?" Grandma Layton whispered, her hand trembling terribly against her face.

Ed Russell, his voice hoarse, answered, "Only the once, Annie. But I think it was nerves, not —"

"And she was shivering badly?"

"Pretty bad."

My grandmother sighed deeply, her eyes closed. When she opened them again she seemed ready to ask more, but raindrops suddenly splattered against the living room window. Moving to it, she groaned, "Oh, no! It's raining *again*? Why of all nights? *Why*?"

Ed, staring forlornly at his wet yellow rain jacket, said, "It's not coming down hard, at least, Annie."

"He'll get absolutely soaked to the bone! He'll be shivering like crazy too — he's so thin, and he's only wearing shorts and a T-shirt! If Valerie's had problems ..."

"It is possible he's found some place to get out of the weather. He just might have found a place, Annie. He just might have."

I heard my parents' bedroom door bang open and the sound of hard footsteps across the floor. Mother came into view, dressed in dry clothes.

"Oh, Valerie!" Grandma Layton quickly pleaded. "You simply cannot go back out! There's enough people alre—"

"*Like hell I can't!*" she blared, grabbing her rain jacket. "I'll be fine! Don't you even think about trying to stop me, Mother! Now where the hell did my boots go, or am I going out in my frickin' socks?"

"Here!" Ed said, promptly delivering them.

"But Valerie ... shivering badly, and passing out like that ... you can't!"

My mother only gave her own a hard stare, and after frantically putting on her boots and jacket shouted up the stairs, "What the Christ is the holdup?"

Seconds later my father all but flew downstairs, a winter jacket tucked under his arm. I'd heard him swearing and firing boxes around in the upstairs closet, and wondered what he was searching for.

"I don't need a stupid winter coat!" Mother snarled. "What the hell is this?"

"Something you're putting on under that rain jacket one goddamn way or another!" my father snarled right back.

She huffed at this but relented, and seconds later pounded out to the porch, with Ed, Dad, and Grandma Layton right behind her. What immediately followed were, for me, only sounds: my grandmother muttering something, the porch door banging shut, and through the Muskoka room screen, Ed and my parents hurrying down the laneway.

Soon Grandma Layton reappeared from the porch, in tears again as often she had been during this evening, and slowly padded back to the living room. Midway she glanced at the clock above the kitchen window, and also greatly concerned, I looked at the lighted clock on the Muskoka room end table. It was 2:45 a.m.

Within an hour of my discovering Sean's footprints that afternoon, the police organized a full search. They used the Taylors' as a base, and quickly it became an extremely busy place. Besides more police a steady stream of volunteers arrived to help. Cars soon lined the road in front of the house and people crowded the yard. With these volunteers the police established teams, each led by an officer with a radio. My parents, the Russells, Cathy, and Rick chose to search together, and their team was the first to leave.

Kevin, Judy, and I watched all this from the Taylors' rear living room window. When the yard became crowded and hectic my father ordered us inside, and we could do nothing but watch and wait. For the most part Marie Taylor and Grandma Layton stayed inside with us, alternating between trips to the window and trips to the phone, which rang almost continuously.

The first few teams had hardly left when, to everyone's dismay, it began to rain. It didn't come down very hard but this time continued much longer than the showers Kevin and I waited out at the cabin. Fortunately most of the volunteers arrived dressed for possible wet weather, so despite these miserable conditions the search carried on.

Several long hours passed. During this time Kevin, Judy, and I seldom moved from the window. Occasionally we'd see a police officer talking on a radio and we'd race to the door, always thinking it was someone reporting they'd found Sean. That never proved true, however, and after the third incident like this we merely remained at the window, restless but quiet.

About nine that evening, when it had become completely dark, the main search ended. It wasn't to continue until first light the next morning. There was no stopping my mother and father, however, and they continued searching using big six-volt flashlights. The Russells, knowing the area much better than my parents, joined them. Several other teams also continued, such as one including Cathy, Rick, and my father's boss, Don Nelson.

Soon after, Grandma Layton took Judy and me home. My sister was losing the battle against sleep by this time and was taken right up to bed. An exceptionally stern grandmother ordered me to do likewise, but there was no way I could sleep. As the night wore on I eventually agreed to lie down on the Muskoka room couch. And although I think Grandma Layton assumed I'd fallen asleep, I was still wide awake to experience those several intense minutes when the Russells and my parents stopped in at our place.

This incident at the house only capped what had been for me a predictably long, agonizing evening. To this day I cannot recall a time in my life when I was more frustrated, more desperate, and more sorry than I was on this night. Being confined to a dark Muskoka room and obviously not able to sleep, I had nothing to do but ponder, and ponder I did like never before. Thoughts included running various imaginary scenarios through my mind — searchers roaming the woods and their whispered comments; taking off into the bush and finding Sean myself; even my brother suddenly appearing at the Muskoka room door and all the things I'd say to him, how I'd give the little bugger proper shit for wandering off. Ultimately dominating my thoughts, however, was how I'd been disgusted with my brother getting scared in the woods, and how I considered his fear silly. This issue came to the forefront abruptly, but would linger the rest of the night.

About midnight, when Grandma Layton went upstairs for what I knew would be a long, pampering check on Judy, I dared to slip outside a minute. Desperately wanting to gain news of the search, I left the back deck and ventured toward the lake, just far enough so I could see or hear anything happening on the main road. I didn't, however, and was left merely standing and shivering in the cool moist air, gazing at the moonlit woods on the lake's far shore.

It was then I recalled something Ed Russell said when I asked about Sean's fear. "Take a look at all that, Lewis," he'd said, pointing to the northern bush, "and tell me it doesn't seem like the woods stretch damn near forever. Try telling me those woods don't seem awfully big and powerful." Gazing at this same bush on this night I unhesitatingly agreed with these comments. I put myself in my brother's place, imagining myself out in that massive forest, in the dark and alone. Intimidating indeed, and when I soon slipped back into the house a new, much more horrifying scenario came in with me: one sensitive to the great vastness and power of the woods, and one portraying my frail little brother stumbling and crying his way through them.

The next morning I woke to the sound of a helicopter flying over the house. Still wearing my clothes from the previous day, I bolted off the couch in time to see the aircraft pass over the east ridge. This helicopter, and the fact no one had woken me in the night, was enough to tell me Sean was still missing. The only good news was that the day was sunny, and drifting in through the Muskoka room screens was warm air.

I found Grandma Layton alone in the kitchen, pacing.

"They're even using a helicopter?" I blurted out, not thinking.

My grandmother had obviously not heard me get up, and at the sound of my voice her head snapped toward me. After exhaling loudly she said in an irritable tone, "The police have had that going an hour now. You've slept through it."

I looked at the clock above the kitchen window. It was quarter after nine.

"Don't look so surprised. It must have been close to midnight when you fell asleep last night."

I only nodded at this, watching Grandma Layton pace once again to the porch window. She moved awkwardly, I noticed, her usual grace absent. When she turned sideways to gaze toward the lake I saw dark spots under her eyes, and a deeply strained look on her face unlike I'd ever seen before. Her curly silver hair, something she prided herself greatly in keeping perfectly neat, was a mess.

Not sure what to say, I nervously whispered, "Everybody's ... still out there, Grandma?"

"Still going. The Morrisons are involved now too. They arrived about a half-hour ago. Reggie's searching, and Carla has your sister."

"So nobody's seen any sign of Sean yet? Like tracks or something?"

Grandma Layton padded back to the living room. "Nothing yet. It rained most of the night and I'm told that probably ruined any tracks."

"Sean likely found a place to sit then. They'll find him under a tree, I bet."

"I'm praying they do, Lewis."

There came a knock on the porch door, and seconds later Laura Russell, dressed in tattered jeans and a thick gray shirt, appeared at the kitchen doorway.

"Come in, come in!" Grandma Layton yelled. "Any news?"

"None about Sean, I'm afraid," she quickly answered. "What I can tell you is there's a heck of a lot of people out searching for him now, Annie. Word's out all over Bracebridge and volunteers are showing up in droves."

"Surely it's simply a matter of time, then," my grandmother declared confidently as she went to the kitchen. Here she sat on a chair and began struggling badly to put on her shoes. I dashed over to help.

"Where are you going, Grandma?" I said, fearing she might be upset enough to head off into the bush on her own. "I'll come with —"

"I'm headed to Marie's. You, young man, are staying right here in this house so we know where you are. Laura's come to stay with you."

Glancing at my neighbour, and realizing a child-watching plan had been established, I turned back and said, desperately, "I could help look, though! If I was with someone I'd be all right! I know my way —"

Grandma Layton gently grabbed my shoulders and pulled me directly in front of her. Softly she said, "I'm sure you'd be a big help, Lewis. I want you to stay here, though, so I know exactly where you are. Would you do that for me — please?"

This request mesmerized me a moment, so unaccustomed was I to my grandmother using a pleading tone with me. Usually she'd simply inform me what it was I'd do, and that would be that.

"Okay," I replied in the same soft tone. "I'll stay if that's what you want, Grandma."

Laura said, "Are you sure you're okay to walk, Annie? I could call Marie's and have someone bring over a car, or at least have someone come to walk with you."

"Thank-you, but I'm fine. The walk will do me good, and it's not far."

"You're sure?"

"I'm sure," and with that Grandma Layton rose and headed to the porch. Before stepping out she said, "I'll phone the second I hear anything."

As we stood in the porch watching her march quickly down the laneway, Laura breathed deeply and said, "Well ... so much for that, Lewis."

"So much for that?"

"I hoped to get your grandmother to lie down a while, but I guess that was wishful thinking, wasn't it?"

"Probably. This is the most upset I've ever seen her in my whole life."

Laura nodded, her glasses in one hand as she rubbed tired-looking eyes with the other. "How about you? Hanging in there?"

Staring at the floor, I said, "No ... I'm feeling pretty dumb, actually."

Laura reached out and stroked my hair. "Now, now. You didn't do anything dumb. Nobody's blaming you or Kevin for this, either — believe me."

"But if it hadn't been for us going to that cabin ..."

"Perhaps, but if there's blame regarding that — and I'm not sure there is — it's with us grownups."

I turned. "Why the heck would it be *your* fault?"

With her glasses on again, Laura gazed at the woods along the back ridge. "It's our fault because we took the chance of letting you kids go to that cabin."

I stared at her. "Took the chance? You mean —?"

"Ed, Marie, and I knew that cabin was there, Lewis — it was Marie's husband Lyall who built it."

Stunned, I said, "Did my parents know too?"

"Yes, your parents knew too. Ed and I took them to see the cabin one afternoon while you kids were out swimming with Cathy. That was early this summer."

I hardly believed my ears. "All of you *went* there?"

"All of us went there, and your Dad was really impressed by the work you boys did to the place. I understand he even left a set of old hinges on some lumber at Marie's for you to find."

This was too much. "And Mom and Dad thought it was okay for us to go there?"

"Naturally they had concerns, but after thinking it over

decided to let it go. They said they knew when moving to Muskoka they couldn't very well tie you kids to chairs and keep you from romping around — especially you. As for Kevin, with the rough time he's having with his mother Marie thought some fun at the cabin would help him, so she didn't stop him either."

"Nobody ever said anything, though. How come my parents didn't just say it was okay?"

Laura looked me in the eye. "Because that would have spoiled the adventure for you. Admit it — that cabin wouldn't have been half the fun if it wasn't your little secret, would it?"

I couldn't help grinning a second. "I suppose not."

"Marie told us on a few occasions she had to go out of her way not to see you boys swiping that old lumber."

"I thought she was always sleeping."

"*Sometimes* she was sleeping, Lewis."

After considering all this, I said, "So ... do you think my parents feel guilty now?"

Laura grimaced. "They probably do, but I don't think they should. All they intended was to give their kids some freedom; a chance to do their own thing. Sure there are risks involved, and some people might think your parents irresponsible, but I don't look at it that way. If you want your kids to develop some backbone you've simply got to stand back sometimes. Even though Sean's in trouble I still think your parents made the right decision, and I admire them."

After this we were both quiet a moment. Finally, while running my foot along the door sill, I said, "Mrs. Russell?"

"Yes?"

"Think ... Sean will be okay?"

"Sure he will be," she answered brightly. "He'll be fine, and so will everyone else."

"I sure hope they find him pretty soon. He's been lost a long time."

"I'm confident everything will turn out well." Laura reached out and dabbed at my cheeks with her sleeve. "Everything will be okay, Lewis."

A short while later Kevin came over. We went into the Muskoka room and tried to watch TV, but naturally neither of us paid much attention, and for several long hours we sat and basically did nothing. Shortly before noon, however, my friend suddenly jumped from his seat and peered out the screen. "Hey Lewis!" he shouted, "I think that's your dad coming up the laneway!"

I sprang to my feet but only caught a glimpse of my father before losing sight because of the thick bush behind the house. By the time I could see him again he was much closer. He was walking slowly, his arms hanging limp at his sides, and he seemed oblivious to the remaining rain puddles on the laneway. Even from a distance you could see he had a very drawn and dazed expression.

My mother had arrived at the house several minutes earlier, and she must have heard Kevin's announcement because we saw her rush outside. I was about to do the same when I caught sight of Ed Russell and Reggie Morrison also walking up the laneway, and when these two saw Kevin and me they waved us back. Gripping the door handle tightly, my heart feeling like it would pound through my chest, I watched my mother meet my father at the end of the driveway. Here he drew her into his arms, whispered a few seconds in her ear, then held her tight as her body went suddenly and completely limp. And eleven years of experience assured me my mother's tears were not those of joy: my brother was dead.

20

Our family held Sean's funeral the following Monday, on one of those perfect late August mornings my brother and I normally treasured. Many people attended, including Gordonier Lake residents, co-workers of my parents, teachers, kids from school and their parents, and many of the police officers and volunteers who took part in the search. The Walshes also attended, making a trip from Scarborough.

Despite my grandmother suggesting I not, I insisted on being a pallbearer, and at the service at St. Thomas Cemetery in Bracebridge I helped carry Sean's tiny oak casket from the hearse to his grave. This experience, mind you, is today only a blur. About all I clearly remember is my father patting me on the shoulder after we'd set the casket down, and Judy, clad in a new blue dress, placing a large bouquet on top of it. The rest of the time I was in a complete daze; once, while the minister spoke, I believe I even scanned the crowd a moment, wondering where the heck my brother was.

Following that service our family held a small gathering back at the lake. Cathy had stayed at our place on this day, and when our family arrived home we found the house spotless and food and drinks ready in the dining room. In doing so she secured forever a place in our hearts; Grandma Layton, especially, was touched.

The afternoon went slowly. The house was crowded and the many conversations made it noisy. I spent most of this time sitting quietly with Kevin on the living room sofa. He was wearing a dark brown suit that, as usual, did not fit him well, and about all I remember him doing the whole afternoon was swinging his arms, trying to stretch his jacket out. As for me, I don't know if I even did that much.

The gathering wound down about four o'clock. I stayed with my parents and Grandma Layton in the porch, seeing people out the door, then slipped up to my room. I laid on my bunk and started flipping through some old magazines, trying desperately but without any luck to get my mind off the day. It was only a short time later, anyway, that I heard footsteps on the stairs, then saw Laura Russell appear at my door.

"Hanging in there, mister?" she said, stepping into the room.

"I'm okay, I guess," I answered, tossing my magazine on the floor and rolling onto my back. "This sure has been a big thing."

"Yes, it's been a big thing." Laura came in and sat on the edge of my bed. She was wearing a red dress that looked out of place on her rugged frame. "Losing someone in your family is always painful, but particularly when it's someone as young as your brother." She studied me, then added, "You were pretty quiet today."

"Didn't mean to be. I just ... didn't feel like talking."

Her eyes still on me, Laura softly said, "I know how you feel. I lost my father when I was about your age, and I remember that leaving me pretty quiet. Later, though, I found talking things out helped me, and I want you know Ed and I are available if and when you feel like doing that. Talking to someone outside the family is sometimes ... easier. I know it was for me."

I whispered, "I suppose, thanks."

Giving me a final glance, Laura started gazing about the room. "Something else I came up to tell you concerns your parents and your grandmother. You may find them acting a little strangely over the next while, especially in the way they treat you and your sister."

Turning onto my side, I said, "Grandma already is. She didn't even give me heck for getting my suit jacket dirty this morning."

This produced a faint smile. "Yes, Lewis. That's exactly the kind of strangeness I mean."

Laura rose and moved to the dresser, where she began looking at some framed family photos. One she soon held up for me. It showed Sean in his lookout tree in the Lord Roberts Woods. "How old was he in this picture?"

"Five. My mother took that one on his birthday."

"What's he doing? I see he's got binoculars hanging from his neck."

"Those were his birthday present, and he's watching a robin's nest in another tree. He used to watch over all the baby birds that were born in it."

Laura smiled and murmured something I didn't make out, then set the picture back on the dresser. Glancing up at Sean's empty bunk and wiping a tear from her cheek, she said, "I'm sure going to miss your brother, Lewis. We're all going to miss him very much."

I never thought I'd see the day, but I was actually glad to start school that fall. Getting into a daily routine again seemed to help me. Having said that, things at school were not the same. Friends were shy about talking — some afraid to talk at all — and during the first month it seemed I could have gotten away with almost anything with my teacher.

As Laura said they would be, things at home were different as well. My father spent more than his usual time reading, Judy spent more than her usual time drawing, and it seemed practically every night Grandma Layton made something special for supper. Relatively speaking, however, these family members seemed to be coping well.

My mother was another matter.

She'd been extremely erratic in her moods; quiet one moment and downright giggly the next. She also threw herself into a frenzied interior decorating mode. It was rare not to find her with a paint brush in her hand, and she had forty-seven little jobs on the go at once. My father didn't help her, however — and wouldn't let anyone else help — because he said she'd then quickly run out of things to do.

Now I found these mood swings and this frenzied decorating bothersome enough, but neither compared to something else my mother developed a habit of doing: staring out my window at night.

The first occasion of this occurred in early September. That evening, a short while after I'd gone to bed, Mother made her usual trip to my room to check on me. As I'd always done to avoid getting in trouble, I pretended to be asleep, and waited for her to come to the bed and give me her standard peck on the cheek. Instead, on this evening she first went to my front window. I knew this because I heard her pull back one of the curtains.

Daring to open my eyes, I could see her by the pale light coming in from the hall. I couldn't see her face, of course, but by the angle of her head I sensed she was looking at the sky, as opposed to the lake or something else. She stood this way, silent and motionless, for what was probably several minutes. It seemed much longer, however, and I was quite relieved when she finally came to the bed, kissed her apparently sleeping son, then quietly slipped downstairs again.

Not wanting to question Dad or Grandma Layton about my mother for fear of upsetting them, I thought I'd accept Laura's invitation to chat with her and Ed. My opportunity came on the final Saturday of September. Ed had visited us that morning and mentioned that, in continued preparation for moving, he intended that day to bring down a dead maple at the edge of his yard. I decided I'd go up and help him.

Since Laura was in town it was only her husband and me chatting that afternoon. For the first half-hour he joked around, trying to cheer me by throwing leaves and teasing about school. Gradually, however, he became more serious, and then even took the initiative in bringing up the topic I wanted to talk about. He asked what my mother was up to that afternoon, and I explained her latest job — painting little dancers on the bathroom walls to please Grandma Layton.

Ed paused from dragging away a branch he'd cut off the recently-felled dead maple. "Perhaps you find that strange, Lewis, but I don't. Doing wacky stuff like that is normal for a parent who's lost a child."

"I suppose," I said, then decided to go right to the crux of my concerns. "She's also been staring out my window at night, though. Don't you think that's strange?"

Dragging the branch to his fire pit, Ed said, "Just stares? What — at the lake?"

"Maybe, but it seems more like she's staring at the sky."

"And how many times has she done this?"

"Three times so far. I've sort of figured out what triggers it. Anytime something happens to really remind my mother of Sean, she ends up looking out my window. The first time she did it, I realized later on it was because she'd gotten my lunch-box out to clean it before I started school, and found my brother's right beside it."

Ed took a seat on the fresh maple stump and stared at the leaves scattered around us. With a pained expression, he said, "I have to contend, Lewis, hearing about this sky-staring habit also doesn't surprise me. I saw this coming with your mother."

"It doesn't surprise you?"

"The rain we got the night your brother was lost — it really bothered your mother. Your grandmother too, but even more so your mother. While we were out searching I did my best to make her think it wasn't a big factor, but she knew better."

"So the rain *was* a big factor, you think? Maybe Sean was already ..."

"May have been. Your mother, though, is convinced the rain made all the difference in the world to what happened; she feels Sean died late in the night, while it was raining. The rain would have made him wet and chilly, and prone to wandering around to stay warm." Ed paused. "And ... it obviously would have made the rocks slippery, Lewis. Your mother, I feel, is guessing at what happened based on intuition — and one shouldn't belittle that, in my experience — but what she's suggesting makes good sense. It's a very logical guess as well."

Sean was found lying near the edge of an eight-foot high outcropping of bedrock, about a quarter-mile northeast of the cabin. It seems he missed it by wandering too far east, and wound up venturing into the deep woods north of the cabin lake. At some point in time — and this was the crucial issue at this moment — he fell off the edge of the bedrock, and died from a fractured skull.

"Not only that," Ed continued, "but obviously the rain made searching for your brother much more difficult, both in terms of searchers getting wet and it ruining his scent for the dogs."

I sat in a nearby pile of fall leaves and looked up at the few scattered clouds. "So Mom's mad about that? That's sort of weird, isn't it? Being mad at ... *clouds*?"

Ed shrugged. "Perhaps. I'm certain your mother doesn't feel the weather was purposely out to harm your brother. I think she's merely disturbed the weather was ... what it was." Gazing at the woods around us, then up at the sky, he added, "It's the indifference of it all, Lewis. Of all the nights it could have rained, why that one? The whole thing runs counter to the way your mother is, you see. She loves her kids, and anything that isn't loving toward them — anything that doesn't *feel* at all — bothers her. Her belief, too, that Sean was simply trying to please you only adds to that feeling of coldness."

I quickly turned. "Simply trying to please me?"

"Your mother's absolutely sure Sean was trying to make up with you and Kevin — especially you. So it's bad enough, in your mother's mind, that good old Mother Nature was indifferent to his welfare. But being indifferent while he was only trying to please his big brother makes what happened seem even ... colder."

"What about Sean being scared, though? Doesn't my mother remember that?"

"Oh, she remembers. By the way she described the incidents where your brother had nightmares she could never have forgotten his fear. That's why up until he got lost she was confident he would never venture anywhere on his own; she noticed he didn't even like playing around the lake on his own. She's now convinced, though, his wanting to impress his big brother was a strong enough urge to overwhelm his fear of the woods."

"But ... Sean wouldn't try going to the cabin only for me. He was way too scared. Besides, why wouldn't he just go with Kevin and me?"

Ed shrugged, slowly running fingers through his hair. "Maybe he wanted to surprise you — I really don't know, though, Lewis. Unfortunately, too, we may never."

Turned out, I didn't have to wait long to get an answer to the mystery surrounding my brother. On the Tuesday evening following my talk with Ed I found out why Sean went to the cabin. Strangely, if it hadn't been for my needing to pee, I might still not know.

Right after supper that evening my mother went to town in the VW with Judy, Grandma Layton, and Marie Taylor to do some grocery shopping. They had no sooner left than my father shocked me by suggesting we make a trip to the cabin. He said he wanted to get a few things he'd forgotten during the search, and that he felt my mother and grandmother would be better off not knowing of the trip. It became dark about seven this time of year, and we knew they wouldn't be gone long, so we had to hurry.

Since trucks made deep ruts in Taylor Avenue during the search, Dad drove his Buick only as far as Marie's driveway. From here we hiked quickly down the road and through the now dimly-lit bush. When reaching the cabin we found quite a pile of Dad's things still lying on the floor, including a large flashlight, batteries, boots, a rain jacket, and an expensive first-aid kit.

As I knelt and began helping my father fill a canvass bag with these things, he said to me, "I understand Laura filled you in on our knowing about this place?"

I shyly nodded, but didn't say anything.

"You boys did some nice work to it — I was really impressed." Dad eyed me. "You do realize, though, that from here on this place is definitely out of bounds?"

"I know," I answered quietly, and it was at this moment, out of sheer nervousness, I suddenly needed to pee. I hurried to the back of the cabin and went, all the while staring at the huge oak and the steadily darkening woods behind it.

Now it was on my way back that I noticed something leaning against the cabin's rear wall.

"Where did this window come from?" I asked my father, who was now outside the cabin door, doing up the straps on the canvass bag.

"Somebody found that in the bush," he answered. When he finished closing the bag he picked it up and immediately started down the path. "C'mon, Lewis. We need to get back."

"Coming," I said, but before leaving I shone my little flashlight on the window a moment. The frame had only a few small patches of faded paint left on it, but enough for me to recognize the colour.

It was the same blue as the Russells' old outhouse.

"Lewis?!"

"Coming," I said again, and then ran full tilt along the dark path until joining my father.

21

"How's that coming?" said Grandma Layton, putting her hand on my arm and trying to read over my shoulder.

"Okay," I answered quietly, using my left forearm as a shield.

Giving up on her peek, she said, "Don't be all night, Lewis Joseph. You're due for bed." She then picked up several empty wine bottles sitting in front of me and took them to the back closet. When I was out of her view I looked at my current sheet of paper again, made a few squiggles, and sighed.

It was late November, and we'd recently seen the entire lake crew out the door. They'd shown up by surprise shortly after our Sunday supper to give us "a boost." They'd apparently sensed our family's spirits were beginning to rise and wanted to push us further. Cathy surely felt this about us, beaming and saying, "You're a bunch of troopers!" Whether I'd go that far, I didn't know.

Now the previous Friday I'd received another surprise: a letter from Joey Farnsted. My city friend, I knew, wasn't the letter-sending type, and I could tell he'd been coached while writing it. It was overly polite, for one, but also lacked any reference to my new woodsy life, something I knew he'd be very curious about. I supposed his parents felt mentioning that topic wasn't a particularly good idea at this time.

Being quite a stickler for returning letters promptly, Grandma Layton sat me down at the kitchen table with pen and paper immediately after the surprise party and made me write a letter to

Joey. "You've had since Friday!" she declared, as though this was an interminable span of time. I admitted to myself, however, I should truly have sent Joey a letter ages ago, as I'd resolved to do the day I went raspberry picking. But somehow that letter had never come about. The reason for my most recent delay in writing my old co-explorer, though, was clear: I didn't have a clue what to say.

At risk of understating, autumn had been unusual. Through perhaps a heightened sensitivity brought on by my brother's tragedy, I essentially experienced again the whole spectrum of feelings toward Muskoka I'd been exposed to since our family moved. And doing so in merely two months, I discovered something not only leading to letter-writing difficulties, but something that would deeply affect the rest of my childhood. Indeed, it would affect the rest of my life.

To begin, there were undoubtedly pleasant experiences during this autumn — sparkling ones, even — when somehow Sean's tragedy was momentarily pushed aside. In early October, for example, I joined Reggie Morrison on his final row of the season, and actually fell asleep in the stern seat, so tranquil was the lake. On another evening I again witnessed the passing of a flock of geese, and was briefly filled with that same envy and longing I'd felt the previous autumn. This time I even cheered the birds, prompting an odd look from my grandmother through our living room window. Lastly, one day in early November Cathy took me to her aunt's cottage again, and spending time there made me very happy for her, celebrating once more her freedom and the place inspiring it.

Sadly, such pleasant experiences were intermingled with an array of ones not-so-pleasant. I came to identify more with the Russells' boredom over the staticness of the lake. Perhaps having been through the cycle of seasons, I began to sense a monotony to this pattern. In the city something different is always happening — your surroundings change, or seem to, much more often. But I now realized Gordonier Lake was Gordonier Lake.

Other experiences were even more negative. One day when alone with Judy I had a sudden and severe fit when she entered the house wearing muddy shoes. "You're getting everything messed up," I shouted at the top of my lungs, "and Grandma's gonna move away!" This outburst definitely frightened my sister and she began crying, and I was left wondering what had come over me.

I now saw nothing strange in my mother's window-staring habit, which unfortunately continued through the fall. I hated her doing this, but with my own odd moods I didn't consider her behaviour alarming. How I longed, however, for a snowy winter night when she and I could again sit in front of the living room window. An image I retained of looking up and seeing her entranced on that New Year's Eve now assumed a dream-like quality. I feared such an evening would never come again, however, and I became angry. Rainy days, most of all, were usually miserable days, but my anger at the indifference of my surroundings expanded to include other things as well.

One day in October my mother had me go with Judy to retrieve some sandals she left months earlier at Lyall Rock. While searching my sister happened upon a perch in the pond we'd seen the bass our first summer at the lake. I immediately knew it was dying — repeatedly it rose to the surface on its side. Judy, alarmed at this, grabbed a small stick and began gently helping the fish swim. When I suggested her actions pointless she said, "Maybe its friends will come help soon." To this I blared, "It doesn't have any *friends*, stupid! Nothing will help it! It'll just sit there and die, or something will come along and eat it! Nothing cares, Judy! Nothing gives a *shit* but you — wake up!" My sister stared at me, terrified, then burst into tears. Angrily she bawled, "You're not very nice, Lewis!"

Nights were the worst, though. For one, the insomnia I'd traditionally suffered became more severe. After one grumpy morning too many, and being sent to my room, my father said from the doorway, "I know this is a bad time, Lewis — I know it is. It's that way for all of us. But your not sleeping and then being miserable with everybody isn't helping — you hear me?" My bad moods got me sent to bed an hour earlier, which, good intentions aside, only worsened the problem. Compounding it further was something I never admitted: I didn't want to sleep, because my sleep was often plagued by nightmares.

In one I recall, I'm running through the woods behind my father. I glance down and see a mud stain on my shirt and I'm worried I'll get in trouble when returning home. For the most part I'm very happy, though — thrilled — because I'm sprinting at full tilt and yet not catching my father. Long gone is his belly and lethargy and he's racing through the woods with me. I'm so happy for him, and for me. I'm exploring deeper into the woods than ever before; everything is so new. But we simply keep running. The woods grow darker, the trees larger, until my father suddenly vanishes ahead of me, swallowed up, seemingly, by a monster I realize is the forest itself.

In another I'm with my brother and Kevin, and we're living at the cabin. It's winter and the snow surrounding the cabin setting is completely undisturbed by human prints. Kevin is happier than I've ever seen him. "The stupid witch'll never find me," he says often. This nightmare splits, with two scenarios alternating back and forth. In one Sean is helping me collect firewood, and a bitterly cold wind has made his bare hands almost blue. I try helping but when we return to the cabin it's somehow been locked. My final image is of trying without success to kick the door open. In the other scenario it's spring, and I'm searching the forest desperately because I can hear Sean calling me. I walk seemingly for hours before coming upon him lying in a shallow, muddy pool, the Russells' small window nearby. His brush cut head is horribly deformed, and his face and neck are riddled with leeches. "Lewis!" he pleads, tears streaming down his face. "Lewis!" Strangely, however, I'm unable to approach him, and despite a deep sense of guilt over his predicament, soon race away in terror.

Although today I might cast off such horrific nightmares as extreme experiences brought on by my brother's death, at the time they affected me equally as much as those gained while awake. They therefore contributed to that slurry of feelings making me realize one undeniable fact: that I had become completely and utterly confused about Muskoka. The question I'd worried over in the months leading to our move I now agonized over. Had moving to Muskoka been a good idea for our family? I could not have given you a clear answer.

Such then was my state of mind when writing a letter to Joey Farnsted on that late fall evening of 1976. I don't specifically remember what I told him. The best I recall is my providing a simple, eleven-year-old account of a number of things I'd seen and done since the move, leading to a brief summary of what happened to my brother. The thoughts and feelings spinning through my head were far too complex for me to digest at that age. But, to paraphrase a certain remark by Ed Russell, although I might not have rationalized my confusion, I certainly still felt it.

"Lewis!" This came from Grandma Layton's bedroom, and I knew it was coming. She'd been reading and I'd just heard her open her little book cabinet.

"Yes, Grandma," I answered. "I'm done."

After simply signing 'Lewis' at the bottom, I folded the letter and sealed it in an envelope my father had given me. I checked the address on the front one more time, then rose and turned off the kitchen light. On my way upstairs I left the letter on the counter. In the morning Dad would mail it for me.

And so, there it was.

I pictured Joey reading the letter in the Lord Roberts Woods, sitting at the exact spot we'd sat so many times speculating about what it'd be like to live in the country. And I hoped he would understand the letter, hoped that somehow, miraculously, he could read between the lines and gain a hint, at least, of what I was going through. But I knew he couldn't possibly.

Part Two

22

One winter afternoon when I was a mere eight years of age, and absent from Lord Roberts School with chicken pox, Grandma Layton blessed me with a long grandmother-to-grandson talk about my future. I can't recall much of what she said on this occasion — I mostly daydreamed through her lectures — but one remark she made did, for whatever reason, stick with me. She claimed that at some point in my life I was bound to meet a person who would profoundly influence the way I viewed the world. She didn't deliver this insight to my eight-year-old ears in these exact words, naturally, but that was the gist of her message. Someone, sooner or later, and for better or worse, would come along and "change me."

Looking back, I believe the summer of 1977, the summer Owen Goddard moved to Gordonier Lake, was when I met my 'fundamental changer'. He more than anyone, I believe, created the filter through which I now view the world. He did not achieve this entirely consciously, however; I learned as much, I think, from observing as listening to him. I also did not learn particularly quickly from Owen. As you will see, our first summer together proved, in the end, a disaster for both of us.

In early May of 1977 the Russells, as expected, put their house on the market. The event surprising everyone was its sale less than a week later. It sold the same day, in fact, the listing came out in the Herald Gazette. Also surprising everyone was Ed's reaction: he instantly shaved off his beard, a vow I learned he made to Laura years earlier.

"Aren't we a tad lucky," my father said as he and I stood at the porch door watching Laura and her barely recognizable husband walk up our driveway. In response they both simply smiled from ear to ear, and continued smiling while stepping past us to enter the kitchen. Already seated at the table with Judy and my mother was Marie Taylor, whom we'd invited to supper to help the Russells celebrate.

Our hilltop neighbours took seats at the table and Grandma Layton poured coffee. My father then dove into the issue captivating him since he returned from work and heard the news.

"So!" he began, folding his arms and leaning back against the kitchen counter, "Who are these eager beavers?"

"Eager beav*er*," Ed answered. "Apparently it's an old-timer from town — Owen Goddard is his name."

Marie's eyes lit up. "Owen Goddard! *Owen Goddard* bought your place?"

"Yes, ma'am. I take it you know him?"

"Sure I know him! We go way back. His family had a farm farther down the Fraserburg road, close to where I grew up."

Laura looked at Marie sternly. "And why, might I ask, are you so shocked he bought our place?"

"Well ... I haven't talked to him in a few years, but the last time I did he didn't mention anything about moving out of town."

"And?"

Marie shrugged her frail shoulders. "And I didn't take him for the type ... that ... would want a place on this lake, that's all. Any idea what he has in mind?"

"Not really," said Ed. "All the real estate guy told us was he plans to live at the house year-round, and didn't exactly spend heaps of time looking at it."

"That part doesn't surprise me," said Marie. "Owen's never been fussy."

"So he's an older guy, you say?" Dad asked her.

She nodded. "He's been around a while."

"And he's coming from Bracebridge?"

"From town, yes. He has — or had — a beautiful little apartment in a house on Quebec Street."

"A beautiful apartment in town!" piped in Grandma Layton, pulling some dinner rolls from the oven. "Why the heck would anybody leave something like that to live at this Godforsaken place?"

My mother frowned. "Maybe Owen doesn't find the apartment beautiful, Mother."

"*Any* place in town is beautiful," she countered, shoving the rolls onto a plate. "He already sounds ... foolish move to me. Some people obviously don't know when they've got it made."

"How true," Dad whispered.

Grandma Layton turned and scowled at him. "What's that?"

My father grinned. "I said I can see a love affair blossoming already."

"Oh, I'll be in love with him, all right." My grandmother now went into her grumbling mode as she yanked plates out of the cupboard.

After giving Dad a harsh look, my mother turned to Laura again. "Getting back to the ranch, dear — when does the sale close?"

"The first of July. We figure on being out by the middle of June, though. We called our friends in British Columbia this afternoon and they said they're ready to take us anytime."

"It's all happening a lot faster than we expected," Ed added. "But we're game to get things rolling right away."

"What about your things? Did this Owen Goddard want all the furniture?"

"He wanted everything we offered up," said Ed, raising his rugged hands in the air. "It's worked out perfect for us. We'll tow our little trailer behind the 'Midnight Blue' and take everything we own out west in one trip. It couldn't be simpler."

My mother smiled. "Just like a couple of teenagers. Must be nice."

"Sounds good to me," Dad quipped. "I promise Mother and

her things will only take up half the back of the truck."

Grandma Layton turned away from the stove and scowled at my father again, this time behind his back. She was holding a large serving fork.

Laura smirked. "You're a braver man than you know, Bruce Farrow."

As planned, the Russells said their goodbyes in mid-June. On their final Saturday we threw a party for them at our place. Everyone on the lake chipped in and bought them a case of their favourite wine and matching Rugby shirts with 'Muskoka' on the front. "That's so people will know you're the tourists that you are," Cathy declared as they walked down the runway for us. Fortunately the Russells were in too cheerful a mood to take offence over this comment. In fact, after their modelling session they cracked open the case of wine, and wound up taking very little of it with them to British Columbia.

It was a mere two weeks after that party, near the start of July, that my father and I got our first glimpse of Owen Goddard. We were returning from town one evening when we saw an old green pickup pull onto the main road from the laneway. A husky, gray-haired man smiled and waved to us, and we knew this had to be Owen. Tipping an imaginary hat to him, Dad said to me, "Looks a little battle-scarred — maybe he ran into your grandmother."

Several days passed before we officially met Owen. Marie was visiting one evening, and when we saw his fully-loaded truck pass on the laneway she predictably suggested we offer help. My mother was in town with Judy at the time, and Grandma Layton had already written off our new neighbour, so it was only Marie, my father, and me making the trip.

When we reached Owen's place we found him adjusting a tarp covering the back of his pickup. Getting a better look at him, I could see he was a big man, not particularly tall but powerfully built. He had broad, meaty shoulders and a neck as wide as his head, and he was using massive hands and forearms to tighten the ropes. There was no mistaking his age, however; his hair was gray and sparse, his skin was weathered and riddled with scars, and he moved with a distinct stiffness. He also had a strained look on his face, and his brown work-shirt was damp in the front and under the arms.

"Long time no see, old timer," Marie shouted as we approached the top of the laneway.

He turned and peered at us, squinting against the late sun. In a deep, booming voice he said, "I guess it's about time I ran into you, Marie. Sorry I didn't drop in the other day."

"I've been snubbed before. How are you keeping?"

"Hanging in there. Folks have counted me out a few times, but I'm still ticking."

Marie smirked, and when we reached Owen she said, "Perhaps they've counted you out because they haven't seen hide nor hair of you. You've been a veritable hermit the last few years."

Owen stared at the driveway. "I know. Just ... been taking it easy. Nothing personal, though." Following an awkward few seconds of silence, he looked up and said with a pained smile, "How about introducing me to your buddies here."

Marie studied her old friend a moment with a puzzled look, then said, "Sure. This is Bruce Farrow, and his son, Lewis."

Owen shook hands with Dad, then turned to me. "Glad to meet you, Mr. Goddard," I said, offering my hand. This was Grandma Layton's training at work.

"No need for any Mr. Goddard stuff with me, Lewis. You just call me Owen like everybody else." And with that Owen Goddard smiled warmly and shook my hand.

In the midst of this introduction Marie had turned to examining the back of his truck, and now said to him, "You *can* afford some new rope, you know." She was referring to his tie-down ropes. They were old and frayed and made up of short pieces tied together, none more than about three feet long.

"Nothin' wrong with those," he said, pulling back on one of the ropes and snapping it against the tarp. "I kept them from the farm."

"Sure," said Dad, tongue firmly in cheek. "All the knots let you get a better hand-hold. They should make'em like that."

After Marie muttered something and shook her head, she said,

"Anyway, we thought we'd come up and offer you a hand."

Owen, while tiredly wiping his shiny forehead with a gray handkerchief, said, "I do appreciate that, folks, but between packing up and cleaning at the other end I'm pretty much cooked for today. I thought I'd get a fresh start tomorrow morning."

"You've got a lot of work ahead of you, old man." Marie was pointing with her cane at a large pile of things at the base of the deck stairs, this pile also covered by a tarp. Her eyes then went up to the house. "This place won't pass mustard as it is, either, you know. Are you sure your old farmer's back is up to all this?"

"Yes, I realize what I'm up against. I have plans," Owen answered quietly. "For the time being, though, why don't you folks come in for coffee. That much I've got organized."

Without telling my father and me what he and Marie were talking about, Owen led the way inside and sat us at the kitchen table. After putting on coffee he poured me a huge glass of lemonade, a drink I would learn he drank by the gallon. He then disappeared into a bedroom a minute and returned wearing a clean navy blue work shirt.

"Judging by those piles out there you can't have brought much furniture, and I guess that's just as well," said Marie. She and I had both been scanning the living room. It looked almost the same as when the Russells had the place — they'd hardly taken anything with them.

"I gave away quite a few things I had at the apartment," said Owen. "Once I saw what furniture the Russells were leaving I knew I'd be fine."

"What happened to that lovely apartment, anyway?" said Marie. "Get the boot or something?"

Owen grinned down at the table. "No. I simply ... felt like moving."

Dad said, "You needed a place of your own again, I bet?"

"Sure," said Owen, suddenly looking up. "This place suited me, too, so I said 'what the hell' and bought it."

"You made happy campers out of the Russells, I'll tell you," my father continued. "They weren't expecting to sell this place quite that quickly."

"Good to hear. Where'd they move off to?"

"Our majestic west coast. To a land far, far away."

"It was something they'd been planning for years," added Marie. Unaware of any change of heart on my part, she said, "Unlike another person around here, they've had their fill of Gordonier Lake."

Owen smiled at me. "Oh? Who might that be?"

"Looks like somebody else enjoyed the great outdoors too," said Dad, looking at a picture on the kitchen wall. It showed a blonde, middle-aged woman seated on a small black horse in front of an old barn.

"Oh, no. She wasn't into woodsy adventures — only horses," said Owen. "That's my ex-wife Jeanne, if you're wondering. I brought that picture here on an earlier trip so it wouldn't get busted amongst the other stuff."

"That's your old farm in the picture, I assume?" When Owen nodded, Dad asked, "How much farther down the road is that?"

"About another three and a half miles. It's —"

"Have you seen or heard from Jeanne lately?" Marie suddenly broke in. I noticed her watching Owen closely. "Is she still in Winnipeg?"

"Still there," came a nearly whispered reply. "And no, I haven't seen or talked her in a while now. The kids see her on occasion, though."

"You should visit her."

"I don't think I'm up to a long drive like that anymore." Owen stared down at the table. "Probably that old truck of mine isn't up to it either."

"So get another one!" said Marie. "Jesus — here we go again." Turning to my father, she said sarcastically, "He's got money for a house, but no money for a truck, of course."

"Why do I need a new truck?" Owen grumbled. "There's nothing wrong with that one." He waved a huge finger toward the window.

For a second dear Marie looked like she wanted to bang her

head against the table. However, she merely said, "*Fine*. There *are* buses and planes that go to Winnipeg, I'm sure. For that matter, I'm sure there are *trains* going there, too."

"Yeah, I know," Owen grumbled again. "*I'm* sure those aren't cheap, either."

Marie, after exhaling loudly, said in a resigned tone, "How about your kids, then? What are they up to these days?"

Owen grimaced. "Tom's hiding in Halifax these days — doing some bookkeeping, I last heard — and Simon felt he needed to manage a gas station just outside Moncton. As for Karen, she and the husband are trying to get rich with a big furniture store in Ottawa. When she's not nagging at me, that is."

"She doesn't nag, I bet. I'm sure Karen only worries about you."

"Oh, no! She nags. She's been trying to get me to move to Ottawa."

"Trying to get you to move there? Then what, might I ask, does she think about you buying this house?"

Owen stared down at the table again, and answered shyly, "Haven't exactly ... told her yet."

Marie stood surprisingly quickly. "Haven't told her! She'll have a fit!"

"So she'll have a fit," Owen said, waving at Marie to sit again. "A little fit never hurt nobody."

"You should call her! She might be trying to reach you!" Marie grabbed the wall phone beside her and held it to her ear. "You *are* hooked up already, mister, so no excuses!"

"Yeah, yeah. I'll phone her soon enough."

Owen rose to grab the coffee pot, and once back at the table pouring he said to my father, "So how about you folks? Been out this way long?"

"About two years," Dad answered. "We moved to the lake from Scarborough."

"Is that right?" I noticed Owen pause in the middle of filling my father's cup.

"Bruce grew up in Muskoka, though," Marie added. "He's got

this area in his blood."

Owen said, "Needed to get out of The Big Smoke, did you?"

"You got it. The Elliotts' place suited us, so we said 'what the hell' and bought it."

Owen smirked. "I do believe we have a smart-ass!"

Marie laughed. "It didn't take you long to get to know Bruce." Then she added, "Wait till you find out about Lewis."

"Really? What about him?"

"Lewis is a professional question-asker. A professional at 'investigating the matter'."

"I don't ask that many questions anymore," I said to Owen, facing him.

Staring right back at me, he said, "That's okay, Lewis. You go ahead and ask me all the questions you want."

"Just don't expect answers, that's all — right?" said Marie, and in the midst of chuckling Owen nodded.

We stayed at his place about another twenty minutes that evening, with him and Marie doing most of the talking. It seemed like these two knew three-quarters of the people in Bracebridge, both living and those in the cemeteries. Finally, after Marie noticed my father's third fake yawn, she suggested we leave.

"That's what happens when two old fogeys get together," she said as Owen saw us out onto the deck.

"You two have known each other quite a while, I take it?" said Dad.

"Right back to when we were kids. Owen had a crush on my sister Fledda. Maybe still does."

"*All right*!" Owen said, and I swear he actually started blushing.

"He was around our place regularly," Marie continued undaunted. "Whenever Fledda was mad at him, though, I ended up talking to him. Apart from the last few years we've stayed in touch ever since. I know this character probably better than anyone."

"Yes, I suppose you do," Owen said, quietly. He then looked out to the far end of the lake, where the sun was nearing the trees, and said in a brighter tone, "Lovely evening, isn't it?"

"Yes, it is," said Marie, stopping halfway down the deck stairs and giving him a strange look. As she soon carefully continued down the stairs, she said, "Now you *will* call Karen — right? I'll find her number and call her myself if you don't. I have files on you, old man." She paused on the stairs again and pointed her cane menacingly at Owen.

"Yeah, yeah. I'll call her first thing tomorrow."

"What's wrong with tonight?"

"No energy for twelve rounds tonight, dear. Tomorrow."

"You promise?"

"I promise."

Owen now turned to me. "Say, Lewis, I could sure use a healthy back for a few days. I'd pay you fair, and the work wouldn't be too hard. Are you available?" He had a pleading tone to his voice I found humorous considering his age compared to mine. I was used to it being the other way around with adults.

I said, "I can come up right after breakfast if you want?"

"Perfect."

"Uh, oh," said Dad. "Your grandmother will be thrilled when she hears this."

"What's that?" said Owen.

"My mother-in-law has already decided you're the hick of the century, I'm afraid. But don't you worry — Lewis and I can handle her."

"They dream they can, at least," Marie added.

As we started down the driveway, Dad said, "Nice meeting you."

"Drop in any time," was Owen's reply. I would learn this was standard.

As usual, Marie refused my father's offer of a ride home that evening when she left our place. Ironically, since it was starting to get dark, she walked at a hurried pace, and I was pressed for time in getting in all the questions I wanted to ask her about Owen. My excuse for going with her was to carry a large coffee table book on dancing she'd borrowed from Grandma Layton.

"Was Owen a farmer his whole life?" I started with, right after we left our driveway and headed toward the main road.

Marie smiled at me and tapped my leg with her cane. “Curious about him already, are we?”

“Sort of. I’ve never met a real farmer before.”

“Well, Owen did farm his whole working life, but he did a lot of other things too. It would have been nearly impossible for him to earn a full living only working a small farm in this area. He had to do all sorts of things to make ends meet, which he barely did. He’s lived a life without much money. You can certainly see the effects of that, too; even though he’s okay for money now, he still *thinks* poor.”

“You mean like not getting a new truck, and using those old ropes?”

“Exactly.”

We soon reached the main road, and I glanced eastward, in the direction of Owen’s old farm. “So is that why he sold his farm, then? So he could make a better living?”

Marie looked at me a second, seemingly undecided whether to give me an answer, then said, “No, that wasn’t the reason, Lewis. He only sold the farm because he ultimately had to. Once he starting getting up there in age and couldn’t work as hard anymore, he couldn’t afford to keep the farm. I’m sure losing it didn’t particularly thrill him, either. I’ve a feeling that’s why I haven’t seen him in a few years — he’s been stewing over his loss.”

“How long ago was all that?”

“Only four years. That gives you some idea of how long he lived poor for the sake of keeping his farm.”

When we reached the midway point on the lake we got a clear view of the place on the hill, and in the dim light I could make out Owen sitting on the front deck. I waved at him, but apparently he didn’t notice me because he didn’t wave back.

“Do you think he’d be lonely up there, living all by himself?” I asked Marie, before remembering she wouldn’t have Kevin with her that summer. Not too swift.

She took the question in stride, thankfully. “We won’t let him get lonely, Lewis. I’m sure he’ll become part of the gang like the

Russells were. He and I are also good friends, remember."

I tried another angle. "Think maybe he moved to this lake because he missed his farm? I mean, this lake is pretty close to it. He said his old farm was only about three and a half miles from here."

"Could be." Marie said this quietly, and not very convincingly.

I mused over this a minute, pretending to look at the dance book. When we reached the far end of the lake and came in view of Marie's place, I gave up on beating around the bush. "Only one more question, if you don't mind."

"Sure you don't need to check your notes?"

"Check my —?"

Marie smiled. "Carry on. Give me the finale."

I took a deep breath, then delivered. "If Owen lived out this way so long, why are you so shocked he moved to this lake?"

At this Marie's smile quickly vanished, and her eyebrows rose. She tried stealing a glance at me but I was watching her closely. I wanted more than the answer she gave Laura Russell.

"Now that ... is the real question," she finally said, stopping at the end of her driveway and taking the dance book from me. "You do know how to investigate the matter, don't you?"

"And?"

"And I think you need to get to know Owen a bit better. Then you may understand why I'm shocked. It's not exactly something I can explain to you in a few minutes, and not something you'll learn from being with Owen a few minutes, either."

"So you won't give me an answer?"

"If you really want one, you hang in there, Lewis," Marie said gravely, planting her cane and starting up her driveway. "I'm certain it'll come."

23

I reported for work at Owen's about eight-thirty the following sunny morning, right after breakfast. I found him in the kitchen, clad in a chestnut shirt and green pants, swearing to himself while struggling to don aged, oil-stained work boots.

"How about being a bosom buddy and pushing those home," he said, resigning. "This goddamn old back's never good first thing."

After pushing on his boots, I also tied them. "That's worth a buck already," he said after. "Sure miss being nimble. How young a guy are you, Lewis?"

"I turned twelve last March."

"Jesus ... twelve," Owen echoed quietly, staring into space. He then eyed me. "I guess it's only fair to tell you my age — seventy-six."

"You don't look that old to me," I said, lying. Between his stiffness and grizzled appearance he seemed even more aged this morning than the previous evening.

Running thick fingers through his sparse gray hair, he said, "Nice of you, but I've already considered Marie Taylor was right about taking on too much with this place. A guy has to learn to accept certain things, maybe."

"Speaking of her, did you keep your promise?"

"Has she got you checking up on me?!"

"No, I'm just curious."

Owen glared at me, slowly rubbing a massive left fist with a massive right palm, before his look fortunately softened. "Well ... I did. I hung up on the daughter about fifteen minutes ago."

"You hung —?!"

"No, *no*." He faked swatting my head. "But I should've."

"She got upset, did she?"

Owen grinned. "Darn tootin'! I'm amazed the Farrow household didn't hear her."

After chuckling over "darn tootin'," I said, "Did you convince her moving to this lake was okay, though?"

Leaning wearily back in his chair, Owen answered, "I wish. She's far from thinking that. She's journeying from our great nation's capital in two weeks to conduct a full federal inspection."

"That soon?"

"That soon, meaning I could sure use your help. It'll do my case wonders if I spruce up this place. One thing it needs is fresh paint, and that'll be a big job."

"I can help," I nervously offered, pondering Grandma Layton's reaction. She'd delivered a serious breakfast lecture about avoiding Owen, worrying his "obviously hick ways" might rub off.

Reading my mind, he said, "Think that'll ignite Grandma?"

"I can take her."

Owen beamed. "There's a buddy."

We started work that morning by carrying inside the boxes he left piled in the driveway. Most held clothes, blankets, and kitchen items. I tried restraining my usual nosy self, but certain things did catch my eye. One box held books, and I noticed every one was about trains; another held a blue quilt with 'Owen and Jeanne' embroidered in handwriting-style letters. "A friend made that for our thirtieth anniversary," Owen quietly explained, catching me snooping.

Once we'd finished moving boxes, he backed his truck to the shed, declaring all remaining gear belonged there. After we removed the tarp I discovered why: other than some folding metal chairs, the entire half-ton was filled with tools — carpentry hand tools, cross-cut and Swede saws, axes, shovels, rakes, and a hundred other implements I couldn't identify. Many looked very old, and I recognized some from a Scarborough antique show I once saw with my father and Jack Walsh. Owen had little to say about them, providing short and quiet answers to all questions. "Just farm stuff I decided to keep" was the most he offered.

We stopped for lunch about twelve-thirty. Strangely, I wasn't feeling hungry yet, but before I could argue Owen was at the stove cranking out a wheelbarrow load of grilled-cheese sandwiches. "A young guy's gotta eat," he rumbled, piling four rough-hewn creations onto my plate alone. Next he mixed a big jug of lemonade and dumped an entire tray of ice-cubes into it, splashing our sandwiches in the process. This brand of hospitality I would get used to.

Although the day had grown hot and bright, the chef insisted we eat outside. I persuaded him, however, to let me slide two white chairs to the deck's south end so at least the maples would shade us.

"Boy oh boy," he groaned while lowering into his chair. "I'm feeling that."

"We could do the rest another day," I offered. While cooking he declared we'd spend the afternoon unpacking boxes.

He eyed me sternly while tucking a small brown pillow behind his lower back. "You quitin' on me?"

"No, I'm not quitting. It's just that maybe ... we shouldn't try doing everything at once."

"Your old man told you to take it easy on me — that's what this is about, isn't it?"

I attempted innocence but failed, and nodded, fearfully.

As earlier Owen glared at me several seconds, but finally said, "Ah, to hell with it. I suppose I should appreciate that." Finishing a bear-sized bite of sandwich, he continued with, "So what does a young guy like you do for fun?"

"I play softball, for one thing. I'm on a team now in Bracebridge."

"A budding Babe Ruth, are you?"

I smiled proudly. "Maybe."

My starting softball was an idea my parents suggested in the spring. They felt getting involved again in a long-time Scarborough pastime would be good for me after our tragic previous summer, and they proved right.

"And so what else do you do?"

"My little sister Judy and I swim a lot at Mrs. Taylor's place."

"How old is she?"

"Six and a half."

"And she swims well?!"

"Heck yes! She could already swim when we moved, and ever since she saw a bass jump from a pond behind Lyall Rock she's had this dumb goal to swim like a fish."

Owen smiled. "But other than your sister ... ?"

"There's a girl up the road Judy plays with — Katie Howard. My mother's taking those two to Santa's Village today. And there's Kevin Taylor, but he won't be at the lake this year. He's living in Cape Breton this summer with his father."

"Kevin Taylor? This is Marie's grandson?"

I nodded. "He lived in Peterborough with his mother, but spent the last two summers here."

"So his parents ... ?"

"They're divorced."

"That's a shame. Did his mother ship him to Muskoka, or did he like coming?"

"He definitely liked coming."

Owen looked toward Marie's place. "I guess, though, it's good he's spending some time with his father."

"Maybe — I don't know if his father is any better — but Kevin didn't have much choice. His mother ... kind of got in trouble last winter, so now he's with his dad."

"Really?! You mean law trouble?"

"Yeah."

"Sounds odd. Not many young mothers do that."

"She's not a normal mother," I muttered, resisting the temptation, for Marie's sake, not to declare Kevin's mother a complete witch.

It was my own mother's idea I mention sweet Debbie. The

previous winter the police arrested her for drug-dealing, and Marie was quite sensitive about the issue. My mother therefore advised me to warn her long-time friend.

"So what all did you do with Kevin when he was around?" Owen asked.

"Mainly we made trips to a cabin at another lake." I pointed toward the north ridge. "He found it, and invited Sean and me."

"It was his escape, was it?"

"Sort of." I smiled at how obvious it really was.

Owen faced me and spoke in a voice I found surprisingly soft for a large, powerful man. "Sean — that was your little brother?"

I stared at him. "You know what happened?"

Looking pained, he nodded. "I remembered the newspaper article, and when your father mentioned last night your family hailed from Scarborough, I made the connection. That's quite a thing that happened."

"Yeah, it was." I now understood Owen's pause the previous evening while pouring coffee.

"Pardon me if this is nosy, but is your family coping well?"

"My Dad, Grandma, and sister seem okay. My mother, though, is still hurting pretty bad."

"And you?"

Looking down I said softly, "I guess I'm okay."

Owen was silent a moment, resuming his lake gazings, but soon said, "Must have been quite a thing coming to Muskoka from the city. Did you like the idea?"

"Mostly. I loved exploring in Scarborough, and by the sounds of Dad's old stories I thought exploring Muskoka would be neat. It was Mother and Grandma who hated the move; Dad had to argue for it."

"Why was that?"

"Mainly because Grandma hates the woods. She thinks everything's really primitive here with all the mud, bush, and animals. My Dad made her a flower garden two springs ago and she calls it her 'lone saviour from the Godforsaken woods'. She thinks it only makes sense to live in a town or city, where there's sidewalks, hedges, and dance schools and stuff. That's why she doesn't understand your leaving Bracebridge."

"I see," said Owen. "And she doesn't want you helping a fool, is that it?"

I nodded shyly.

"Marie Taylor lives at this lake, and you help her."

"Grandma says Mrs. Taylor's a prisoner to her house, though. Sort of like Grandma herself is a prisoner to her grandkids. But I wouldn't worry; Grandma can't stop me from helping you." This was a lie, but for the fool's sake I thought it best to remain optimistic.

Having finished eating, Owen opened a pocketknife and began sharpening a carpentry pencil used earlier to make house-chore notes. As he whittled I couldn't help watching his hands, which until now I hadn't given much attention other than noticing they were three times larger than mine. I now noted how rough and riddled they were with scars. What mainly drew my attention, however, was his left hand — his index finger was completely missing.

Catching me staring, he said, "Got it pinched off fixing a tractor. Trust me, Mr. Question-Asker, you don't want more information than that."

"That's fine," I croaked.

Owen paused from his pencil sharpening and eyed me. "The *reason* it happened, though, Lewis, is I was working half-asleep that day. That's something I did too often, I'm sorry to say."

"Farming was that hard?"

He grimaced. "I've come to think I worked a little too hard for my own good. And I don't just mean losing a finger and developing a bad back."

I decided not to ask what else he meant, and instead said, "Are we ... gonna —?"

"No, *no* — we won't be working like that," he broke in, firing another fake swat with one of his huge paws. "After all, you're on summer vacation, aren't you?"

I grinned in relief. "Darn tootin'."

As Owen requested, we continued work that afternoon by beginning to organize his inside belongings. During this time he asked countless questions about myself and other lake residents, making me wonder who was the real "Mr. Question-Asker." With an 'If you're gonna ask'em, be prepared to answer 'em', attitude, though, I obliged by first telling about my father. I explained how he'd changed so much since moving to Muskoka, how he'd become so fit, smart-alecky, and ambitious, and how he denied changing. The Russells followed, and I described how Ed and Laura, out of sheer boredom, left Gordonier Lake after twenty-five years of residence. Moving to the Morrisons, I explained Reggie's relationship with his boat and Carla's relationship with her pickerelweeds. Owen listened attentively before offering a sly assessment. "Strikes me as a hell of a funny bunch, Lewis my boy."

Lastly, I told Owen about Cathy, thinking that similar to Marie he should be sensitive to her plight. Early the previous December dear Aunt Jenny passed away. As Cathy's sister Andrea sadly speculated during the cottage visit, Aunt Jenny's riverside walk indeed proved her last. And as Cathy similarly wondered, the Christmas of 1975 — when she gifted the reading pillow — proved her aunt's final such holiday. Predictably, the winter was rough for Cathy. She made dozens of trips to an Oakville hospital, her old truck providing frequent problems, and she became exhausted and irritable, her trademark smile entirely absent. Although during the spring her spirits began brightening somewhat, she was still far from recovered. In May the lake crew gave her a party to celebrate her 30th birthday, along with a 'new' used fridge, but she was clearly not her festive self.

My introduction went further than merely ensuring Owen knew about her aunt's death. I couldn't resist, gossipy as it was, telling him about certain controlling parents, and how the woods surrounding Aunt Jenny's cottage had inspired in Cathy a sense of freedom. I also couldn't resist bragging about a particular cob of corn, and despite showing genuine sorrow over Aunt Jenny's death, this little story elicited a hearty chortle from Owen. "Good on yuh, lad! Keep that up and you'll have balls the size of Purbrook pumpkins!" Perhaps, I thought, this epitomized the influence worrying Grandma Layton.

Now despite his many questions early this afternoon, Owen later grew increasingly quiet, especially when we returned to working outside. I became concerned I'd somehow upset him, since the earlier glares suggested this wouldn't be difficult. But, when I left for home late that afternoon he forced a smile, paid me, and said he'd dearly appreciate more help the next day. When asking he even used the same pleading voice as the previous evening.

While descending the laneway hill I turned, puzzled by this burly old man's moodiness, and glanced back. The same as I'd seen while walking Marie Taylor home the night before, Owen sat in his deck chair, gazing toward the lake. Unlike the previous night, however, I was now close enough to clearly see his face. He looked very solemn, and by the way his head slowly turned back and forth I sensed, odd as it seemed, he was searching for something.

24

Following Gordonier Lake tradition, on Saturday evening of that week we surprised Owen with a housewarming. Everyone on the lake gathered at our house about seven and then went up to his place together. When reaching the driveway my sister, determined to arrive first, ran ahead onto the deck and before my mother could stop her she'd tapped on the living room window. I happened to notice Owen in the kitchen, and long before Judy saw him, he saw her. Nonetheless, he went to the living room window and pretended to be completely in the dark when Judy, in professional style, threw her arms out and screamed, "Suuurrrrprise!"

That was the start of what proved a mostly enjoyable evening. Owen seemed genuinely thrilled to have us "drop in." Marie Taylor looked after introductions, and as she contended our new neighbour instantly fit right in with the lake gang. One exception, of course, was my grandmother. She came with us to Owen's place under protest and her lack of enthusiasm definitely showed when Marie introduced her to him. He merely smiled, though, and said, "Very nice to meet you, Annie," and even continued to smile as Grandma Layton began cleaning and reorganizing his "bushcamp kitchen."

The first anxious moment on this evening came about half an hour following our arrival. After presenting Owen with a cake she'd made for the occasion, Marie, without her cane in hand, stumbled on a small box lying near the front window. Fortunately my father was standing nearby and caught her in time, but she came very close to crashing into the window. She went away a little shaken, and more than a little embarrassed.

Soon after this I went with Owen to get the folding chairs we stored in the shed. Once inside he said to me in a quiet but angry voice, "*Jesus*! I'd like to heave that goddamn box in the lake!"

"It's not really your fault," I said. "Mrs. Taylor's a little awkward on her feet. She's got ... bad ones."

Giving me a puzzled stare, Owen said, "You know what happened to her?"

I nodded, and at the same time realized he, having known Marie so long, naturally knew about her tragic winter experience.

Handing me a chair, he said, "How'd you find out? Fledda?"

I again nodded. "I overheard her explaining to my grandmother one night what happened — I heard about that old lady Mrs. Taylor helped. Mrs. Garrett told my grandmother so she'd understand why Mrs. Taylor gets so uptight about winter."

"Marie does get awfully wound up, doesn't she? I've witnessed that plenty of times over the years."

"Maybe she does, but after I heard what happened I sure stopped arguing about bundling up."

"Yes, I suppose bundling up is wise," Owen said, and before grabbing another chair he again showed me a puzzled look.

About eight o'clock that evening, after beating my father and Rick at horseshoes, Cathy and I decided we wouldn't press our luck and left them to play some one on one. We climbed to the deck to join the other lake residents. Here we found Marie and my mother sitting on the wooden deck chairs, with Owen and a slick-looking Reggie Morrison sitting on the railing bench. Judy was on Owen's knee, holding a small piece of driftwood he'd given her. As for my grandmother, she was still in the kitchen and being contained by Carla.

"I'll have to give you a boat tour sometime," I heard Reggie say to Owen as Cathy and I approached the group.

"Be sure to wear your swim trunks, though," my mother quipped.

"She's a fine, seaworthy ship," Reggie defended. "Eh, Lewis?"

I only smiled.

"Sure, Owen," said Cathy. "Just ask the lead bailer here."

Reggie gave her a stern squint. "She's held up a lot of years! You won't —"

Cathy smirked. "*Yes*, okay, Reggie! Don't get yourself wound up, or that boat is exactly where we'll stick you."

"Don't you play with me, missy! I was only offering my new buddy here a toot around the lake. If he's walked *around* it a few times maybe he'd like to go *on* it."

"Sounds good, Reg. I'll look forward to that," Owen said in a soothing voice. He'd been studying again a picture Judy had given him as a housewarming present — his house with green and orange polka dots and a small Ferris wheel built into the deck.

"You've been walking around the lake?" Marie asked him, showing a surprised look that was becoming common.

"Just … having a look," he answered, seeming to avoid her stare. "I got Lewis and Judy to give me the dime tour a few days ago."

"That's how we found the driftwood!" said Judy, getting off Owen's large knee and showing Marie the stick.

"You were out early this morning, too, Carla tells me," said Reggie.

"She was up?"

"Up? She's the one who wakes the birds here."

"Jeez. If I'd known I'd have invited her out," said Owen. "I saw a few things along shore that would have thrilled her."

"How about the Russells' old trail?" Cathy asked. "Have you hiked it yet?"

"Trail?"

Reggie pointed behind the house. "It starts beside that big beech tree."

"And ends at a creek, and a big raspberry patch," Cathy added.

Owen looked to where Reggie was pointing, then eyed me. "Huh! I wasn't aware."

"Have any trails like that on your farm?" Reggie asked.

"One. At the back end of the property there's an old one for taking out firewood — much like what Lyall Taylor made."

Cathy said, "You owned the farm right across from the Fraserburg United Church, didn't you? The one with the little cemetery? I remember seeing 'Goddard' on the mailbox."

"That's the one."

"My sister and I always waved to someone at that farm when we passed on the way to our aunt and uncle's cottage. Was that you? Did you used to wear a big blue hat? And drive a rusty old tractor?"

Owen smiled. "Brown station wagon — right?"

"Hah! You remember us?"

"Pretty hard not to." Owen grinned at the rest of us. "They'd be half out the window and yelling and waving with both arms. Full of beans every time."

"Animals let out of our cages is what we were," said Cathy.

Mother said to Owen, "So did you enjoy having a farm?"

"There's ... a certain satisfaction, I suppose."

"I remember a few times we saw someone riding a horse," said Cathy. "Was that your daughter?"

"Her, or my wife."

"Probably Jeanne," added Marie. "She loved the horse Owen got her."

"On the other hand, I'm sure that farm was a lot of work," said Reggie. "My brother had a farm, and it wasn't big, but it sure kept him busy."

"Any farm is a lot of farm," Owen said.

"You must have taken a fair bit of pride in the place," my mother said. "It was hard to leave, I assume?"

Owen glanced at Marie before answering, "Yes, it was. But I suppose things have to come to an end eventually. Maybe it's for the best, too."

"And now you've started a whole new chapter," said Reggie. "Although, I've heard through the Gordonier Grapevine you've got a big test coming up."

"You're wrong there, my boy," said Owen, a faint smile

returning to his face. "The daughter doesn't stand a chance."

Marie smirked. "Oh, we'll see about that. You've still got plenty of work to do before satisfying Karen. And unless you've found a way to drop twenty years —"

"Everything's under control," Owen broke in firmly, sitting up straight. "Lewis and I are starting the painting on Monday. I went into Canadian Tire for the paint this morning. All we need is some decent weather."

Marie shook her finger at him. "You just take it easy, mister. All this work — by the time you learn your lesson it may be too late."

Owen looked sad and desperate. Almost whispering, he said, "I know, Marie, but ... I really want things to work out at the lake, and my buddy here says he'll help me, so ... I'm optimistic they will."

Everyone was silent after this, so I don't think I was alone in being both surprised and moved by his remark. Wanting to lighten the conversation again, I brightly added, "We're gonna have the place running like a well-oiled locomotive!"

Marie brought a tiny hand to her forehead. "Oh, *no*! You've already been lecturing the boy on trains? Lord help us!"

"Nothing wrong with a little knowledge," Owen defended.

"A certified train fanatic," Marie informed everyone, motioning toward her old friend with her thumb. "A walking railroad encyclopedia, as a matter of fact."

"Nothing wrong with that," said Reggie, grinning as he leaned over the railing. He'd been studying Owen's rock and root infested lawn, and now said to him, "Speaking of your work a minute ago, I see you haven't met Mr. Lawn From Hell yet. Eddie and Laura needed three days to psyche themselves up before mowing this thing."

Owen merely shrugged. "I guess a guy never gets done cutting hay in this life, Reggie my boy."

"But what do you think?" Marie asked me. "Because I know darn well who'll be cutting the hay at this house."

Doing my best to keep a straight face, I boldly said, "I think it's especially tough ... considering I'm underpaid and everything."

Owen's eyes lit up. "Underpaid? You think —"

Feeling brave, I mimicked one of his fake head swats and said, "Only kidding. A guy never gets done being kidded in this life, Owen my boy."

As everyone laughed my old and feeble friend clamped onto my neck with his powerful right hand and drew me into a vice-like headlock. He then started twisting my nose with his other hand. At that moment, Carla Morrison and my grandmother came out the kitchen door.

"Lewis Joseph Farrow!" Grandma Layton screamed. "Don't you be horsing around like that!"

Unable to turn my head to face her, I choked, "But he —!"

"I'm okay, Annie," Owen said calmly, but keeping me in the suffocating headlock. "Young L.J. here will go easy on me."

My grandmother grumbled, "But that boy needs to learn that ... *older* people aren't up to wrestling." Immediately turning her back on Owen, who finally let me out of the vice, she started down the side deck stairs with Carla.

"Annie's decided to head home," Carla said, smiling back at us. "I'll walk with her."

"Thanks very much for coming, Annie," Owen boomed, sounding sincere. "I appreciate it."

Without turning Grandma Layton lifted her hand in a mild wave and started down the driveway. And although I'm sure she tried to say it quietly to Carla, everyone on the deck managed to hear "pathetic old coot" before she was out of range.

My mother's face turned beet red, which she then covered with her hands. "I am *so* sorry, Owen! I'm sure she doesn't mean —"

Before she could finish, though, our new neighbour turned to me and slyly responded, "What was it you said a minute ago, Lewis?"

25

Right on schedule, the following Monday morning I helped Owen begin painting his house. We made decent progress, and to not let the painting get monotonous we occasionally did other jobs, such as cleaning and organizing various areas inside. We also went to the great effort of finally cutting the lawn, thinking this would please my grandmother, but it didn't have much effect. Every morning at breakfast she duly reminded me of Owen's "lack of appreciation for civilized life." The only person who enjoyed these lectures was Dad, because it meant Grandma Layton wasn't bothering him. Luckily I managed to make it out the door every day, and Owen always breathed a sigh of relief when he saw me.

Despite all this work, on several evenings that week he also made an effort to become better acquainted with other lake residents. Upon returning to the lake after a softball game on Tuesday evening, for example, I saw he took Reggie Morrison up on his lake cruise invitation. On Thursday evening he walked to Lyall Rock to watch Judy, Cathy, and me swim. My mother was also there, and she and Owen had a fairly long chat. It might have been a pleasant chat, too, except for being interrupted by Judy with requests for swimming praise, and by Cathy with tongue-in-cheek requests for spare cash. This prompted Owen to later repeat his comment about the lake crew being a "funny bunch."

By noon on Friday Owen's place looked pretty good. We had all the painting finished, all his things unpacked and arranged, and the yard looking neat as a pin. My father visited in mid-morning, right before a city trip to see Jack Walsh, and declared the place the "Taj Mahal of Fraserburg Road."

Studying the house and yard from his deck chair at lunch, Owen echoed Dad's statement, saying, "Yup, things have shaped up real nice. The last thing she can say is the place is run down." By "she" Owen meant his daughter, of course, who was arriving the next day.

"Really think she'll like this place, though?" I said.

"We shall see, Lewis. There's nothing much more I can do to please her, so what will be, will be." With that Owen leaned back in his chair, closed his eyes against the bright sun, and breathed deeply.

Now that afternoon, immediately following lunch, he surprised me: he suggested we hike down the Russells' old trail, saying we could check how the raspberries were coming along. I knew his back had been hurting him that morning, and having finished the house I assumed he'd take it easy the rest of the afternoon. No sooner had we returned our empty plates to the kitchen, however, than he proposed walking the trail.

So, after Owen changed into his "raspberry-inspecting" shirt, and he'd filled a huge, ancient-looking thermos with his standard thirst quencher, we set off down the trail. My older friend amazed me again by walking at a good pace, taking perhaps two strides for every three of mine, and in only about twenty minutes we reached the creek and raspberry patch.

"Here you are — this is the pot of gold at the end of the rainbow," I said, remembering how Ed Russell had introduced the berry patch to my brother, sister, and me years earlier.

Owen seemed to sense I'd borrowed this line, because he smirked before saying, "Do you pick these every year?" He was grasping one of the berries, which proved not quite ripe yet.

"No — not really," I answered.

"Well, we'll have to come back in a few weeks and get some. I might be able to butter up your grandmother with some of these."

"Have fun. The summer we moved to Muskoka she said she'd only bake with them when hell froze over."

"Is that right? She's that uptight about Muskoka, is she?"

"She's that uptight."

Owen took a seat on the large boulder at the edge of the creek, the same one I shared with Ed when first visiting the berry patch. He then asked for the big thermos of lemonade I'd been carrying. Telling him I didn't want any yet, he filled only one of two metal cups that unscrewed from top and bottom. "This was an awfully good idea," he said quietly before quickly downing his cup.

Noticing some beads of sweat on his forehead, and remembering my father's warnings, I said, "You're finding it hot?"

"No, I'm finding *me* thirsty," he answered gruffly. "You've gotta stop worrying about me so much." With that, he turned away and studied the two young birches shading us.

A breeze came through and tipped over Owen's empty cup. When it landed on a creek stone it made a clanking sound, spooking several birds from a tall nearby maple. They flew off, and I watched them as they circled above us before leaving our view.

"Starlings," I whispered, out of reflex.

"Starlings?" Owen gave me a puzzled look. "You know your birds, do you?"

"Sort of. My parents gave my brother a book on birds one year for his birthday. He used to get me to read it to him, so I got to know birds pretty well."

"A fan, was he?"

"For some reason Sean really loved birds. At the end of our Scarborough street was a small patch of forest called the Lord Roberts Woods, and he used to keep guard over a robin's nest all the time. Mom eventually even got him a little pair of binoculars."

"How about that!" Owen said as he poured himself more lemonade. After another drink, he continued. "It's funny your mother — not liking the idea of moving to Muskoka. She strikes me as the type that would."

"She looks out for Grandma, though, and she sure —"

"Didn't want to come here," Owen finished.

"But I think Mom was starting to like it in Muskoka after we moved. There were times when she seemed interested in things.

She thought a collection of woodsy stuff Cathy's sister made was pretty neat — a 'Stones, Bones, and Cones' collection. Our first New Year's Eve at the lake, too, I sat with her and just watched it snow."

"Is that right? You know, it's a shame the way things turned out. You told me last week your mother is having a particularly tough time?"

I looked at Owen and nodded, and he returned such a caring look I immediately decided to tell him about my mother. Pushing several creek stones with the tip of my shoe, I said, "She looks out my window at night sometimes."

"Looks out your window? What do you mean?"

"She comes into my room every night to check on me, and sometimes before she comes to my bed she stands at my front window for a few minutes."

"And does what?"

"Just stands ... and stares at the sky."

I looked up at Owen again and saw a pained expression. After staying silent a few seconds he said, "That's a heck of a shame, Lewis."

I only nodded, then went back to looking down at the creek.

"Are you sure when she does that she's thinking about your brother, though?"

I nodded again, without looking up. "She only does it when something reminds her of him."

"Does she get moody like that at other times?"

"Only at my window at night now, really. Mr. Russell seemed to think Mom was bitter about the way things were the night Sean was lost."

"What way was that?"

"It rained that night, and the rain really got to my mother. Later it got to me, too. I mean, why the heck did it have to rain when Sean was lost? He was only trying to help Kevin and me! And the rain would have made him cold, and the rocks would have become slippery, and ..."

"I see," Owen said quietly. "I guess that would get to a person."

"There's even more to it than that, though," I said, deciding to reveal all. "Sean ... started getting afraid of the woods after we moved, and Mom knew about it."

"Afraid? You mean at night?"

"No, I mean anytime. Mr. Russell was the one who also explained to me about Sean. He said the woods were too big for him."

"Too big?"

"Sean was weird whenever we went into the woods — he stayed close to other people, and he stumbled a lot. When I found out what his problem was, I thought it was pretty stupid."

Owen said, "He was nervous, in other words?"

"Really nervous. He didn't even pay attention to birds anymore."

Owen, staring at his cup, said, "So why'd he go into the woods on his own then?"

"He wanted to get back in with Kevin and me at that cabin I told you about. We were fixing the place up, and I mentioned to him one night that one of the things we still needed was a window. The Russells took down their old outhouse that summer, and when Mr. Russell just piled everything in the bush behind their place, Sean decided to take the window from it. That must be what happened."

"Do your parents know about that?"

"Dad saw the window — somebody found it — but I never told him Sean was carrying it. And Mom only knows he was afraid, and that he must have wanted to make up with Kevin and me, and ... I just —"

Owen turned away to look at the raspberry patch as a certain young man beside him added several drops of water to the creek. Soon, though, with his huge right hand rubbing my shoulder, he said something shocking me, so perceptive was it.

Looking right at me, he said, "Between all the different people you've met on the lake, and all the things that have happened, you've had quite a strange time — haven't you? People mad at the sky, people relaxing in boats, people fretting about winter, people getting their batteries charged without knowing it, and so on. I imagine you're pretty confused — you don't know what the hell to think about Muskoka, or what the hell to feel."

I could only stare at Owen; he saw something in me no one else had apparently seen. Somehow he had come to recognize all the different influences I'd been exposed to, and in so doing recognized my predicament. It was almost as though, I thought even at this time, he could relate to this problem.

I nodded and whispered, "It's been weird." Rubbing my wet eyes, I added, "I guess ... I'm one of the 'funny bunch'."

Owen smiled, then caught me off guard with another comment. Eyeing me again, he said, "And you haven't been into exploring the woods since your brother died — have you, Lewis Farrow?"

I looked at him a few seconds, then shook my head. "I guess I ... just haven't felt like it." Pawing some creek stones again, I said, "How could you tell, though?"

He pointed to the path. "Your not telling me about this trail, for starters. But mostly because when an old guy like me has to slow down for a young guy like you, he knows something's not quite right."

To this I could only offer a shy grin.

My perceptive older friend glanced upcreek again a moment. Motioning with his thumb, he said, "Ever been up that way, Lewis?"

"Have I ever been up the creek before?" I managed a full smile as I wiped my cheeks with the bottom of my shirt.

Owen pressed a thumb and forefinger against his eyes. "You've got a fair bit of your old man in you — do you know that? Now, in all seriousness, have you ever been up that way?"

"No," I said, seriously. "Anytime I've hiked down this trail I haven't gone farther than the berry patch."

"Feel like having a look?"

"What for?"

"What for? Explorers need a reason? I thought you liked 'investigating the matter'."

Quietly, I said, "Yeah, I do."

"So you don't feel like it?" Owen used that same pleading

expression and tone as the times he'd asked me to work for him.

I said, "Well ... we can ... if you want. How come you want to?"

He merely shrugged. "Can't a guy simply be curious? Who knows what we'll find along that creek."

So, after another few minutes rest at the berry patch, Owen and I started a trip up the creek that afternoon. Mostly we could walk along the edge in knee-high grass, but in places thick bushes grew here and we had to leave the creek and travel through the much dimmer forest. The bed of the creek varied also; in some places it was wide, shallow, and littered with smooth, half-submerged rocks, and in other places it was narrow and deep. Changing the flow of the water as well were occasional fallen trees, which created musky, algae-covered pools. Mostly, the creek followed a very twisting course, and it was rare we could see more than fifty feet of it. This made me anxious to forge ahead, always impatient to see around the next bend, but I did keep Owen in mind on this day — for the most part, at least.

The first real surprise of the trip was a peculiar tree. We reached a portion of the creek where it passed alongside a marshy clearing, and here, right at the edge of the creek opposite the clearing, was a white pine growing at an angle of about thirty degrees. Not only that, it grew on a smooth section of bedrock, with a tangle of roots stretching into the bank of soil behind it. Despite this the tree appeared perfectly healthy, and it was simply begging to be climbed. I tried talking Owen into joining me, but he only laughed and watched as I easily clambered about twenty feet up the tree.

Since maples surrounded this pine, the forest floor, creek, and long grasses at the edge of the marsh were completely speckled by leaf shadows. I had no branches below me to obstruct this view — which with normal, climbable trees there would have been — and I found this speckled pattern dizzying. This was especially true when a light breeze came through and made the maples sway. I actually had to cling tightly to the rough bark of the pine to keep from falling.

The marsh clearing was not large, and continuing along the creek we were soon back in solid woods. What we now encountered, however, was a stretch of young maples not much taller than Owen, and they were so thick they made hiking difficult. My partner was better than me at making his way through these trees, and he wound up slightly ahead. I only caught up to him because he suddenly stopped. "Hey — look here, Lewis!" When I reached him he pointed down to some deer tracks — some large, some small. "I'm guessing a doe and two fawns," he said, studying the prints.

Sure enough, only about five minutes later, right after we'd cleared the young maples, a doe and two fawns suddenly bolted away from the creek ahead of us. I expected them gone and out of sight in a matter of seconds, but something happened I thought strange. While the doe and one fawn continued to dash off, the other fawn suddenly turned and approached us, only veering when about thirty feet away. It then disappeared into the woods behind us while the doe and other fawn disappeared ahead of us.

I said to Owen, "Why would it —?"

"Shh." He motioned to me to sit with him on the trunk of a dead beech lying nearby. Here we sat silently three or four minutes. Finally, the fawn that came toward us reappeared, and in a cautious yet slightly frolicsome manner, crept through the woods in the same direction the doe and other fawn went. When it was out of sight again I said, "What the heck was that all about? Why'd it come right toward us?"

Owen stood up, and while starting down the creek again he said, "You can never say for sure about these things, Lewis, but I will guess at this much. I'd say that fawn and I have a lot in common — we're both living on time we're not supposed to have." He wouldn't elaborate on this remark, and it kept me quiet and musing for a while afterward.

The biggest surprise of the afternoon came perhaps fifteen minutes later, or about an hour after we'd started along the creek. We reached a patch of solid spruce, and as we made our way through it we couldn't see any more than about ten feet ahead.

That didn't bother me, however, because long before we reached it I could hear the waterfall. At first I thought the faint hiss I was hearing was simply the breeze passing through leafed trees ahead of us, but as we continued the hiss turned into the sound of rushing water. Getting impatient, I ran ahead, weaving my way through the spruces. At last leaving the patch I came to a small, bright clearing beside the creek. "Holy cow!" I shouted back to Owen.

The waterfall was close to ten feet high, running over the edge of an outcropping of bedrock. At its base was a jumbled pile of sharp boulders, large and small, that had very apparently cleaved off the edge of the bedrock. These boulders made the water deflect in all directions, and between this and all the sun-brightened spray, the falls appeared to have a much greater volume than they really did.

"Isn't that something!" said Owen when he reached where I was standing. "You wouldn't have thought there was any sort of waterfall in here, would you?"

"Jeez no!" I said. "I had no idea there was anything like this near our lake!"

There was no stopping me, of course. I explored below, around, and above the falls — running down the length of the bedrock cliff until I discovered a section I could climb. As for Owen, he found himself a shaded spot below the falls and sat down with his back against a tree. Slightly worried about this I asked him several times if he wanted to head back, but he insisted I carry on. He seemed to especially get a kick out of watching me wade through the shallow pool at the top of the falls.

"I get tuckered out just watching you," he said when I returned. "Did you leave any stone unturned up there."

"The pool at the top has minnows in it! They must have to swim against the current all the time!"

"And you got tuckered out just watching them, I hope," Owen said wearily. He was still leaning against his maple and had his hands behind his head. His eyes were open, however, and when I looked up at the blue sky, to where he was looking, I saw several small clouds drifting southward.

When I looked down again he said, “So I can’t get your grandmother any wild raspberries, huh? I’ll have to work on something else, then.”

“You’re thinking about that? Why does it matter what Grandma thinks about you?”

Owen turned to me. “Oh, it matters. For one thing, I need your help, and your grandmother’s been making your help hard to come by. That means managing at the lake may involve more than winning over my daughter. A simpler reason is that a guy doesn’t like being called a fool all the live long day.”

“She says you’re an old coot, actually,” I said, grinning, and this caused a spruce cone to bounce off my head.

I picked up the cone and rolled it between my fingers. “Speaking of your daughter, what do you suppose she’ll say about your sore back tomorrow?”

Owen answered with a confident tone. “I’ll be fine by tomorrow. And when she asks you how I’m doing, you tell her I’ve been jumping around like a spring lamb — you hear?”

“Got it.”

“Don’t be chuckling like that. This is a serious matter.”

“Okay, okay.” I brought my hand to my mouth.

“Expect to be invited up for lunch tomorrow, too — I need you to cover me.”

“Cover you?”

Owen showed a sneaky grin. “She can’t yell at me if you’re there, dum-dum.”

I smiled. “It really means that much for you to live at the lake? I mean, fighting your back and your daughter and my Grandma just for the sake of being there, Owen?”

He gave me a very sad look, similar to the one he’d given Marie Taylor at his housewarming party. Softly he said, “I sure hope it proves worth it, Lewis.” Seemingly more to himself than to me, he added, “If I can’t have a train, maybe I can have Gordonier Lake.”

Totally puzzled by this, I said, “What do you mean by that?”

“Oh, I guess don’t know what the hell I mean.” Owen let out a short laugh, wiping a tear from his eye.

I said, "You know, there's something I've been wondering about."

"Uh, oh."

"If you like trains so much, how come you never went to work at the railroad as an engineer or mechanic or something?"

Owen stared at me. "I wanted to. Marie and Fledda had an uncle who worked for CN, and I talked to him a few times and he liked it. I also think it'd be an important job. A guy would feel like he was keeping the whole country moving ... and growing. I'll remind you — this country was built by railroad, young man."

I nodded. While working on his house he'd reminded me about eight times. I said, "So why didn't you get a job like that? Were they not willing to take you? Or did you need too much school for it?"

"Don't know how much training would have been involved, or whether I'd have gotten a job, because I never looked into either."

"Never looked?!"

Owen solemnly answered, "It'd have been tough to give up the farm, Lewis."

"But I thought you said the farm was too much hard work, and never to become a farmer?"

"I know I said that. But ... well, it's hard to explain. The bottom line is that a guy doesn't always get to do what he really wants to do, Lewis. Sometimes you have to make sacrifices."

I mulled this over a moment, staring at Owen's four-fingered left hand. When I looked up again I could see his expression had become very somber and vacant, much like the time I saw him on his deck from the laneway hill. He was gazing toward the waterfall, his eyes darting about but never settling on anything. He did this several minutes.

Worrying I had upset him, I said, "Want ... some more lemonade, Owen?"

He faced me again and a smile slowly returned to his face. "We should save it for the trip back, maybe. I suppose she's time."

"Trip back! Aren't we going any farther?"

"Oh, jeez!" Owen stood and dusted off his work pants. "I've uncaged the beast."

Pointing beyond the falls, I shouted, "There might be more stuff up there, though!"

Owen started downstream, however, saying, "Another day, maybe. I need some energy left for tomorrow, remember."

Realizing he was probably right, I gave up on the idea and caught up to him. As we entered the patch of spruce again, he said, somewhat apologetically, "We've had some fun, though — right?"

"Fun? This has been a hoot!" As we weaved our way back through the spruces I decided to get downright philosophical. "You know, Owen — exploring this creek? It feels just like the old days — back when I first moved to Muskoka."

"Nice to hear," he uttered calmly, but soon after began chuckling.

"What?" I said.

"The *old* days!" he answered. "You're a gem, Lewis."

26

Owen's daughter arrived the next day in mid-morning. My father and I were on the front lawn playing catch with a softball when we saw a big blue Thunderbird pass on the laneway. Dad, pausing with the ball to watch the car, said, "If it's true you are what you drive, Lewis, then the old boy's in trouble." This notion proved accurate on this day; only an hour later a frazzled-looking Owen, true to his warning at the waterfall the previous day, came down and invited me for lunch.

"How is she?" I said as we started toward his place.

"Currently worn down to a trot," he answered while wiping his shiny forehead with a handkerchief, "but for damn sure she'll get a second wind."

As we neared Owen's place I saw his daughter sitting at the white deck table, cupping one hand above her eyes to block the sun while she studied the view. My first impression was surprise over how young she seemed; she didn't look much older than my mother. Owen later explained his daughter was a "late arrival." Adding to her youthful appearance was ponytailed blonde hair, running shoes, jeans, and a white T-shirt. This white shirt also helped bring out the redness in her face, but she did manage a pained smile as I stepped onto the deck.

After introducing me Owen said, "Why don't you two have a lovely chat while I work on lunch." He then promptly snuck away to the kitchen.

Once her father was out of earshot Karen Leonard gave me a

pleasant but penetrating look. She had her father's hazel eyes, I noticed, along with his fair complexion. Apparently she also shared his sharpness, because the first thing she said was, "You're the rescuer, are you?"

"Rescuer?" I responded innocently.

She frowned. "*Yes*, all right then."

Already off to a rough start, I decided to use one of my father's suggestions. "Did you ... have a nice drive from Ottawa?"

Karen took this sudden change in direction in stride. "Yes, it was a nice drive, thank you. With our store so busy I don't get out of the city often anymore. Although, that doesn't bother me too much."

"You really like Ottawa?"

"Sure. It's a —" Karen broke off and turned toward the front door. With a considerably louder voice, she said, "Ottawa's a *beautiful* city, Lewis!"

I looked to the door, but saw no sign of any reaction from Owen — none that he revealed, anyway.

Shifting in her seat, Karen said, "So Father mentioned your family moved to this lake from Scarborough."

"Owen told you about us?"

"Sure he did. He's told me about everyone on the lake, and I don't think merely to change the topic, either. He's seems to have taken quite a liking to what he calls 'the funny bunch'." In a more serious tone, Karen softly added, "Dad also mentioned your little brother. I was really sorry to hear. I hope you don't mind him telling me?"

"That's okay."

"Aside from what happened, are you glad you moved to Muskoka?"

"Sometimes," I answered quietly. "Owen, though, he told me last night that, all in all, I should consider myself lucky to live here."

Karen's eyes widened. "Really!"

"How about you? Did you like growing up in Muskoka?"

Owen's daughter remained oddly silent a moment, seemingly

in recovery, then said, "To some degree. Our family wasn't exactly floating in money, and that made it tough at times. I guess my fondest memory was the horse we had. My mother loved horses, and Dad saved up for years before getting her one."

"So your ... Mom and Dad got along pretty good?"

"Sure, they were very close. To some degree they still are. I know they still have feelings for each other, although you'd never get either to admit that — especially Dad. It was only the farm that caused the breakup, Lewis."

"Your mother didn't like it?"

"At first she did, but I'm afraid she grew to hate it with a passion. As the years went by she saw less and less sense in keeping it. And when she reached her limit, and stubborn old Dad refused to sell ..." Karen looked solemnly toward the maples at the end of the deck.

Trying to lighten our conversation again, I said, "When they were together, did they go on many train rides?"

Her eyes brightened. "Hah! Has Dad been carrying on about trains with you?"

"He talked a lot about them while we worked on the house. He told me he wanted to work for the railroad when he was younger."

Chuckling, Karen said, "Yes he did, and he can talk a person's ear off about trains." After looking out to the lake, she eyed me. "You mentioned working on this house a second ago — you were the one, then, helping Dad spruce it up to impress me?"

I could only nod, realizing my mistake.

Karen smirked. "Surely you didn't think I wouldn't catch on? With the shape Dad's in he could never have done all this work in a couple of weeks."

"Owen's as sturdy as an ox," I said, trying to redeem myself. "I can't believe how much energy he has."

"Yes, *yes*." Karen gave me a familiar fake swat. "Oh well. I hope he hasn't been working you to the bone, at least. He's used to working hard and for long hours; he was like that his whole life. The problem is, he thinks he can still work that way."

"We didn't work too hard," I said truthfully. "Actually, on some afternoons we've gone hiking."

"Hiking?"

"A few times we've circled the lake, and yesterday we went down a path behind this house, and then along a creek." I threw in, "We even discovered a waterfall!"

"Huh!" Karen once again became wide-eyed. "What the heck's that all about? Scouting out firewood?"

I shrugged. "He's never said anything about firewood."

"Now what the —?" Karen broke off, because her father trudged out onto the deck hauling a large salad bowl and plates. After roughly plunking everything down he took a chair and tapped the table with his massive knuckles. "Dig in kiddies. Don't be shy."

"Yes, because the more you eat the less you say ... and the less you ask," Karen added. She then did as her father desired and spent most of lunch gazing out over the lake, a very strained and puzzled look on her face.

Following lunch that day Owen insisted he needed a nap. He might have been fibbing, but by this time he did look tired. Taking charge of entertaining Karen, I escorted her down to the Morrisons' place, where my mother and Marie Taylor were visiting. I knew Marie and Karen were already acquainted, of course, but I soon learned they hadn't seen one another in quite some time. Over the next hour these two chatted nonstop about everything from clothes to how Karen's furniture store in Ottawa was doing. But their conversation eventually turned to the issue of Owen. Marie initiated the topic by asking Karen about her two Maritiming brothers, Tom and Simon, who Owen briefly spoke of the evening I met him. Tom, you may remember, was "hiding in Halifax," working as a bookkeeper, and Simon "felt he needed" to manage a gas station near Moncton.

Seated on the couch, Marie asked, "So how often do they see your father?"

Karen, who'd remained standing this entire visit, grimaced.

"Very rarely. Dad talks to them on the phone once in a blue moon, and gets the odd letter, but that's about it."

"They're still feeling guilty about not carrying on with the farm?"

"'Fraid so."

"That's a shame. How about your mother — how's she doing? Owen mentioned you see her occasionally."

"Paul and I went to Winnipeg last Christmas, and she's fine. She still often asks about Dad but seems settled enough. She's sharing a house with three other seniors." Karen took a cup of coffee from Carla. "Now if I could only get Dad settled the same way as Mother ..."

"It's really bothering you, is it?" my mother inquired from her recliner.

"To put it mildly. Right when I thought I was making some progress getting him to move to Ottawa, he pulls this little stunt. I don't know what the heck to do with him."

Getting bold, I said from my floor seat, "Why do you have to do something with him?"

Karen glared at me momentarily, then said, sternly, "Okay, tell me this, Lewis. If your father was seventy-six years old and had a bad back — besides other health problems — would you be comfortable with him at this lake all on his own?"

Before I could argue back, Mother intervened. "We're quite willing to help your Dad if he needs it, Karen. I don't think he'll be a problem. As for Lewis, working around the lake is nothing new to him. He does all kinds of jobs for Marie."

"I realize," said Karen, "and do I appreciate that. But what if my father gets sick? It just ... worries me with him being out here on his own. I'd feel a lot more comfortable having him near us in Ottawa, and I know Dad could find a place there to his liking."

Marie said, "How long have you been pushing for this?"

"Over a year. I went to work on him about a year ago last spring."

"How about you and your husband moving to Muskoka?" Carla asked from the kitchen, sporting a sly grin. "We've got a lot right between us and your Dad we could sell you."

"You know, in all seriousness, if it wasn't for this store we've got I might even go for moving back to Muskoka. Paul's put a ton of work into the business, though, and I don't think it'd be fair to ask him to give all that up."

Marie said, "So have you managed to get your father looking at houses or apartments in Ottawa?"

"No, I've never made it that far. For one thing, Paul and I have only been able to get Dad to the city twice since I brought up the idea of moving. On both occasions, too, he invented an excuse for not looking at places to live. The last time we had him at the house was March, and he claimed he had a headache the whole weekend, which was bull."

My mother said, "You think he's simply not big on the city, maybe?"

While moving to the living room window, Karen answered, "No, he seems to enjoy Ottawa. I think he'd be fine. It's not like Dad's ever had a problem with cities, really. He's simply been tied to the farm."

Mother continued. "So what do you suppose *is* the problem?"

Karen shrugged, her back now to everyone as she looked toward her father's hilltop house. "I don't know. And as time goes on, and things keep changing with Dad, I get more and more confused. I've really started to worry about his health, and I don't mean merely physical."

Marie smirked. "You think he's getting a little senile, is that it? Like all us old folk get?"

"Now, now! I'm not saying he's that way because he's getting up there in age. Some of the sharpest people I know are his age. I'm just saying he's been doing some strange things the past while. Moving to this lake is only the latest thing."

"That's not a unique observation," Carla added, returning to the living room. "Val's mother thinks your Dad is completely strange."

Karen again shrugged. "Yeah? Well, she might be right."

"Pardon me if this is nosy," my mother said, "but what sort of 'strange' things has your father been doing?"

Karen sighed. "For starters, he's been awfully quiet the last few years. Sometimes when I'm with him he drifts off and I almost have to yell to bring him back. And now all of a sudden he's moved out to this lake, and Lewis tells me they've been going for walks in the bush for no apparent reason. With anyone else I wouldn't consider that odd, but with Dad it's another matter; it's simply not like him to do stuff like that. Maybe I'm over-reacting, but hearing these kinds of things about him scares me, and — " Karen paused to catch her breath, then suddenly turned to me. "Has he taken you to see the old farm yet?"

"No, and he hasn't mentioned wanting to take me."

Hearing this Karen just shook her head, looking frustrated and puzzled, then resumed peering out the window toward the hill.

After watching her a moment, Marie said, "Your good old Dad's tough to figure out, isn't he?"

Karen immediately turned. "You know what the hell I'm talking about here, don't you? I forgot about that!"

"I'm afraid I do, my dear," Marie quietly answered. "And yes, I'm every bit as confused as you."

27

I continued spending considerable time with Owen during the remainder of that summer. We tackled various projects around his house, such as building another small shed to compensate for the first one being jammed with his old tools. We'd no sooner finish a project like that, however, than he would dream up a new one. When I asked my father about this, he said, "You don't work hard on a farm most of your life then all of a sudden stop, Lewis." During our work I learned a number of other things about Owen. One was he could repair virtually anything under the sun. Another was he could build things, such as a shed, with a minimum of materials. Lastly, I discovered he could, in fact, talk about trains for hours on end, and eventually I needed a lesson from my father on "suggestive yawning."

Karen made a second visit in early August that summer, and once again Owen survived the ordeal. His only concession was to make an appointment with his doctor the following week. Fortunately his checkup went well, and put him in such a cheery mood I invited him for supper that evening. Although Grandma Layton made me wonder if this wasn't the worse thing I could have done for his spirits, he simply smiled his way through her pokes, like the one about him having a "hayfield lawn," and even another "old coot."

Aside from all this, Owen and I continued exploring the woods surrounding the lake. One afternoon, when my older friend was feeling especially energetic, we explored the creek beyond the waterfall and discovered an interesting little section where the creek split into two; another time we hiked in the woods southeast of Gordonier Lake and saw a moose. I loved these trips, and despite continuing to have somber moments, Owen seemed to enjoy them as much as I did. This was something Marie Taylor never got over, I should add. Often after cutting her lawn I'd tell her about the trips Owen and I made, and she would sit wide-eyed, listening to every word while twiddling her cane. When I finished she'd shake her head and say something like, "It's a strange world, Lewis. It's a strange world."

On a Saturday morning in late August, the day of that summer's corn roast, I finally got a chance to see Owen's old farm. The previous afternoon the new owner, John Vincent, dropped by Owen's place while he and I were having lunch on the deck. John asked him if he had time to look at the farmhouse water pump, which was acting up. He promised a trip the next morning, and I recognized my opportunity.

Now although Owen said I could see the farm, I questioned his enthusiasm. Something about his stare when I asked made me wonder if the idea bothered him. When I asked again and he insisted it was okay, I also reserved a spot in the truck for my father, knowing he too was curious.

Rumbling up the Fraserburg road the next morning, Owen explained about the pump. "Back when I sold the farm I made the mistake of telling the Vincents they could call me if they ever had a problem with it. She's an oldie, and temperamental."

"Why a mistake?" said Dad, pulling his visor down against the sun.

"At the time it seemed a good idea; it gave me an excuse to see the farm again. But these days I'd prefer to keep my distance. No question, too, this couple can afford a new pump. John's a pharmacist and Nancy's a nurse, and their kids are out of the house. I don't see how they'd be hurting for money."

"So why *don't* they buy a new one?" I said, squirming to get more comfortable. Owen and Dad had stuffed me between them.

"They don't for the same reason they haven't changed much of anything at the farm, Lewis. They're sort of antique buffs, and they like keeping the farm as original as possible."

"Ever thought of dropping a hint?" asked Dad.

Owen shrugged. "They're pleasant enough, so if they want help keeping this old pump running, then what the hell — I'll help them out. I know eventually I won't be able to fix it, and then this kind of thing will be over with."

Dad said, "How'd this John Vincent find you?"

"He fills Marie's prescriptions, and it seems she's been rather chatty." Owen grinned, glancing at me. "Apparently I've become one of the Seven Wonders of Fraserburg."

We soon reached the farm, which I remembered seeing during trips to Cathy's cottage. A small church and cemetery to the left, Owen turned into a long gravel driveway opposite these. An aged, two-storey white house, very close to the main road, sat on the driveway's right side. At the end of it, about fifty yards away, was an ancient-looking barn and several rundown sheds. To our left, stretching well back from the road, was a long, narrow hayfield of perhaps a hundred acres, bordered neatly on the sides and far end by thick woods.

Owen parked beside the house. As we left the truck John Vincent stepped out a screen door and onto the long open porch running down the side of the house. Behind him was a smiling, brown-haired woman wearing a large green apron, one boasting a picture of Bugs Bunny eating a carrot. Instantly I found myself liking her.

"Really appreciate this," John said as he stepped off the porch. He was wearing oil-stained overalls and his black hair was sticking up in places. The day before he wore a white shirt and dress pants, and for a pharmacist I thought he now looked funny. I had to hide a grin.

"Not a problem," Owen answered in a polite tone before introducing everyone.

"Curious?" Nancy Vincent asked my father, still wearing her warm smile.

He nodded. "Hope we're not intruding."

"You're not intruding any more than we are," said John. "Isn't that right, Owen?"

"No, no," he replied firmly, starting toward the porch. "This is your place now. You two need to try forgetting about me."

We went in the house through the screened door, with Nancy leading the way. The room we entered was the kitchen, and its large size amazed me. Along the wall facing the driveway ran a deep counter, perhaps twenty feet long, with pale green cupboards above it. Against the wall facing the main road stood a huge black cast-iron stove and a bathtub-sized washbasin. In the middle of the room, with plenty of room to spare around it, was a long wooden table that could have seated a dozen people with ease.

"All this is only the kitchen?!" I said to Nancy.

"That's how all farmhouses were in the old days, Lewis," she answered. "The kitchen was the main room of the house." Glancing at Owen she added, "When you work hard you eat big, too — right?"

"When you've got it to eat, you do," he whispered with a forced smile.

Nancy led us to a doorway on the room's front side, that closest to the Fraserburg road. This opened to a small living room that included a wooden staircase leading to the second floor. Covering the furniture and floor was a large sheet of clear plastic that had bits of plaster scattered across it. Looking up I saw the ceiling was torn down, exposing the upper-floor joists.

Owen, behind me, said, "What's this you're up to?"

"Just redoing the ceiling," Nancy answered. "We didn't have much choice — it was falling apart. Hope that doesn't bother you?"

"Don't be so worried about me. You do whatever you need to. Things don't last forever."

"It'd be nice if they did, Owen. I could handle that."

"'Fraid I can't agree with you there. I for one am glad they don't," he countered, and Nancy gave him a curious look.

Owen soon went to a door at the back of the kitchen, one I hadn't noticed when we first came in because it blended so well with the wall. When he opened it and switched on a light I could see a rough set of stairs leading to the basement. He started down, followed by John and my father.

I was about to follow them when Nancy said, “You’re welcome to look around outside, Lewis. I don’t think you’d find an old pump very interesting.”

“Don’t wander too far,” said Dad from halfway down the stairs, already knowing what I thought of this idea, “and stay out of trouble.”

So, Nancy saw me to the door and I hurried off to explore the farm. The place calling my name the loudest was the barn, and I went in through a small creaky door at the near end. It was divided into three main sections — with me in the centre one — by several four-foot high walls running the entire length of the building. I ran my hand along the top of one wall and found it smooth and rounded at the edges. These walls served as bases for large posts that in turn supported runs of high beams, and these beams also looked well worn. While studying them I saw a pair of swallows up at the distant roof. They flew along the peak until disappearing out the far end wall, where several boards were missing.

Except for a few broken bales of old hay the barn appeared empty. When I hopped over the right divider, though, I discovered this was not entirely true. Lying next to it, and looking very out of place, were two rusty train wheels. They were huge, of course, and after giving up trying to budge one I chuckled to myself. Leave it to Owen, I thought, to have train wheels in his barn.

At the rear outer corner of this right section of the barn was a low wooden enclosure with a gate, and here I found a narrow set of stairs leading to the basement. It was not dark, since the land dropped off at this corner, and when reaching the bottom of the stairs I was still above ground. A strong, damp musty smell — a mix of old hay, old wood, and old manure — took some getting used to.

The basement was small and contained only three livestock stalls, each with its own window. Two stalls were completely empty and swept clean, but the third still had some hay in a low trough and several horseshoes hanging on one wall. The window frame had tiny painted flowers, and on a small stool hung a muddied pair of light blue slacks. I quickly realized this was where Owen's wife Jeanne kept her horse, but also that many years had passed since she and this horse departed. Besides everything wearing a thick coating of dust, the flowers around the window were dirtied and fading, and to the whole place there was a deep quiet.

Beside the entrance to this horse stall was a large door, and after getting past a blatantly Owen-crafted latch, I eased it open. It led to the field behind the barn, and stepping into the bright sun I had to cover my eyes until they adjusted. When they did I discovered what I thought the crown jewel of my exploring mission: about a hundred feet from the barn, nestled in long hay, was a large stone foundation.

Although only about six feet high, and measuring maybe thirty feet long by twenty wide, its walls were over two feet thick. Leaning against the outside of one wall was a giant, roughly-squared slab of stone, and I guessed it once spanned the top of the doorway next to it.

I managed to climb the east end wall. The tops of all the walls, I discovered, were cracked and crumbling. From this vantage point I could see through the hay, allowing me to spot a rusty wagon wheel near the base of the north wall. It was half-buried and hay was growing up through its rotted spokes.

I have no idea how long that afternoon I circled, climbed, and studied that old foundation; I found the whole thing fascinating. I do know that by the time I returned to the house, Owen, Dad, and the Vincents were out on the porch and looked like they'd been there a while. They sat in old wooden chairs, gathered around a small round table that seemingly wore twenty coats of white paint. John was pouring iced tea.

When I drew close I heard my father say to the Vincents, "Really — you should come out."

"You shouldn't have said that," said Nancy. "We might just show up. We haven't been to a corn roast in years."

"Then c'mon out."

"Is your place on that laneway leading to Owen's?" This came from John.

"It's not at our house — the buggers won't let us have a turn yet. Marie Taylor is holding it this year. She's at the west end of the lake, not far off the main road."

"I know the house," said John. "Are you sure Marie wouldn't mind, though?"

My father shrugged. "She told me yesterday the more the merrier, and I'm confident everyone else on the lake feels the same way."

"Sure, we'd love to have you over," Owen added, but rather lifelessly.

Dad turned to me. "So? What'd you break?"

"Nothing!"

"Where all did you go?" said Nancy, pouring me a glass of the iced tea.

"Only in and around the barn."

Dad smiled. "And around all the sheds, and the fields, and the — "

"No!" I gave my father a light jab, then asked Owen, "Why is there an old foundation behind the barn? What used to be there?"

When he only offered a long face, Nancy said, "That was the foundation of the first barn the Goddards built." She turned to Owen. "What year did that go up again? I should remember these things."

"Eighteen seventy-three," came a quiet answer.

My father's eyes lit up. "Eighteen seventy-three? Your family goes *that* far back in this area?"

John said to Dad, "The Goddards were original settlers in Muskoka — you didn't know that?"

"No, I was *not* aware. When people don't tell you things, you aren't aware of them."

Owen shrugged. "Didn't think it would interest you."

Dad sat up in his chair. "Sure it interests me. These were your grandparents who started here?"

Owen nodded, then motioned with a huge finger to the cemetery across the road. "And ended here, too."

My father stared vacantly at the worn floor of the porch. "The things you learn when you go for a drive down the road. I had no idea you had roots that deep in Muskoka, Owen."

"He's got'em," said Nancy. "They're roots we plan to respect to the utmost, as well. Owen didn't ask but we gave him our word."

Dad said, "Do you know what we're talking about, Lewis? Owen's family were pioneers — just like in those books you used to bring home from the library in Scarborough."

"You mean they had to clear the wilderness and everything?"

In a cold, harsh voice Owen broke in. "They cleared exactly what you still bloody well see cleared today."

Surprised at his severity, I continued nervously. "Were ... you sort of a pioneer too?"

Owen looked out to the field, his face drawn tight. "No, not me."

"The real pioneer era was over by the time he was born," John took over. "He never lived through those times."

"But he knows all about them, I bet," Nancy added.

Owen grimaced as he slowly ran his thick fingers through his hair. "Yes, I suppose I do."

"Now I understand better why you two are trying to preserve this place," Dad said to the Vincents. "You've got a veritable piece of Muskoka heritage here."

"She's a treasure," said Nancy, smiling at Owen.

He only shrugged at this, then suddenly rose from his chair. "We really should be going, boys, as I think of it. There're things I promised Marie I'd look after at her place so it'll be ready for tonight."

"I suppose if we're attending we shouldn't stand in your way," said Nancy. "Need any help?"

"No, no. That's fine," he said, starting for the driveway.

"All of you are welcome anytime," said John.

My father quipped, "You shouldn't have said that. We might just show up. Eh, Owen?"

He offered only a faint grin, not saying a word. And that wasn't much less than what he had to say during the drive home.

28

Marie Taylor's corn roast didn't truly get rolling until about eight that evening. That was when the Vincents arrived. They blended well with the lake crew, chatting like they'd known everyone years. They also brought more corn, which made the resident corn-shucker (Judy) happier, and more beverages, which made the resident drinkers happier. And John Vincent, it turned out, hiked in the Yukon in his younger years, and until my mother rescued him this naturally boosted the evening for the resident explorer.

Owen was also in a better mood, helping me with the fire and Judy with marshmallow sticks. Too, halfway through the evening Marie played an old record, and trying to impress Grandma Layton, Owen did a little jig in front of the fire. He showed fine form, and I wondered if my grandmother's involuntary dance finger might even rise. The potential for this dissolved, however, when his pants fell to his knees, leaving everyone rolling on the lawn. Everyone, that is, except Grandma Layton; she used it as an excuse to head home. "Apparently Mother didn't care for the music," my father said, wiping tears.

About ten o'clock Dad, Cathy, and John Vincent coaxed me into getting another bottle of wine from the kitchen fridge. I found my mother having tea with Marie and Nancy Vincent. With them was Reggie Morrison, sitting at the table's opposite end, eyes puffy and closed, shoving back small mountains of milk-soaked cornflakes with a big serving spoon. I noticed he drank heavily on this night, as he always seemed to at corn roasts or any evening events, and that he spent most of his time indoors. I also noticed, several times, a familiar dark, grave face.

"How's the bonfire?" Marie asked me. "I'm afraid to look."

"Cathy says it's the biggest one at the lake ever!"

"Let's just hope the fire department doesn't wind up saying the same," my mother warned. "I know you've had a good summer, but don't get silly out there."

"Better tell everybody else too," I warned in return, reaching into the fridge for the wine. Dad and Cathy had started eyeing Lyall Taylor's long-retired wooden rowboat.

"It's my fault," Marie whispered to my mother. "I made the mistake of telling them to burn up any rotten lumber. You add some booze to the situation and —"

"Oh, go on!" Mother broke in. "It doesn't affect these guys the slightest bit. Eh Reg?"

"Hhmph," he answered, puffy eyes remaining closed, and working on another big spoonful of cornflakes.

"It's a good thing this isn't at our place, then," said Nancy Vincent. "There's certainly piles of stuff at the farm we could burn. We're always afraid to, though, because of Owen. We're never sure how he'll react."

I said, "He told you today to do whatever you want."

"*He* says that, Lewis. But his eyes say otherwise."

"Have you made many changes to the house?" Marie asked.

"Only where necessary. We had to redo an upstairs closet, and I imagine a new pump is in the works. Beyond that there's the living room ceiling, which we're currently redoing."

"Well," Marie continued, "if things need doing they need doing. You may just have to put Owen out of your mind. It's your farm now."

"I suppose," said Nancy, quietly.

While Mother poured more tea and the three women chatted about the weather a moment, I heard Reggie Morrison's jaw suddenly crunch into something hard. Only I noticed, and when he made a screwy face I leaned back in my chair, expecting bad things. Luckily he merely dipped his head below the table and spit out, and a plastic-wrapped whistle bounced harmlessly off my chair leg.

"How about you?" Nancy asked Marie. "Have you changed much in this house?"

"Very little. It was Lyall's treasure; I strongly doubt he'd like changes."

"But he's not here to stop you," Mother said, winking at Nancy before delivering, "You may just have to put Lyall out of your mind. It's your house now."

"Oh, but he *is* here!" Marie pointed to her large silver locket, and Mother and Nancy let out a long, corny "ahhh."

They'd no sooner quieted than John Vincent stormed in. "What the hell happened to our go-fer?"

I smiled, holding up the wine bottle. "Sorry."

"Hey, John," said Nancy. "You should get the box — this is as good a time as any."

"Sure — can do."

"Box?" said Marie.

Nancy grinned. "We have a little surprise for Owen. Something we think he'll get a kick out of."

"It'll only take a second to get it from the car," said John. "Where the heck *is* Owen, anyway? He's not —"

"I know where," I broke in, anxious to see this surprise. "I'll get him."

Owen was playing tag with Judy and Katie Howard among the young spruces behind Lyall Taylor's old workshop. This was the latest the girls had been allowed to stay up at a corn roast and they were making the most of it. With their coaxing Owen had worked up a sweat chasing them.

By the time I had him in the kitchen everyone else had assembled. On the table sat a very old-looking wooden box with a sheet of red wrapping paper taped over the top. Owen didn't immediately notice it, his eyes fluttering while adjusting to the bright kitchen lights. He said, "Someone's found an instant cure for a bad back, did I hear?"

"We may have something that'll interest you even more," said John, pushing the box toward him.

"What's that?"

"Open it and see."

Owen slowly tore off the wrapping paper and everyone crowded in to see. Although the box was large it contained only four things: a metal comb, a pen with stand and inkwell, a black leather belt, and a brown leather wallet. All items had a musty, aged smell.

"We found this box when we tore out the living room ceiling," said John. "It was nailed between the joists."

Looking stunned, Owen lifted out the items one at a time, repeatedly turning them over in his massive hands before sending them through the group.

He last removed the brown leather wallet. One side was plain, but the other, in crudely branded letters, displayed 'George Goddard'.

Owen whispered, "I'll be damned."

For nearly a minute he held the wallet, weighing it in his hand and rubbing the leather, all this time seemingly deep in thought. Finally he handed it to Carla Morrison, who in turn started it around the table. As he did this I happened to notice Marie; she was eyeing him closely.

Owen said to John, "You say the box was hidden in the living room ceiling? The floor of the main bedroom?"

He nodded. "And hidden well, too. Must have been George's secret hiding spot. When we discovered the box I went upstairs to see how someone would get inside. I moved the bed and pulled back the throw rug, but even knowing where the box was it still took me a few minutes to find a little hatch in the floor. Your George was clever."

"Yes," said Owen, vacantly. "Can't say I ever noticed anything."

"Hope we've done the right thing by showing you this tonight," said Nancy. "We intended to surprise you this morning, but with Bruce's invite we left it for tonight instead."

Owen answered quietly. "You did the right thing."

"Is this really old?" asked Judy, who now held the wallet.

"Yes, Judy, it's very old." Owen sunk into a kitchen chair and wiped his forehead with a paper napkin. "Much older than me, even."

"We do occasionally find old items around the farm," Nancy said, "but we knew right away these were special, and that you should have them."

"Yes, I appreciate that," Owen said, his eyes distant now as he smiled faintly. "Very nice of you."

29

"George was Owen's uncle; his grandfather's oldest son," Marie Taylor explained on her front patio the following evening. I'd recently finished cutting her lawn and she was cooling me down with some apple juice.

"Is he in the cemetery across from Owen's old farm? He said his pioneer family was buried there."

"*Some* of Owen's early relatives are in there. His parents and grandparents are, but his Aunt Patty moved away after she married and she's buried with her husband out west somewhere. As for George, he isn't in that cemetery either. I'm afraid I don't know where he is."

"Owen was really close to him, though? He seemed pretty sad after the Vincents showed him that box."

"In a way he was close to him, Lewis. Although, he never actually met him."

"Never met him?! Then why was Owen so upset by his things?"

Marie paused, studying a blue toque she was knitting, then said, "Because ... there's a story about George that Owen knows well."

I sat up in my seat. "A story? One you know too?"

She nodded. "I heard it when I was about your age. Our family was at the Goddards' place for supper one night, and my father, who loved to hear about early settlement times, persuaded Owen's Aunt Patty to tell a story. So she told the story about George."

I beamed my warmest smile. "Is this a story you could tell me?"

Marie glanced at my presentation a second before turning back to her knitting. "You're worse than Father was."

I waited quietly, staring at the grass and twiddling my thumbs. Finally I heard, "*Yes*, Lewis, I'm only kidding. I'll tell you about George."

And so, that evening, after finishing her tea and resuming knitting, Marie Taylor told me the story about George Goddard, one I'll share with you as best I remember it.

"One fall in the late 1860's," she began, "Tom and Dorothy Goddard, Owen's grandparents, made a huge decision, Lewis: they would move their family to Canada. The idea first arose when the Goddards saw an ad in a London paper. The Ontario Government was granting free land in Muskoka. A family could get two hundred free acres provided they built a house, lived in it at least six months of the year, and every year cleared and cultivated at least two acres. Like many people back then, Tom and Dorothy were enticed by this opportunity. They'd faced years of hard times in England and the idea of owning their own farm really caught their fancy. They saw the chance for a better life, and not merely for themselves but also for their children and future grandchildren. Concerning the challenge, Tom felt they could handle it. He worked as a stone mason in London and wasn't the world's weakest or least capable person. Too, both Tom and Dorothy tended to learn new things quickly, and both also had a great deal of grit and stubbornness.

"They had three kids — George, Patty, and Harold. Harold was five at the time I'm speaking and Patty was eleven. George was fifteen and already an independent and capable young man. Tom and Dorothy thought the world of him and his strengths contributed to their decision to come to Canada; they had great faith George would handle the life well.

"So, the Goddards settled in Muskoka in the spring of 1868. Their journey across the Atlantic and into Muskoka was trying, to say the least, but the trip was nothing compared to the challenges of their earliest days here. When they first reached Muskoka they were shocked. Roads and buildings were few and rough, and never before had they seen woods like what they saw in this area. You need to understand, Lewis, coming from England they didn't have a clue what true wilderness was like. The trees then would make the ones around us now look like toothpicks, and outside the towns the bush was so thick the sun had difficulty shining through the canopy. Patty said the experience terrified her.

"When they managed to reach the lot they'd located on — the one you saw yesterday, Lewis — they were again shocked. They'd made the mistake of locating their land before leaving England, and what they received was rocky, partly swamp, and of course, mostly smothered with thick forest. Patty said her father, even stubborn as he was, wanted to head right back to town. It was George who somehow convinced him they could make a go of it, and so the family stayed. They built a large campfire and kept it going all night, fighting back a darkness unlike they'd ever experienced before, and in the morning went to work."

"So they were all on their own?" I broke in.

"No, no. I'm getting to that — be patient." After shifting in her seat Marie continued.

"The first task at hand for the family was to build a little shanty to live in until they could put up something more substantial. In doing this they received much help, both labour and know-how, from the first family of settlers they met — the Samuels. On the Goddards' third day Gordon Samuel and his two sons appeared at the lot with some trout and the group had a cook-out together. From that day forward the Samuels offered the Goddards help in getting a shanty built and a crop started.

"The Samuels had been settled three years at that point. Their cabin was about half a mile from where the Goddards made their camp. A few days after the cook-out George and Patty went with Dorothy to meet Mrs. Samuel and her daughter, Melissa, who was a little younger than Patty. They had a pleasant visit, finding Mrs. Samuel and Melissa friendly, but they came away from the experience disturbed over the family's living conditions. Patty said she'd never seen such destitute people in all her life; they had next to nothing. Their clothes were rags, their cabin had only a mud floor, and they seemed to have little food. Things looked so bad for them that Patty said she had a hard time not crying on the way home that day, and she said George and Dorothy hardly spoke a word.

"Anyhow, George became good friends with the Samuel boys — Loren and Fred. Patty said they were nice boys and George got along well with them. During that spring and summer the three often fished together on the various lakes nearby and on the Muskoka River. They also shared time cutting firewood and helping build a proper cabin for the Goddards to live in, which was finished by September.

"The Goddards' first crop that fall proved almost a complete failure. Patty said the family worked hard, but between their inexperience and the difficult conditions they gained a meagre harvest. What the family did harvest they pitted in the ground, but they made the pits too shallow and when winter arrived the vegetables froze, and then in a mid-winter thaw they spoiled. They later learned this was a common mistake for new settlers.

"Since Tom and Dorothy still had money, however, the family didn't fare too badly over their first winter. They made the occasional trip into town to stock up on supplies and so lived out the season reasonably well. In fact, when Tom hired the Samuels to help him and George clear more land during the winter, the elder Goddard paid mostly with food. Patty said George even managed to occasionally give Loren and Fred a little extra without it being missed. She said her brother really felt sorry for the boys, who always looked so hungry.

"When spring arrived the whole family went to work burning logs and brush and getting a second crop going. They'd managed to clear a few acres over the winter, but it was a miserable two acres to work. Besides being riddled with stumps there was no end to rocks, and the soil itself proved poor. Also, with the lot's little patch of swamp, and so many lakes and creeks nearby, the mosquitoes were terrible, and Patty said the blackflies made a thick cloud around your head. They persisted, though, planting vegetables such as corn, turnips, carrots, and potatoes in what good patches of ground they had. Tom and George insisted on putting in much longer hours than the rest of the family. Patty said the two sometimes almost crawled into the cabin at night, riddled with bug bites, only to be up and out again at first light the next morning.

"In late June Gordon Samuel and his two boys stopped by the clearing with an announcement doing nothing to raise the Goddards' spirits: the family was packing up and moving back to the States. They were leaving in only a few days and had come to say goodbye. Patty said George was heartbroken; Loren and Fred were the only friends he'd made and now they were leaving. That the Samuels didn't ask for help also frustrated him, since the Goddards were still relatively well off. Tom and Dorothy maintained it wouldn't have made any difference, noting how desperate the Samuels were, but they had a difficult time convincing George."

"So did they ever see them again?" I asked.

"No, never again," Marie answered, pulling another ball of yarn from her knitting bin. "I don't believe the Goddards ever heard what became of them, either, but that wasn't unusual in those days, Lewis. I'm sure George realized when the Samuel boys left he'd lost them forever.

"Despite this setback, however, that second summer the Goddards continued to work hard weeding their crop and improving the lot and cabin. They were becoming used to this work and Patty said things were going relatively well. Also, in late July Tom and George helped a crew of men build a bridge several miles farther down the road, and through this work the family made new friends.

"But, in early August, George had an accident. While clearing rocks from the lot he got his foot caught between two small boulders, then lost his balance and fell. He suffered a badly broken ankle. Tom took him to the doctor in Bracebridge right away and got him looked after, but George knew he'd be unable to do any serious work for some time. Patty said this injury made her brother miserable, and an incident a short time later didn't help matters.

"One day he decided to go fishing on the Muskoka River. Patty and Harold went with him and while he fished Patty picked blueberries a hundred yards upriver from where he sat. Harold, still just six at this point, started out helping Patty but soon became bored and ended up merely playing along the shore. They'd been at the river about an hour — with George catching few fish, I might add — when Harold somehow managed to slip and fall in. The river was banked by steep bedrock at the point he went in and the water quickly became deep. Harold couldn't swim yet and he began screeching and thrashing in the water. George desperately tried running to his little brother but because of his bad ankle he fell twice. Patty was the one who saved Harold. She ran down the shore, jumped in the water, and pulled him out. All in all, the little boy came out none the worse for wear, but Patty said George was extremely upset about the whole incident. Later he threw a tantrum inside the cabin and Dorothy made him sit outside until he cooled off.

"The Goddards did their best at farming but in the fall the harvest was only slightly better than the family's first. They still had much to learn. George, as if needing more disappointment, was particularly unimpressed. After working so hard over the summer he was disgusted with how the family received such little reward. Patty said he became progressively quieter after that. One afternoon in late October she noticed him sitting on a rock and just staring at the clearing. It struck her as especially odd because the day was cool, and he had no shirt on.

"The family had little money left and Tom had no choice but to get work in one of the lumber camps. He would not be home again until spring. Patty said her father was distraught about leaving and asked Dorothy repeatedly whether the family would be okay. She insisted they'd manage somehow, but little did she know how terrible things would get.

"The family's second winter proved much harder than the first. Less snow fell than the first winter but there were many more bitterly cold days. The Goddards' firewood supply ran out by late January and every day they had to scrounge the bush for deadwood. Patty said it was all they could do to keep the cabin tolerable during the day, and at night the family had to sleep together to stay warm. Also, they worried about their little stove and crude chimney. They learned of a family whose cabin burned down late one night and how they'd walked several miles to the nearest neighbour wearing only their sleeping clothes. Patty said the story really bothered George and kept him up at night watching the stove.

"With a poor second harvest their food supply was hardly sufficient. Many times George tried hunting and trapping, but his ankle hadn't healed properly and he wasn't good on snowshoes. Patty said it was downright painful at times to watch him shuffling along. As well, her city-raised brother barely knew the first thing about hunting and trapping. After a month he managed to catch only a few small rabbits, and with his ankle hurting so badly he had to give up.

"That left the family with a small store of vegetables, some flour and soda, and what fish they could catch to get them through the rest of the winter. All of them lost weight. Patty said George looked thin as a rake, and Harold had little energy to play. Dorothy, though, suffered the worst. With such bad nutrition, and the mother putting the welfare of the kids first, she eventually became quite sick. Patty and George didn't know what illness she had, but she was weak and bedridden for nearly a month, and the kids worried night and day they would lose their mother.

"I don't know how, Lewis, but the family did manage to scrape through that winter, Dorothy included. Patty claimed she was never happier to see spring in all her life. Tom returned from the lumber camp exhausted but uninjured, and brought with him a good stock of food, including some candy and a small bolt of fabric for Dorothy. The family had a veritable feast, and after they finished eating Patty even sang a few songs — something she hadn't done since leaving London."

I broke in. "Why are you smiling, Mrs. Taylor?"

"You'd have to know Patty," she answered. "She loved singing more than anything, and was a treat to listen to."

Marie inspected her knitting, then gazed at the lake, which had settled into its evening calm. She might have kept right on gazing had it not been for a low "ahem" from the chair next to her.

"You wear me out, Lewis," was the immediate response. Following a deep breath, however, Marie continued the story, and as she did I noticed her smile quickly faded.

"To cheer up George that spring, Tom proposed he take over the original shanty. He seemed comfortable in it during the family's first summer and Tom felt he'd be happier having more space to himself. Patty also thought it a good idea considering how quiet her brother had become; he rarely spoke more than a few words to anyone now.

"So George moved next door and the family, once again, set about preparing a crop. The familiar routine of long working days resumed and the family struggled to keep up their spirits. By this time they'd seen more families quit and move away, and they hated the thought of this happening to them. The Goddards might have been tired and worn but they were still very determined.

"It was in mid-June of that third spring when Patty woke one night just before dawn. She sat up to see Tom quickly getting dressed, with Dorothy helping.

"'What's the matter?' she whispered to her parents.

"'Something's nosing around outside', her father quietly answered.

"Tom got out his gun, grabbed the only two shells he had, and told the others to stay inside. There was no stopping Patty, though; she stubbornly insisted on going out too, and her father relented.

"There was a three-quarter moon that night so they could see fairly well. They went over to the shanty to get George up, but his door wouldn't open. After knocking on the door and calling him several times they still received no answer. Knowing George slept like a stone, though, they gave up and carried on.

"Tom and Patty crept toward the far edge of the clearing, to the spot where the continuing rustling sounds were coming from.

The two worried it was a bear, naturally, and Tom had his rifle aimed and ready. When they drew close, however, they saw something taking their breath away more than any bear would have. It was George making the noise. He was on his hands and knees, and was scratching at the ground with his bare fingers.

"'What are you doing there, George?' Tom asked his son.

"When George turned they could see his face in the moonlight. Patty said his eyes were frantic and distant, and he didn't seem to recognize her or Tom. He only silently peered at his father and sister a few seconds, then went back to scratching at the ground.

"Tom, stunned, didn't know what to do. He tried grabbing his son but he broke loose and took off into the bush. Seeing no sense in trying to chase him, Tom and Patty waited outside the cabin, surrounded by mosquitoes, hoping George would come back on his own. They waited till dawn but they neither saw nor heard any sign. Once it became light they discovered why they were unable to open the shanty door: it opened inwardly but had been yanked outward so hard it jammed in the frame. Tom Goddard, a good-sized man, actually needed an axe to force the door open again.

"It was about two hours later, in mid-morning, that little Harold stumbled upon George. He was sleeping in the bush behind the shanty. His clothes were soaked and muddy, his hands were swollen and covered with dried blood, and his neck was practically matted with mosquito bites. Tom let him rest, then took him into town to see the doctor.

"Soon after they left, Dorothy collapsed in what seemed to Patty a nervous breakdown. And poor little Harold, not understanding what was going on, kept trying to comfort her. Patty coaxed her mother to sit up and drink some tea, but she said it was hours before Dorothy even stopped shaking.

"Now Tom Goddard wasn't much of a talker at the best of times — *I* can tell you that, Lewis — but Patty said when he returned in late afternoon he was especially quiet and brooding. He wouldn't say a word about George. Later Patty saw her father standing at the edge of the clearing — at the spot where they'd discovered George the night before — and he appeared to wipe tears from his eyes. It was the first time she'd ever seen him that upset.

"That day was the last Patty ever saw her brother. She eventually learned from the Bracebridge doctor that George was sent away to a hospital in Toronto, but what ultimately became of him she never found out. As for the rest of the Goddards, Patty said what happened to George only made them all the more determined to continue, and the farm you saw yesterday is proof the family did."

Marie rose and put on the sweater draped over the back of her chair. For several minutes after she'd finished the story I didn't speak, trying to digest what I'd heard. During this time I looked out to Lyall Rock and the lake, which had become shiny in the dimming light.

I said, "Did the woods make a lot of people go crazy back then, Mrs. Taylor?"

Sitting again, she said, "What happened to George didn't happen to many people in pioneering times, but I can tell you it wasn't the only incident of its kind. Life back then was tough on the body, Lewis, but it was even tougher on the spirit. A person can only take so much."

"But if George never came back, then who stored his things away in that box?"

"My feeling is Harold did. He went on to become Owen's father. And since he died young in a tree-felling accident, he probably never thought to tell anyone up to that time he'd hidden his older brother's things in the floor of the farmhouse."

"Think Owen's mad the Vincents brought those things over last night? He seemed kind of quiet with them at the farm yesterday."

"I really don't know whether Owen is glad about John and Nancy finding and giving him George's things. As for being quiet with them, I'm sure it was the farm making Owen that way, not the Vincents. They've been extremely considerate toward Owen, and I think he knows that."

Marie shifted in her seat to face me again. "What you need to understand, Lewis, is that George's story is only one of many stories of the Goddards' hardships Owen heard as a boy. People often coaxed Dorothy and Patty into telling them. The night she told the story about George, Owen sat right beside me, and I'm sure it wasn't the first time he heard the story, nor the last.

"Now you try imagining yourself hearing even just this one story I've told you, and it being *your* Uncle George, and *your* family that's involved. You think about that. You couldn't avoid developing the same bitterness toward the woods your family developed; it would get right into your blood just like it did theirs. Owen certainly kept the farm all his life as a tribute to his family's hard work, but I believe there was far more to it. I think every time he looked at the woods lining their field he'd remember all the agony they caused his family. What he saw were much younger woods than those of pioneering times, of course, but they were still *the woods*. And I think he felt a duty to his family to continue battling them."

"But ... Owen and I went into the woods a lot this summer, and he never said anything bad about them."

"What he's up to these days I don't have a clue about. I told you that when Owen moved to this lake. What I am sure about is that the bad feelings I've mentioned — the kind Owen's had his whole life — don't simply go away. I don't believe they could *ever* go away. You only need consider how much resolve he had in keeping that farm. It cost him his health, the opportunity to make a decent wage, and the chance to pursue things he dreamed about — like working for the railroad. It also ultimately cost him his dear wife; she left him because she became tired of the farm and he refused to sell. A person needs a strong grudge to make those kinds of sacrifices."

I pondered this a moment, looking at the darkening lake again, then said, "Think I could ask him about all this?"

Marie stared at me. "I strongly recommend you don't. It's a sensitive issue with Owen, and I'm certain you wouldn't get answers. All you'd do is get in his bad books. I've known him most of my life and I wouldn't dare raise that topic, and I'm sure Karen wouldn't either. I'll ask him about his ex-wife and kids, like I did the evening you met him, but I'd never bring up his early family and what they faced."

"So Mrs. Leonard and Owen's sons know all this stuff?"

"Certainly. That's why Tom and Simon feel so guilty about not carrying on with the farm, and why they live so far away — they knew the kind of feelings their father had. Tom especially; he grew up constantly reminded he was named in honour of Owen's wilderness-battling grandfather. As for Karen, she's not exactly a fan of the woods herself — I don't believe her for a second when she says she'd move back to Muskoka. I could tell when she visited, too, she found it not only annoying but strange her father moved to the lake and is going for pleasure hikes with you in the woods. She's apparently convinced that must surely mean he's become a little senile."

"And you're sure he hasn't?"

Marie nodded confidently. "He's seems as sharp as ever to me. Maybe, I'm inclined to say, even more so. He strikes me as more ... of a *thinker* these days than when he was young. Then he was all work, all fight; too busy to contemplate anything."

At this time my tiny, elderly neighbour again rose from her chair, cane in one hand and knitting bin in the other. "So with all this, Lewis, at least you now know why I'm confused Owen moved to Gordonier Lake. You've got the answer to the big question you asked me the night you met him. The answer to the mystery itself, though — why is he here, considering his past? — I couldn't tell you. For the life of me I can't figure it out."

30

Despite school, and Grandma Layton's strictness concerning homework, I still visited Owen often that fall and winter. To begin, he proved a major Toronto Maple Leaf fan, and it was a rare Saturday night I didn't join him for Hockey Night in Canada. He also continued to enjoy doing things outside with me. When not too cold we'd go for walks along the Fraserburg road, and when the ice was thick we sometimes snowshoed around the lake. One winter evening Owen even surprised Judy and me by joining us on a few toboggan runs down the laneway hill, an event later inducing the standard disbelief in Marie Taylor.

In contrast, Owen was business as usual when it came to living at the lake; he seemed determined as ever to carry on. Besides working against his bad back he survived several more encounters with his daughter, including a week-long visit during the holiday season. He even continued trying to gain favour with his helper's grandmother, buying her an expensive cookbook at Christmas (to no avail) and attempting to chat with her several times (to no avail.) To all of this my father commented, "Your buddy is as stubborn a person as I've met, Lewis."

Despite Owen's enthusiasm toward spending time outdoors, and his great determination to continue doing so, his mood was not always pleasant. But learning his background I better understood what caused him pain. I saw, for instance, that his bad back not only hindered his living at the lake, but also reminded him of his farming past, and in turn his motive for that farming past. I understood how his frugal ways, once merely a curiosity, also similarly served as an unwanted reminder. So too his sacrificed career, particularly evident by his solemn expression one day in Bracebridge, when we sat silently in his truck at a railway crossing watching a train pass. Concerning his ex-wife Jeanne, I saw how moved he was when receiving her Christmas card. He kept it in his giant hands close to an hour, and often glanced at the kitchen wall photo showing his former spouse with her horse. This was also a rare time seeing Owen drink; he downed several shots from an ancient-looking bottle of whiskey. Lastly, I now understood his sad spells of gazing at the lake and woods. More than any other, I believed this immediate and unavoidable stimulus reminded him of his early family's suffering.

With Owen seemingly inescapably immersed in his past, I ultimately became equally confused as Marie Taylor about why he wanted — and apparently wanted dearly — to live at Gordonier Lake. Taking Marie's advice, I never made inquiries. But I reasoned his motive wasn't merely, as he claimed the evening I met him, to have his own place again. I believed his motive must surely be deeper to make him battle so hard. He could, for example, have simply bought a small, relatively maintenance-free house in Bracebridge. A clue I kept in mind was something he said at the waterfall: "If I can't have a train, maybe I can have Gordonier Lake." Another was one drawn from his gazing spells, especially when directed at the lake. Like at the end of my first workday with him, I sensed he was searching for something; his eyes didn't remain fixed but scanned back and forth. His downcast expression during these occasions, however, also suggested to me that, whatever he was searching for, he hadn't found it. I therefore believed that although successfully living at the lake, his summer had, in the end, been one of failure.

Concerning myself, during the fall and winter I couldn't help thinking often about the Goddards' past, especially the story about George. Pondering their extreme hardships, and with Owen's constant presence, I also couldn't help getting swept into sharing his sense of bitterness toward the woods. Such a feeling was obviously in great contrast to that within me most of the summer of

1977. Up until hearing about Owen's background my renewed interest in exploring had somewhat overshadowed everything else, even my mother's problem and my brother's death. I'd come to feel quite positive about living in Muskoka, and to increasingly believe Owen was right when he said I was lucky, despite what happened to Sean, to have moved. Learning my older friend's past, though, and eventually sharing in his sense of bitterness, unquestionably changed my thinking. I now wondered whether exploring the woods was nothing more than some romantic pursuit, or mere fun and games. I became, in short, once again utterly confused about my feelings toward the woods, and our family's move to Muskoka.

My renewed confusion and subsequent despair were evidently not lost on Owen. Although I never confessed to hearing the story about his uncle, he seemed to know I did. He had perhaps guessed I'd hound Marie after the corn roast for more information concerning George. I didn't blame him for my problem, however. Only reluctantly allowing me to visit his old farm, he'd tried to avoid my learning his past, and was obviously upset that afternoon I did. Also, he obviously never expected the Vincents to present him with a box of George's things. Nonetheless, that he felt bad about my renewed confusion over Muskoka was clear; he was now exceptionally generous and tolerant with me. At times he was even openly apologetic, and particularly so one evening in February.

On that Saturday I made my usual trip to his place to watch the hockey game. What was not usual was him dozing off halfway through the second period. This only coincided, though, with how he'd been the entire day. I'd found him acting strangely. He visited our family during the afternoon, for example, and was rather irritable, especially with my father. I couldn't see why he bothered coming down.

This evening, just when I assumed him fast asleep, he suddenly spoke. Out of the blue, and with eyes closed, he softly said, "I'm so sorry."

I glanced at him, completely puzzled. "You're so sorry?"

Eyes remaining closed, my older friend repeated, just as softly, "I'm so sorry, Lewis."

Part Three

31

The summer of 1978, the final summer at Gordonier Lake I will present to you, is one I still consider the strangest yet of any in my life. It seemed a near magical time, a time when perhaps being so disposed to noticing how I and others felt about their wild surroundings that I gained insights into that which I was formerly blind. To begin, I believe I learned as much or more about my fellow lake residents during this time as I did since moving from Scarborough. This was especially true of my parents, because it was near the end of this summer I learned 'what I didn't know about the move'. It was during this season, too, I became enlightened as to why Owen Goddard moved to Gordonier Lake. But the particulars of these revelations aside, it is because of their collective impact that I deem this summer so strange. For at the end I was no less confused about how I felt toward my new home than at the start — indeed, perhaps even more confused. And yet, with what I learned on my own, and with an older friend's help, I would start high school in the fall feeling oddly at peace with Muskoka.

I'd say that summer began in early May, on the Morrisons' first weekend of the season. They arrived in late afternoon on a Friday, just in time to share supper with us, and just in time to share the year's first major thunderstorm. During supper we watched and listened to this storm approaching, a huge dark mass of lightning-riddled clouds drifting in from the west, and only several minutes after we finished eating it arrived. The rain poured so hard you could barely see the lake, and the thunder was extremely loud and mixed with bright flashes of lightning. Not surprisingly, the power went out within several minutes. This prompted a snide remark from Grandma Layton about the "hick hydro," and for the next half-hour everyone just sat in the living room watching the storm. My grandmother aside I think all found the event rather fun. About eight o'clock, however, this festive mood quickly dissolved.

Just when the rain had stopped and the storm seemed over, we suddenly heard a huge boom outside. It was powerful enough to shake the entire house, and make a vase on the Muskoka room coffee table topple and shatter.

Poor Grandma Layton almost fell out of her 70th-birthday wicker chair. She shouted, "What the heck was *that*?"

"I'd say we've been hit by lightning," my father declared, jumping to his feet. He rushed to the porch and grabbed the fire extinguisher, then flew out the door, with Reggie Morrison and me right behind.

The instant we stepped out we smelled smoke. Frantically circling the house, however, we couldn't find anything burning. "Here!" Dad finally shouted. He'd turned to checking the woods behind the house. "Jesus did this ever get hit!".

My father stood at the base of the huge pine, the tree dwarfing all others in our back woodlot. The lightning had blasted a giant chunk out of this tree about four feet off the ground. All around the base were strewn bits of wood, none larger than my fist, and many were blackened and smoking. Dad was hopping about stomping out the live ones.

"That was one *hell* of a blast," he said when Reggie and I reached him. My mother, Carla, and Judy were right behind.

"It wasn't the house, at least," my mother said in a shaky voice, staring at the pine and the blackened bits of wood.

"For sure you've lost a tree, though," Carla added. "Look at the size of the chunk out of it — my God!"

My father nodded. "It got it good, and what scares me is it

likely wouldn't take much to finish the thing off. If we get more rough weather tonight ..." He paused a moment, surveying the tree and house. "You know — I'm bringing this thing down *right now*. That way I can at least have some say in where it lands."

Reggie whistled, gazing up at the huge pine. "Can you handle that, Bruce? That's an awfully big tree."

"I've taken a few trees this size down before. I'll be okay," Dad replied, and without giving anyone a chance to argue, he turned and headed for the shed to get the chain-saw.

And so, a few minutes later, the rest of our family and the Morrisons found ourselves standing on our front lawn in the drizzle, listening to my father run the chain-saw behind the house. He revved the saw several times and I sensed he was studying the tree. Then I heard the saw bite into wood.

"Sure hope he knows what he's doing," Carla said, and Mother cast a glance suggesting she didn't need this comment.

After a long minute of sporadic cutting, we watched as the tree trembled slightly, then began falling. It hit the ground with a tremendous 'whoomp' combined with the sound of snapping branches.

"All okay!" Dad yelled.

"Thank goodness!" said Carla, and my mother now looked at her with chin high.

Everyone went to look at the tree. Lying down the pine seemed larger than ever. Even falling toward the laneway at a forty-five degree angle the tip of the tree still reached the ditch.

"The Bunyan lad has nothing on me," my father said, grinning through a face covered in wet sawdust. "What do you say, Reg? Eighty feet?"

"Easy. Around this lake now that's a big tree."

"It *was* a big tree." Dad began walking down the trunk. "Heck of a shame losing a large healthy pine. I'm only kidding when I brag about cutting this down."

Reggie shrugged. "As good as dead anyway, Bruce."

My father, upon reaching about the three-quarter point up the pine, said, "Hey! What the hell have we got going here?"

Everyone quickly went to where he stood. There, nailed close to the trunk on two thick branches, was a wide, four-foot long plank. It was painted flat black.

Turning to me, Dad said, sternly, "Were you kids starting to build yourselves a fort or something?"

"No," I answered truthfully. "I didn't put that there."

My mother glared at me. "You're sure, Lewis Farrow?"

"Honest! I don't know how that got there!"

Dad, again studying the wet plank, said, "Bloody high enough. Do you suppose kids visiting the Elliotts might have done this, Reg?"

"Could have," came a very quiet answer.

"Whoever it was, they were brave," my father continued as he started back to the shed with the chain-saw. "You'd only fall down from there once."

It was late on Sunday that weekend before the weather cleared. After supper I helped Reggie launch his boat, and as usual joined him for his first row of the season. As always after long rains the lake was especially smooth and shiny on this evening, and except for faint dripping sounds all was quiet. For the first few minutes we merely soaked up this peaceful atmosphere. I lounged in the bow, trailing my fingers through the water while Reggie took his standard long, slow sweeps with the oars. When we reached the far end of the lake, however, the rower stopped, bailed out several pailfuls of water, then pulled his cigarettes from his shirt pocket.

"Looks a lot different, doesn't it?" he said, motioning with his lighter toward our place.

"It looks weird," I answered, turning to face the house. "Seems empty back there now."

"I suppose it'll take some getting used to. That was a big old tree."

"I still can't believe no one ever noticed that plank."

"Would have been hard to see it so far up the tree and painted black like that."

"I guess the kids who put it up there didn't want anybody to see it or they'd get in trouble." Receiving no response I turned and added, "Don't you think?"

Reggie took a long drag off his cigarette and squinted at me. "I'll tell you something, Lewis. I don't think it was kids who put the plank in that pine."

"It wasn't kids? Then who?"

"I think — no, I *know* — it was the Elliotts themselves."

I sat up in my seat. "You mean Mr. and Mrs. Elliott?"

"Yes, sir. Greg and Linda themselves."

"Why the heck would they do that?"

Reggie paused again, puffing on his cigarette, then said, "Well ... I have a theory about the whole thing, and one you're not likely to buy into, but here goes. Greg and Linda were very curious people. They were both well-educated and had a lot of different interests. They loved to dabble; you might have called them explorers — sort of like you. They had a penchant, though, for exploring stuff you and most people would find ... odd. They loved mysterious things — things most people don't really know much about. Now over the last few summers the Elliotts were at Gordonier, I think they dabbled in the idea of there being more to the woods than meets the eye. I'm speaking of spiritual matters."

"Spiritual stuff?"

Reggie nodded.

"But what did the plank have to do with that?"

"The big pine, Lewis, is at least one of the places they used to do their bit at night."

My prankster neighbour had no sooner capped this last line than the signal flags went up for me. He was going for all the money tonight — his tallest tale yet.

"You're trying to tell me," I said, "that the Elliotts used to climb into the pine at night and sit on the plank. Is that right?"

Reggie nodded again.

"And do what?"

"Sit up there and ... meditate or whatever. I don't know how this stuff is done, Lewis! I'm only telling you that sometimes these people would go up there."

"How do you know?"

"I'd *hear* them! I used to go out for a smoke at night and on four definite occasions I heard them either climbing or talking in that tree. That was over the course of their last two summers at the lake. Don't you doubt that's possible, either — you know how sound carries around this lake at night."

I beamed a big smile. "I'm getting a little old for this, you know."

Reggie raised his hand in the air and closed his eyes. "I'm not pulling your leg, Lewis. I swear on my mother's grave — they'd climb that goddamn frigging tree at night."

I pondered this a moment, then decided, out of curiosity, to let Reggie play out his little joke for the time being. Smartly, I said, "So, did you ever ... ask the Elliotts about all this?"

"I asked Greg Elliott about it the first time I heard them, and he deserved an award for how quick he changed the topic. They didn't know anybody could hear them, you see."

"I guess then it was good they ran into money problems. They sound like weird neighbours."

Reggie again squinted at me. "That's the next thing — I don't think they had money problems."

"But the day I met you and Mrs. Morrison, she said they told her that."

"Sure, that's what they *told* her, but they had to give some sort of excuse for moving away."

"Okay, so why do you think they left?"

Reggie looked across the lake toward our place. "My theory ... is they left because they had themselves a bad experience."

"What do you mean by 'a bad experience'?"

"I mean if you go exploring this spiritual stuff enough, maybe ... you find something you wish you hadn't."

I grinned. "You mean they had an encounter with the evil spirits of the forest?"

"Now, now. You go on and scoff at this all you want, mister. I used to scoff at this stuff too. I've seen some weird things go on over the years, though. That bass jumping out of that pond a few years back, for instance — I'd say there was something pretty strange going on that day. And on Friday it was kind of coincidental that particular tree was hit in the storm, wasn't it? Food for thought, my boy."

"Maybe it got hit because it was such a big target?"

"I'll remind you the tree got hit right at the base. I might be wrong, but I don't think how big or tall the tree was had anything to do with it getting hit."

"Maybe."

Reggie, continuing to gaze toward our place, said, "A bloody chill went down my spine when I saw it was the big pine the lightning hit."

Now something about the way he said this — a quiver in his voice, perhaps — made me begin wondering whether he really was playing with me. He might have simply been showing mastery at his craft, but I can tell you ahead of time that if he was putting one over on me, he never capitalized on it. Not only did he not tease me later, but after this night I never heard him mention the Elliotts again. Also, what he said next he said with an eerily familiar dark, grave face.

"You know, Lewis, the whole thing with the Elliotts is something I've put a lot of thought into the last few years. You can't help it when you see people doing the kind of thing they were doing. You start to wonder yourself whether there isn't more to the woods than meets the eye."

"Native Indians sure think there is," I offered.

"That's right. Maybe, too, not all these things you can't see are good things. You look around this lake. Everything seems so quiet and pleasant, but you try telling me you can't see the potential for some evil beneath it all as well. It's enough to put a guy on edge." Reggie stubbed out his cigarette on his well-worn rowing seat, and after taking up the oars again, quietly added, "For half my goddamn life I came to this lake and never gave it a thought. But let me tell you, these days I sure as hell occasionally do."

Not long before the Morrisons left for the city later that evening, Carla visited. My mother invited her into the Muskoka room, where I was leafing through my father's week-old Toronto newspapers. Carla and Mother occupied the sofa while I sat in the armchair farthest from the window.

"Feel like tea?" my mother asked.

"I'm fine, thanks. Besides, Reggie'll be calling for me anytime. He's eager to get going."

"Couldn't you go back early tomorrow morning? I'm sure there'd be less traffic."

"I'd like to do it that way, being up so early anyway, but I'm not the driver so I guess I can't say much. For whatever reason, Reggie wants to head home tonight. He's downright cranky about leaving, actually — that's why I popped over."

"Doesn't surprise me," my mother said. "The weather didn't cooperate too well this weekend. By the way — how did your place fair in the storm? Any problems?"

"The roof didn't leak — at least not that we could see — and the TV still works. I sometimes think Reggie would be more upset about losing that than the roof leaking. God forbid he couldn't stay up half the night watching his late movies."

My mother smiled. "A real movie-aholic, is he?"

"Seems so. But maybe only to hide another problem." Carla whispered now, supposedly so I couldn't hear, and apparently thinking I didn't already know, "Someone's been drinking a lot more the last few years."

My mother whispered, "He does seem to dive right in at the corn roasts, I've noticed."

Carla sighed. "Ah, but if the TV, the booze, and that stupid, leaky boat help him relax from whatever work problems arise, then I guess so be it. That's what the cottage is all about — right? He doesn't have any of these habits at home, so it's hard to argue he has a problem." Glancing at me, she said, "Speaking of that stupid, leaky boat — I was sorry to see it floated again this spring. I'd really like to see Reggie get himself another one."

Mother grinned. "So why doesn't he? Too cheap?"

"No, the problem isn't cheapness. Anytime I complain about the boat he reminds me of the dear memories he has of it. He says it takes him back to the 'good old days', whatever the heck that's supposed to mean. As I recall, he faced the same occasional work problems in the 'good old days' as he does now." Carla smirked. "For some husbands it's cars, for others it's boats, I guess."

Several loud honks came from the direction of her place. "Guess I'm being paged," she said, slowly rising from the sofa. "Thanks for the break."

As we soon watched her start down the driveway, as usual carefully scanning the ground, Mother leaned out the porch door. "Want a flashlight? It's awfully dark — new moon, must be."

"I'm fine, thanks. Toodle-oo."

She was hardly out sight when my mother turned to me. "So Mr. Up-Too-Late. I don't care for grumps in this house — know where you're going?"

I reluctantly nodded.

Before heading upstairs, however, I returned to the Muskoka room to put away my father's newspapers. Soon after, my mother came in.

"By the way," she said, watching me, "since when are you into reading newspapers?"

I answered quietly. "I don't know — just felt like it tonight."

"You wouldn't be desperate to escape bed, would you?"

"No."

"And why so pale? Not feeling well?"

"I'm okay."

My mother gave me a short, puzzled look, then picked up a plate of tarts she'd put out for Carla. "How about getting those lamps and the back light for me," she said before heading to the kitchen.

After finishing putting away the newspapers I turned off the two lamps. I then went to the switch for the back light, which was next to the screen door, and flicked it off. It was just then, as I quickly headed out of the dark room, that the Morrisons passed on the laneway. Their headlights shone into the Muskoka room, and for a brief moment shadows of pine branches appeared on the inner wall.

32

As was unfortunately becoming tradition, on the May long weekend Grandma Layton whipped the entire family into a thorough spring cleaning. She issued orders immediately after breakfast Saturday morning, reading from a notebook to ensure she didn't miss anything or anyone. My first job, as I feared it might, was a complete overhaul of the large upstairs closet; "somebody," she claimed, kept just pitching things into it. As the day went, however, this closet would become a distant third to Somebody's concerns. For starters, in mid-morning I received a major surprise: a phone call from Kevin Taylor.

I believe I only touched three steps on my way downstairs after my mother yelled for me to come to the phone. She'd been talking with Marie, who'd called from Peterborough; Kevin wanted a quick word with me. Our chat proved exactly that; my mother didn't allow me to run up long distance charges. But I still gained news my friend would be arriving at the lake the following evening to begin a two-day visit, and this was all my mind needed to go to work.

Kevin was currently going through yet another lifestyle change. Although I hadn't talked with him since shortly after my brother's funeral, I occasionally heard bits of news from his grandmother. He and his father had recently moved back to Ontario from the east coast and bought a house in Peterborough, one about a mile from the apartment Kevin had shared with his mother. This weekend was Marie's first visit to this new residence, having been picked up by Kevin's father on Friday.

How my friend felt about living with his father I couldn't have told you for sure, but I guessed he was suffering as badly as before. Anyone who would marry "the witch," I reasoned, must be equally as evil. When I added to this suspicion the news Kevin would yet again be denied a summer at Gordonier Lake, I expected he was at the breaking point. I didn't think he'd bolt from the car when arriving at his grandmother's and disappear into the bush, but I did think he'd have this in mind for some point during the weekend. And as crazy as this notion may sound, I soon learned it also crossed my mother's mind he might be distraught enough to run off, and that her son might be concerned enough to help him.

"How's the scheme coming?" she blurted out, suddenly appearing at the door of the big upstairs closet. With the noise I'd been making moving things I hadn't heard her climb the stairs.

"Scheme?" I said, trying my utmost to look innocent.

Two small green eyes drilled holes in me. "Don't give me that, mister. I know darn well what's on your mind. You're thinking Kevin will make a run for it this weekend, aren't you?"

"No."

"You're also thinking of a way to help him."

I shook my head, staring at the floor. When you're born, I considered at this moment, perhaps part of your brain stays inside your mother for her to tap into at will.

The mind-reader moved on. "I'm here to *strongly* suggest you not try anything."

Resigning at denial, I said, "But his mother's in jail, and his father's probably on his way! Kev'll go nuts! He needs — "

Mother broke in with a hushed but severe voice. "One kid lost in the bush is enough for my lifetime, thank you, Lewis! Now, do we have an understanding? No foolishness! Kevin may be still in the same mess as before, but running off won't cure the problem."

To this I merely nodded, and thankfully my mother seemed reasonably content. I hadn't, however, truly given in. I figured, first, that with Kevin having been so adept at finding his way through the bush to the cabin, there wasn't much chance of him getting lost wherever he now went. Second, I expected he'd be hell-bent on taking off regardless of whether I helped him, so I might as well.

If my mother had left me at this point I may have continued pondering this issue, but right when she seemed ready to do so I suddenly heard, "Speaking of lost kids, is that some of Sean's things you're trying to hide from me?"

I turned and saw my mother once again staring at me. Without a word she approached the box I'd been cradling in my arms since she arrived at the closet. When she reached me I gave in and relieved my tired arms by putting the heavy box on the floor.

I said, "It's ... just a few little things."

"Just a few, huh?" My mother peered down into the open box, which was almost full. It held a wide assortment of things, topmost being a rubber ball with 'Sean' on it, an old Montreal Expos hat of mine my brother insisted on keeping, and a tiny sweater Grandma Layton knitted. As I feared she would, my mother slowly started removing things from the box.

"Oh, this is a good picture!" she said, taking out a framed photo of her sons standing in front of the Scarborough house, both dressed formally for Grandma Layton's 65th birthday. "Although, as I recall, that day you two were really at each other."

I nodded. "Sean was being an idiot. He started telling everybody on the block we were dressed up because I'd discovered gold when I was out exploring and struck it rich."

Mother smiled. "He really thought you were something, Lewis Farrow." She then playfully added with a smirk, "Why, though, I have no idea."

We continued this way, gradually emptying the box until my mother finally pulled out Sean's binoculars, which lay on the bottom, along with his bird book — the one I used to read to him.

"Now this was a birthday present that went over well," she said, goofily peering through the binoculars at the upstairs hall. "I'd never seen your brother so excited as when he got these." Putting the binoculars down, she spent a minute silently perusing the book — an expensive bird encyclopedia that made my father cough for ten minutes after learning my mother bought it. She said, "You should keep this book out somewhere — other people in the family may want to look at it. Judy could use it for a school project or something." She spoke in a normal enough voice, but I saw her eyes had become wet. Before she realized I was watching she wiped them with the back of her hand.

"Okay, Mom," I said softly, turning away when she caught me staring, "I'll ... put it on my shelf somewhere," and when she gave me the book I didn't return it to the box.

I would do that in a few days.

That evening, as I feared, my mother spent several minutes gazing out my front window. It was the same as always, with her standing perfectly still and peering out at the night sky. Even though I knew I'd get in trouble for being awake, on this night I really wanted to talk to her about this habit. I didn't, though, and was greatly relieved when she at last came to the bed, kissed my cheek, and returned downstairs.

The next morning, thinking he might have something to offer, I decided to mention the whole incident to Owen.

"Losing a child's no small thing, Lewis," he said from his deck chair. "It'd be a mighty hard memory to live with, I'm sure." Gazing out to the lake a few seconds, he added, "You couldn't manage to hide that box?"

I shook my head. "She caught me right in the middle of moving it. I was about to bury it among some other ones, like Grandma told me to." Leaning back in my chair, I grumbled, "It's been *two years*, and she's still staring out my window at the stupid sky. Mother just had her fortieth birthday last Friday, too. I mean, she's getting *old*!"

At this my elderly friend briefly brought his hand to his forehead, but then said, "Two years for someone your age may seem like a long time, but as you get older it won't. It's quite possible your mother will mourn your brother's death the same way for the rest of her life. You should be prepared for that. I also know something else — there's no shame in your being upset, either."

Owen had apparently spotted me wiping a few out-of-nowhere drops of water off my cheeks. I croaked, "I only wish ... she was the same way she used to be. There was a New Year's Eve ... she and I just sat and watched it snow. Nothing else — just sat and watched the stupid snow come down like it was the first time we'd ever seen it." Turning to Owen, I said, "Suppose you could talk to her about what she's doing? Maybe with someone like you she'd open up a bit."

Owen slowly shrugged his massive shoulders, staring down at the deck. "Don't know if I could be much help — I've never been through what she has, and she knows that." Looking out to the lake again, he said, "All I do know is your mother's a heck of a nice person, and it's a shame she's hurting. We'll see, Lewis."

On Sunday evening of that long weekend the entire lake crew went into Bracebridge together to see the Victoria Day fireworks, put on by the local Kinsmen Club. During her Saturday morning phone call Marie arranged for us to meet her, Kevin, and his father at the door of Monck School, the site of that year's holiday event. Luckily this group did finally arrive — they were half an hour late — and together we set up camp on the lawn beside the school, amid a steadily growing crowd.

Kevin's father, Bill Warren, was a tall, smartly-dressed man with neatly-trimmed black hair. For a minute he actually fooled me into thinking there was nothing wrong with him. Between his tidy appearance and how he cheerfully greeted everyone after Marie's introductions, you would have thought him downright respectable. What woke me up — drug-dealing Debbie's former husband couldn't fool the great investigator for long — was a closer look at his son.

The first change in Kevin I saw was that he'd gained weight. He looked downright strong now, actually, filling out his clothes well. Those clothes themselves were healthier too. Long gone were the ill-fitting, secondhand things he'd worn when he was with his mother. He wore a new white shirt and blue shorts, and his running shoes were a brand my parents couldn't afford for me.

What I saw in him, in short, were the effects of his father obviously having money to burn, and the question popping into my head was: where did that money come from? Sizing up my friend's father while he chatted with the lake residents, I didn't allow myself to be fooled by his smiles, or by his tidy, smart clothes. Lots of criminals were clean-cut; that was their camouflage.

At first opportunity I led poor Kevin well away from the lake residents so we could talk. I drew him to the edge of the school playground where many kids, including my sister, had gathered and were making plenty of cover noise. I desperately wanted to learn what he had in mind. A dawn breakout after spending the night at our place? A midnight escape from his grandmother's, with me on lookout? Since it was starting to get dark, and I knew we'd have to return to the group when the fireworks started, I wasted no time in seeing what option he was considering.

"*Take off into the bush!* What in the friggin' *hell* are you talking about, you idiot? Why would I take off on my Dad?"

I simply stared at Kevin, shocked at my friend's naiveté, then said, matter-of-factly, "'Cause he's a goddamn, good-for-nothin' crook."

Kevin eyes almost popped out of his head. "My Dad's not a crook! You take that back!" He drew his hands into fists and glared at me, and for a second I feared there'd be, as Owen would put it, "a development." How that development would unfold was also far from predictable; my friend was no longer the skinny rake of years past.

In sheer desperation, I said, "I wasn't saying anything bad to *you*, Kev. I was only —"

"There's nothing wrong with my father!"

"But Kev, he's not letting you spend the summer at the lake — is he? It's only a matter of time, too, before he gets into trouble like your witch of a mother."

"My Dad's not doing anything wrong! And I was the one who decided not to spend the summer at Grandma Taylor's!" Kevin's chest swelled. "*I've* got a full-time summer job at a hardware store."

This stunned me. "You got a job at a hardware store? A real

one? With people around and everything?"

Chin high, he said, "I'm gonna stock shelves and help with deliveries and stuff."

I had no idea what to say to him at this point. Unsociable Kevin willingly working at a store? Seemed almost impossible to believe. Following this brag about his job, though, he added to my confusion, as he would the remainder of our weekend together. Gradually calming down, he told me about how he'd joined a softball team, and was helping his father fix up their new house. I tried to picture him helping do carpentry and couldn't; his skills must have improved dramatically since our cabin days. The final touch was when he explained his father was coming to Muskoka the following weekend to borrow some of Lyall Taylor's old tools, and would be making the trip alone. Kevin had already volunteered to help a poor, elderly lady on his street till her vegetable garden!

Who the heck was this guy?

When we returned to the lake crew we found Kevin's father talking up a storm with Dad, Rick, and Reggie, all seated in lawn chairs. While Kevin joined them I went over to Owen, who, as often was the case these days, sat alone looking somewhat downcast.

"Seen a ghost?" he said when I reached him, seeming to snap out of deep thought.

"Maybe," I answered quietly.

He looked puzzled. "What's up?"

"Kevin! He's acting really weird."

"Oh? How's that?"

"He's going on about all the stuff he's doing at home, like playing softball and working at a hardware store and helping old ladies."

"What's so weird about that?"

"Nothing ... for most people. But I thought he wouldn't like living with his father any more than with his mother. I thought he'd be dying to get away from him. Hearing him go on like that — he sure never talked about his mother and her neighbourhood that way."

Owen answered casually, "All parents and neighbourhoods aren't the same, though. He simply had the misfortune of getting into a bad situation."

I nodded at this while watching Kevin, who was sitting on the grass beside his father's chair. Owen must have seen me looking because he said, "Your friend should be all right. His Dad seems like a good guy, and where they're living seems nice enough. While you two were away Bill mentioned Kevin's settling in real well in the new house. He's getting involved in all kinds of stuff. He was playing softball with some new friends before they came up to Muskoka tonight — that's the main reason they were so late."

I nodded again, and reminded of Marie's remark the previous summer about Owen, said softly, "It's a strange world, Lewis. It's a strange world."

"What's that?" Owen asked.

"Nothing."

I wanted to ask what else Bill said, but the first firework went off with a loud bang and made a huge red flower high over the field in front of us.

"Apparently we're on," Owen said, smiling, then let out a long "oooh" with the rest of the crowd.

The following Saturday I went over to Marie's place in mid-morning. Bill had arrived at the house a half-hour earlier and was struggling to get Lyall Taylor's old table saw into his truck. "Could you lend him a hand, Lewis, before he hurts his back?" was the plea I received from Marie by phone. When we had the saw loaded — a huge, old brute of a thing — she insisted we also load the last bit of Lyall's old lumber; Cathy recently claimed she didn't need any more. By the time we finished all this it was noon, and Marie invited me to stay for lunch. "God, say yes," Bill whispered to me. "I'll never finish it all on my own." He was referring to the way his former mother-in-law had joyfully cooked up a storm; she was in the best mood I'd ever seen her in. At one point I'd heard her singing inside, and later even saw her moving about the house without her cane. Later my mother would say to me, "You mean you're surprised? She's thrilled things are working out for Kevin. Very relieved too — she agonized over not having the money or health to keep him with her."

It was after this big lunch — right after Marie went upstairs for her traditional afternoon nap, more precisely — that Bill surprised me with a request: he wanted to see the cabin. He was apologetic after asking, saying, "We don't have to go, Lewis. I understand if you'd rather not." I did hesitate a moment, but agreed on the condition he never mention the trip to my mother. What swayed me was realizing that despite what happened to Sean, part of me missed the cabin.

So, similar to old times, Kevin's father and I started off down Taylor Avenue. There was a slight breeze on this somewhat overcast day, and that was convenient because the mosquitoes had begun making their spring appearance. Bill setting a fast pace helped too; he wanted to visit the cabin and get back to the house before Marie finished her nap. Once again just like old times, I thought.

I hadn't been to the cabin, of course, since the evening my father and I went to retrieve his things after the search. The first thing I noticed was how much shorter the trip now seemed. Two years earlier it had felt like the cabin was about five miles back in the bush. Bill and I didn't walk any faster on this day than Kevin and I used to, but in no time we arrived at the cabin.

My former project, I was sorry to see, was in sad shape. The roof showed signs of leaking badly, and the door frame had split and parted company with the door again. The small outhouse window still leaned against the back wall, but I didn't mention it to Kevin's father. After a quick study of the cabin I followed him to the lake, which itself seemed the same as ever — quiet and pristine.

"So no one has a house or cottage at this lake?" Bill said, scanning the shore.

"No, and we never saw signs of anyone else coming here."

Bill beamed an all-knowing smile. "Kevin had himself quite a find then, didn't he?"

Sensing he was more than aware of his son's past desires, I

nodded. "I was surprised he showed it to Sean and me."

"Am I right in assuming, though, you and Kevin didn't come to this cabin after your brother's accident?"

"I sure didn't. But Kevin ... *might* have a few times — he really loved this place."

Bill turned to me, his hair fluttering slightly in the breeze coming off the lake. "He had every right loving this place, and wanting to run off and live here. The way things were with Debbie, I felt like doing the same myself; she really went bad. If you're wondering why the heck I was with her ... well, the person she is these days isn't the person I married. I don't know what the heck happened with Debbie. It sure screwed me up, and I know it did a number on Kevin too."

I asked something I'd been wondering about all week, beginning right after realizing Bill was not, in fact, the crook of the century. Carefully I said, "Sorry if this is nosy, but how come Kevin didn't just live with you from the start?"

Bill frowned. "Before Debbie got caught I had no way of proving she was involved in the drug trade, and she won custody when we split up." With his frown transforming into a smirk, he added, "Kevin's sure as hell with me now, though."

"Also seems to be ... liking it," I said, having a hard time with the words. I still hadn't gotten over the change in Kevin.

"Yes, he's enjoying the new neighbourhood. He's made himself quite a few friends already, and he's even got a job lined up at a hardware store at the end of our block. Did he brag to you about that?"

I nodded. "He told me about his softball team and about helping some lady. He's kind of ... changed."

"Yes, I'm aware. I want you to know, though — it wasn't only me and the east coast that changed him. He told me how you taught him a lot of things about softball, and how you helped him with carpentry." Bill grinned. "I thought it a tad ironic the way he went on about how big a help you were in fixing up this cabin. This, when he only wanted the place so he could supposedly get away from other people."

I also couldn't help grinning, surprised at not having realized this irony on my own. And when I finished patting myself on the back for how I'd supposedly helped Kevin, I said, "So with you two living in Peterborough, will he still get to come to Muskoka?"

"Oh, sure — you'll still see him. For one thing, we'll obviously be occasionally visiting Marie. But I don't think you'll have Kevin at Gordonier Lake for a whole summer again. Marie's not really up to having him with her, but for that matter, I don't know whether he even wants to spend a summer in Muskoka again. By the way he talks I think he's fairly happy, and I'm glad."

"So you don't think he still wants to live at this cabin?" I said this only half-jokingly.

Bill turned and again studied the cabin. "You know — you read sometimes about people moving way up north and building themselves a little place like this in the woods. We might laugh at Kevin's plans of living here, but there's people who actually do that sort of thing. Many are people fed up with all the ills of society. The thing is, though, most of them eventually come back. Sometimes they invent excuses about why — like for the sake of their kids — but for the most part I think it's because they miss too many things." Bill paused a moment, staring at the silent, pristine woods around us. "The problem, you see, Lewis, is that when you walk away from the bad stuff of society, you're also walking away from the good stuff. And I think maybe that's what Kevin finally realized."

I said to Bill, "I have one more question if you don't mind."

"What's that?"

"If Kevin's happy where he is, how come you wanted to see this cabin?"

Bill smiled faintly but as he turned to start back to Marie's, he spoke with the same half-joking tone I'd used a minute earlier. "For *now* Kevin's content where he is, Lewis, but if he ever changes his mind, at least I know where to look for him — don't I?"

33

While the spring season made my father particularly restless, its effect on Marie Taylor was quite opposite. Daily pacings between thermometer and window ceased, no longer did she fret over what I or anyone else wore outside, and she relaxed enough to resume retiring for an afternoon nap.

Marie's sister Fledda evidently shared in this annual sigh of relief; every year she visited in early summer to "celebrate the end to another season of torture for my dear little sister." She also renewed her campaign to end that torture by getting Marie to move south. "Her lasting love for Lyall is touching," she once said to Grandma Layton, "but it's time she let go of his pride-and-joy house." My anti-rural grandmother was naturally in agreement but I too saw sense in it, and even more so this summer of 1978. I'd now experienced three winters of Marie's anxiety, and even though I knew I'd miss her, I wished she would take her sister's advice.

Fledda's visit this summer came on a Sunday in mid-June. I learned of her arrival when she phoned Owen's place. "Could you two please come over and assess some damage?" she pleaded. She provided no further details and when I reported the call to Owen, he said, "For sure she's up to something."

Owen, it dawned on me, already knew Fledda. I remembered Marie teasing him about having dated her older sister when they were teenagers. I only now realized this connection because Owen hadn't yet encountered Fledda since moving to the lake. She'd taken sick with the flu the previous February, and instead of her usual winter visit Marie had spent a week in Barrie.

No sooner had we arrived at Marie's than we learned the "damage" was a problem with the fancy French doors leading to her balcony. The house had heaved or settled slightly over the winter and the doors were jammed shut. But although this problem was genuine, I soon realized Owen was correct in suspecting Fledda was up to something.

"So the place has pretty much had it, is that what you're saying, dear?" She said this right after Owen declared the doors in rough shape. "Not much left you can do, I suppose?"

Owen, on his knees examining the sill, looked up with a frown.

"You don't have to fix the doors if you don't want to," Marie said. "I can hire a carpenter from town."

Before Owen could answer Fledda said, "Oh, but why on *earth* spend money on a lost cause? Fixing the doors — or, it pains me deeply to say, anything around this house — would be simply and obviously silly." Patting her sister lovingly on the shoulder, she added, "There just ... comes a time, I'm afraid."

Owen, having difficulty studying the top of the door-frame, asked, "Am I okay to stand on this little stool, Marie?" He was referring to a tiny one beside her bed.

"If we could fit, we'd all stand on that stool without breaking it," Marie promptly declared before offering what evidently was unquestionable proof. "Lyall made that for me."

Fledda smirked. "Ah, but he also built the house and put in these doors, didn't he?"

"And built everything well! He can't help it if the place has heaved a bit!"

"Heaved a bit!" Fledda put a hand to her heart for added effect. "It's all but heaved into the blessed lake, dear!"

Owen stepped off the little stool. "I'm not the carpenter Lyall was, but I can fix this, Marie."

"Are you sure? I can hire someone to come out."

"Nope — no need," Owen insisted, and after a sly glance at his old girlfriend, started downstairs.

When we were back outside Owen headed to his truck, saying

he'd go home for his own tools. He suggested I stay and set up a workbench on the lawn. This proved a bigger job than expected, because two saw-horses I needed were buried under dozens of other things in Lyall Taylor's old workshop. I didn't have to contend with this clutter alone, though; Fledda soon entered and started angrily flinging things out of the way for me. You may remember, she was by no means the frail little thing Marie was, and even in her mid-seventies she still packed a wallop. She was, as Owen later described her, a "rugged, true-blue Muskoka woman," and she actually made me a touch nervous on this day.

"*I can fix this, Marie!*" she mimicked in a childish voice. "*I'm not the carpenter Lyall was, but I can fix this!*" Fledda viciously fired a piece of old pine siding against the shed's back wall. "I'd liked to fix his bloody neck!"

After looking to her co-worker for comment, and receiving not so much as a peep, she said, "It was a simple assignment! All I asked him to say was, 'Sorry, Marie, but the doors are cooked, and so's the rest of the stupid house I'm sorry to say, dear — I'm afraid you'll have to move'. But noooo! That would have been way too easy!" After tossing an old lamp out of the way, she continued with, "Why the hell is that old bugger living out here anyway? He's the last person you'd expect to see on this bush lake, and here he is helping Marie stay!"

Without thinking, I asked what should have been obvious. "You ... know all about Owen and his past then?"

Fledda looked stunned. "Know about him? I *lived* him! Not only did we date a few years, but my family saw his all the time. We were on McKay Lake, just up the road from the old Goddard farm. Oh, I know Owen! I've never seen anyone hate the bush more than that bugger. You wouldn't *believe* the stuff he used to do!"

It was my turn to be surprised. "Wouldn't believe what? What did Owen used to do?"

Apparently sensing some doubt in me, Fledda's eyes blazed. "He'd hunt drunk sometimes, I can tell you that, mister. He'd shoot almost anything that moved, too. He'd shoot little birds for the sake of killing something. He was also known to cut down big trees out of sheer spite, especially after his father Harold was killed felling one. He'd go into a complete rage sometimes, and don't you even think about doubting what I'm saying. I'll inform you again — I know Owen Goddard!"

Although I valued my life, Fledda got my back up talking about Owen this way and I became daring. "You're sure about the trees, Mrs. Garrett? And you saw him shoot little birds, did you?"

For a second I honestly feared I'd get a close-up of an old wooden mitre box Fledda currently held.

"I *know*, my dear, because my father hunted with your buddy. He hunted with Owen, that is, until he decided the man was nuts. And, for your stupid information, a few of the big trees I mentioned were ones I saw him take down in person."

Fledda evidently decided she'd thrown the knockout punch, because after yanking a saw-horse clear of the final clutter with the power of a small farm tractor, she stomped out of the workshop with it. This left me to stew over what she'd said, and stew I did. Naturally I questioned her claims; I knew she might simply be retaliating against Owen for fixing her sister's house and spoiling her plan. But the more I considered her claims, the more weight they gained. As I'd seen while working on his house, Owen unquestionably had a temperamental side. Add to this Marie's account of his bitterness and I could picture him doing some scary things. Especially when he was still working the farm and his negative feelings toward the bush must have been strongest. I therefore reluctantly had to admit something to myself: what Fledda said was probably true.

When I rejoined Marie's sister with the second saw-horse I discovered her carrying with seeming ease a wide, eight-foot plank. This was one Kevin's father and I left because it was too rotten; apparently Fledda thought it just right for the occasion. "There — a rotten plank for the rotten carpenter to fix the rotten doors on." After fetching a second plank and setting up the workbench, I felt a change of topic was needed, so I asked her about Marie's fate with her house.

"Even if Owen or anyone else couldn't fix the doors, or other things that are wrong with the house, think that would persuade Mrs. Taylor to move anyway? I mean, at the corn roast she had last summer she said she wouldn't even *change* the house, let alone sell it."

Fledda gave me a cold stare. "You really know how to put cheer in an old girl, don't you?" She took a long breath. "Ah, but I'm afraid you're right. Every year I try talking some sense into Marie, and every year nothing happens. As you said, I probably couldn't even get her to change a stupid light fixture in that stupid house — 'Lyall might not have liked it', she'd say. Good old Lyall and his pride-and-joy house."

"It *is* well-built."

"Well-built maybe, but overdone if you ask me. Just look at that silly thing." Fledda waved a hand toward Marie's elegantly-trimmed balcony and French doors.

"I admit that stuff looks a bit fancy compared to the rest of the house. Why'd Mr. Taylor add them?"

Fledda grimaced. "In theory, at least, Loverboy added them as a birthday present for my sister shortly after she made the mistake of marrying him. He built everything during a week Marie was away visiting me in Barrie. When I brought her home he didn't say a word, but let Marie discover the doors and balcony when she went up to their bedroom later. Big surprise it was. She told me her sweetie tied a giant red bow to the railing. That's about as corny as it gets, I'd say, but that was Lyall and Marie. They were, supposedly, as close a couple as any."

"And did she like the balcony and doors?"

"She'd never admit not liking anything her dear Lyall built for her, but I somehow doubt she liked this particular birthday present. Why would she? The doors are just begging to let in winter drafts, and as you know, Marie's not exactly a huge fan of that season. Not that Lyall cared. To me, after he married Marie he should have done the honourable thing and sold his pride-and-joy. He could then have moved his dear new wife to a place with milder winters than Muskoka. Or even no winters at all. But no, he never did anything to help Marie with her problem. Pretty selfish for a guy who was supposedly madly in love with his wife."

Hearing what surely was Owen's out-of-view truck crunching the gravel on Marie's driveway, I quietly said, "So you don't think they really were all that close?"

Fledda shrugged. "Pretty one-sided as I saw it, Lewis. No question Marie thought the world of Lyall, lugging that locket around all the time and naming swimming holes after him, but I have my doubts it went both ways. Like I said about the balcony and French doors, in theory they were for Marie, but really I think they were just something Lyall wanted for himself. Probably saw a picture in a magazine one day and thought a balcony and fancy doors would serve as the final touch to his masterpiece. Who the hell knows."

As Owen approached us toting one of his ancient wooden tool-boxes, Fledda turned her back on him. "And now here comes the Muskoka Madman to help good old helpful Marie by fixing what was really only for Lyall. Myself, I was tempted to just kick the stupid bloody doors open."

The next morning, after Fledda returned home, I continued stacking some precious firewood Marie recently had delivered. The day was hot, but a cool breeze blew in from the lake. By noon I was nearly finished so I told Marie at lunch I'd stay and stack what remained. This clearly pleased her, and heading upstairs for her afternoon nap she told me, as usual, to help myself to the fridge.

I'd continued work about a half-hour when the phone rang. So it wouldn't wake Marie I rushed into the kitchen to answer. Turned out, it was her closest friend — Grandma Layton.

"Did Marie leave a skirt out for you to bring home?"

"No, she didn't mention anything."

"Could you do me a favour then? Go upstairs and get it? She keeps it in the hall closet. It's a gray one — you'll see it."

"But ... Mrs. Taylor is sleeping!"

"Then be quiet! The Euchre Club girls are picking me up

soon and I need the skirt. I'm sure Marie wouldn't mind."

So, reluctantly I made my way up Marie's old stairs. They creaked so I went slowly, carefully choosing where I stepped. When reaching the closet I quickly found the skirt. Not only was there merely one gray one, but half the closet was filled with what clearly were Lyall's clothes. Moreover, most of the boots and shoes on the floor were also his, and hanging from a wall hook was a worn carpentry apron.

Now I'd just closed the closet door and was about to start back downstairs with the skirt when I heard a sound coming from Marie's room. It was an odd noise, one I didn't recognize.

Softly I said, "Mrs. Taylor?"

No answer.

I crept toward her bedroom door, which was slightly open, and called again. Still I received no answer. Somewhat concerned, I poked my head in her door. To my relief Marie was sleeping peacefully on her bed. The sound came from some papers fluttering on the dresser next to the bed. But what next caught my attention was the reason the papers were fluttering.

Both balcony doors were wide open, letting in the cool breeze coming off the lake.

Besides making the papers flutter, this breeze made something else move: gently swinging from the right door handle was Marie's cane, one of her daily reminders of a lake breeze long ago.

I also noticed Lyall's homemade footstool sitting in the middle of the balcony doorway. It was apparently just beyond the swing of the doors, and also built just high enough to allow his tiny wife to reach the top barrel bolt.

As the breeze drifted in again, and the papers on the dresser again fluttered, I decided to quiet them with a weight. And the most convenient item was a large, silver locket laying open nearby, one showing a young couple walking hand in hand down the Fraserburg road.

34

Judy waded through some pickerelweeds near Lyall Rock, and Carla Morrison squirmed in her green boots.

"How can she *do* that?" Carla gasped. "And in *bare feet*!"

"Guess she figures the water snakes need company," Owen quipped, earning his ribs a third jab.

It was the first Saturday of July, and a day marking the Walshes' 50th wedding anniversary. In early afternoon our family's adults headed for the Scarborough party, leaving Judy and me in Carla's overnight care. Only us three would occupy her cottage; Reggie drove home Friday to take care of work problems and wouldn't be returning until Sunday.

After this Saturday's supper Cathy visited to invite us swimming at Lyall Rock. By 'us', of course, she meant Judy and me. My sister immediately began sweet-talking our squeamish neighbour, however, and within ten minutes miraculously coaxed her into Reggie's boat. Not wanting Owen to miss the occasion, I phoned and he joined us by foot. Now, after swimming a half-hour, we were nursing the remaining daylight. Owen, Carla, and I sat high on the spacious front rock, while Cathy lay spread-eagled waterside. Judy, of course, entertained other friends.

"Speaking of water snakes," said Cathy, "I haven't seen one in years."

"Nice try," Carla scoffed, still defending a terrestrial version of swimming.

"Really! I occasionally saw one during my first years here, but

I haven't in ages. They've maybe died out in this lake, Carla."

"Oh, stop. You'll bring me to tears."

"All gone except this one behind me," said Owen, straight-faced.

Carla actually turned to check, then delivered yet another jab.

Owen surprised us this evening by arriving in swim shorts. "Brand spanking new," he proudly announced. He was even first in the water, and although displaying rusty skills, swam ten minutes before getting out to pester Carla.

"How's the back these days?" Cathy asked.

"Better'n ever. Thinking of taking up water-skiing."

"I just bet."

"Or maybe —"

"Stop right there, you!" This harsh yell came from Carla, and was delivered to my approaching sister. "What have you got?"

Judy carried a pickerelweed stem, and it was obvious what Carla thought she had.

"Only a plant, Carla," said Owen.

"It looked like she had something else, and it's not like it'd be a first! Did you hear what happened years ago?"

Owen grinned. "Heard the story. I was feeling down one day and Lewis cheered me up."

"Sure — joke away! I almost had a nervous breakdown!"

"It was only a snake and some frogs," said Judy.

"Only a snake *eating* some frogs."

Approaching us, Judy mischievously held out the stem. "Wanna look closer, Mrs. Morrison?"

Carla smirked. "Oh, I do appreciate the gift, dear, but maybe your brother needs it. He's probably hungry again by now."

My sister consented, and after psyching myself up, I folded the stem and jammed it in my mouth, algae slime included. I even managed several fake chews before spitting out.

Owen almost busted a gut and Carla almost fainted. "You people are sick! Absolutely sick!" she shouted.

Wiping tears, Owen said, "You're definitely a member of the 'funny bunch', Carla. Yes indeed."

When she recovered she turned to Cathy. "So I hear you're taking Lewis and Judy to your Aunt Jenny's cottage?"

"Yuppers. I managed to get next weekend off at the bakery so I'm taking these guys out. Been promising a long time."

"Your aunt would be pleased."

Cathy only nodded.

As I'd already noticed earlier in this summer, she was still very much in mourning over her aunt's death — even a year and a half later. At times, strangely, she was more sensitive than ever. When anyone mentioned her aunt's cottage, for instance, she invariably became downcast and irritable. Although I knew she'd long promised my sister and me a cottage weekend, she still surprised me when actually inviting us.

Carla brightly offered, "Do you have snakes and frogs and *caterpillars* at that cottage too?" She shuddered after this last item.

Thankfully, Cathy beamed a smile. "Yes, ma'am!"

"Then Judy's in paradise."

Owen let out yet another chuckle. Similar to Cathy, I hadn't seen him laugh like this in months, and felt glad for phoning him.

Carla now caught Judy returning to the water. "Oh, no you don't! You're up too late already. It's pushing eight-thirty. Time for bed, Miss Farrow."

"Home?" Judy cried. "But we just got here, Mrs. Morrison! Why can't we —?"

"We've been Lyall Rocking enough. Come on — load the boat. We're done."

Judy and I reluctantly obeyed, and were soon seated in the boat with Carla, me at the oars. Owen was not aboard; he opted to walk home. Cathy needed to see Marie Taylor, so she also stayed ashore.

"Owen's sure moody, isn't he?" she whispered, holding the boat's stern with her foot while watching him slowly hike the southern shore.

"He often goes for walks — I can tell you that," said Carla, also watching Owen. "Sometimes I see him walking very early in the morning."

"For sure he's got things on his mind. No lack of energy, though. I was amazed to see him swim tonight, even though he wasn't the greatest at it."

"He mentioned he rarely swam as a kid. His father only pushed him to learn so he wouldn't drown if he tipped a canoe while fishing."

Cathy smiled. "Sounds practical. Odd he'd do it for fun now."

"Better late than never, maybe," I said vacantly, also studying Owen a moment. I then stared at Carla.

"Don't hold your breath, mister!" she scoffed, then motioned that I start rowing.

"I guess you three are on your lonesome tonight," Cathy said, glancing back as she started toward Marie's place. "The boogeyman's liable to visit."

"Naw, the boogeyman doesn't worry me," said Carla, before adding with a smirk, "It's the boog*er*man that's the problem."

My sister and I laughed so hard we almost fell out of the boat.

"What'd I miss?" Owen hollered from the far shore.

"Boogerman!" Judy and I yelled.

It was only dawn when I woke the next morning. At first I thought it still night, but after opening a curtain on the Morrisons' spare bedroom window I saw the sun's halo behind the back ridge.

I heard kitchen sounds so I padded out, slipping from the bed quietly so not to rouse my sister. I found Carla sitting at the table. She wore a housecoat and slippers and had her blonde hair in curlers. On the table was toast and tea, but she hadn't turned on any lights and the room was still very dim. I saw she'd opened the kitchen curtains already, however, and that she sat facing the large window.

"Oh, dear!" she whispered. "Sorry about that, honey. Should have known a growing boy would wake to the smell of food."

"That's okay," I said, rubbing my eyes. "Now I see what Mr. Morrison means about you being a morning person."

She sipped her tea, then said, "Only here at the lake. At home I'd sleep another hour."

I sat at the table and peered out the window. The lake's end bay was just becoming visible.

Carla said, "Are you hungry? You could have some toast for now."

"Sounds good."

"Then again, maybe you'd rather harvest the lake."

"Very funny." I went to the kitchen counter and filled the toaster.

"My poor stomach still hasn't settled since you pulled that stunt."

"Sorry," I replied sincerely. The truth was, neither had mine.

Carla turned. "What time does Judy usually wake?"

"Early, but not quite this early. Except at Christmas, of course."

Our host resumed window-watching. "Shame."

When my toast emerged I sat again at the kitchen table and began buttering. Midway, though, I stopped and stared out the window, just as Carla was doing.

The sun must have topped the back ridge because the lake and shoreline trees suddenly brightened. This basic event, however, wasn't what caught my attention.

It was the quality of the light.

Everything — water, rocks, leaves, even a bullfrog I noticed floating among some pickerelweed — was absolutely glowing. I'd never seen this during my lake time, and could hardly believe my eyes.

"Amazing, isn't it?" said Carla, apparently sensing my surprise. "Few rise in time to see this, and that's a shame."

I moved closer to the window. "It doesn't even look ... *real.*"

Carla smiled. "It's a strange effect, isn't it? The first time I saw a sunrise at this cottage we were still building. We had no beds yet and I didn't sleep well on the floor. I was up at dawn one morning and came out to the kitchen to make tea. When I looked out this window I couldn't believe how beautiful everything was. I'd seen sunrises other places, obviously, but I'd never seen such a glow."

I leaned closer to the window. "What makes it do that?"

Carla shrugged. "Sometimes in those early days I'd stroll the laneway, trying to figure it out. This glow lasts only a few minutes, so you don't have much time. The best I could tell was it involves how the sun filters through the trees on the back ridge. But I'm not sure and I've long stopped trying to solve the mystery. What I do know is that I love Gordonier Lake sunrises, and since that first morning I've always gotten up to see them."

She was right about the glow being short-lived. While we talked it gradually dissolved and all looked normal again — bullfrog and pickerelweed included.

"I think it's neat now I did wake up to see it," I said before starting into my toast.

With the hint of a grin behind her teacup, Carla answered, "Yes. Neat how that happened."

For the next hour that morning Carla and I chatted on numerous fronts, all the while watching the day brighten. When Judy arose our neighbour cooked a big breakfast, and it was almost nine o'clock before I left the kitchen table to dress.

35

As Cathy promised, the following Friday Judy and I found ourselves bouncing down the Fraserburg road in her rusty truck, heading for her late Aunt Jenny's cottage. The day was hot and humid and we suffered the dust for the sake of having, as the driver put it, "both air conditioners going full blast." Jokes like this came often from our formerly wealthy neighbour, as did her trademark smiles. And yet, I sensed quite early into this trip she was not nearly as joyous as she tried to appear.

Now I'd already dismissed the notion Cathy regretted inviting my sister and me out for the weekend. She readied all food and gear in advance, and picked us up only minutes after arriving home from the bakery. All bubbly and sporting a genuine smile, she insisted we "Hurry up, hurry up!" It was only later her jokes and smiles seemed forced — several times, too, I caught her staring quite solemnly out her side window. Feeling confident my sister and I were not the problem, I naturally assumed she couldn't help thinking of her aunt at this time. But soon she said something making me also question this notion. Halfway to the cottage we passed Owen's old farm and saw John Vincent replacing some siding on one of the storage sheds beside the barn. Right after I waved to him Cathy blurted out, with definite bitterness in her voice, "Those dummies are fighting a losing battle trying to keep up that place, Lewis." So sudden and nasty was this remark that Cathy herself seemed surprised by it. When I glanced at her she immediately forced out another wide smile, then burst into talking about the hot weather.

Following what she claimed was a long-standing tradition, right after arriving at the cottage we went swimming in the river. Judy and I were already dressed for the occasion so were first in, but Cathy wasn't far behind. After a quick change she came charging down the front rock wearing her wacky blue swimsuit, the one she'd embroidered umpteen little orange and yellow fish into. Screaming something unintelligible, she cannonballed off the end of the dock. The splash was so huge and loud that half a dozen crows suddenly exploded from a tall maple near shore. "You'd think by now they'd be used to me!" she giggled girlishly when she resurfaced and saw the birds flying away.

We swam close to an hour before giving in to hunger. We'd absorbed enough hot sun by this time so we ate supper inside, taking seats on creaky wooden chairs surrounding the main room's equally creaky wooden table. Although we opened all the windows upon arrival, the cabin still had a strong musty smell, and I had difficulty eating. My appetite wasn't the only one affected. Cathy was seemingly used to it and unbothered, but Judy soon claimed she wasn't hungry, and following a quick bite proceeded to nose about the cabin. Then she actually voiced her distaste over the odour.

A second after Cathy glanced at my sister, and noticed a thumb and forefinger pinching a nose, she said, "What's the matter, Jude?"

"Something ... really ... smells in here." She lay on the old flower-print couch sitting against the cabin's centre wall. She'd been toying with a wood carving of a fish she discovered but had now put it down and was blatantly pinching her nose. Evidently she saw nothing impolite, also, in telling the host in a nose-pinched tone her cottage smelled.

Cathy said, "Don't worry, sweetie. Things are always musty in here till the cabin airs out. It'll be okay."

Judy sat up and sniffed loudly in all directions. "No, it's more than just musty, Cath. Something ... *smells*."

Cathy rose from her chair and went to the couch. Sniffing the air a few times herself, she grimaced. "Jesus — you're right."

Asking Judy to stand, she removed the cushions. She discovered nothing out of the ordinary, however, and so pulled one side of the couch back from the wall. Seconds after kneeling on it and looking behind, she said, "Oh, oh!"

I knelt on the couch beside her and Judy. The fabric covering the back was torn at the bottom, and lying inside were the remains of what I guessed was a deer mouse. Tufts of reddish-brown hair, a long tail, and a skeleton were all that was left, along with an acrid smell.

"Yuck!" said Judy.

"Yuck is right," Cathy echoed. She rose from the couch and went to a tiny closet beside the bathroom. She returned with a garbage bag, small broom, and dustpan, and after I helped her draw the couch well away from the wall, we cleaned everything up as best we could. Cathy virtually soaked the back fabric with air freshener, then put a box of baking soda inside as well. Luckily these measures worked; although the cabin itself still had a distinctly musty odour, it smelled considerably better than it had. Judy even repaid our host by returning to the table and eating some supper — the mere sight of a decomposed animal evidently not a problem for her.

Loudly chomping on some celery, she said, "So how come a mouse tried living in the couch, Cath? And how would it get in the cabin?"

"Don't know," came a quiet answer. "As for getting in, there's holes all over the place."

"But why wouldn't it live outside somewhere?"

Cathy frowned. "Maybe because to the mouse there's no real difference between this cottage and outside." When my sister seemed puzzled, Cathy muttered, "Oh well, though. Just another nail in the coffin, I suppose." Like her comment about the Vincents, I glanced at her in surprise, and again she quickly recovered and forced out a smile.

That evening, continuing with what she declared was tradition, the three of us stayed up late playing board games at the kitchen table and goofing around outside. Judy and I had fun, but

Cathy was clearly wound up the most. About ten o'clock, after we'd finished playing tag, she suddenly beamed her mile-wide smile at my sister and me. "Okay, so who's up for a skinny dip?" When Judy declared firmly she wasn't swimming in front of me in her bare bum, our host reacted by chasing her around the cottage some more. And so the night went.

About eleven, when Judy's yawn rate was getting high, Cathy conceded to call it a night. My sister and I climbed the ladder to the attic, where the two beds were already made, and about thirty seconds after Judy's head hit the pillow she was asleep. I wasn't so lucky, of course, and wound up sitting by the window and watching fireflies for a while. When I finally climbed into bed it must have been nearly midnight. Cathy was still up at this time; I heard her moving around downstairs. Strangely, I also heard her swear to herself a few times, and the last thing I recalled was the sound of her briskly sweeping the bare cabin floor.

The following sunny morning Cathy had her guests up by seven-thirty. After a quick breakfast she took us for a walk along Cridiford road, the pastime I clearly remembered was her Aunt Jenny's favourite. Without question this was why Cathy proposed the walk, because she mentioned her aunt many times — particular trees Aunt Jenny loved, her favourite sections of the river, and so on. She was especially reflective when we reached the end of the road, and ventured close to a long stretch of rapids.

"These are the May Chutes," she explained, leading us toward the end of the rapids by way of a large, smooth patch of bedrock. This rock would be underwater in the spring, I guessed, but in midsummer the river only thundered down a narrow centre channel.

While preventing Judy from getting too close, Cathy smiled sadly and said, "Aunt Jenny could watch these rapids forever."

I said, "Your aunt loved coming to the cottage as much as you and Andrea, didn't she?"

Cathy nodded. "Uncle Neil too."

"Was that true before they started bringing you and Andrea to Muskoka, though?"

"Heck yes. Their history with this place goes way beyond Andrea and me. They built the cabin in the late thirties, and came to Muskoka regularly."

Kneeling, and out of sheer curiosity tossing a small stick into the chutes, I said, "That time I first saw the cabin, your Aunt Jenny really seemed to enjoy it."

"Well, sure. Aunt Jenny and Uncle Neil were extremely attached to this place, and took a lot of pride in it. Money was tight so they really treasured having a cottage."

"Did they ever get to know Mr. Fox?" I looked up and showed Cathy a devilish grin.

She seemed slightly embarrassed. "Andrea had to tell you about him, didn't she?"

"Who's Mr. Fox, Cath?" Judy asked. "Somebody who lives around here?"

"Yes, Judy, somebody who lives around here, or who did, at least. He was a good friend."

Watching my stick emerge from the chutes, I said, "Too bad, though, another buddy decided to live in your couch."

I intended this as a joke, but when Cathy turned to me she was not laughing. Indeed, for several seconds she looked like she wanted to see how I'd fair in the chutes, and this time not even a forced smile followed.

Since it was hot again we spent most of the afternoon swimming. This included taking turns swinging off a rope attached to a shoreline tree. We took turns, that is, until the rope broke with Cathy aboard. She tried making little of the incident but actually came close to getting seriously hurt, only narrowly missing some sharp rocks. "The place is falling apart!" she weakly joked. Falling apart for sure, and yours truly would soon learn the hard way just how badly.

In late afternoon, while taking a break from swimming, Judy and I tossed a Frisbee around in front of the cabin. Doing this, I should admit, was my idea, because I already knew she couldn't throw a Frisbee worth beans, and it amused me to see her bettered at something. It sure didn't amuse her, however, and she eventually let loose in frustration, firing the Frisbee into the top of a birch tree behind the cabin. Unfortunately — you'll soon learn why — the Frisbee dropped out of the branches and landed on the back side of the cabin roof.

I'd already noticed an old wooden ladder leaning on its side against the cabin's back wall, and after setting it up I daringly climbed the half-rotted rungs. The Frisbee landed near the peak of the roof, and when reaching it I flung it onto the front rock again, warning Judy at the same time not to fire it anywhere else. What happened next, though, is in memory merely a blur. As I turned and started back to the ladder, my right foot suddenly went through the shingles, and just as suddenly I was falling headfirst toward the edge of the roof.

Probably the only reason I'm able to relate this incident to you is that one Neil Stevens, at some point in time, drove a large spike into the back cabin fascia. Later Cathy explained her uncle put it there to hang a big flowerpot. Luckily for me big flowerpots are heavy, because even being old and rusty and sunk into bad wood, the spike still held when I eventually hung upside down from it by my belt buckle.

I reckon the yell I let out gave Carla Morrison's garter snake scream years earlier a run for its money.

Cathy was inside at this time, and from the sound of the side screened door banging open I wasn't sure she didn't break it off its hinges. When I yelled a second time, and she saw me hanging from the edge of the roof, she screamed, "*Lewis! Oh, shit! Shit!*"

My yelling apparently did not go unheard by the neighbours, because only a split second after Cathy's scream I heard someone come crashing through the back woodlot. When this person reached the ladder at about the same time as Cathy, I saw it was a large, nearly bald man, perhaps in his sixties, wearing gray work clothes and tall black rubber boots. He immediately started up the ladder, and the day took another turn for the worse.

As you may guess, the old, half-rotted ladder that supports a thirteen-year-old boy does not necessarily support a large man, and only four rungs up, this large man made this discovery. Down to the ground he went, landing on his back and knocking the wind out of himself. He rolled onto his side, clutching his stomach as he fought to regain his breath.

For a moment I feared Cathy was in the worst state of anyone. She started a bout of nearly psychotic screaming as she knelt beside her neighbour. She didn't know what to do for him and neither did I. Thankfully, within a minute he regained his breath, and after getting to his feet with no apparent injuries, he again studied my predicament. When the Belt-Buckle Hanger said, "Are you okay, sir?" he even cranked out a grin.

Cathy, however, was definitely not grinning. Running to her truck, she yelled, "I'm going for your ladder, Tom!" She spun her tires all the way out of the driveway and was back in several minutes. At last, while Judy asked why retrieving a "stupid Frisbee" was such a big deal, Tom helped me to the ground. Other than countless scratches on my chest and stomach from sliding down the rough shingles, I was thankfully none the worse for wear. My rescuer also recovered, and Cathy invited him to the side deck for a drink. He was Tom Hutchings, the man Andrea mentioned at Cathy's corn roast, the one singing so loud at a cabin corn roast with Cathy's Uncle Neil that the police dropped by.

He was now drinking on this afternoon too, but certainly not singing. After a sip of his Scotch he daringly leaned back in one of the old cottage lawn chairs and said, "This, by the way, wasn't what I intended to do today."

"I'm so sorry!" Cathy said. "That stupid bloody ladder! And the roof and poor Lewis — that fall must have scared you half to death!"

"I'm used to stuff like that," I said coolly, lying my rear end off. Truth was, I probably could have downed a Scotch myself on this day. My fib did seem to soothe Cathy somewhat, though, and she walked well back of the cabin to study the hole in the roof.

"She's a doozy," Tom informed her, keeping his puffy eyes lovingly on his beverage. "I got a look at it while I was up on the ladder. A rafter must have broken for a hole that wide, not just sheathing. You'd be wise to patch it up soon, too — I've got a small tarp at our place I can lend you. I think it's supposed to stay clear for the weekend, but who knows after that. We're due for some rain."

Nodding at this, Cathy said, "It's amazing Lewis didn't fall right into the attic."

"Hundred to one would have been better off."

"Think the whole roof is rotted, Tom?"

"Hundred to one too, and I believe I can tell you why."

Cathy returned to the deck. "Okay."

Tom motioned to the birch behind the cabin. "The roof's way too shaded at the back. You were only asking for problems. Should've brought that tree down years ago."

Cathy's eyes lit up. "But Aunt Jenny loved that birch! No way I'd have ever cut it down!"

"Yes, I realize Jenny loved it. I was present when she and Neil started work on the cabin footings, and made the decision to leave the birch standing. Jenny said, 'Well, we certainly can't cut down that beautiful little birch'. I argued she should drop the tree before it became a beautiful big birch, but she wouldn't listen. 'We're not here to wreck the woods', she said. But I think today, Cathy, I can safely declare I was right. That tree only brought your aunt, and now you, grief."

She replied to this with a noticeably angry tone. "I know that, Tom, and it seems a lot of things around this cottage I let have their way have begun bringing me grief. There's not much point, though, in me spanking myself for it at this stage, is there?"

"No, I suppose not," Tom said quietly, seeming to regret coming across so strong. When Cathy went inside, probably to check the attic, he shrugged. "Only tried to tell her ... what was what. My real mistake, maybe, was not telling her years ago."

That evening Cathy and I grabbed several chairs off the deck and sat out on the front rock. Judy was not with us; she was completely exhausted from so much swimming, both on this day and all week, and our host pushed her into bed soon after supper.

The Walshes were coming to visit from Scarborough the following Friday, and Jack Walsh, you may remember, was Judy's old swimming instructor. So my sister had naturally been practising up the last week so she could impress him.

After explaining this to Cathy she began by saying, "Andrea and I loved swimming almost as much," and continued with stories of sneaking out of the cabin at night to go skinny-dipping. These she followed with many others about her aunt and uncle's cottage adventures, and several hours passed quickly. The occasion reminded me of her corn roast years back, and my first trip to the cabin, when she laughed and cried with her aunt and sister for hours at a time.

It was ten o'clock, and completely dark, when she ran out of steam and went inside to get drinks. While she was gone I noticed there were few stars visible in the sky, and becoming unsure of Tom Hutchings' forecast of clear weather, when Cathy returned I asked about the roof. Little did I realize I would soon receive a bomb.

"So when do you think you'll be able to fix the hole I made? I can help, you know."

"First off — it obviously wasn't your fault. Second, fixing it doesn't much matter now. I called Rick a while ago and he's coming tomorrow to patch it up for me, but he won't be doing anything major."

"How come? Do you have to wait till you have more money?"

"No ... it's not because of that." Cathy paused, gazing at the moth-covered front cabin light, before quietly saying, "It's because Andrea and I have sold this place, Lewis."

I quickly turned. "Sold it?"

"To a couple from Guelph."

"But ... how come?"

"Didn't really have any choice. The cottage is done. That damp musty smell in there isn't just from dead animals and the roof leaking — the whole place is rotting away. Too, even if I had the money to build something new, it simply wouldn't be the same here." Staring sullenly back at the cottage, Cathy added, "If you're wondering, the night I stayed behind at Lyall Rock to talk to Marie? That was to give her the news the cottage had sold, and to thank her for all the lumber and other stuff she'd given me. She really tried to help me save this place, but ... it was hopeless."

With these words her eyes blazed, and instantly reminded me of a day years earlier. When my brother and I first spied Cathy, you may recall, she was crying, and soon viciously fired a hammer into her lumber-laden pickup before heading down the Fraserburg road. The problem with her Aunt's cabin was far from being a new one.

I dared to ask, "What about Andrea, though? What did she think about all this?"

"Oh, she was resigned to it as well. She knew selling this place was inevitable. She wanted to keep it as much as I did, but also knew there was no way. Even if she'd paid to have the cabin rebuilt — which she offered to do — the place, like I said, simply wouldn't be the same. It wouldn't be Aunt Jenny and Uncle Neil's little treasure anymore. It'd just be a small cottage like any other."

"Do you think your Aun—?" I stopped myself.

Cathy turned to me. "Do I think Aunt Jenny would mind my selling? Is that what you were going to ask?"

I nodded, looking down at the dark bedrock.

"I think she saw this coming, Lewis. Actually, I'm sure of it. That final time Andrea and I brought her here — after my corn roast — we tried to gloss things over. But Aunt Jenny could see the cottage was in sad shape. It also really hurt us watching her look the place over, and watching her almost break through that old picnic table seat. After all the good years she and Uncle Neil had at this place ... " Cathy stared at me. "I think her knowing what was in store for the cottage was why she encouraged me to have you kids out for a weekend sometime. She saw it as a chance for me to have one last hurrah; to relive old times."

This last part I should have seen coming, of course. The way Cathy had insisted on keeping to traditions the whole weekend, I should have seen what she was trying to do.

Quietly I asked, "Are you losing the cottage soon, Cath?"

"Next Wednesday." With a very sad smile and wiping a tear from her cheek, she added, softly, "But I've had a great time this weekend, Lewis — this has been special for me — and I really want to thank you and Judy for that."

The next morning I woke to the sound of an alarm clock ringing below me. I listened close to half a minute before deciding Cathy must be outside and unable to hear it. Glancing out the attic's gable window, and seeing it was barely dawn, I found it odd she would be up and out already. Another Carla Morrison she was not.

I climbed down the ladder and silenced a small travel alarm in the main bedroom, where Cathy had slept. It was set for 6:00 a.m. — early enough, I thought, but she had apparently risen on her own even earlier. I went to the front window to see if I could spot her, and after pulling back one of the drapes I soon did. She was sitting on an old bench swing down by the still misty river. She had her back to me, but as she gently rocked on the swing I saw her bring a hand to her eyes several times. I considered going out to her but didn't, and when I later 'woke up' she was back in the cabin, and I didn't say a word about seeing her.

Rick arrived a touch after eleven that morning. He had some roof sheathing and several bundles of shingles in his truck, and I helped him carry these materials to the back of the cottage. We set up an aluminum ladder he also brought, and I followed him up onto the roof. This I did nervously, mind you.

Removing Tom Hutchings' small tarp and beginning a study of the huge hole I'd made, Rick spoke to me quietly, and with a hint of anger in his voice. I'd already noticed while moving the lumber and shingles he was somewhat irritable.

"How's Cathy been this weekend?"

"Not so good," I whispered. "She tried to seem cheery, but I don't think she really was. And this morning she's been pretty quiet — she and Judy have just been packing stuff up inside."

Cathy's boyfriend only sighed, continuing to peer into the hole at the rotted rafters.

I said, "So Cathy really had to sell this place?"

"'Fraid so, Lewis." Rick currently had his scruffy, brown-haired head right inside the hole.

"There's nothing you can do?"

"Nope. It's way beyond fixing up. Cathy worked a heap of extra hours at the bakery the last while thinking she'd fight it, but in the end she realized there was no point. Even if rich Andrea gave her some money it wouldn't have made any difference."

"The people who bought the cabin will try fixing it up, though — right?"

Rick tore off a few of the broken shingles and tossed them off the roof. "I seriously doubt that. I'm sure these people bought the place only for the property. They'll rip the cabin down and put up something new."

"Does Cathy realize the new owners will do that?"

"She knows."

"But ... why did this place get so run down? Because Aunt Jenny didn't have much money?"

"That was part of it. If you ask me, though, the main problem was the whole cottage gang being too damn determined to let things have their own way." Rick motioned to the birch behind us, the one Tom Hutchings had pointed out was shading the roof too much. "Stuff like that. I don't like killing trees any more than they do, but if one was ruining my place I sure as hell would. Same for the mice wrecking things inside, and the porcupine that's been crawling under the cabin and slowly eating the goddamn floor away. I'd fix that prick soon enough."

"Eating the floor?!"

"Sure — they love plywood." Rick headed for the ladder. "The bottom line, Lewis, is that there's a downside to all this freedom business, and Cathy's found that out the hard way. If you set up shop in the middle of the woods, like Aunt Jenny and Uncle Neil did at this spot, and then don't hold the woods back, they'll creep in on you. Sure as shit they will. And a wrecked cabin is what you'll end up with."

We left the cottage about four that afternoon. By this time I'd helped Rick mend the hole in the roof, and since he then had to meet his boss in town, only Judy and I remained with Cathy. Along with our weekend things we helped her carry a small end table and several boxes filled with dishes, pictures, and ornaments to the truck. "I'm coming back tomorrow to get the rest of the stuff," she explained. Later, however, while my sister and I waited in the truck, she went down to the river, insisting she needed to get one last thing. I eventually saw it was a light sweater she'd left on the bench swing early that morning, a small blue one Aunt Jenny once knitted for her. Before returning, an older Cathy gazed across the river a minute, studying the place that so long ago gave her a sense of freedom, and which she sacrificed her family's fortune to live near. I now understood, though, she was also studying the place whose very wildness broke her heart. And when she started back to the truck, the face I saw did not clearly bear a celebrative, mile-wide smile, nor clearly a tearful look of anger. What I saw was something oddly in between — a look suggesting she wasn't sure what in the world to feel.

36

The Walshes arrived about eleven the following sunny Saturday morning. Grandma Layton was first to greet them in the driveway, and proceeded to treat silver-haired, fancily-dressed Rita Walsh like she'd journeyed to the roughest place on earth. "Poor thing! You must be completely exhausted!" she said soothingly while leading Rita directly inside. Lunch proved the most formal affair she'd yet staged at our new residence, with all her fanciest dishes and cutlery making an appearance. After, she continued with the formalities, displaying her flower garden, then having Judy do several dance routines in the living room. She and Rita sat prim and proper with their tea while my sister performed, and naturally, waving about was the infamous dance finger.

As embarrassing a show of rural refinement this may have been, the show that followed outdid it. No sooner had Judy finished her last dance than she was tugging at her former swimming instructor's arm to go for a dip. And no sooner had she, Jack Walsh, and I arrived at Lyall Rock than she was requesting praise for swimming skills. "How about *this*, Mr. Walsh?" she said while sidestroking, and later, after butterflying, "That's *way* better than before — right Mr. Walsh?" This went on close to an hour, and an hour too long as far as I was concerned. It was times like this I wanted to disclaim any relation to my sister.

Luckily both Jack and I were saved by my mother. She appeared carrying a plastic jug and cups, and seemingly knowing in advance the show taking place, beckoned Judy to take a break. We all sat on the bedrock, catching shade from the big centre pine.

"I got tired of listening to it," my mother said after Jack inquired about her unexpected visit. "Bringing drinks here was my excuse."

Jack smiled. "They're really carrying on, are they?"

"Oh, God — it's awful. Mother's well on her way to convincing Rita she's paying for a lifetime of sins."

Grinning, Jack nodded, then quickly downed an apple juice. My mother said, "Someone around here wearing you out, by chance, Jack?"

Still smiling, he smoothed what little gray hair he had left while glancing at Judy. "Not entirely her fault — I do believe I'm getting out of shape. Don't get to the pool very often these days."

"Do much diving in the Bahamas last winter?"

"Some. But not as much as I used to. I'm not getting any younger, my dear."

Referring to Jack's long-time promise, Judy said, "But you're still gonna teach me how to scuba, though — right, Mr. Walsh?"

"Of course, sweetie. Maybe Lewis will want to learn too. There's lots to explore in the ocean, and it's amazing the things you discover. I can tell you this — every time I dive I see something I've never seen before."

To this Judy declared, through what I hoped was only temporary insanity, "I had a dream one time about swimming to the bottom of the ocean. And maybe if I get so I can swim as good as a fish, I could!"

While I snorted in disgust Jack showed my sister a quizzical grin, apparently not having learned her Muskoka-grown goal in life. Delicately he said, "That ... might be a tad ambitious, sweetie."

Judy glared at him. "But you said I'm getting better ..."

Mother drew her into her arms and stroked her long brown hair — hair, I should add, no longer in a ponytail. Soon after reaching the ripe old age of seven the previous winter my sister declared ponytails a "little girl thing." This change was one of many she'd decided upon recently, all part of a new 'big girl' image. She'd begun marking her height each week on an old wall ruler, for instance, and competitive as always, never failed to point out her marks were higher than mine at age seven. She was, that is, becoming more of a pain than ever.

Holding her, my mother said, “Mr. Walsh isn’t teasing, Judy. He simply doesn’t want you getting your hopes up about things that can’t happen. We used to let you dream like this, but maybe now you need to start ... accepting a few things.”

I’d heard enough niceties. “You need to *wake up*, is what she’s saying, idiot.”

While Mother gave me the expected stern look, Jack said softly, “I know you’re keen to do all this stuff, Judy, but you have to accept there’s places in lakes and oceans you simply can’t go — not without equipment, at least. Only fish and a few other kinds of animals can. You’re not one of those, and can’t ever be, I’m afraid.”

I simply couldn’t resist adding to this; as cruel as it sounds, I relished seeing my sister in rare defeat. I also remembered two summer days of bedroom confinement several years earlier because of this same dispute. Waiting until I’d caught her eye, I said, very smartly, “Toldyuh.”

This hit the mark.

Judy jumped to her feet, stomped over, and screamed, “Blow it out your bum, Grumpface!”

“Judith Ann Farrow!” Mother cried. “Don’t you talk —!”

“You think I care if some stupid fish is better’n me? I don’t ... give a *shit* what some stupid fish can do!”

Unlike Grandma Layton my mother didn’t have dentures to fall out, but she certainly had the same disciplinary voice.

“You’re going home right away, missy! How *dare* you talk like that, especially in front of company! March!”

And so ended the swimming portion of that day’s program. Did I feel guilty? Yes, I’d prompted Judy’s outburst, and yes, I believe she mimicked my own at Lyall Rock the autumn after Sean’s death. Nonetheless, I confess to snickering my way home on this afternoon. I felt it high time she lost at something, and clearly she would never be able to swim as well as a fish, despite all efforts. My painfully competitive sister had, at last, met her match.

Or so it seemed.

As I expected, Grandma Layton turned supper that evening into a formal affair similar to lunch. After this meal she continued trying to impress Rita, and forced me, my mother, and a quietly stewing sister to sit with them in the living room. Soon, however, I copied my mother's tactic and took drinks to the back deck. There my father was talking with Jack, as he'd been doing almost nonstop since arriving home from work.

Jack Walsh not only taught my sister how to swim during our time in Scarborough, but also became good friends with my father. He'd lived and worked in many parts of Toronto and knew the city well. On numerous occasions he'd taken my father, along with various combinations of our family's other members, on excursions. Although I felt Dad only went on these outings out of politeness, I thoroughly enjoyed them. One memorable occasion was an evening Jack took my father and me to the roof of the office building he worked in, and we spent an hour gazing at the city lights. He and my father talked about how many people's lives depended on this place, how many important decisions were made here, how it often served as a representative for the country. Through this and subsequent talks I felt Jack did my father a great service. He helped Dad adjust to a place he had little experience with, and more, kept up his spirits. He'd only left Muskoka, of course, for lack of steady work, and I was certain his heart remained there.

So I was not surprised when delivering drinks to find my father talking with Jack about the city. Although Dad obviously no longer required his 'adjustment' services, the city was virtually the only topic these two had ever spoken about, and I supposed they continued out of sheer habit.

"You should've seen it!" I heard Jack howl as I stepped onto the back deck. "A dorky little guy running around in a tutu!"

"This was right downtown?"

Jacked nodded. "Near the Eaton Centre. But that's Friday night on Yonge for you, though — right? Anything that can happen, will happen. Simply give it time."

My father said, "Hey — as I see it Toronto's a place you can be whoever you are without shame. I argue it's one of the many things that sets it apart from smaller towns."

"I suppose." Jack turned to me and accepted his drink. "Your Dad's been hounding me about my latest adventures downtown."

Taking his own drink Dad said, "Just wanting to keep in touch. Nothing wrong with that."

Jack smirked. "Keep in touch? When *were* you in touch?"

"I ... had a handle on things in the city!"

"You didn't strike me as in touch at our party, Mr. Farrow."

Dad glared at Jack. "That was no big deal. Why make a big —?"

"What's this?" I broke in.

Jack stared at my father. "What? You didn't tell him?"

Dad frowned and shrugged. "What's there to tell?"

I said to Jack, "Didn't tell me what, Mr. Walsh?"

"Your Dad gave us quite a laugh at the anniversary party a few weeks ago. Very late in the evening — or very early in the morning may be more accurate — your father, gentleman that he is, offered to walk home an older couple we had over. They only live one block south and two blocks west of us, but on the way back it seems your old man became a little disoriented."

"I didn't get lost," Dad defended. "I just got ... a little tired."

"Sure!" Jack chortled before turning back to me. "He was feeling pretty jolly by this time, you see, and couldn't focus too well. He did make it to the Lord Roberts Woods, though, and that's exactly where we found him, fast asleep."

My father again shrugged. "Nothin' wrong with that."

"You're damn lucky we found you. When Val and I were out looking I only went in those woods because I needed a pee. As a matter of fact, you almost got watered."

Dad's eyes lit up. "So what was I supposed to do? I figured I'd just wait it out till dawn!"

"I believe anybody else would have freaked and flagged down a car or knocked on a door or something, Bruce."

"At three in the morning? Who the hell would stop their car

or open their front door? I wouldn't!"

Jack laughed heartily. "Sound asleep in a little bloody patch of woods in the middle of a big city. Only you, Bruce. Only you would do that."

"There was no problem! I'd have been back in time for breakfast!"

"Oh, you're a country boy if there ever was one," Jack said, continuing to chuckle as he looked toward the back woods. "Your home is most definitely Muskoka. This is where you're in touch, Bruce; this is where you belong."

The Walshes left about eight that evening. Better put, they *tried* to leave at eight. Grandma Layton was the culprit, standing in the driveway gabbing with Rita a good twenty minutes. By the way she talked you'd think she was being left for the wolves. Finally my mother dragged her away, and several toots of the horn later the Walshes were gone.

I found our house especially quiet that evening. Usually my father would goof around with the rest of the family to ease the emptiness a house takes on after company leaves. On this evening, however, he sat in the Muskoka room and gazed off into space. It was my mother who livened things up by challenging Dad and me to a game of Monopoly at the kitchen table. This was a game she normally didn't care for, but for reasons unknown to me, on this night she insisted we play.

Now it was about eleven o'clock, right after Mother bankrupted us, that my sister made a surprise appearance. She'd walked so softly down the stairs none of us heard her. In her hand was a large Bristol board picture, and when she entered the kitchen I could see it was the one she'd made during our first week in Muskoka. This was the picture, you may remember, depicting the lake setting: our floating red house with triangular windows and rooftop bus, Z-shaped black grass with giant chickens, an orange lake with floating candy canes, and lastly, those wonderful flagpoles with bushes around them. The family had declared it one of Judy's all-time classic works, and she'd taken it to heart.

Knowing she was still very uptight about the day's events, I assumed she was merely acting up, convinced that displaying her masterpiece justified her being up late. I said, "That's pretty lame, Jude."

She pretended not to hear me, though, and continued into the porch. It was after she plopped herself down on the floor and started putting on her shoes that I realized what was really going on. Her eyes were distant and she seemed to look right through everything. Also, the porch windows were open to the screens, allowing in cool air, and although wearing only light pyjamas she seemed totally unbothered.

The Midnight Muffin-Maker, in short, was at it again.

I had no idea where the baker intended on going, but before she even had one shoe on my mother was pulling it off. "No, no, dear."

My sister muttered something I couldn't make out and resumed trying to put on her shoe, but Mother again stopped her.

"No!" Judy grumbled, trying to slide away.

"You can show your picture to the fish tomorrow," Mother said softly. She then managed to get my sister back on her feet and to steer her upstairs, the great masterpiece left lying on the porch floor.

"Show her picture to the fish?!" I said to Dad, but he only answered, "Who knows?"

Soon after this, when I'd finished helping my father put away the game, he sent me up to bed. When I reached the top of the stairs I crept over to Judy's door. She was back in bed, her light off, and my mother was sitting beside her, gently stroking her hair.

Mother glanced at me as I poked my head in the doorway. I said, "Why —?"

"Shhh. Not so loud."

I whispered, "Why would she want to show one of her drawings to some fish? Fish can't make or understand pictures — especially wacky ones like hers."

My mother slowly turned to me. "I believe, Lewis, that's the idea," and she then resumed stroking Judy's hair.

37

Kneeling and stroking a chin that had remained beardless, Ed Russell picked up a fist-sized rock lying near the shore of the lake, close to his old dock. He remained silent and I watched as he slowly turned the rock over several times in his rugged hand, studying it closely with a puzzled expression. At last he returned it to the exact spot he found it and looked up. Shaking his head, he said, "Just a stupid rock, Lewis. Nothing but a stupid goddamn rock."

We'd been through a peculiar day on this final Sunday of July. It effectively began when the Russells made a surprise visit about two in the afternoon. My sister sounded the alarm, spotting the distinctive 'Midnight Blue' pulling into the Morrisons' driveway, and seconds later Carla phoned and invited our family. She also called everyone else on the lake, and within a half-hour all had arrived. "The tourists have come home!" Cathy declared, waving a bottle of the Russells' favourite wine she'd been saving. And so the party began.

The first several hours of this afternoon were chaotic but pleasant. Our woodsy former neighbours told countless stories and jokes, and displayed several dozen postcard-like photographs Ed had taken. These included views of a house in British Columbia they'd bought — a tidy bungalow nestled amongst young evergreens — and of a lush mountain valley a short drive away. Unlike on previous occasions of looking at their photos, this time they were happy to describe them at length, Laura fighting a lingering cough from a recent summer cold. They even let me practice my trade dozens of times. How high is that mountain? What kinds of fish are in that river? What species of tree is that? And so on. Answers, however, were often disappointing; neither Laura nor Ed seemed sure sometimes what to tell me, and on several occasions they even mildly argued with one another. Certainly they'd never have hesitated explaining anything around Gordonier Lake, and Cathy and Carla were quick to point this out. They resumed making their usual remarks about where the Russells truly belonged. And, like at their 25th anniversary corn roast several years earlier, I once again noticed sour looks from both Ed and Laura.

By four o'clock most of the crowd had adjourned to the shore of the lake, sitting in a long row of lawn chairs. Carla, Cathy, and Laura remained chatting in the kitchen, however, starting to work on supper, and they commissioned me to slice salad vegetables. It was about a half-hour into these preparations that Carla made what proved the final and most fateful tease of the day. While Cathy chuckled, Carla said to Laura, "So — have you asked Owen yet about renting a room?"

I expected Laura to merely utter some short, sarcastic rebuttal, but instead she lost her cool altogether. Unlike the 25th anniversary corn roast, when she'd let off steam with my mother, she now had it out with Carla and Cathy face to face.

After a short cough, she croaked, "Yes, that's very funny, Carla. Very funny! Now why don't you stroll outside and take a frickin' leap into your pickerelweeds."

Carla spun around, a shocked look on her face. "What the hell's with you? I was only joking!"

"Of course you are! But you two go on and on. What makes you so damn sure Eddie and I are unhappy out west? Have you been out west with us?"

Cathy said, "Laura, we —"

"Have you two seen how things have been going? No, you haven't. You haven't, so ... just shut your mouths, for once!"

Carla's eyes bulged. "Don't you tell me to shut up in my own cottage. What the hell do you think —?"

"What's going on?" This came from Ed as he opened the front screened door. "Something wrong, Laura?"

"The usual bullshit is what's going on!" his wife answered, on her way to the bathroom.

After she slammed the door Ed quickly said, "She's only tired, Carla. We've had some long days of driving. Maybe we should have come back across the country at a slower pace. We hurried a bit, I think."

"You can bloody well hurry right back if you're going to be belligerent! I won't be talked to that way in my own cottage. I was only joking!"

"I know, I know," Ed said soothingly. "I'm sorry, and I'm sure Laura will be too when she settles down."

"I'm starting to get the message why you two left, at least," Carla continued, turning her back on Ed. To Cathy she said, smartly, "Amazing they condescended to bless us with a visit!"

Ed moaned. "Carla!"

"Maybe you live way up on a hill most of your life and you start looking down on other people in more ways than one."

"That's not the slightest bit true and you know it!" Ed said with a hushed voice. "Laura's only ... tired. Trust me — she'll be good and sorry when she cools down. You'll see."

"Damn well better be!" Carla muttered harshly. She then fired potatoes into a pot of water so hard she splashed the entire stove.

Oddly, but right in line with how this day was going, by the time supper hit the table Laura was on speaking terms again with Cathy and Carla. Predictably, though, fight wounds were far from healed. Like Grandma Layton and Marie Taylor were when they had their winter dispute years back, the three women were excessively polite with one another. The way Laura went on about the supper Carla cooked you'd think the Farrow family lived beside Canada's finest chef. But with a non-hostile atmosphere restored, at least, after supper Grandma Layton and Marie Taylor played board games with Judy in the kitchen while others played cards at the Morrisons' big (and garter snake-free) living room table. This crowd did not include everyone, however; as usual Ed wore his emotions on his sleeve, and invited me on a walk with him around the lake to "get some air."

During the first half of this walk he was his usual quiet self when hiking. Totally unlike past occasions, though, such as when he took Sean, Judy, and me raspberry picking, he paid a great deal of attention to everything around him. He became, seemingly, the Ed Russell in the old camping and hiking pictures I'd viewed years ago. Some jewelweeds between the Morrisons' and his old dock received several minutes close inspection, and a set of small racoon tracks occupied his attention nearly three. "Probably a young one of the pair living behind our old place," he whispered. He did all this studying in apparent puzzlement, however, and even sometimes anger. It was when we neared his old dock that he stopped to look at a certain small rock I've already mentioned. So strange was his mood that I didn't say a word, but merely followed behind him as he took his peculiar lakeside walk.

When we reached Lyall Rock we seated ourselves underneath the large central pine. The lake was now completely still and shiny, and for a few minutes we both gazed silently at the water and dimly-lit woods. Like during the walk, Ed was especially attentive, and hardly a ripple in the water or rustling in the woods escaped his notice.

By this time his anger, if not his puzzlement, seemed to have dissolved, so I dared to ask about the afternoon's events. Since their son, 'Jermany Jimmy', was flying into Toronto from Munich on Tuesday, the Russells were only staying at the lake until Monday evening. I therefore worried they wouldn't have enough time to patch up strained friendships.

"We're just a little on the stressed out side, Lewis. I'm sure everything will be fine between Laura and Carla — Cathy too."

"But Mrs. Russell almost went through the roof! I've never seen her that mad before!"

"Yes — I realize. But things will smooth over nonetheless.

Cathy and Carla teasing us about belonging at this lake is nothing new, of course. Laura's only especially upset right now because of something she can't bring herself to admit to the two bloody teasers."

"And what's that?"

Ed frowned. "That they're right."

"They're right?" I did my best not to shout. "But you told me you and Mrs. Russell were bored stiff of this place!"

"I did, and we still are. What we didn't expect, though, is to miss the lake anyway — and all the woods, and ... that stupid goddamn rock back there."

"You miss all that stuff?"

"I'm painfully afraid so."

"But there're tons of lakes and woods in British Columbia! All those pictures you brought ...!"

Ed looked at me. "Yeah, Lewis, there are — but not *this* lake, and *these* woods."

"What's the heck's the difference?"

Looking up and studying the darkening crown of the big pine at our backs, Ed said, "The difference is things simply don't feel the same out west. Laura and I have settled into the new house fine, and the area we're in has been interesting, but ... we simply don't feel the same. We don't feel the same connection to things out west that we do at this lake. Not knowing the area well is part of it — I'm sure you noticed how crappy our answers were to your photo questions earlier." Reaching into the long grass beside him, he picked up and studied a feather from the lake's great blue heron, a bird he could have given me a book's worth of answers about. "You know, it's funny. Those photo albums you and Cathy brought out at that corn roast a few years back? Laura and I hadn't looked at those in probably fifteen years. I bet, though, we've looked at them fifteen times just since we left this lake. It's like this spot, without our realizing it, became ... part of our family."

I said, "Don't you think you'll end up feeling that way about where you're living out west, though?"

"Eventually we would, I suppose. But I don't think the kind of feeling I'm talking about — the one we have toward this place — is the kind you get after a few days or a few months. I'm sure it would take years and years of living out west to develop the bond we have with this lake. It might take another lifetime, actually, and we don't happen to have another one handy."

Capping this unusual day, I asked a fittingly bizarre question, one I thought I'd never hear myself ask the obsessively west-bound Ed or Laura Russell. Carefully, feeling there'd been enough fighting for one day, I said, "So ... are you saying ... you and Mrs. Russell are sorry you moved out west?"

Ed watched a beaver cruise the south side of the end bay. Running his fingers through tangled dark hair, he quietly said, "Oh, I wouldn't say we're sorry. We've learned some things, and we're staying out west for the time being. It's depressing, though, and damn frustrating — as I think you've seen with Laura. She's been very edgy lately and sick with a cold half the summer. After all the years dreaming about getting away from this place ..." He rose and looked sadly toward his old hilltop house. "My mother once told me that when you get bored of a place, it sometimes means that place has become part of you, and I think I know now what she meant." Turning to me, he added, "Cathy and Carla may only be up to their usual teasing when they call us tourists, Lewis, but really — they're right. They're goddamn right. That's exactly what we are out west, and exactly what we'd be anywhere except Gordonier Lake."

38

After breakfast the following morning I went into town with Owen. He wanted some lumber for a firewood box, our next project, and had other assorted errands. As usual he needed me so he could "be more efficient about it." The previous summer my father offered an explanation. "Old-style farmers like him didn't go to town often, Lewis, and when they did the trip was strictly business. No farting around — go in, grab what you need, and get the hell back to work."

So, I wasn't surprised when we finished our town errands and returned home by nine-thirty. The surprise followed. Unloading the truck we heard strange sounds from behind the house — short huffs. I guessed a doe, the sounds much like those we'd heard during our first waterfall hike. Owen evidently guessed the same, because after pressing his finger to his lips, he drew in the air the shape of a deer.

Slowly creeping to the house, we poked our heads around the corner. Our suspicions were confirmed.

It was a doe all right: Laura Russell.

She was kneeling in the woods closely examining a pine sapling, the same way her husband had studied things the previous evening. The strange sounds were coughs from her summer cold. And when spotting the two heads she made another sound: a loud "Oh!" as she fell backward into some brush.

After we helped her up and recovered her glasses, she said very casually, "You're back already! That was ... fast! I was just ... you know ... out for a walk. Gorgeous morning, don't you think?"

Owen let her squirm, then uttered his trademark welcome. "Drop in anytime, Laura."

What followed were more excuses for her presence, but these Owen ignored and Laura finally moved on. Scanning the house and yard, she said, "I see you've got the place looking pretty smart."

"Not much choice; I've a daughter to impress."

"Yes, so I heard. Must be an awful pile of work, though. This lawn especially — isn't it miserable?"

Owen nodded, a suspicious look forming. "Lewis here has been helping, though, so I'm managing."

"That's so nice of him to do that, isn't it? Very nice of him."

Owen eyeballed Laura. "And since I'm managing, I'm stayin'."

"Of course you are. I mean, why not?" She turned away and moved to the edge of the lawn, much like an actor in a play, I thought. Solemnly — perhaps too solemnly — she said, "Must feel weird, though, living in one place like that for so long, then moving away. How long were you at the farm?"

Tiredly, Owen answered, "Most of seventy years."

"Seventy years! My God! I can't even imagine." Laura turned back to Owen. Delicately she said, "You don't miss it?"

"Wouldn't matter if I did. Had no choice but to sell — couldn't keep the place up."

"Oh, that's right! I'm so sorry! And naturally there'd be no way around that. Mind you, if —"

"Like I said," Owen broke in firmly, "I'm stayin'."

"I wasn't implying you weren't! I wouldn't think like *that*. No siree."

Owen started toward the house. "Why don't you come in for coffee, Laura. You're wearing me out."

In a whisper came, "So I'm getting somewhere, then."

Owen spun around. "What's that?"

"She said coffee would be very nice," I answered, and without even glancing at Laura, led her into her old house.

While Owen made coffee his surprise guest quietly wandered about his living room, seemingly caught between not wanting to be nosy and needing to be. Occasionally I saw her sneaking glances into the back rooms, and after making sure the new owner wasn't watching, she even straightened on the wall a framed landscape photo Ed had abandoned. Almost all the furnishings, you may remember, the Russells included in the sale — another measure they'd taken in making a wholesale lifestyle change. So the house interior Laura saw on this day was little changed from the one she'd left. I supposed this made it easy for her to imagine, too, she never had. But although watching her gaze lovingly at her old belongings made me sympathetic, when she began gazing lovingly out the large front window I felt extremely sorry for her. Unlike with Ed the night before, when I'd seen puzzlement and anger, all I saw on Laura's face was puzzlement and sadness.

When she took a seat at the kitchen table Owen poured coffee, and a smile slowly appeared on her lean, tomboyish face. It was the same crazy-eyed smile I'd witnessed all through breakfast, which she, Ed, and the Morrisons had at our place. I quickly surmised, considering Ed's comments the night before, that his wife's giddy mood was simply an attempt to hide stress and depression, something she'd obviously failed at the previous afternoon. I think everyone else present, even without Ed's comments, somehow surmised this too, and all seemed to silently agree to let Laura be as silly as she pleased. Sadly, her mood would produce an unfortunate incident.

Along with being downright hyper-active, scurrying about our kitchen and generally getting in Grandma Layton's way, Laura talked nonstop. Mostly she spoke of old times at the lake, stories dating from when she and Ed built their place. But eventually they became recent.

Laura mentioned tobogganing with my brother one January afternoon. I was not present — only Judy was with Sean — so what she said was also new to me. She described how Sean had coaxed her onto his toboggan, and the two had veered off course partway down the hill. When plunging into the side bank both went ass over tea-kettle. "And while I shook snow out of my hair," Laura capped her story, "Sean, the brush cut little rascal, laughed his bloomin' head off!"

My mother did her best to take the story in stride, but soon I saw her blowing her nose in the bathroom and I knew it had taken a toll. She was also especially quiet by the time she headed off to work with my father. And although Laura may not have witnessed the short bathroom cry, she did notice my mother's quietness. I know this because after my parents stepped out, she had her own little bathroom cry.

Peering out Owen's side kitchen window, she said, "God, I'm so sorry about breakfast, Lewis. I got so wound up I never considered I might be upsetting people by mentioning your brother. I feel like such a bloody dope."

Knowing by "people" she truly meant my mother, after glancing at Owen I lied and said, "You don't have to worry, Mrs. Russell. Mom's pretty tough about him these days."

"I sure miss that little guy." Laura removed her glasses and wiped a tear under her eye. "Sean was darn good company, Owen. He was a good boy."

"He really liked you too," I offered softly, and truthfully. "Mr. Russell as well."

This seemed to comfort Laura, and with wet eyes but a giddy smile again she said, "I suppose it wouldn't hurt to tell you another story — your brother and I, Lewis, had some nice afternoons in this kitchen together."

"Some nice afternoons?"

"Sean used to visit sometimes — mostly Saturdays, and during the week in January he had the chickenpox — to watch birds come to our feeder."

I stared at Laura, hardly believing my ears. "Watch birds? Sean never said anything about that!"

"Yes, I know he didn't. He said he always gave you some excuse why he wanted to visit me — such as my needing help with something. He said he wanted to keep his bird watching a secret from you, and insisted I not, as he put it, 'blab'. I had a hard time not telling you when I looked at his picture after his funeral, the one showing him in that lookout tree. But somehow it seemed too soon, too much like betraying him. I feel now, though, he wouldn't mind me 'blabbing'. When you hear about your brother, I think you should be proud of him."

Stuck on another issue, I said, "Sean was terrible at keeping secrets, though! He was the one always blabbing things he wasn't supposed to — especially to me."

"Well, this was one secret he apparently did keep."

"But why?"

Laura showed me a long face. "I didn't know why at the time, and he wouldn't say, but I now think he was ashamed to tell you."

"Ashamed? I saw him watching birds all the time in the city!"

"I know, but that was before he became afraid of the woods, and his big brother became aware he was afraid. I think he felt you'd be ashamed of him if he told you he came to my place to watch birds. Probably felt you'd call him a sissy."

Lying, I said, "I wouldna done that!"

"I didn't think you would either, but silent is the way Sean wanted me, so I obliged."

"And you knew Sean was scared, too?"

"Not when we lived at the lake. Ed kept his promise to your mother not to tell anyone about your brother's fear, but after we moved he saw no harm in telling me. I wasn't particularly surprised. As Ed mentioned he told you, we had a nephew of his — Gordie — develop the same problem one summer at the lake. The woods were a bit much for him too." Laura turned to Owen, "Speaking of the feeder, did you not see it in the shed, or not feel like putting it up?"

Owen shrugged. "Bird feeder?"

"We left it on the top shelf. In it there's even a coffee can with some birdseed. I'm amazed you didn't notice."

"Never looked up there, and we filled the shed with my old tools pretty quick."

I broke in. "But ... I thought Sean stopped liking birds, Mrs. Russell. He never seemed to pay any attention to them when we went exploring around this lake, or around the cabin."

Laura nodded. "I think he did lose interest in them for a while. When he became scared his fear likely overwhelmed any other feelings. But then one cold day in December when he delivered a Christmas card for your mother, I sat him down at this kitchen table to warm up. And only a few seconds later a bird landed at the feeder — it hung from the railing post in front of this side kitchen window. All the rest, as they say, is history. He watched birds come to the feeder for close to an hour that day. I eventually phoned your place and told your father Sean decided to visit longer, and longer was the proper word. I had to pick Ed up from the studio in town and damn near had to push your brother out the door. He also took offence at my doing that; he seemed to think I didn't care about what already were *his* birds. As he followed me to the driveway he told me how those boys knocked that robin's nest down in the Lord Roberts Woods. 'Some people don't care much about us little guys', he said. God I laughed."

"So even though he was scared, he still liked watching birds? How —?"

After coughing, Laura said, "My feeling, Lewis, is on that December day your brother discovered — or rediscovered — another side to the woods. He realized wild things can be big and powerful, but also tiny and fragile. Just like him." Laura smiled. "You should have seen Ed when I told him; he had no idea. He worked all the Saturdays Sean came up, and not being aware of your brother's fear, I saw nothing in him watching birds. But last winter, when we saw some birds at a friend's feeder, I mentioned your brother's habit. Eddie's eyes lit up. 'I'll be goddamned — he did see something!' At first I didn't know what he meant, but after he revealed Sean's fear I did: there's a softer, more delicate side to the woods. Ed was hoping your brother would see that side, and was very proud of him when hearing he finally did." Laura stared at me. "And you, big brother, should be proud of the 'stupid wimp' too."

Evidently Ed had told his wife pretty much everything, and stubbornly I whispered, "I'll think about it."

Laura uttered a familiar, "What's that?"

"He said he's more than proud of his little brother," Owen answered right on cue, ruffling my hair with one of his massive hands. Even more clever, he then added, "It seems some of us just have a hard time admitting things."

Laura soon declared she needed to return to the Morrisons' place. She and Carla, I was glad to hear, were going shopping in town. But despite insisting she needed to leave, she still spent several minutes leaning against the front railing of the deck, peering at the lake and surrounding woods. This she did silently, and seemingly deep in thought.

At last she said, "You may have painted the house and tidied the yard, Owen, but you sure haven't changed the view."

"Not yet, at least — chain-saw's on the fritz."

Laura quickly turned, and a faint but distinctly devilish grin appeared on Owen's face.

The victim playfully tried stomping on his work boots, saying, "Bloody well better be joking, mister!"

When she gave up on retaliation and headed for the stairs, Owen, still chuckling, said, "Remember — you're welcome to drop in anytime. Hell, you can drop in every day if you like."

Laura paused on the stairs. "It's a fairly long commute from B.C., but I appreciate the thought."

Owen smirked. "Who said anything about commuting?"

Fighting a grin, Laura fired back, "Oh, don't start! There's two twerps at this lake already." Her eyes twinkled slightly, and I thought for a second, considering Owen's little remark earlier, she might actually confess to regretting the move. Instead, as she continued down her old stairs she merely said, "Besides, Eddie and I have everything out west! *Real* mountains, for one, not molehills like what we suckered you into." A short doe-like cough, then, "Christ — I can't wait to get back."

In denial to the end.

The Russells left that evening about an hour after supper, one Cathy hosted for almost the entire lake crew. Laura distributed hugs, leaving two particular lake residents to last so she could spend an extra minute with them. Then all at once our old neighbours left for Toronto to meet up with their son, Ed honking the horn on the 'Midnight Blue' about eleven times while Laura did all the waving. And although I now knew it was truly 'tourists' who were leaving us again, I never heard anyone call them that. Everyone, I believe, knew there was no need this time.

Shortly after the Russells' departure, I returned to Owen's to deliver several receipts I'd forgotten to give him following our town errands. He'd politely turned down an invitation to Cathy's, claiming he felt a bit tired. I had no reason now to consider this an excuse, because I found him lightly snoozing on the living room couch. After I presented the receipts, he merely grunted a quick thank-you and dozed off again, and I quietly slipped out.

It was about eight-thirty and the day was nearing an end. The lake had reached its evening calm, the air was cool and fresh, and the only sounds were occasional faint rustlings in the bush. As always on clear summer evenings from the lake hilltop, the woods to the north were richly coloured; you saw a hundred shades of green by the time your eyes reached the horizon.

Now right after crossing the deck and starting down the stairs, something new about the house caught my eye, something I somehow hadn't spotted on my way in.

Near the side kitchen window, hanging from its tall, specially-made railing post, was the Russells' old bird feeder.

Evidently Owen filled it with the bird seed the Russells left, too, because a white-throated sparrow, or Canada bird, suddenly landed at the feeder. I watched this tiny, frail bird as it flitted about picking up seeds, and then I watched as it flew away, weaving through the maples behind the house, and finally boldly disappearing into the deep woods.

39

On the Friday morning following the Russells' visit I helped Owen cut his lawn. On this day he tackled the trimming while I ran the mower, and as usual, the protruding bedrock and tree roots made work slow and difficult. We were only half finished when Owen signalled for a break and we retired to the deck chairs.

Although it was not yet ten o'clock the day was already quite warm. Occasionally a soft breeze blew from the south, however, and we had just sat when this breeze again came through. With it arrived a Monarch butterfly, one of many we'd seen on this morning, and for a silent moment we watched it flutter across the deck. When it left our view Owen wiped his forehead with his handkerchief, stretched his legs, and took a long, deep breath. He then surprised me by saying, "So — what's Mr. Lewis so down about this morning?"

Turning away, I answered, "I'm not —"

"Don't try denying it. You've been dragging your chin since you got here. What's up? Sick of cutting this miserable lawn?"

"No, it's not that." Hesitating, unsure whether to once more trouble him with my problems, I grumbled, "Mom stared out my window again last night."

"Oh?"

"She was fine for a few nights after Mrs. Russell mentioned Sean — especially the first one. I even heard her playing records in the Muskoka room. But last night, for some reason she got messed up."

"You were awake late again, were you?"

"I think I'm always awake when she does it. I can never sleep for the first hour after I go to bed, and she checks on me inside that time."

Owen faced me and quietly said, "I think you'll just have to show a little patience, Lewis. I have a feeling things will smooth out eventually. And you should work on getting to sleep — grumpy mornings won't help you or your mother."

When I glared at him over this comment, and he simply glared back, I gave in and said, "Do you suppose it'd help if I told Mom what Mrs. Russell said about Sean?"

"No, no. I'd leave that alone. Be patient, Lewis. Be patient."

It was soon after this chat, and just before Owen and I intended to resume work, that we spotted Grandma Layton marching up the laneway hill.

"Uh, oh," Owen whispered. "Apparently there's been a development."

Grandma Layton looked frazzled. Her usually perfectly-curled silver hair was a mess, and although heading uphill, she walked at a hurried pace. In her hands was a clear-lidded plastic bowl. When she reached us on the deck I saw it was actually a set of bowls nested together.

"Hello, Annie. Nice of you to drop in," Owen brightly began. Referring to my grandmother's past "hayfield lawn" comments, he apologetically offered, "Lewis and I were working on the crop —"

"I'm not here about your yard," Grandma Layton broke in. Pausing to fully catch her breath, she added with a strained voice, "I'm here because I need a favour."

Owen and I glanced at each other. This was definitely a development.

"Well, sure!" Owen said, leaning forward. "What can I do for you, Annie?"

"My situation is this. We're throwing a little moving-away party tonight for one of the girls in the Euchre Club. Fran Hollings? Marie mentioned you know her."

"Sure do, and I think a party is a very considerate idea."

"Thank you. Anyway, her favourite thing in the world is raspberry tarts, and considering a terrible experience she had on our laneway several years ago, I'm determined to make her some. Valerie just called from town, though, and said she can't find anybody with raspberries today. So I'm stuck. The party's tonight and I've got no berries."

"That's a damn shame."

"Now I understand there's a patch of ... *somewhat* wild raspberries at the end of the Russells' old path."

Owen nodded, and slyly added, "Sure, and I happen to know those entirely wild berries are good and ripe now, too."

This subtle correction produced the desired wince, but Grandma Layton nonetheless persevered. With eyes closed, and her face noticeably tightened, she slowly and painfully said, "So ... I was wondering ... if you might be kind enough to take Lewis and, well ... get some for me."

After she delivered this climactic line Owen sat musing a moment, looking first at me, then at my grandmother, then at the deck. You could almost hear him tallying "old coots" in his head, and I feared things might turn sour. It was only a few seconds later, however, that a devilish smirk suddenly formed on his face and I sensed a compromise had been reached.

"Annie, my dear," he said, rising to his feet, "Lewis and I'd be happy to help you pick some berries."

My grandmother's mouth dropped open. "Surely you don't expect me —?"

"It's not too far," Owen continued firmly, stretching his back. "You'll be fine. A little exercise never hurt nobody. I've even got the wife's old gardening shoes inside you can borrow."

And with that, and before Grandma Layton could argue the issue, he turned and quickly strode into the house.

It took us over half an hour to reach the raspberry patch that afternoon. Grandma Layton looked funny in the shoes Owen gave her to wear. They were made of blue rubber, with fake red flowers attached to the top, and they squeaked as my grandmother walked.

You only heard the squeaks, though, when she wasn't complaining, which wasn't often during the trip. Despite her usual grace when walking she seemed to have a talent for tripping on tree roots, and for finding the path's few muddy spots. It was therefore as much a relief to Owen and me as it was to her when we reached the berries.

"Here you are, Annie," Owen announced brightly while sneaking me a wink. "The veritable pot of gold at the end of the rainbow."

My grandmother stared at the gold in disgust. "You've dragged me to the blessed boondocks for *this*? It's hardly anything!"

"Your eyes are deceiving you, my dear. There's enough raspberries in this patch to fill a wheelbarrow. And fine berries at that."

To this judgement Grandma Layton predictably scoffed, but nonetheless followed Owen and me to the edge of the creek. Before crossing, however, Owen first made a loud whistle and clapped his hands several times. I knew what he was up to, but in obvious puzzlement my grandmother asked, "What the heck is that all about?"

"Bears love berries," Owen answered matter-of-factly. "A guy has to be careful."

Grandma Layton stared at him dumbfoundedly a few seconds, then likewise at her grandson. "That's just great!" she blared, bringing her hand to her forehead. "That's just beautiful!"

"Settle down, Annie, settle down," Owen gently pleaded, seemingly sincere. "I'm sure we'll be fine." As my grandmother began a round of grumbling to herself, though, he secretly showed me a devilish grin and quietly snickered in my ear, "Better'n Christmas morning, Lewis my boy."

Fortunately Grandma Layton crossed the creek without too much trouble, holding my outstretched hand and nervously but safely stepping on the large stones positioned in the middle. When the three of us were across I distributed the plastic bowls, which I'd been carrying, and we all began harvesting the raspberries. We made good progress the first fifteen minutes or so, since it was easy to get at the outside berries. But soon we had to start working our way into the thick, tangled bushes, and we were constantly unsticking them from our clothes.

"Ouch! Stupid things!" Grandma Layton moaned. "I'll have more scratches after this than I've gotten my whole life! If you're not a bear when you arrive you are when you leave! Had I known it would come to this foolishness I'd have asked Valerie to go out of town for berries. The garden ones are far better anyway. They're bigger, and *cleaner*."

To this I offered, "But I don't think they taste as good as these ones, Grandma," and quickly regretted it. Same for the berry juice I blatantly wiped from my chin.

"You! If I didn't need these so bad for Fran I'd tar and feather you! We'll be here a month at this rate!"

"Settle down — there's plenty to spare," Owen chortled. As Grandma Layton scowled at him, he quietly added, "And I *guarantee* you we won't be at this a month."

After moving out of our view, he soon continued with, "So speaking of dear Fran — I think Marie told me she's moving to Toronto. Is that right, Annie?"

"That's correct. She's found herself a beautiful little apartment in Scarborough. The dear lady's had enough of living so close to the sticks and ... stumbling into ditches at formal occasions. If my grandchildren didn't live here I'd be going with her, too."

"You'd really leave the lake?"

"In a second! As far as I'm concerned there's nothing here except muck, bugs, and swampland."

"And pathetic old coots?"

"And path—" Grandma Layton broke off, apparently remembering the favour being granted on this afternoon, and instead merely offered Owen a huff, and her back.

We continued picking in silence about ten minutes, gradually working our way deeper into the berry patch. After noticing my grandmother wincing on occasion, I inquired about her problem.

"My feet. They're hurting from that stupid path, and these stupid shoes."

"Can't recall Jeanne ever hurting in them," said Owen.

"Sounds like you've got tender tootsies. Need to get yourself out and about more."

"I surely hope you don't mean more of this sort of thing. I'd rather get more root canals than romp around in this Godforsaken bush!"

"Oh, c'mon," Owen said, stopping work and giving my grandmother a confronting eye. "You're *honestly* telling me you're not finding this a pleasant little trip?"

"Pleasant trip?" Grandma Layton snorted disbelievingly. "*Pleasant*? Why you ... just go straight to *hell*, Owen Goddard!"

Immediately upon hearing this outburst I considered boldly pointing out some 'improper vocabulary'. It seemed only fair, considering the countless hours I'd spent confined to my room over similar language. Owen, however, beat me to the return punch, recalling my grandmother's "when hell freezes over" response to berry picking years earlier, which I'd shared with him. With surprising calm after Grandma Layton's nastiest of remarks, and with his usual slyness, he said, "Go to hell, Annie? I don't know — am I dressed warm enough right now?"

After another long hour of picking and sampling, we managed to fill all three bowls. Instantly Grandma Layton snapped on the lids and gave her helpers suspicious glares, saying, "And those will be *staying* on." We solemnly vowed they would, but for several minutes thereafter we nonetheless received watchful eyes.

It was early afternoon and the day's heat had peaked. Aside from issuing the berry-stealing warning, through suffering this heat Grandma Layton had become fairly quiet. She also looked tired and I knew by her continued wincing her feet truly were hurting. So, although it'd been fun drawing her into the woods, I felt the game should now end. Owen apparently felt likewise, because after seeing her wince yet again, he said, "I'll get you fixed up, Annie. I know just the cure." His cure proved to be the creek, and after we'd crossed back over he drew Grandma Layton to a spot of smooth bedrock at the creek's edge.

"Sit yourself down right here," he said, sweeping a few stones aside with one of his huge work boots.

"I'm not sitting *there*," Grandma Layton snootily declared, glaring at the rock.

Owen's voice deepened. "Don't be so bloody stubborn. Do as you're told."

My grandmother muttered something resembling "look who's talking about being stubborn," but did concede, and eased herself down onto the bedrock. Owen then had me slip off the rubber shoes.

"Now you just slide those puppies into that stream," he commanded. "Do'em wonders."

Grandma Layton hesitated, but gradually eased her feet into the water. I then removed my shoes and socks and did the same. During this time Owen sat beside me and untied his laces. "Brace yourselves," he warned before slipping off his boots.

Once he had his feet in the water both he and I lay back, putting our hands under our heads to act as pillows. The bedrock was warm and surprisingly comfortable and our faces nicely caught the shade of the bushes behind us. Owen then began coaxing Grandma Layton to lie back with us, which she was very reluctant to do. She seemed concerned about what might be in the creek or what might come floating down it. Finally, after several trial runs, she resigned and lay back. Placing her hands under her head, she stretched out her legs, and took a long, deep breath.

With my grandmother settled I relaxed and gazed up at the sky. It was clear blue except for a string of tiny cloudlets drifting slowly westward, and several gulls soaring in circles to the south.

"Now that is sure a fine day," Owen declared. "As fine a day for berry picking as you could hope for, Annie." While saying this he dumped about a dozen berries into my hand, and it was all I could do not break out laughing.

"It's been an odd day, actually," she said softly. "The forecast called for rain, but it hasn't even hinted at wanting to do that."

"No, it's downright perfect." Lifting his head slightly, Owen added, "And here comes one of your buddies, Lewis. He obviously feels the same way."

With a thick finger he motioned downstream, and when I lifted my head I saw a Monarch butterfly fluttering alongside the creek, just above the long grasses. It was slowly approaching us.

"Might even be the same one," Owen said teasingly. "He may have followed you here."

"What's that all about?" Grandma Layton asked.

Quickly swallowing several berries I'd snuck into my mouth, I said, "Owen's only kidding, Grandma. We've seen a lot of Monarchs today, and he's talking about one we saw right before you came up to see us."

"Well — a bug is a bug, I say."

Owen sighed. "Yes, all right, Annie."

Turning his head toward me, my employer said, "Feel like finishing that lawn when we get back, Mr. Lewis?"

"Not really," I shyly answered, smiling. Besides enjoying the sun, I was loving the feel of the creek flowing around my feet.

My grandmother said, "You can work a boy too hard, you know, Owen Goddard."

"Yes, believe me, I know," he quietly replied. "I've been there. I won't do that to Lewis."

The breeze from the morning had continued into the afternoon, and as it came through again it made the tops of the trees gently sway. The leaves rustled, and for a moment you could hardly hear the trickling sounds of the creek.

Soon after this short breeze Owen poked me in the leg with his finger. I opened my hand, expecting more raspberries, but he merely poked me again. When I looked at him he motioned with his nose toward Grandma Layton. Turning my head the other way I saw she was watching the butterfly, which had passed and was fluttering its way farther upcreek. This, however, wasn't what really caught Owen's attention.

She was following the butterfly with her right index finger, tracing in the air its path as it dipped and twisted among the raspberry bushes. It was the same as so many times before with Judy, and she continued with this close to a minute, lost, seemingly as much as ever, in a paradise of grace and refinement.

When the Monarch went out of view she noticed the two curious onlookers, and said, “What?”

“Nothing, Grandma,” I merely answered. Then, along with Owen, I simply laid back again on the warm, smooth bedrock, closed my eyes, and took a long, deep breath.

40

"Just one!" pleaded Dad. "Just one won't make any difference."

The Farrow family was slowly driving along the busy main street of Bracebridge in my father's green Buick, heading for Grandma Layton's party. My parents sat in front while Judy and I sat in back with our grandmother, who along with perfume, jewelry, and a fancy blue dress, wore a flowered tin of raspberry tarts on her lap.

"You're not getting any!" Grandma Layton harshly answered for about the fifth time. "So you can shut it. I've barely enough as it is. Lewis and that pathetic old coot ate half my berries!"

"It's amazing you put up with them, Mother."

"Amazing I put up with certain other people!"

We now hung a right onto a side-street. Shortly before reaching the next intersection my grandmother pointed to a large red-brick townhouse with a spacious, well-manicured yard. It was the sort of house, I knew from pictures, she'd lived in most of her life.

Dad pulled up to the front walkway. "Fancy joint."

"It's a lovely, fancy *house* is what it is," Grandma Layton declared. "A *real* house, with a perfect yard and sitting nice and close to all the stores."

"Sounds great. Have they a room for rent?"

Grandma Layton leaned forward in her seat and scowled. "Don't you joke, mister — I'd be tempted!"

"I didn't mean for you," Dad quipped, and his mother-in-law

looked ready to smack him with her raspberry tin.

At this time, however, a tall, gray-haired lady wearing high heels and an ornate green dress stepped out of the front entrance to the house and strolled down the walkway. It was Nora Keaton, the lady who put her Cadillac in the ditch after my grandmother's 70th birthday party. I later learned she was the owner of this fine townhouse.

Coming to my mother's open window, she said, "Don't worry about Annie getting home, Val — I'll look after her."

"Much appreciated," Mother replied.

"Sure takes a load off my mind too, thanks," Dad added sarcastically. In this same standard tone, and while my mother winced, he then yelled to Grandma Layton, who had vacated the car. "You have a terrifically wonderful time, Mother!"

My grandmother merely started up the walkway, and as we drove away Dad uttered what would prove the signature line of the day. "Lewis, my son," he said, glancing at me by way of the rear-view mirror, "it seems some people just don't know where they're best off."

After dropping my mother and sister off downtown to do some shopping, my father and I made a trip to his boss's house. Don Nelson had taken that Friday off and had called our place shortly after Dad arrived home, saying he needed two office files from my father's briefcase. The Nelsons owned a tan-brick bungalow on Santa's Village road, which ran alongside the Muskoka River, and we reached the house in only about five minutes. We found a rather unoffice-like Don, dressed in sandals, black shorts, and a navy blue muscle shirt, sweeping out his garage.

As we walked up the driveway, Dad said, "What the hell? House-cleaning? How come you're not out in the boat, Donny?"

"Outboard's acting up these days — needs servicing," his boss answered, stopping his sweeping a second. "Beautiful day though, don't you think?"

"You have a knack for picking the Fridays to take off — I'll give you that."

"Yup, she's a beaut', all right." The sweeping continued.

My father looked at his employer quizzically a moment, then said, "Lewis here has the files you were peeing yourself over."

"Super!" came the reply, and when I handed over the folders Don instantly plunked them down on an old vinyl recliner sitting at the back of the garage. He then continued sweeping — somewhat nervously, it even seemed.

"Jeez, Donny," said Dad. "Try not to dig into those too fast."

He smiled. "So your ... mother-in-law's at a party today, is she?"

"She is."

"Well, they sure picked a fine day for it." Don now began whistling while he swept, and occasionally, I noticed, glanced out to the road.

"Something on your mind, Donny?" My father eyeballed him.

"No, there's noth—"

Before he finished, we heard a high-pitched yell from inside the house. "Daaawneee! Walter called! He'll be here in a minute."

"Walter?" Dad bellowed. "Walter's coming here? Is that what the hell you're up to?"

"Maybe," Don squeaked. He now had his arms wrapped around his head, and the broom lay on the garage floor.

"You set me up, you bastard!"

"I ... suppose. But if I'd told you in advance, would you have come over?"

"Christ no! Walter's all I need!"

"Now, now. He called me yesterday. He and Dora drove over from Alberta to do the family thing for a week, and he wanted to stop by after his golf. So I invited him for supper tonight. When I mentioned you and I were working together again, he said 'Hell, 'vite him over', and I promised I would."

"*Walter Harris* said that? I'll bet."

"You can ask him yourself," Don replied smartly, pointing to the road, "because here he is."

A big white Oldsmobile pulled into the driveway and parked behind Don's car. A short, stocky man with wiry silver hair got out and walked up the driveway. He was wearing a yellow shirt, gray dress pants, and white golf shoes.

"Bruce Farrow! I'll be damned," he said in a gravelly voice and sporting a superior, gold-toothed grin. "Thought you were a goddamn city boy these days?"

"Hello, Walter," my father answered in a suddenly very tired voice. With similar enthusiasm, after the two men shook hands Dad turned to me and said, "Lewis, this is Mr. Harris. He was my boss before I moved to the city."

"Before your father decided to get silly, is what he means," Walter said, giving me a firm handshake. Winking at me he added, "I see he at least got something accomplished in The Big Smoke, though."

"Three somethings," Dad answered carefully, as he always did now when commenting on how many kids he had. "Lewis here is my oldest. He turned *thirteen* in the spring."

As I'm sure my father intended, this slyly emphasized revelation left Walter silent a moment, seemingly dazed by just how far into the past was Bruce Farrow's employment with Harris Business Services. This escape tactic almost worked, too. Walter, glancing at me before gazing toward the river, said, "Yup, a hefty chunk of years have passed for sure." He then eyed our Buick, which my father had slowly but surely sidled over to. "You were just on your way out, were you, son?"

Before my father could provide a predictable answer, Don quickly said, "Hell no! He told me a minute ago he has loads of time to spare. Don't you, Brucey?"

In obvious defeat, my father could only nod.

Don led everyone to his covered side patio, where we took seats in white plastic chairs surrounding a matching table. Like his office, this patio had orange and yellow potted marigolds hanging everywhere. Even with these flowers we still had a fine view of the river, and when a runabout cruised past my father made an energetic and lengthy production of waving to a young couple.

"So," Walter said after my father finally settled into his chair.

"You're back."

"I'm back."

"And working with Donny again."

"Back with Donny again."

Walter smirked. "Right back where you started, in other words."

Vacantly, Dad said, "Basically."

"Basically nothing. You're right back to what you were doing before."

Don Nelson caught my eye and smiled. "Don't worry, Lewis. Your Dad can take him — easy."

"Take me, my ass!" Walter snorted. "I could still womp you two little farts with one hand."

Don countered with a mischievous grin, and again glancing at me, made a churning motion with his hands.

I saw a fire ignite in Walter Harris's eyes. "Fine! We may as well get this out and over with." He sat up in his seat and focused on my father. "I'm not mad at you anymore, Bruce. I'm not one to hold a grudge. I admit, I got a little upset at the time —"

"A little upset?" Don howled. "You chased him down the frigging street, Walter!"

"All right ... I know I did!" My father's old boss had his eyes closed now and was holding his hands up. "But that's all over and done with. That was a long time ago — Bruce has a teen-aged son, for bloody sakes — and like I say, I'm not one to hold a grudge."

Don chuckled, but before Walter could retaliate a red-gowned Gloria Nelson came out with a jug of iced tea and some glasses.

"Would you like to stay for supper as well?" she said to my father while filling his glass. "There's plenty enough for everyone."

"Thanks, but no thanks," Dad answered quickly. "I promised the kids pizza. My mother-in-law is out tonight and that's about the only time they get to have pizza."

This, of course, was news to me.

When Gloria returned inside my father's reprieve ended and Walter went back on attack. "Anyway, Mr. Farrow, I thought I was giving you a pretty fine job, and I still hold to that — I had tons of people after it when you took off. Donny can vouch for me."

"I have to admit he's right on that one, Bruce. We did take in a lot of applications."

"And I thought," Walter continued, "that maybe you were being kind of foolish, and maybe kind of ungrateful — that's all."

"And maybe you kind of ticked him off," Don added.

Now to all this my father sat with an obviously forced smile, not saying a word. He also contributed little when Walter and Don soon talked about other things — like Walter's new house in Red Deer. Most of the time he either gazed out to the river or stared at the patio floor. By the time we got up to leave he looked humbled and downright depressed, a mood in great contrast to earlier when he wisecracked my grandmother. Walter was chatting up a storm with Gloria Nelson by this time, so only her husband came out to the driveway with us.

"You haven't gotten your feathers ruffled, have you?" he said seriously as my father got into the car. "You know how Walter is — he's only screwing around."

"Oh, I realize. It's more me I'm bothered by than him."

"Well, get over yourself and come back after supper. We'll play some darts and get Walter plastered for old times sake. Think back to how things were before you dropped the moving-off-to-the-city bomb on him — you two got along great."

My father shifted the car into reverse. "I realize that too — I'll think about it."

"By the way," Don added with a sly grin, "what are you boys gettin' on those pizzas?"

"Bugger off," Dad answered, then backed the car out of the driveway.

He hummed and hawed for a while after supper that night before finally deciding to return to the Nelsons' place. Drinking meant he'd have to spend the night there, and I was amazed at how agreeable my mother was to his proposal. She uttered a pleasant "that's fine" and started in on the dishes.

After he departed, and Judy went upstairs to play in her room,

I decided to help my mother with those dishes. As usual on these rare occasions she simply stood at the sink smiling and waiting for me to ask whatever questions she knew I wanted to ask. And since I knew she knew, and didn't like drying dishes, I wasted no time. Interrogating my mother, I must add, was Plan B; my father wouldn't utter a word the whole way home.

"Mom? Do you know a Walter Harris?"

"I can't say I've met him in person," she answered, handing me a wet plate, "but I've heard your father mention him. He was the man your father used to work for." Pausing from the dishes and glancing at me, she added, "Why?"

"When we were at Don Nelson's today, Mr. Harris showed up and started bugging Dad about when he moved away to the city. His old boss was mad at him because he quit his job. I thought Dad got laid-off because there wasn't enough work. That's not right?"

My mother only frowned, so I continued. "I started thinking maybe Dad really quit because he didn't like his old boss, but as we were leaving Don Nelson said Dad and Mr. Harris got along great together in the old days."

"I see." Mother rubbed her forehead. "And I have a hunch you're demanding to know what that's all about, aren't you?"

"Well ... yeah," I said firmly. "I'd like to know what's going on. I'm starting to think somebody's been tellin' fibs around here."

"All right, mister. Don't get in a huff." My mother was silent, in that same mulling-over-what-to-say mode I'd often seen in years past. At last she said, "I suppose you're old enough to know a few things. You have to promise me, though, not to say anything I tell you to your grandmother — okay?"

"I won't." At this point I paid very little attention to my drying.

My mother took a deep breath, then said, "Your father didn't move to the city because he had to, he moved because he wanted to. He left a good year-round job in Bracebridge when he went to the city, and I guess that got Walter Harris pretty riled up. He obviously thought your father was making a silly move."

"Dad *wanted* to move to the city? That's sure not what

Grandma told me years back!"

"Yes, I know she didn't, and that's because I didn't tell her the truth." My mother paused, once again seemingly collecting her thoughts. "When I first met your father he spoke very highly of Toronto. He talked often about how there was so much going on, how the rest of Ontario and even the whole country paid so much attention to the city. He always said 'Toronto is where all the important stuff happens'. He used to drag me downtown simply to walk around and soak up whatever was going on. When we bought the house in Scarborough, he loved chumming with Jack Walsh because he knew the city so well.

"But, anytime we visited Muskoka before his precious aunt and uncle moved west, I noticed a definite change in him. Somehow he was more energetic and confident; he also slept and ate better. All this, too, when he was visiting the same area where his parents died in that terrible accident. And although the energy and confidence also made him even more of a smart aleck, I really enjoyed him in that Muskoka mode. I also felt strongly he was much better off. So, when Donny Nelson sent a letter a few years back with a Bracebridge job offer, I planted my feet and pushed your father to take it."

"You pushed him?! But you —?!"

My mother looked me straight in the eye. "It was my idea to move to Muskoka, Lewis."

I almost dropped an expensive bowl I'd been drying.

"I argued with your father umpteen times till I was blue in the face before he gave in and agreed to move. I don't imagine you ever heard any of that, though. We didn't want you kids having bad thoughts."

Not revealing I'd heard that one argument in the fall of 1974, and still in disbelief, I said, "But all those stories Dad used to tell! He wanted to move back to Muskoka for the sake of us kids!"

"No! Just like your father doesn't realize how living in the country changes him, he didn't realize back in the city how often, or in the lively way, he told stories of growing up in Muskoka. Getting you excited about this area was not his intention; he wanted you kids to grow up in the city. Once again — where all the important stuff happens."

"He did seem to like it here when he was a boy, though."

"Maybe, but that's exactly what Muskoka is to your father: child's play. It's a place to perhaps go on holidays, but not a place to take seriously. I can tell you this — he convinced Jack Walsh he was thoroughly against moving away from the city. Our old neighbour didn't believe me when I told him your father needed to move here. From what I gathered during their visit a few weeks back he believes me about your father now. He's seen the evidence; your father's quite a different person these days than the one he was in the city. Going to sleep in the Lord Roberts Woods that night a month ago only put the icing on the cake."

Drying dishes had become my least concern, and putting down my towel, I said, "So what about Grandma? Why didn't you tell her why Dad *really* moved to the city, and how moving to Muskoka was your idea?"

My mother also stopped working. "I learned after first visiting Muskoka that your father became upset when I mentioned how this place affected him — just like he does now. He was embarrassed the city wasn't good for him when he so wanted it to be. And upsetting him ruined the positive influence this area had. I realized if ever I was to move us back to Muskoka, his pride would have to stay intact. That's where my mother came in. If I'd told her your father needed Muskoka she'd have nagged him about being weak, spoiling the whole move. She may nag at him anyway, but not about being weak. I also knew that to lay the groundwork for the move I'd have to lie to my mother, leading her to believe your father always had returning here in mind. I told her he only moved to the city because he was laid off work, and she deduced the rest. The result was your father could keep his chin up and not worry about being teased after moving. No question, as well, the move has been good for him; he's far better off living at this lake than he was living in Scarborough."

I said, "Other people tease Dad about changing, though."

"They *did* tease him. I politely hushed everyone on the lake during our first spring here when they were all teasing him about being the 'Ed Allen of Fraserburg'. As for Don Nelson, I plan to have a talk with that bugger. He sure didn't help your father today by subjecting him to Walter Harris — look at how quiet and depressed your father was at supper. Donny also wasn't supposed to make the call about when you learned everything I've told you tonight, which he effectively did today. He knows all about you and your questions. I'm going to call him tomorrow and give him proper hell."

I didn't doubt my mother, becoming stronger in my eyes by the minute, would do this, too.

I now said, "But ... even if the move's been good for Dad, it didn't bother you to push Grandma Layton to come here?"

Mother shook her head. "Like I believe I told you before we moved, my mother is much more adaptable than you realize, and I think she's slowly adapted to living in Muskoka. You'll never hear her admit that, of course, but I think she truly enjoys some things around the lake. I've spied on her a few times when she's worked on her flower bed, and seen her studying wildflowers in the back woodlot. They're things here she cares for besides her grandchildren."

"Ever seen her watching ... butterflies?"

My mother look puzzled. "Butterflies? No — can't say I've seen that."

Wanting to explore another matter, I quickly said, "And what about you — you didn't really mind moving to Muskoka?"

"I was basically neutral myself. Only having been to Muskoka those few times to see your father's aunt and uncle, and Haliburton maybe a dozen times when I was a kid, I really didn't know what rural life would be like. But I'm speaking, naturally, of how I felt when we moved. These days I simply don't know, Lewis. Things ... didn't exactly go as I planned. I kept your brother's fear of the woods a secret from your father so he wouldn't gain any ammunition in arguing we'd made a bad decision. But what happened next I obviously couldn't hide. Your father never blamed me for Sean, at least, and thankfully your grandmother was decent enough not to blame your father. I agonized over her doing that — blaming your brother's death on him when moving here was really my idea. I damn near told her it was all my fault one day. I realized, though, that would simply have made an even bigger mess of our lives. The bottom line, Lewis, is that your stupid mother may have rescued a husband, but she lost a son doing it."

I could see my mother's eyes welling up, and I said, softly, "I sure don't think what happened to Sean was your fault, Mom. If ... that means anything to you, that is."

She smiled faintly while gently stroking my hair. "Oh, it means something, mister."

With her upset I figured I'd asked enough questions, but after a quick wipe over her eyes she continued. Her voice cracking slightly, she said, "Anyway, Lewis, with your father it's basically like this. He wants the city but needs the country. He *wants* to live amid 'important' things, but *needs* the energy and confidence he scarcely realizes the country gives him. Do you ... understand that?"

I nodded, but said nothing. This was all too much.

"And it doesn't much matter whether he likes the idea of living in Muskoka, because this is where he belongs, so this is where we're staying. He can make as many phony trips to the city as he likes, but here is where we're living. Need beats want."

"Whether he likes the idea? You mean ... he might not?"

My mother again eyed me, and I noticed a familiar mischievous sparkle. "The stupid bugger would end up miserable, but if I let him, he'd probably move us back to the city." Grinning while wiping a tear, she said in a low voice, "Lewis, my son, it seems some people just don't know where they're best off."

41

"He's in 28," the silver-haired lady at the hospital reception desk informed us. "Go around the corner and you'll see the stairs on your left."

After my mother uttered a quick thank-you, she, Dad, and I started down the hall, with the youngest well in front. I hurried, as I'd been hurrying at everything since hearing the news. Although this mid-August Sunday was unseasonably cool, I was sweating badly nonetheless. "Slow down there, Charlie," came my mother's call. I impatiently waited for her and my father at the bottom of the stairs, then with them rose to the second floor.

Immediately after I opened the stairwell door we met the Morrisons headed in the opposite direction. Carla whispered, "Oh! We didn't mean for you to come rushing right in."

"How's Owen?" I instantly blurted out.

"He seems ... relatively okay. The doctor said it was a mild heart attack, and that he might have had it in his sleep yesterday evening."

I said, "But yesterday we changed some rotten boards on his deck, and I didn't notice anything wrong with him!"

Carla shrugged. "Sometime during the evening he did develop a problem, though, and it was darn lucky Reggie discovered him."

"When was this?" said Dad.

"A touch after one," Reggie answered. "I stayed up to watch a movie, and when it was over I happened to look out the kitchen window and notice all the old boy's lights were still on. I took a walk up there and found him lying on the couch. He was awake but in real rough shape. So, I ran home for the car, got Carla up to help, and we rushed him to the hospital."

"I wanted to call an ambulance, but Owen wouldn't have any part of it," Carla added. "The stubborn bugger argued about going in at all, actually."

"It's amazing we didn't hear you pass us," said my mother.

Reggie shook his head. "Near your place Owen insisted I flick off the headlights. 'Don't be wakin' the whole goddamn neighbourhood over me', he blared."

Mother sighed, then asked Carla, "Have you managed to reach Karen yet?"

"She's here. Owen insisted I not call her right away so I waited until six this morning. She arrived about ten minutes ago."

"And she's pretty ticked with Daddy, I'll tell you," Reggie added with a smirk. "She seems caught between hugging him and belting him. I'm sorry to say it, but the old boy's Gordonier Lake days are probably numbered now."

"They're not num—" I quickly countered, before a soft hand squeezed my neck. Instead my mother offered, in a surprisingly sad tone I'd only later understand, "I suppose we shall see, Reggie."

We left the Morrisons, who were heading back to the lake, several long minutes later. We continued down the hall, passing a nurse pushing a food trolley which a now very impatient thirteen-year-old bumped into. When we came to Owen's room my mother insisted on first poking her head in the door to make sure our timing was okay, then we stepped in.

Owen was sitting up in bed. He was running his huge fingers through his hair — hair that seemed sparser and grayer than ever at this moment — and he appeared lost in thought, a frown on his pale, drained-looking face. When he saw the Farrow clan his frown worsened, and after groaning he put his four-fingered left hand on his forehead and barked, "Oh for Christ's sake! You people didn't have to come all the way into town just for *this*. What the hell —?"

"Don't be silly," my mother gently interrupted. "Of course we've come in."

"You just be thankful there're people who care about you," Karen said in a scolding tone. She was sitting in a black chair on the window side of Owen's bed, dressed in jeans and a blue T-shirt, and Reggie was definitely right about her not appearing very impressed. She'd hastily drawn her blonde hair into a sloppy ponytail — perhaps while driving — and she sported a dark-eyed scowl that would have given Grandma Layton a run for her money.

My parents and I gathered around Owen's bed and my mother leaned over to give him a hug and kiss. During what I thought an awkwardly mushy moment I studied the room. My friend's bed was one of two, the other occupied by a thin, elderly man watching a nearby wall-mounted TV. He seemed only half-conscious and I wasn't sure he'd even noticed our family yet. As I studied him — rude and nosy as this was — I suddenly felt a deep pain; *that*, I realized, could well be the life to which Owen was headed.

When I turned to his bed again the greeting segment of the visit was complete, and my father said to him, "So — you had yourself an incident, did you?"

"Apparently that's the case. Can't say I remember having one, though."

"Don't worry," Karen said smartly. "You'll be getting plenty of reminders."

"How's ... the food?" my mother asked in a brighter tone, referring to Owen's lunch tray. It looked barely touched.

"Can't say I've much of an appetite, but it looks good. I'll polish it off soon enough."

"He means he'll have me eat it before the doctor comes in." This naturally came from Karen, who was now facing the window.

"So are they treating you well?" my father said, glancing toward the nurse's station in the hall.

Winking at me Owen answered, "They're treating me like a king. It's a damn shame I'm going home this afternoon — a guy can't do any better than this."

Karen spun around and glared at her father. "The only place you're going over the next week is to the biffy. And that's if you're lucky."

In a much softer voice my mother said, “Is there anything we can get you, or do for you, Owen?”

“I’m fine, thanks. If you’re really keen, though, you could give that old duffer over there a smack across the head. He hasn’t said two words since they transferred me in here this morning.”

Karen’s eyes lit up, and in a quiet but harsh voice she said, “Look who’s talking about being an old duffer! You could easily have five years on that man. You’re not a young guy anymore, Dad. That’s what you need to wake up and realize.”

To this Owen breathed deeply, and training sad hazel eyes in turn on his drug-dazed roommate and then on me, said, “Oh ... don’t you worry, my dear. I’m wide awake now.”

With thankfully no further hostilities between father and daughter, we visited about another fifteen minutes before my mother suggested we leave. Reluctantly I said goodbye, then followed my parents downstairs. Karen, wanting a coffee, came with us.

“When are you headed back to Ottawa?” my mother asked her in the foyer, near some assorted vending machines.

“Tomorrow, unfortunately. Things are crazy at the store right now — we’re in the midst of a major sale. I’ll be back Friday, though, and although I’ll be damned if I’ll admit this to him, I think Dad’s basically okay.”

My father asked, “Any thoughts on the future?”

“Sure, I’ve had thoughts. I’ve decided to look at a few apartments when I get home. Having something specific to confront Dad with will give me a lot better chance of getting him to move.”

“Is that what you have in mind?” my father continued, pushing Karen’s hand away and feeding coins into a coffee machine. “We weren’t sure.”

“I think it’s the natural next step from here. Obviously he’s having trouble coping at the lake.”

“Maybe,” my mother said. “I’ll remind you, though, that no one on the lake minds helping your father.”

“I can do all the work he wants,” I quickly added.

"That's very nice of you," Karen said, "but you shouldn't have to help him. Dad's living his last years, and I think I should be the one looking after him. He served his family all his life. Now maybe it should serve him."

I saw Owen twice during the week. The first visit was on Tuesday evening and I joined Cathy and Grandma Layton. Owen was pleasant but said little; he still looked drawn, and hardly even teased my grandmother. My second visit, with my mother, was on Thursday evening and this time he looked and sounded much better. He completely finished his supper and even had me run to a store several blocks from the hospital for some lemonade. When my mother commented on him having more energy, he said, "I'm going to need it, too — aren't I?" Mother and I gave him sympathetic smiles.

Right on schedule, Karen arrived back at the lake early Friday evening. When we caught sight of her blue Thunderbird approaching on the laneway, Mother ran out and flagged her down.

"So they figure he's okay to come home?" she asked her as she sat down to supper with us.

"The doctor's saying he sees no reason to keep him any longer. He said this afternoon Dad could come home tomorrow if he wants. And as soon as he heard that, of course, it was settled."

"Have any luck with the apartment idea?"

"Yes, I did. I looked at one about two blocks from our place, a two-bedroom on the first floor of a pretty tidy building. I think it would be perfect for Dad."

My father grinned. "And when, may I ask, are you going to spring this on him?"

Karen's pale, youthful face turned slightly redder. "Tomorrow. I know it's awfully early to be bugging him about moving but that's the way you have to do things with Dad. Cruel as it sounds, you need to work on him when he's down and out. If I wait a month I won't have a prayer."

Dad snickered. "Beating up on your old man — shame!"

"Hey — don't underestimate this particular old man. Down and out as he may be, he knows this is coming, and he's been sitting in bed a week working on an argument. This still won't be any easy thing."

"Why he'd be stubborn about leaving this Godforsaken puddle is beyond me," said Grandma Layton. "I'm sure that apartment is wonderful, and if he had any sense at all he'd take it."

"Also take you with him?" said Dad, showing crossed fingers when my grandmother had her back turned.

"Leave her," said Mother, tossing her serviette at him. While he picked it up off the floor, my mother turned to Karen and quipped, "If you want help persuading your father to move, just let me know — I have experience with these matters."

"Is that so?" Karen whispered back. "I'll keep that in mind."

As expected, Owen came home with his daughter the following morning. Mother and I were in the Muskoka room at the time and we watched them pass on the laneway. Owen, looking out of place on the passenger side, showed us a big smile then reached over to toot the horn several times.

Less than a second after I started for the door my mother stopped me in my tracks. "Hold it right there, mister — you leave those two alone for the day. Karen needs to talk with her father and she won't be able to if you're there. I don't want Owen leaving the lake any more than you, but fair is fair." Heading back to the Muskoka room, she added, "And if you must you can tell Owen I was the one who spoiled the plan."

So much for that.

For the entire day I did as told and stayed near the house, all the time wondering, naturally, how my older friend was faring. That he might actually have to leave the lake had sunk in, and to say the least, not being able to do anything about it frustrated me. I knew Karen had to leave the next day, but that still gave her plenty of time.

So, I was very nervous the following morning when Owen's daughter stopped at our place on her way home. My mother, equally as eager for news, marched out to the driveway with me to meet her.

"So?" she immediately asked.

Karen looked down at the driveway, and to my delight, slowly shook her head. "Stubborn old fart." She then spotted my grandmother sticking her nose out the porch door. "Sorry, Annie, I —"

"Words well chosen!" Grandma Layton declared, then disappeared inside the house.

Almost floating on air, I asked Karen, "Is it okay if I go up and see him?"

"*Yes*, Lewis," she answered in a defeated tone. "You go right ahead. Dad even had the nerve to request I send you up there."

As I trotted down the driveway my mother firmly added, "Don't let him get doing anything, though — you hear?" I quickly nodded and continued on.

I found Owen seated in his deck chair at our usual shaded spot. The day was already bright and warm, and on the arm of his chair was his standard glass of lemonade. A wide, damp forehead spoke of his most recent, and undoubtedly most crucial, battle with his daughter, and once again I was both puzzled and amazed at his resolve to continue living at the lake. Not even a heart attack, apparently, could make him budge an inch.

"Thirsty?" he said as I took a seat in the other chair. "There's more of this stuff inside — Karen sloshed it up before she stormed away."

"I'm okay," I answered. "Sorry about yesterday — got tied up with a few things."

"Your mother ties good knots I bet, too," Owen said, giving me a sly glance. He then turned toward the lake and sighed. "Guess I raised a bit of a stir, didn't I?"

"Sort of. But Mrs. Leonard said you're not moving to Ottawa — is that for sure?"

"For sure. I'm still here. Don't get things wrong, though — if it comes to the point where everyone at this lake is baby-sitting me,

I'll leave. I know now that if I'm to live here I'll have to be more careful. Besides, hospitals don't suit me."

I grinned. "Grandma said it the other way around."

"She did, did she? I'm amazed she didn't rip into me when she visited during the week. Marie Taylor too. Both were pretty quiet, though. Everybody's been quiet, as a matter of fact."

Owen turned and stared to his right, and I said, "Me?"

"Two weeks worth, I'd say. Other than working on this deck I've hardly seen you. What's up? Sick of me?"

Suddenly feeling a need to study my running shoes, I answered, "I'm not sick of you. I've only been ... thinking about stuff."

"Figured that much. I saw you sitting at Lyall Rock one day all on your lonesome. You looked like you'd lost a dog or something. Care to share?"

As he did during the talk prior to our first creek-exploring mission the previous summer, Owen gave me such a tender look that I once again decided to tell him everything. Still studying my shoes, I quietly said, "I've been through a lot of weird stuff this summer ... but the big thing — I found out Dad didn't really want to move back to Muskoka. The whole idea was actually my mother's. He wanted to stay in the city, even though living in Muskoka is obviously better for him, and now ... now I don't know which way is up around here. I'm more mixed up than ever."

"I see. You found out about your Dad, did you? Figured you would."

I looked up. "Figured I would? You mean you knew what went on?"

"Your mother explained about your father one night earlier this summer. I figured it was only a matter of time before you found out."

"What night was that?"

Owen turned away from me — awkwardly, I thought — and said, "Oh, I don't remember exactly when it was. You were in bed at the time, I'm sure. That's quite a thing to find out, though, isn't it?"

"Yeah, it was. But only one more thing, really. It's been strange since we moved."

"Yes, I suppose it has," Owen echoed passively. He then surprised me by suddenly adding, "I guess my situation hasn't been of much help to you either, has it?"

"Your situation?" I did my best to look innocent.

Owen squinted at me. "Don't think I don't know you're aware of my past, Mr. Question-Asker. Right from that first night I saw you walking Marie home I knew you'd be asking questions about me. After the Vincents gave me George's things at the corn roast I also knew you'd badger Marie to tell you about him."

Nervously I said, "Are you mad at me for that?"

"I was a bit at first, I have to admit. That's why I didn't wave back to you the night you walked Marie home. I've since come to regret that, though. You were only being the curious young guy that you are. I'd been doing my best to keep quiet about the farm and my past, but I guess that was sort of silly, wasn't it?"

"I don't know," I quickly answered, but sensing an opportunity, I decided to get bold. Mustering the courage to abandon Marie's previous summer advice, I said, "So if you felt so bad about the woods, Owen, how come you moved to this lake? Why'd you go for all those hikes with me?"

To this I received a penetrating stare. "That's a tough one, Lewis."

I stared right back. "I'm ... not doing anything."

For a moment Owen merely responded with a faint smile, then turned to watch a car pass on the Fraserburg road. Finally, after a deep breath, he said, "Well, I guess the first thing I should confess is that this lake is far from being a new place for me. I've been coming here since before I was even your age."

"You came here way back then?"

"I hunted in these woods many a time with my father, and even on a few occasions with my grandfather. I don't imagine there's any part of this bush I haven't seen."

I pondered the implications of this, then leapt from my chair. "Does that mean you already knew about the waterfall?"

Owen nodded with a slightly red face and said, the same way I had earlier, "Mad at me for that?"

"Maybe," I answered sternly, slumping back into my chair. "How come you didn't just tell me? I feel like a goof now."

"You're not a goof, Lewis, and the reason I didn't tell you was because I thought you needed a lift considering the things you told me that day about your mother and brother, and being so confused about the woods. Seeing your face, too, when you discovered that tree, and the deer, and then the waterfall — I felt I'd done the right thing."

After I reluctantly nodded, Owen said, "But moving on, there was a day, back when I was close to your age, that I made a trip to this lake with my Dad and Grandpa. We had permission to come on this land from an old settler — Verne Janson. He was the one who named the lake, and he and my grandfather were close friends.

"Anyway, we came to do some fishing. This lake had some decent trout back then, and over the course of the morning we caught ourselves a nice string. We fished right at the bottom of this hill, where the water's deep and cool, and when we headed home we passed this very spot we're at now. Grandpa wasn't in the finest of health that year — it proved his last year, in fact — and when we made it to the top of this hill we had to stop so he could rest. We all found ourselves a tree and sat down against it, mine being a birch that grew right behind the house here. As he often did, Grandpa then nodded off for a spell, while Dad, not liking to waste time, started cleaning the fish. I, though, didn't feel like doing anything, so I only sat back against my tree and looked north, toward the lake.

"You need to realize — this spot didn't look much like it does today. None of these houses and cottages were here, for starters, and the road was a pretty rough thing in those days. The bush was a lot sparser, and there was debris lying in it from the logging days."

I followed Owen's gaze out to the lake, and he said, softly, "But, there were still plenty of young trees — birches and maples mainly — and that summer they were exceptionally full with leaves. Also on this sunny afternoon a fresh breeze blew from the east, and when it blew these young trees swayed and rustled. There was still plenty of wildlife here as well — a big snapping turtle sat on what became Lyall Rock, and a pair of wood ducks toured the end bay. And the breeze brought in a few small clouds, and you could watch their shadows move over the eastern ridge, deepening the green tops of those swaying, rustling young trees.

"And to all this, Lewis, I found myself watching, and listening. I must actually have fallen into a trance of some kind, believe it or not, because next thing I knew, Dad and Grandpa were barking at me to catch up with them."

Owen paused for a breath, then showed me the warmest, most joyful smile I'd even seen from him. "I couldn't have given you words for what I felt that afternoon, and for that matter I still can't. All I knew then, and know now, is that I felt something good, and that was definitely an odd thing for me. All those early family stories I heard when I was young really did the job on me. I came to feel as bad about the woods as maybe a guy can feel. No amount of hard living or hard work or missing the railroad or even missing Jeanne made me stop hating the bush, or in turn stop trying to maintain the fort my family built against it. For whatever reason, though, on that one afternoon here at this lake when I was a boy, I felt something good."

I turned to Owen. "So ... that's why you moved here? Just because this place made you feel better?"

With a shy nod, but a hint of relief in his voice, Owen answered, "That's basically it, Lewis."

I looked out to the lake, scanning this view to the north as I'd seen him do so many times since meeting him. My mind was spinning, and I said, "Why didn't you just come here years and years ago, though, Owen — before the Russells were here? Why only now?"

"Because the idea didn't hit me until a few years ago. When I first left the farm I was the most bitter I've probably ever been; I felt I'd failed my early family by losing the place. I didn't feel like doing anything for quite a while. That's why Marie and Fledda didn't see me for a few years — I was plain miserable. But then, one day in early spring a few years ago I made a trip out to the farm to help the Vincents with the old pump. On the way home I slowed the truck along the road here and looked at this lake a minute. It was funny, because naturally I'd been past this lake thousands of times before but never paid it much mind. On this return trip from the Vincents, though, I did, and I got thinking back to that afternoon when I was a boy. Later, too, I kept on thinking about it. The only explanation I can give you is that maybe my head was starting to clear. Before that time, you see, everything got lost in the blur of trying to keep up the farm.

"When I saw this place listed in the paper the following spring I couldn't believe my eyes, considering how long the Russells were here. I saw I had the opportunity to own this little spot, and perhaps feel again what I'd felt as a boy. I knew, of course, it'd be tough sledding considering my age and health. But like I said about the fawn that doe sacrificed last summer, I felt I was on time my worn old farming body wasn't supposed to have, and that puts some added kick in your step. Just maybe, I thought, I could ... change. In the same way my family's pioneer homestead can't survive forever, despite the Vincents' efforts, I felt the way of thinking that built it might not be invincible either. Just maybe.

"Now some people may think that silly — an old farm duffer moving to a place simply to feel better about the woods — but for me it wasn't silly at all. When a guy feels bad about something for seventy or so years, feeling good about it is a pretty special thing."

Already believing I knew the answer to this question, considering Owen's sad, searching gazes the previous summer, and his general moodiness since then, I nonetheless asked, "So have things worked out?"

Owen showed a pained smile. "There have been some pleasant times, I'm happy to report. A stretch of good feeling now and then, and I'm grateful for those. But I've learned it's no easy thing to change a heart full of bad feelings; mine are just too deeply rooted. I've done what I can to avoid things that stir up the bad memories, like the farm and those old tools in the shed I can't bring myself to part with. With our hikes, too, and staring at this view to the north so much, I've given myself every chance to feel something positive about the woods. But now and then, as I'm sure you've seen, all the bad feelings take over again. Sometimes merely being outside, or even near a window, reminds me of the old days, and all the bitterness comes back."

Thinking to the previous summer, when Owen so accurately guessed at my problem, I said, "When those bad feelings get mixed with the good ones, you become ... confused, do you?"

Owen looked at me, and brightened hazel eyes told me I'd hit the mark.

"And you're messed up then, just like me?"

My weathered friend was silent a moment, studying in turn his massive, scarred hands and then a pine sapling near the deck. At last he said, "This summer I've come to believe, Lewis, that if a guy tries sorting out his feelings toward good old Mother Nature he'll be sorting a long time. I don't say that in a defeated way, like I've given up in frustration, but in a respectful way — realizing and accepting that the way we look at wild places is complicated. I now sometimes wonder if mixed feelings isn't how it is for everyone, whether they realize it or not. It seems that notion holds true on this lake. Kevin and mixed feelings about that cabin, your Dad's situation with moving to Muskoka, and your city-bred grandmother and butterflies, to name a few. I think it might simply be the plight of us folks to be confused about the woods, a fact of life. And in an odd way, I find, a guy can take some comfort in that. I'm not alone, at least."

I suppose I gave Owen a quizzical look, and slyly as usual, he capped our afternoon conversation. "I'm afraid the truth is — yours truly, along with probably everyone else in the world, are all part of the 'funny bunch', Lewis."

42

When we reached the north end of Bracebridge my mother turned right, easing through the open gate of St. Thomas Cemetery. Once inside she drove slowly, passing row after row of headstones before parking at the lane's edge.

"Don't forget the bouquet," she said to Judy.

With my sister carrying the flowers we walked to Sean's grave. His headstone was small and made of silvery granite.

In Loving Memory of
Sean Andrew Farrow
April 10, 1968 - August 27, 1976

"Put it wherever you think is best, sweetie," Mother said, and Judy placed the bouquet against the side of the headstone.

This was a Sunday afternoon in late August, slightly over a week since Owen came home from the hospital. My mother was now starting her holidays and she'd coaxed Judy and me into town, supposedly to get ice-cream. The date, however, told me the true reason for the trip.

The sky, overcast during the morning, had started clearing and as we stood at Sean's grave the sun even came out.

Following a long minute of silence, my mother softly said, "Hard to believe it's been two years already. Seems like yesterday we even moved to Muskoka."

"We've been here oogles," said Judy. "I was only little when we moved."

"That's very true, dear," Mother replied, pressing my sister's head against her hip. "All this was back when you were only little."

Judy looked up. "Sean got lost in the woods, then slipped on a wet rock — right, Mom?"

Gazing up at the remaining clouds, my mother answered, "That's pretty much the gist of it, dear."

"Why would Sean go off on his own, though?"

Mother glanced at me. "He simply wanted to please someone, that's all, sweetie. But it's not the someone's fault, because the someone didn't know."

"So ... it was really Sean's fault for what happened?"

My mother again looked down, and I saw her cheeks were now wet. Her long, shiny brown hair, too, had somehow become mussy. "I don't know whether it was anybody's fault, Judy. I just ... I just don't know. I'm hoping you won't look at it in terms of fault. I'm not sure that's a good thing."

"But do y—" Judy continued, but someone caught her eye and motioned for her to hush.

What followed was yet another silent moment, which this time ended when a large blue car entered the cemetery and parked behind us. Three formally-dressed, elderly people — one man and two women — got out and approached a large headstone only ten feet from Sean's. One women was sobbing uncontrollably.

In a shaky voice my mother whispered to Judy and me, "Maybe we should go, guys."

Heading to the car I struggled desperately to think of something we could do on a Sunday that would lift my mother's spirits. Finally I offered, "Feel like going window shopping along the main street, Mom? Judy and I won't get bored."

But without looking at me, and reading my mind as always, she wiped those small green eyes of hers and said, softly, "I'll be okay, Lewis."

That evening, a half-hour after I went to bed, my mother made her usual trip upstairs to check on Judy and me. She spent a minute in my sister's room before coming to mine, and naturally when she entered I closed my eyes and pretended to be asleep. As I fully expected that night, instead of coming straight to the bed she first went to my front window. I waited for the sound of her drawing back the curtains before again opening my eyes. By the light from the hall I could see her standing at the window, as she had so many times in the past, with her head tilted skyward. She stood this way, silent and motionless as always, for several long minutes.

I closed my eyes again as she finally turned and came to the bed. I sensed her lean over me, and when smelling her peach-scented hair I waited for the standard peck on the cheek.

This time, though, I instead received a nudge.

"I know you're faking, Lewis Farrow," she whispered.

I opened my eyes slowly, trying for a good performance, but her smirk told me it was no use.

"How'd you know?" I said.

"Because you never sleep on your side. That's how I know."

"I ... couldn't get to sleep. It's —"

"Never mind." After seemingly mulling over something, she added, "If you're awake you might as well come out with me."

I sat up. "Come out with you? Come out where?"

I received no answer, my mother merely turning on the lamp and pulling jeans and a pullover from my dresser. "Here," she said, "you'll need something warm — it's cool tonight."

"Need something warm for what?"

"It's a surprise," Mother said, grinning. "So don't ask questions. Just hurry up and get dressed."

All the lights were off downstairs except for a lamp in my parents' bedroom, where I supposed Dad was reading. I tiptoed behind my mother to the porch and here she pulled her jacket from the closet. We then quietly slipped out.

The night was cool and very dark. As we started down the driveway I looked to the sky, which had completely cleared, and found the moon was only in its first quarter. Once leaving the reach of the porch light Mother produced a flashlight from her jacket pocket and switched it on. I followed her out to the laneway and then up toward Owen's place. Neither of us spoke and the only sound was gravel crunching under our feet.

Making our way up the hill I noticed Owen's outside light was off. When we reached his driveway I saw all his inside lights were also off. Nonetheless, my mother led me up the stairs and onto the deck. I was about to ask again what we were doing when our neighbour's large, weathered face suddenly appeared in front of the flashlight. He was sitting in his deck chair.

"I was about to call you," he said to Mother. "Wasn't sure you'd noticed."

"Oh, I noticed all right. I also noticed a certain someone awake when he was supposed to be asleep."

"Yes, I see that. But I'm afraid he's over the age of twelve, ma'am, so that'll mean the adult admission price."

"He'll take it off his lawn-mowing bill."

"Touché."

I'd heard enough. "Pardon me, but would someone kindly tell me what the heck is going on?"

"Come here where you can see better," said Mother. She pulled me to the front railing and pointed to the far side of the lake. "Look above the trees."

I looked toward the northern ridge, and there I saw faint streaks of bluish-green light shooting into the sky.

"You've never seen those before, have you? Those are the Northern Lights."

"Isn't that something, Lewis?" Owen remarked from his chair behind us. "Might not be as impressive in Muskoka as they are in the high north, but they're still a hell of a sight."

"Owen invited me to watch the lights one time near the start of this summer," said Mother, "and now I always watch for them."

"You mean he showed you —?"

In shock, I thought back to occasions earlier in the summer when I'd talked to Owen about my mother's problem. On the Sunday of the May long weekend — the morning before meeting Kevin at the fireworks — I remembered he'd said "we'll see" when I requested he talk to my mother. And later came the morning, before taking my grandmother raspberry picking, that he'd said, "I think you'll simply have to show a little patience, Lewis. I have a feeling things will smooth out eventually."

He had a feeling all right.

Looking behind me, I saw in the pale light the hint of a smile, and at that moment Owen Goddard seemed ten feet tall.

To my mother I quietly said, "Why didn't you tell me about this?!"

Gazing toward the lights, she answered, "I didn't because you'd ask to come with me, and then you'd be a grump the next day. Exactly like you'll be tomorrow."

"I won't be a grump on you. Not when you do stuff like this."

"Ahhh ... that's the spirit, lad," Owen broke in. "Now why don't you two lovey-doveys sit down. You're blocking the view."

"Yes, Mr. Goddard," Mother replied, and she and I sat at the top of the front stairs. My head, of course, was spinning by this time, but before I could even begin asking my mother questions she whispered a familiar, "Shh, just watch."

With that said, the three of us sat in silence and took in the lights. With my eyes fully adjusted to the night the strands of light now seemed brighter. They burst up seemingly from nowhere, waving and curling at random, and you couldn't predict exactly where or when the next strand would appear. After reaching its peak each strand lingered a moment, glowing in bluish-green, then slowly dissolved again into the darkness.

Despite this magical display, or perhaps because of it, I soon became sleepy and rested my head on my mother's lap. Turning just enough to see her face without her noticing, I recognized a look I hadn't seen since our first year on the lake.

It was the same unwavering, wide-eyed stare she'd maintained so many times in the Lord Roberts Woods, and the same when watching snow fall one fine New Year's Eve.

I don't know how long we sat out on Owen's deck that night. I do swear for the whole time, however, my mother never once took her eyes off the Northern Lights. And when morning arrived, and I woke back in my bed, a grump is the last thing in the world you would have called me.

EPILOGUE

The Farrow clan finally received a chance to hold the corn roast that year. We held it the first Friday of September, later than usual to give Owen some recovery time. The occasion passed in fine style, and although he kept himself fairly reserved, he still had a good time. He was there to grab a leg when we tossed Dad in the lake, and when I last saw him he was on the back deck watering Grandma Layton's flowers, chuckling so hard he was hitting the railing as well.

It was in the spring of 1980, almost two years after that corn roast, that we lost Owen. He became ill in mid-May with heart problems and passed away in his sleep several weeks later. He was buried in Fraserburg United Cemetery, right alongside his family and farm, and to this day anytime I'm out that way I make a point of 'dropping in' on him. As a final note, my old friend was home when he died, as I'm sure was his wish. He was having an afternoon snooze on his couch, with the front drapes wide open. And I like to think his last view of Gordonier Lake that afternoon was a pleasant one, that he went to sleep feeling something he'd felt as a young boy.

Within the remainder of that new decade we lost Marie Taylor too, and on a peaceful autumn evening in 1991 I went for a row with Reggie Morrison that proved his last; he left us only a month later. Carla and Cathy are still at the lake, however, as are my parents and grandmother. Grandma Layton recently celebrated in graceful style her 92nd birthday, and despite being "worn and torn by the ravages of the Godforsaken sticks," seems destined to remain with us many years to come. Judy is now married and has two sons, which she often reminds me is "two more than you have." She paints and swims through life in Peterborough, only a short distance from an old cabin buddy of mine who, if you can believe it, owns and runs a summer camp for needy kids. Lastly, if you'll allow me to backtrack in time, soon after Owen's death a rugged, fifty-something couple bought the place on the hill at Gordonier Lake. They moved in one sunny morning in August, and so I later heard, crept slowly and quietly along the laneway in a midnight blue pickup, their heads barely above the dash. I happened to be admiring the view from their hilltop that fine morning, however, and told them, "You just keep the little bugger's bird feeder filled and I won't tell anyone you're up here." And with that I shook hands with two new lake residents.

Concerning yours truly, my early education in carpentry led to full-time summer jobs in high-school, which in turn led to my becoming a house contractor in my mid-twenties. At the ripe old age of thirty-three, I now live about forty kilometres north of Bracebridge, just outside the town of Huntsville. It was while coaching at a softball tournament in this town that I met, and later married, a local girl named Carrie Milton. "She's more than you deserve" was Grandma Layton's first comment after meeting Carrie one evening, and so my fate was sealed.

Now as I mentioned in the introduction to this account, I still make regular visits these days to Gordonier Lake. You may better understand, however, that I make such trips more than for the sake of visiting family and other lake residents. Each return also provides the opportunity to once again explore and reflect on the setting for what I truly believe were the most important years of my life. Always wanting Carrie to understand what happened during my early lake years, and becoming upset when my "woodsy ramblings" failed, is, in itself, one indicator of the influence of those years. But the real proof lies in the impact they've made on my everyday adult life.

To begin, it seems hardly a month passes now when I don't

ponder, momentarily or at length, my natural surroundings and my feelings toward them. Such ponderings are not my only ones, of course — I won't tell you I'm completely preoccupied with woodsy thoughts. For a span of about ten years, in fact, I barely gave the Muskoka woods much thought at all; as with most people, the years between fifteen and twenty-five passed in a blur of school, parties, and assorted jobs. But as I've grown older and somewhat more settled, I've found myself reflecting often on wild places I visit and the varied feelings they instill in me, either immediately or later. Even during months I've built houses in Toronto I haven't felt totally alienated; clouds still pass overhead, rain still falls, and when you dig you can still smell the raw earth upon which the city was built. I find, then, I'm never entirely out of touch with wild nature, and therefore it never ceases to enter my thoughts and influence my moods.

Predictably, I also pay attention now to the varied feelings of others toward wild places. Carrie and fellow workers are obviously prime subjects, and frequently I'm amazed, if not quietly amused, by their subtle contradictions between preach and practice, between seemingly conscious and unconscious reactions toward the Muskoka woods. I also tend to notice, however, how people in other areas of the world react to their wild surroundings. During winter Carrie and I sometimes travel overseas, and each occasion leads me to increasingly speculate on the universality of people having complex emotional relationships with wild nature. I once watched, for instance, a Nepalese woman spend a silent, tearful moment kneeling on a narrow Himalayan trail where her husband fell to his death, then later listened to her passionately expound on the spiritual greatness of her mountain home, the widow's eyes now shining with utter reverence. Throughout Africa I've met local people who, while wearing jewelry depicting animal figures, relate their bafflement over tourists coming so far merely to see wildlife. And in Peru, after an El Niño, I once joined indigenous families angrily digging through the muddied remains of their flood-ravaged farms, helping them start over in a fertile land they declared they'd surely never leave. Such broader observations and subsequent musings also are not limited to the present. A small museum I visited several years ago boasted a life-size model of a prehistoric family gathered around an evening fire. Modellers had given these people fearful faces and weapons to clutch as they stared out at the wild blackness around them. But in reflecting upon this display, I wondered whether these ancient people, like others I know, also sometimes rose early simply to witness the beauty of the rising sun, or were energized, without realizing it, by the arrival of spring.

Yet another lasting impact of my Gordonier Lake experiences is my attentiveness to the influences that shape our feelings toward wild nature. In particular, I've made a study of the role social influence plays, especially during our most impressionable years. I believe strongly the array of feelings I experienced as a child toward my wild surroundings was much broader than if merely experiencing them on my own. Without question the people I interacted with introduced me to different ways of perceiving my new home. Having experienced this myself, I now wonder whether this happens to all of us as kids. Near where Carrie and I live are many young families, and the 'woods' for all these kids are the same. Yet when you dare to subtly probe into their feelings about their surroundings (at risk of seeming a bit cuckoo) you discover they all feel quite different things. And not too surprisingly, their feelings tend to coincide with those of their parents and other adults close to them. Someday, as an experiment, I'd like to send the same group of kids from Kevin Taylor's summer camp down the same camp trail once a day for a week. Adult guides, distinguished by their dominant pursuits in life, would take turns accompanying these kids and interpreting the trail — a biologist, a farmer, a naturalist, an urban developer, a trophy hunter, a stock broker, and lastly, say, a landscape painter. After that week I'd like to ask each child how he or she felt about the woods. For example, "Do you think the woods are a good place or a bad place?" I wonder whether I'd discover a familiar confusion. I wonder, in short, whether with each of these kids I'd be talking to essentially my childhood self.

Finally, I now often ponder my ponderings; I question, that is, why after all these years I continue to explore and question my feelings, and those of others, toward wild places. I know from experience this isn't typical. In the past, while talking with friends about the woods and the way they affect us emotionally, I'd usually hear something like, "Well, that's all very interesting, Lewis, but ... *so*?" In defence I tended to offer standard arguments, such as our feelings being critical to the fate of dear 'Mother Nature'. But today I confess to having no clear answer to why our emotional relationship with wild nature matters, no more than I clearly understand that relationship itself. Perhaps, in the end, it is mere curiosity, yet another parcel of mystery to human existence — how and why and if we fit in with the rest of nature. What I am sure, on a personal level, is that my attentiveness to wild places provides me with a profound sense of being involved in those places. Wild nature, that is, has unquestionably become as much a shaping force in my life, both in pleasant and unpleasant ways, as I similarly shape its destiny. It is a relationship, too, seemingly only strengthened by my curiosity toward it, seemingly only stirred, exposed, and expanded through my explorations. And so for myself, and in memory of an old friend, I continue to investigate the matter.

About the Cover Artist

Although essentially self-taught, Richard Robinson studied fine art at the University of Windsor and took further courses in oil painting both in Brampton and at Georgian College. He has worked with charcoal and pastels but prefers the rich, vibrant colours offered by oils. One of Richard's specialities is commissioned paintings of clients' homes, cottages, and favourite scenes. With over 200 such paintings to his credit his works can be found not only in Canada but also in the United States, Great Britain, Europe, and South America.

Richard Robinson's association with Muskoka dates back to 1964. An immediate love for the region led to Richard and wife Marlene purchasing a cottage near Baysville in autumn of 1977. When Richard retired in 2000 after 32 years as a secondary school teacher of French and Spanish, he and Marlene decided to make Muskoka their year-round home. A recent addition to their lakeside residence includes both a gallery and studio, where Richard can pursue his love of capturing on canvas the natural beauty of Muskoka.

For commissions or general inquiries please contact:

Richard Robinson
1030 Dickie Lake Road, R.R.#1
Baysville, Ontario
P0B 1A0
(705)-767-3000
richardrobinson@dickielake.com

About the Author

Born in Scarborough in 1964, Robert Rea moved to Muskoka at age five. Upon completing high school he attended the University of Waterloo, where he earned a Bachelor of Science (BSc) and a Bachelor of Environmental Studies (BES). Since graduating he has travelled extensively throughout the world, with special focus on traditional-lifestyle aboriginal peoples.

The author is pleased to receive comments regarding any of his current books, or to receive inquiries into upcoming publications. He may be contacted at either of the following addresses:

Regular mail: Robert Rea
Box 921
Bracebridge, Ontario
Canada
P1L 1V2

E-Mail: maplelnd@muskoka.com

From the author of the National Best-Selling

A VIEW TO THE NORTH

comes

SUN DREAMS

"Stories are to a land as facets are to a diamond ...
Each may reflect from a different angle, but all lend
sparkle to the same precious stone."

So the stage is set for **SUN DREAMS**, a rich assembly of stories blending mystery, humour, romance, tragedy, and adventure. A colourful cast offers not only a collective portrait of Muskoka but insight into the many 'faces' all lands possess. Written in the informal, down-to-earth style for which the author has become known, **SUN DREAMS** explores the human role in the nature of place.

"... as a group [the stories] provide a rich and varied tapestry of the characters who populate the shorelines and backroads of cottage country."
Sally Gower, *The Cottage Times*

"... an ensemble of characters sure to touch every reader lucky enough to meet them. ... In these seven stories Rea demonstrates his mastery of character development ... "
Louise Gleeson, *The Muskokan*